KANSAS CITY COVER-UP

BY
JULIE MILLER

MILLS &
BOON®

Published in Great Britain 2015
by Mills & Boon, an imprint of Harlequin (UK) Limited,
Eton House, 18-24 Paradise Road, Richmond, Surrey, TW9 1SR

© 2015 Julie Miller

ISBN: 978-0-263-25302-3

46-0415

Harlequin (UK) Limited's policy is to use papers that are natural, renewable and recyclable products and made from wood grown in sustainable forests. The logging and manufacturing processes conform to the legal environmental regulations of the country of origin.

Printed and bound in Spain
by CPI, Barcelona

The moment the idea of Gabe Knight stripping off her clothes and joining her on top of this table popped into her hazy thoughts, she knew she had to end the embrace.

"Gabe." She offered him one last breathless kiss, then pushed her fingers between their lips. "Gabe, we have to stop."

"I know." With a throaty growl, he pulled away, dropping little kisses to her fingertips as he retreated. "I know you're right. I don't like it. But you're right."

Despite the rumpled coal-dark hair and the collar she'd wrinkled with her eager hand, his deep blue eyes were as clear and focused as ever. "So why did you kiss me? And yes, I know, it was a team effort. But I'm interested in your motives."

Motives? She hadn't thought that far ahead. Still trying to regulate her own breathing, Olivia ran her fingers through her own hair, dismissing the probing question. "Don't analyze it, okay? Just accept the thank-you."

"That was more than a thank-you."

Julie Miller is an award-winning *USA TODAY* best-selling author of breathtaking romantic suspense—with a National Readers' Choice Award and a Daphne du Maurier Award, among other prizes. She has also earned an *RT Book Reviews* Career Achievement Award. For a complete list of her books, monthly newsletter and more, go to www.juliemiller.org.

I wanted to take a moment to remind readers that my Precinct books, while set in a real place, are works of fiction. Kansas City is a safe, welcoming place to visit—full of history, art, music, theater, beautiful fountains, fun activities, great sports, fabulous places to shop, yummy barbecue and some of the friendliest people in the country.

With thanks to my family and friends in Kansas City.

Thanks, too, to the police, fire and rescue, city engineers and other public servants who serve KC and the surrounding metropolitan area.

My stories may be fiction, but Kansas City is real and wonderful—a great city to live in or visit.

Hope to see you there!

Chapter One

"How is this a cold case?" Detective Olivia Watson squatted down beside the body with the bashed-in head lying on the plush office carpet.

The pool of blood looked fresh enough. The alleged murder weapon, a civic volunteerism trophy from the dead man's own desk, had already been bagged and packed away by the CSI trading notes with the medical examiner nearby. A uniformed officer and two building security guards were holding back a bevy of shocked and grieving office staff from the Kober & Associates PR firm, as well as curious onlookers from other businesses in the building beyond the yellow crime scene tape that blocked off the victim's outer office door. The two Kansas City PD detectives on the far side of the room interviewing the distraught secretary who'd discovered her boss's body after her half-day spa appointment seemed to have the crime scene well under control. So why call in representatives from the Fourth Precinct's Cold Case Squad?

Olivia rested her forearms on the thighs of her dark wash jeans and studied the sixtyish man's still features again. The glass-and-steel high-rise in downtown Kansas City was almost as new as the murder itself. She was used to working cases with pictures out of dusty boxes and autopsy reports that raised a lot of unanswered questions. She'd worked with skeletal remains and mummified corpses and alleged victims whose bodies had never been found at all. Most people assumed the Cold Case Squad was an easier gig than working a fresh investigation. She liked to think of it as a *smarter* assignment, requiring more insight and diligence than other divisions at KCPD.

Olivia was a third generation cop, like two of her three brothers. And the third one worked in the medical examiner's office. After two years in a uniform, five years in vice and the past year working cold cases, she'd learned that killers who'd eluded capture and thought they'd gotten away with murder often proved to be more devious and more dangerous than any other criminal out there. It was her job to track down those killers and finally get justice for those forgotten victims whose memory often died with their closest family and friends.

So why was she here to assist two perfectly capable detectives when there was a stack of her own investigations back at HQ to sort through?

"There must be a connection to one of our dead file cases. But if there is, I don't see it yet." She glanced up at her new partner, Jim Parker—back from the dead himself after a particularly harrowing undercover assignment for the Missouri Bureau of Investigation. "Do you?"

Jim's green eyes surveyed the room the way she had. "I recognize Ron Kober from the newspapers. Besides owning a Top 50 company here in KC, he helped get Adrian McCoy elected to the State Senate a few years back. Looks like he was doing pretty well on his own, without the senator."

Olivia arched a dark eyebrow. "Until today."

She liked Jim well enough, respected his reputation as a cop, appreciated that he got her sarcastic sense of humor. But after that humiliating debacle with her last partner, learning to trust him was hard. Thankfully, Jim was a newlywed, completely crazy about his wife, Natalie, and showed nothing but a friendly professional interest in his relationship with Olivia. Still, she found herself thinking about her words before she spoke to him, guarding her thoughts and feelings, which was no mean task for a woman with her volatile Irish roots.

"A man with this kind of money probably has plenty of enemies," Jim suggested.

An angle which she was sure the lead detectives were already exploring. Still didn't explain why she and Jim were here. She looked back down at the body, willing the corpse to speak and share his secrets. But she wasn't psychic and dead men didn't talk. However…

Her eyes went past Kober's body to a scrap of torn paper underneath the desk. She snapped a picture with her cell phone before reaching over the dead body to pick it up with the sterile gloves she wore.

Jim crouched down beside her. "What did you find?"

Olivia turned the tiny square over between her thumb and index finger. "Four numbers. I don't know. It may just be a piece of trash."

"Looks like a torn-up piece of stationery." Jim picked up the wastebasket beside the desk and set it between them to sort through its contents.

But there were no other little hand-torn shreds like this one. "Could be the last digits of a phone number."

Jim replaced the wastebasket and stood. "Or part of an address or social security number."

"Or a locker number or part of a combination lock." Olivia straightened beside him, spotting a pad of dove-gray paper on the desk that matched the piece in her hand. She picked it up and angled it in the light to see if she could read any indentations in the surface. But there were too many marks from previous notes to make out anything specific. "Maybe it's just a testament to their housekeeping service not doing its job, and isn't related to the crime at all."

Just in case, though, she jotted the 3620 in her notebook before handing the scrap of paper and Kober's scratch pad over to the CSI.

She tucked her own notepad into the pocket of her short leather jacket and peeled off her gloves, following Jim to the door. "So if this isn't our case, why are we here?"

Jim nodded to the detectives hovering over the weeping woman across the room. "Hendricks and Kincaid are taking lead on Kober's murder here. Sawyer Kincaid called us in as a courtesy."

Frowning, Olivia stuffed the gloves into the back pocket of her jeans. "And he didn't say why?"

"He just said it was a directive from higher up." He touched her shoulder to indicate he was taking a detour. "Looks like they're wrapping up that interview. I'll go ask if they can make sense of any of this yet."

While her golden-haired partner crossed the room, Olivia indicated she'd head on downstairs and meet him at the car.

She shouldn't have acknowledged the visceral impact of the short black hair and chiseled cheekbones of the man waiting just outside the office door as she passed him. Admitting any kind of gut-kick attraction to a man was, at least, an inconvenience, and, at most, a huge mistake. Her relationship with Marcus had taught her that.

But the man's piercing blue gaze locked on and followed her through the doorway. The skin at the nape beneath her short hair tingled with awareness at his interest. Only, she wasn't sure if it was sensual nerves fluttering to attention, or an alarm going off. Either way, she wasn't about to flutter for any man, and she wasn't going to ignore those survival instincts that warned her of danger.

Olivia stopped in the middle of the assistant's office and turned to face Mr. Tall Dark and Staring. "May I help you?"

He pulled back the front of his tan corduroy sport coat and tucked his hands into the pockets of his jeans, assuming a casual stance she wouldn't match. "I can tell you why you're here, Detective Watson."

Her chin jerked up ever so slightly at the stranger calling her by name. Un-uh. That wasn't an advantage she'd allow. Her hand instinctively came to rest over the Glock holstered to her belt. "Do I know you, Mister…?"

"Not really." The man straightened from the wall where he'd been leaning, and she could see he stood a good five or six inches over her five-foot-seven-inch height. "Ron Kober is the man my fiancée Danielle Reese was getting inside information from for a story she was writing when she was murdered six years ago."

"Danielle Reese?" Why did that name sound familiar? Didn't matter. This guy was still a couple steps ahead of her in the conversation, and she didn't like it. "You didn't answer my question. Who are you?"

"Gabriel Knight."

Was that supposed to mean something to her? That deep, succinct announcement made it sound as though he thought he was somebody important. But she'd have remembered a face like that. Not exactly handsome with all those sharp, unsmiling angles, but definitely interesting.

Olivia blinked, silently reprimanding herself for even noticing such irrelevance. It was more important to note that she saw no sign that he was wearing a gun, and since he hadn't flashed a badge to identify himself, he couldn't be a cop. Gabriel Knight must be a curiosity seeker who'd probably lied to the uniformed guard about having some kind of information on the case so he could get close enough to see the dead body.

"Sir, did one of the detectives ask you to come past the crime scene tape for questioning?" He didn't answer. Proof enough for her that Gabriel Knight was trespassing on the crime scene. She thumbed over her shoulder to the hallway. "Then you can't be in here."

"I've got press credentials." He tugged at the cord hanging around his neck and pulled a plastic card from his shirt pocket. "I'm covering the murder for the *Journal.*"

A reporter? "Yeah, well my badge outranks your little piece of plastic. If you'll wait out front with the other reporters, the press liaison will be downstairs to give a briefing in a few minutes." She took him by the arm and turned to escort him into the hallway, but the man didn't budge.

"You need to talk to me." His voice was low and articulate, and, without being a breathy whisper, was for her ears alone. "I have information on this case. That's why the officer out front let me through."

"Then you should talk to Detective Kincaid or Detective Hendricks." She released him to point out the big man with the dark hair and the black man with the diamond stud in his left earlobe in the other room. "I can introduce you when they're through with their witness."

But Gabriel Knight grabbed her elbow and pulled her back beside him. "You may not read the paper, but

I know who you are, Detective Watson. You and your partner are part of the cold case team, working older, unsolved crimes. Like the murder of Dani Reese. She was an investigative reporter, a colleague of mine. The woman I loved. She was found dead at an abandoned warehouse down on the river docks six years ago. Shot through the head like some common criminal. I'm the one who called Chief Taylor and suggested he send a team from your department here this afternoon."

Olivia jerked her arm from his grasp.

"You called the Fourth Precinct chief?" Who'd filtered the request down through Sawyer Kincaid and on to Jim and her. She hated anyone who felt they were entitled enough to break the rules of standard police procedure whenever it suited them. She could do the low, threatening voice, too. "You know, we have real work to do, Mr. Knight. KCPD is not at your beck and call to dig up sidebars for whatever story you're working on."

"Trust me, Detective, there is nothing more real to me than finding Dani's killer. If your people won't do it, I will."

Her people? Cops? Like her friends and father and grandfather and brothers? The same men and women who'd solved her own mother's brutal slaying two decades earlier? This guy was bashing them?

And then something else he said registered, cooling the defensive anger that had flashed through her veins. *The woman I loved.*

She empathized with the kind of senseless violence, anger and grief Gabriel Knight had suffered more than he knew. It only took one deep breath, one thought of her mother's smiling face, to remember her sensitivity training. "Every victim believes the death of his or her loved one is our most important case. I'm sorry for your

loss. But if the department hasn't made enough progress on Ms. Reese's death to suit you, it's only because
there haven't been any substantial leads. Not because
we've given up."

"*This* is a lead. There has to be a connection to Kober.
Find it."

"I promise you, if we get new information on your
fiancée's death, we'll look into it."

"Coming from you, that's not terribly reassuring."

Bristling at the dig that felt inexplicably personal,
coming from a man she'd never met, Olivia gestured
toward the yellow tape. She bit down on the urge to demand an explanation and invited him to walk beside her.
"We never give up on a case. Ever. But some take longer to solve than others. It's a matter of prioritization.
We review cases every day and try to focus our time,
money and manpower where it can do the most good."

"You're preaching departmental protocol, Detective Watson. And that's not a good enough answer." He
stopped at the outer door, dipping his head slightly as
he faced her one more time. "You find out who killed
Kober, and I guarantee you'll find a lead on Dani's murderer. It may even be the same man who committed
both crimes."

With that warning, he ducked beneath the tape and
stalked away. Olivia shook her head at the uniformed officer's questioning look about whether or not he needed
to stop Knight before he pushed his way through the
gathering of onlookers and got on the elevator.

She was still processing the oddly charged and cryptic encounter when she felt a tap at her elbow. She nodded to Jim and he lifted the crime scene tape for her to
exit in front of him. "You know who you were talking
to, don't you?"

"Yeah. He said his name was Gabriel Knight. He's a reporter."

"Not just any reporter." They stepped onto the elevator and Jim pushed the button for the ground floor. "Gabe Knight writes the Crime Beat column for the *Kansas City Journal*."

Her instincts about men must still be out of whack after dumping Marcus. Otherwise, she'd have pieced together the name with the clues he'd dropped.

"He's the guy who wrote all those editorials about KCPD not being able to catch the Rose Red Rapist?" And when the task force did finally catch the creep and put him on trial, there hadn't been one word of praise or apology, merely a recitation of facts and something like, *"About damn time."* Olivia groaned at her ineptitude as she walked out with Jim. Somehow she felt as if she'd betrayed her brethren cops by even having a conversation with the department's most outspoken critic. "And I was nice to him. Well, I was civil. He thinks Kober's murder is related to the unsolved death of his fiancée a few years back. Danielle Reese? He's the one who got us invited to the crime scene."

They circled the gathering of television cameras and reporters on their way to her SUV. She felt Knight's blue eyes following her from the crowd awaiting the press conference as they crossed the street, but studiously ignored the urge to meet his watchful gaze.

"He probably approached you because he thought you'd be softhearted and sympathetic to his cause." She glared at Jim over the hood of the car before they both climbed in. "Clearly, he doesn't know you very well."

Okay, so Jim's dry wit could make her laugh, too, just like her brothers' teasing guff usually did.

Olivia's smile faded as they fastened their seat belts.

"He's poking his nose into our crime scene, trying to get the scoop on the rest of the press—and then he turns around and criticizes us for not catching every last bad guy, or doing it fast enough to suit his idealistic time-table? That just sticks in my craw."

She looked through the windshield to glare at the presumptuous Mr. Knight. But those smug blue eyes were nowhere to be seen. Even with a second search among the reporters gathered in front of the building, she didn't spot his rich, coal-black hair. "That son of a…" Had that self-important buttinsky snuck back inside the building? Un-uh. Not on her watch.

Olivia pulled her keys from the ignition and opened her door. "Can you get a ride with somebody? I'm going to have a couple more words with Mr. Knight."

Jim climbed out on the opposite side. "Do you need me to go with you?"

"No, I can handle him." As soon as he'd closed his door, she hit the locks and hurried around the hood of the car.

"Olivia, we're a team, remember? I've got your back."

"I know."

"How come I don't quite believe you mean that?"

Olivia stopped midcharge. Marcus Brower had supposedly had her back, too. And while her former partner had never once let her down out on the streets, his betrayal behind closed doors would probably always taint her ability to trust a man who wasn't family again.

But Jim Parker didn't deserve to be blown off because some other guy was a two-timing jackass she'd put her career on hold for. "Sorry. You and I are still in the getting-to-know-you phase, I suppose. Sometimes, people like Gabriel Knight don't take a woman cop seriously. I need him to understand that when I tell him to go away and let us handle things, I mean it."

Seemingly satisfied with the apology and that much of an explanation, Jim nodded and pulled out his cell phone. "The man's a cool customer from what I hear. Don't let him rile that Irish blood of yours."

"Too late for that. Say, maybe you can pull out the file on Dani Reese's murder so I can get up to speed on whatever it is Knight is blaming us for. See if we can find that connection to Kober he claims, too." She waved goodbye as Jim placed his call. "I'll catch up with you back at HQ."

"Roger that." She heard an amused voice behind her as she darted across the street. "Good luck, Mr. Knight."

Chapter Two

"Are you deaf or stupid, Mr. Knight?" Gabe halted on the seventh floor's concrete landing at Olivia Watson's voice. "I'll bet it's neither one. You're just too damn arrogant to think that the rules apply to you, aren't you?"

It was the husky undertones coloring that voice, not the words themselves, that turned him to face the detective.

She glared at him from the bottom of the stairs, her chest subtly expanding and contracting beneath that trim leather jacket. It hadn't taken the police as long as he'd expected to notice him sneaking through to the back stairs and chase him up six flights of steel and concrete. This one was smart. Determined. Ticked off.

"Detective," was all the verbal acknowledgment he gave her. Because the hammer of his traitorous pulse was already acknowledging way more than it should, given that she was a cop, she was a Watson and she wanted to shut down his investigation.

The badge she wore like a necklace, the gun resting on the curve of her hip, and the accusation filling her green? gray? gold?—curiously indefinable eyes did little to diminish her striking beauty. She might wear her sable dark hair in that mannish cut and talk the same sarcasm and suspicion the male cops he knew used, but there was no mistaking the femininity in that husky voice and her leggy, athletic build—or his damnable reaction to them.

For the six years he'd been obsessed with finding Dani's killer, he'd been anything but a fan of KCPD. That another woman, a cop—Thomas Watson's daughter, no less—should get him thinking randy thoughts about stripping off all that hardware and attitude didn't sit real well with his celibate devotion to the fiancée he should have saved. His curious fascination with the mysteries surrounding the lady detective who'd tracked him down rankled his long-held contempt for the police department that had failed to bring Dani's killer to justice.

"I need you back downstairs," she ordered. "Now."

Thanks. The sharp command took the sexy out of her voice and made it easier for Gabe to dismiss his far too male reaction to her.

He moved to the edge of the landing, toward the woman attempting to stop his return to the taped-off office suite on the tenth floor. "There's no such thing as a perfect crime, Detective. Only an inability to see and understand the clues that are there. If you aren't willing to find the connection between the two murders, I will."

With a curt nod, he turned to the next set of steps, skipping a stair and another pointless conversation with KCPD.

"Don't make me pull my gun, Mr. Knight."

He stopped and leaned over the railing. "Why don't you join me and do some real police work, instead of standing there, trying to make me think you can stop me."

"Trying?" The curse that followed definitely wasn't feminine. Gabe laughed and climbed the steps. He heard her charging up the stairs after him.

Good. He'd goaded at least one KCPD cop into taking

some action. Even if she argued every step of the way, Detective Watson's presence would get him back into Ron Kober's office so he could pick up what the CSIs and detectives were saying, and he could get a closer look at the crime scene for himself.

But Gabe's smug smile flatlined when he felt a strong tug at his shoulders. "What the—"

"You are officially trespassing in a restricted area." Olivia yanked his jacket halfway down his arms, twisting them back and restricting his movement long enough to snap a pair of handcuffs around his wrists. She wrapped her hand around his elbow and turned him to face her. "And you're annoying the hell out of me. Now, either go out front with the other reporters, or I'll happily escort you to a jail cell myself."

Locking his hands behind his back wasn't going to stop his investigation. "I know Dani Reese is in your cold case files."

"Fine. I'll look it up when I get back to the precinct. You're still leaving."

With a tug on his arm and a dare to defy her challenge bringing out the green in her eyes, Gabe reluctantly fell into step beside her and headed back down the stairs. She might have changed his direction, but she hadn't silenced his voice. He calmly explained his reasons for ignoring her order to clear the building. Again. In case Olivia Watson had more bravado than brain cells going for her. "I'm trying to speed the process here, Detective. Dani was getting inside information on strong-arm tactics and a possible mob connection to Senator McCoy's campaign. Six years ago. And now he's running for re-election?"

"I get your timeline. And I get that the events are too serious to dismiss as coincidence. You said Kober was feeding your fiancée intel on the senator's campaign?" Her fingers tightened around his arm as they turned the corner—probably standard procedure to provide extra balance to a man in handcuffs. But his pulse leaped at Olivia's firm grasp on him, momentarily distracting him from the questions laced with skepticism. "How do you know that? Were you working the story, too?"

"No. It was Dani's big scoop. She was trying to make a name for herself. I didn't even realize what she was onto until it was too late." Taking a deep breath, he pushed aside his lusty reaction to Detective Watson's touch and let his heart fill with its customary guilt and grief. It wasn't hard to replace Detective Watson's changeable eye color with the sky blue beauty of Dani's soft gaze in his mind. "I started reading the notes she had saved on a zip drive one night. I found Kober and Senator McCoy's name, along with the draft of a story on kickbacks from Leland Asher."

Olivia's pace slowed. "The alleged crime boss?"

"You know there's nothing *alleged* about the way he conducts business. That man has more ways to launder money than an industrial linen service. When I confronted Dani about the scope of what she was working on—and warned her of the danger—she got mad and stormed out. By the time I found out where she was meeting her contact, it was too late." He stopped on the landing, needing to set his feet to withstand the memory that chilled his blood like a ghost passing through his body. He should have stopped Dani that night. He should have gone with her. He should have covered the damn story himself and not let a junior reporter—no matter how good her instincts might be—take that kind of risk. When he found his breath again, when he could firmly close the door on the gruesome images from the past, Gabe continued. "The next time I saw Dani, she was lying on a slab in the morgue. She'd been shot three times. The ME had to identify her by the dragon tattoo on her ankle and what was left of her teeth."

"I'm sorry." Olivia's fingers curled into a fist and she pulled away. "I know that's rough. Losing someone you love is tough enough. Seeing them in the morgue…"

Gabe glanced down to see her unfocused gaze staring off into the corner. Was that real empathy? Some haunting remembrance of another case she'd worked? An official training technique to gain his cooperation? Didn't matter.

"Save your pity. Do your job." As soon as he spoke, her gaze snapped back to his. "A couple of dock workers found Dani lying beside her abandoned car near an old warehouse. The killer had taken her engagement ring and billfold, and tried to make it look like a robbery. That's how KCPD investigated her death, as a carjacking gone bad. But I tell you, it was all about the story she was writing. That's why you people never solved the case."

"You people?" He watched her bristle at the dig against cops, against someone much closer to the case than she probably realized. Detective Watson wrapped her hand around his arm again and pulled him into step beside her. Ah, hell. She hadn't really been listening. She was just humoring him. "Less talking and more moving, okay, Knight?"

Gabe lengthened his stride to get ahead of her. He stopped on the next landing and turned, forcing her to halt on the step above him. He had no problem getting in her face and making his point. "Connect the dots, Olivia. If Ron Kober knew enough about Leland Asher's influence on the campaign to share it with the press six years ago, I don't imagine either Senator McCoy or Asher would want Kober around now. McCoy is already under investigation. If Kober told anyone what he knew? What Dani knew? You know how the press is ready to jump on any hint of a scandal during a campaign."

To her credit, she didn't back down from the confrontation. "Look, I understand why you think there could be a shared motive between the two deaths. I promise, I will read through your fiancée's case file. But I told you, I'm not even assigned to Kober's murder. All I can do is inform Detectives Hendricks and Kincaid that—" She stopped abruptly and angled her head to the side.

"I'm telling *you*."

She leaned toward the steel railing. "Shh."

He leaned with her, demanding she pay attention. "It makes sense that the same person who wanted Kober dead might also have wanted to silence Dani. The two murders—"

"Shut. Up." She pushed him back against the wall with a hand over his mouth.

And then he heard it, too. The double click of a door opening and closing. Footsteps in the stairwell below their position.

Running footsteps.

Even the pretense of listening to his outpouring of information had ended. She was in full cop mode now. Olivia pulled her hands from his chest and chin and plucked the radio off her belt. "This is Detective Watson. Has the building been cleared?" While other officers in the building responded, she pulled a ring of keys from her jeans and unlocked his cuffs. Her next question was to him. "Did you bring any of your reporter friends with you?"

Gabe shook his head. He shrugged his corduroy

jacket back onto his shoulders and zeroed in on the sounds of huffing breaths and hurrying footfalls below.

There was the punch of another door handle and a muttered curse before Olivia got back on the radio. "I've got activity in the south stairwell. Maybe somebody who shouldn't be here snuck in." Her gaze tilted up to his. Okay, so she could do the subtle dig thing, too. "Or our perp is trying to sneak out. I'll get eyes on it. Watson out." She pushed open the door marked with a three and pointed into the main building, dismissing him. "Can I trust you to find your way to the front door all by yourself?"

She must have accepted his silence as an agreement because she put away her handcuffs and radio and pulled her gun in the same fluid movement. Then those long legs were booking it down the stairs.

OLIVIA PUSHED ASIDE the charged energy that hummed through her system after trading words with Gabe Knight and focused on her pursuit of the unknown subject. She saw the second-floor door swinging shut and pressed her back against the concrete block wall, keeping her attention on both the door and the stairs, uncertain which way the intruder had gone until she heard the deep, ragged panting of a man trying to catch his breath from a location below her. He'd heard her coming and had ducked into a corner to hide.

"KCPD. You on the stairs—show yourself." She crept down to the midfloor landing, her gun leading the way. "Hands up where I can see them."

She smelled the sweat of fear and desperation coming off the intruder as she neared the rear exit on the first floor. Maybe this was just a homeless guy who'd wandered in off the street. Nothing like discovering a hoped-for haven swarming with cops to make a guy nervous. "I'm Detective Watson with KCPD. My goal isn't to hurt you, but you're trespassing. I'd like you to identify yourself, and I need to ask you some questions."

For a few seconds, the heavy breathing stopped. Olivia focused in on the body odor wafting from the recess between the rear exit and the side of the stairs and turned. There was a guttural roar and a flash of gray before the intruder's arms swung over the railing with a metal folding chair and knocked her down the last couple of steps.

Olivia pitched forward, landing on her hip and shoulder, hitting the floor hard. Her knuckles banged against the concrete. She lost her grip on the gun and the weapon slid beyond her reach.

Instead of capitalizing on his advantage and hitting her again, the perp in the gray hoodie ran past her. But Olivia wasn't about to ignore an opportunity to take control of the situation. She kicked out her feet, twisted her legs through his and tripped him.

In a tumble of clanking metal and furious curses, her attacker went down. For the split second he was stunned by the impact with the unforgiving concrete, Olivia went after her Glock. The attacker extricated himself from the chair and pushed to his feet while she rolled toward her weapon and scooped it up.

"Hey! Stop!" A blur of denim and corduroy shot past her.

Olivia flipped over, bracing her gun between her hands. But the only shot she had was Gabriel Knight's back as he shoved her attacker against the door. "Son of a…"

She scrambled to her feet, hating that any man thought he had to save her.

"He's got a gun!" Gabe shouted.

Ah, hell. She saw it, too. "Move!"

Adrenaline or stubbornness kept him from obeying her command. With his forearm wedged against the other man's throat, Gabriel grabbed her attacker's wrist and slammed it against the wall. Once. Twice. The small Saturday night special popped free and skittered across the floor. The pesky reporter was taller and broader than the other man, blocking out any chance to get a good read on the perp beyond faded jeans and the sweatshirt. Olivia picked the snub-nosed semiautomatic up by the barrel and tucked it into the back of her belt.

She was about to put her shoulder into the reporter's ribs and knock him away from the perp when she saw the flash of steel arcing between the two men. "Knife!" She raised her gun again. "Drop it!"

Gabe Knight cursed as the smaller man shoved him into Olivia, knocking them both against the rack of folding chairs. The storage rack shifted and they wound up tangled on the floor beneath an avalanche of more chairs. The attacker flung the door open and charged into the alley behind the building before she could push Gabe off her and roll to her feet. "Get out of my way!"

"Damn it. Olivia!"

She left Gabe's outstretched fingers behind and flew out the door after the man with the knife. "Police. Stop!"

Why was it that skinny guys could always fly?

She shifted into high gear, her boots crunching gravel and debris against the asphalt. But it was no good. Even running at full tilt, he easily widened the gap between them. And she couldn't fire off even a warning shot without a clear line of sight to the cars driving past on the street beyond and whoever might be walking along the sidewalk and accidentally step into her line of fire. In a matter of seconds, like a shadow swallowed up by the bright afternoon sunlight, the perp shot around the corner and was gone.

Olivia lowered her gun, skidding to a halt as she reached the sidewalk. She glanced up and down and across the street through the beginnings of rush-hour traffic. "You lousy, lucky chameleon."

He'd either ducked inside a nearby shop or had a ride waiting for him. At the very least, he'd dropped the hood and merged with the crowd of pedestrians crossing the street as the light turned green. Since she hadn't seen his face, she had no way to identify him—not even by hair color.

"Damn you, Gabriel Knight." Breathing deeply from the wind sprint, her voice was barely a whisper. But the gun and the badge made shocked and curious passersby walk a wide berth around her. She put up her hand to reassure them she meant them no harm and holstered her gun.

But the would-be rescuer who'd gotten in the way of her doing her job was another story. Olivia raked her bangs off her forehead, blew out a heated breath and decided to tell Gabe Knight exactly where he could stick his machismo. Maybe she'd even take him in for interfering with a police officer and allowing the person she wanted to question escape.

With a decisive nod, she spun around...and plowed into the middle of Gabriel Knight's chest. There was a brief bombardment of sensations—soft corduroy and unyielding muscle; long, sinewed fingers; the faint scents of coffee and soap; heated skin beneath starched cotton—before she jerked back into her own space and shored up her defenses with the frustration and annoyance still sparking through her. Olivia planted her hands at her hips and tipped her face to his. "You followed me?"

"Are you hurt?" Gabe asked, dropping his hands from her shoulders, ignoring the accusation.

"Am I—" His nostrils flared with what must have been a fast run for him, too. The lines beside his eyes etched with concern as that piercing blue gaze swept over her. But her irritation with the man dissipated when she saw the blood dripping from his sleeve onto the asphalt at his feet. Shaking her head at the injury that could have been avoided if he'd just done what she'd said, she moved to his side to inspect the clean slice through the sleeves of his coat and shirt. "He cut you."

"I'm fine."

She'd tended enough scrapes with her three older brothers growing up that she knew that was a lie. "Let me see." She put his hand up so gravity would help control the blood flow, and peeled back the shirt cuff that was no longer white. Although the perp hadn't nicked the main vein or artery, the three-inch gash across Gabe's forearm was deep enough to need stitches. "I don't suppose your chivalry extends to carrying a handkerchief, does it?"

He smirked, reaching behind him to pull a palmful of folded white cotton from the rear pocket of his jeans. Gabe shook it open and pressed it against the wound with a wince. "You're welcome."

"For what?" Olivia took over rolling up the handkerchief and wrapping it around his forearm. "I'm going to have bruises on my tailbone and elbows, thanks to you."

"Me?" he scoffed. "That guy attacked you. He had a gun. You didn't have any backup."

"I didn't need any backup." She'd been half joking when she'd asked for the hanky. The old-fashioned habit of carrying one reminded Olivia of her Grandpa Seamus, touching a mushy place inside her…for about two seconds. Gabriel Knight was certainly no sweet, old grandfather. With a determined shrug of her shoulders, Olivia denied any softening in the animosity she felt toward this man and pulled the knot tight, drawing the skin on either side of the cut together and stemming the ooze of blood. "He was running, not fighting. I had him."

"You were on the floor."

Unlike her vocal brothers, a tightening of his lips was the only complaint Gabe made about her nursing technique. As soon as he started to lower his arm, Olivia pushed it back up. "I had the vantage point to retrieve my weapon. But you got in the way and I couldn't use my gun. Now a potential killer, or a possible witness, at the very least, is on the loose and we've got no way to track him."

"That was no innocent bystander." Gabe curled his fingers into a claw in front of her face. "My hand was on the knife with his. I've got his DNA under my nails."

Olivia released him and backed away a step. "Is that why you jumped into a situation I had under control? Just so you could swipe some DNA from a suspect?"

"Call a CSI and find out if he's in the system. At the very least, I can give a description. White male. Late twenties, early thirties. About five-nine, wiry build, receding hairline." The intensity around those cobalt eyes relaxed and he grinned at her dubious glare. "I'm a professional observer. I've got an excellent eye for detail."

The leather of her jacket creaked as she crossed her arms in front of her. He thought he'd one-upped her? Solving crimes was her job, not his. And she was damn good at it. "Yeah, well did your eye for detail notice the perp didn't have any blood on him until you got cut?

Bashing in somebody's head creates a lot of spatter. If he killed Ron Kober upstairs, then he changed his clothes and stashed them somewhere. That's probably why he was opening and closing doors." Olivia's gaze dropped to the buttons on Gabriel Knight's shirt as her thoughts took a left turn into facts that made less sense. "Why club the victim over the head when he already had two weapons on him?"

Although it had been a rhetorical question, Mr. Thought-he-knew-better-than-she-did answered, "Weapon of opportunity? Were there signs of a struggle up there?"

More like signs of a good clean-up job. Not exactly the kind of painstaking task she'd associate with their panicked, high-speed attacker. Olivia pulled her phone from her pocket. "I'm calling Detective Kincaid to give him a description of the intruder, and let him know to search the building and vehicles in the area for soiled clothes."

Fully in detective mode now, Olivia glanced around the alley, poking inside trash bags and around a stack of discarded office furniture while she reported the incident to Sawyer Kincaid. Once she hung up, she went to the nearby Dumpster to look inside. But Gabriel Knight had eavesdropped on every word; his eyes had watched every move. Now he came up beside her, lifting the lid from her hand and holding it open while she searched.

"This is a police investigation, Mr. Knight. Your services are not needed, nor are they welcome." She pointed to the stain on his coat. "You'd better go have a doctor look at that."

"If solving Kober's murder leads me to solving Danielle's, I'm not going anywhere."

A drop of blood fell from the crimson moisture

soaking his sleeve into the stinky remnants of office lunches and cleaning supplies. Groaning in resignation, she palmed his shoulder and pushed him back, catching the lid and closing it.

"You're contaminating another potential crime scene." She moved between him and the Dumpster, forcing him to retreat one more step. "Along with any DNA you *might* have picked up from your attacker."

"Your attacker, too."

Shaking her head, Olivia pulled her radio off her belt and made another call to Sawyer Kincaid and the other officers in and around the building. "This is Detective Watson. I was searching the trash in the alley behind the building. But I've got an injured civilian in need of medical attention I have to see to. I'll leave the gun the perp dropped with one of the CSI's out front, but you'll have to get somebody else to comb the area back here." She shivered beneath the unblinking intensity of Mr. Knight's piercing blue eyes. Didn't the man have business of his own to tend to besides insinuating himself into hers? "By the way, your eye for detail missed the jimmy marks on the door. That's why he had the knife, and most likely how he got inside. Still can't explain the gun, though. What I saw upstairs was a crime of passion, of opportunity. Why get your hands dirty when you can kill someone from a distance?" That probing gaze never wavered from her face, even when she drifted into her thoughts and back again. "What, you've got nothing to say for once?"

"You're not getting rid of me, Olivia." He leaned in, refusing to back down. "Either I'm part of this investigation, or I'm a long, tall shadow dogging your every move."

Feeling the chill of his real shadow falling over her

upturned face, a proximity alert went off inside her. An unexpected urge tingled through the tips of her fingers. Shaking her head, Olivia stepped to the side before she forgot she was a cop and did something stupid like slap that arrogant taunt off his face…or touch his chest to see if his heart was thumping as wildly against his rib cage as hers suddenly was.

Every self-preserving instinct she had warned her to leave Gabriel Knight and those annoying shivers he triggered right here in the alley. But Olivia had a badge and responsibilities and a hardwired sense of right and wrong she had to answer to that made her feel obligated to drive him to the ER to get his wound stitched up. "Come on. My car's out front. Keep it elevated." She took his elbow and pushed his injured forearm up and helped him hold it above the tempting location of his heart. "I'll take you to the hospital."

Chapter Three

Olivia sat on a metal stool outside the curtain of one of the ER bays at the Truman Medical Center and texted a preliminary report about the events that had transpired in the stairwell and back alley of Ron Kober's office building to her work email while the facts were still clear in her head. Although her shift was officially over, the long hours had become a habit. She'd be in before roll call meeting in the morning, too, to type her notes into a formal report for the case file.

Annoying reporter trespassed on crime scene and interfered with officer in pursuit of suspect. Recommend citing him for being a PITA.

She listened in on the more professional exchange of medical information from the other side of the curtain.

"That should do it, Mr. Knight," the lady doctor who'd introduced herself as Emilia Rodriguez-Grant intoned in a soft but succinct voice. Olivia breathed in, waiting for the words of dismissal that would signify an end to this obligation to the man who'd gotten hurt while in her custody. She heard the clank of a medical instrument being set onto a metal tray as Dr. Rodriguez-Grant continued. "Try not to get it wet for twenty-four hours. It'll leave a scar, but the stitches will keep the mark thin and less noticeable—and certainly reduce your chances of the wound becoming infected."

"Thanks, Doctor," Gabe's deep voice replied.

Scar? Wound? Olivia's lungs emptied out with a sigh of guilty resignation. She was well-trained and fully capable of defending herself against a violent suspect. But she'd only seen the folding chair and the gun. Chances were, that knife would have sliced through *her* skin if Gabriel Knight hadn't intervened.

She deleted the last two sentences from the text and replaced them with a more accurate, less petulant account.

Reporter Gabe Knight injured in assistance of officer on scene. Recommend follow-up on allegations of ties twixt Ron Kober's death and murder of Dani Reese.

After sending the text to her computer, Olivia stood, smoothing out the wrinkles in her jeans and stretching to ease the kinks in her neck and back. Her new partner, Jim Parker, was right. She'd let her emotions interfere with the calm, logical pursuit of the facts and her duty to a citizen she'd sworn to protect and serve.

Common sense meant she couldn't just dump Gabe Knight off at the hospital. As much as he'd butted heads and gotten in her way, she still needed an official witness statement from him, in case the man who'd escaped did have some bearing on Kober's murder—or the death of Gabe's fiancée. The DNA the tech from the crime lab had scraped from beneath his nails might provide a vital clue to identify the killer of one or both victims, so it had been necessary to keep him with her to maintain the chain of custody of that potential evidence. Besides, with his penchant for taking the police department to task for its shortcomings, Gabriel Knight was the last man she could risk abandoning. If he was injured worse than anything a few stitches could fix, or he blamed her for getting cut in the first place, then abandoning him at the hospital might put the department in danger of some kind of lawsuit. He'd probably make her front-page news on a dereliction of duty accusation.

Before a renewed wave of guilt and irritation could sideline her thoughts again, Olivia pulled aside the privacy curtain. "How much longer do you think you'll be…?"

Olivia's brain blanked for a split second when she saw Gabe Knight stripped to the trim waist of his blue jeans. She winced at the bruising he'd earned from his struggle with the perp, and suspected she had many similar marks herself.

But it wasn't pain—or even empathy—that quickened her pulse. *Focus on the woman in the green hospital scrubs and lab coat. Ignore the tapering T-shaped back of the man sitting on the stool beside the examination table.* So much smooth, tanned skin. She'd bet it was warm skin, too, since there was nary a goose bump, in spite of the chill from the hospital's air conditioning. *Olivia Mary Watson!*

Obeying her own mental reprimand, Olivia tore her gaze from the long stretch of Gabe Knight's bare back, forcing her attention to the petite brunette doctor. "Um, are you about done, Dr. Grant?"

The wide shoulders shrugged and Gabe rose and turned to face her. "Kept you waiting too long, Detective?"

"Hold on, Mr. Knight." Olivia's wayward eyes got some naked chest time, too, before Dr. Rodriguez-Grant tugged Gabe's arm back across the table to wrap a long piece of self-sticking gauze around his forearm. She cut the piece off the roll and patted the protective bandage into place before releasing him. "Now you're done. We just need to finish the paperwork."

Stop ogling! What was she, in junior high? Olivia raked her fingers through her hair, using the movement to distract her. She hardly qualified as a gawking innocent. It wasn't as if she'd never seen a man's naked chest before. She'd grown up with three brothers, a dad and a grandpa in the house, after all. And she'd been with Marcus for almost seven months before that relationship had blown up in her face. But Gabe Knight was taller, leaner than Marcus. His black hair was a smoky dust across some nicely honed pecs that indicated he got more exercise than sitting behind a desk all day, writing crime reports and editorials critical of KCPD.

And though she prided herself on her eye for detail, those were *not* the details she was supposed to be paying attention to. She needed to get away from this man and get a good night's sleep to recharge her energy and ability to concentrate.

"No rush. I just need to call my partner and let him know my status if I'm going to be much longer." That part was true. Jim had already texted her twice, asking if she was still with the reporter and if everything was okay. He'd gone house hunting after work with his wife, but would be there pronto if she needed him. He'd also pulled up Danielle Reese's case file and wanted to get her up to speed on the dead-end investigation. "I can go outside to make my call."

But the ER doctor stopped her before she reached the hallway. "Hang on a sec. I have some information for you, too, Detective Watson." Olivia stepped back into the treatment bay and made a point of watching Dr. Rodriguez-Grant roll the tray table out of her way and cross to a stainless steel counter to retrieve a prescription pad. "Are you up to date on your tetanus shot, Mr. Knight?"

Gabe nodded. "My work takes me out of the country sometimes, so I'm current."

"Good." The petite doctor jotted a note on the prescription pad and tore off the top sheet. "Take the full round of antibiotics and see your doctor in about ten days to remove the stitches. Of course, if it shows any signs of swelling or infection in the meantime, come back and see me."

He took the prescription note the doctor handed him and stuffed it into the front pocket of his jeans. "Thanks."

The doctor tucked her short, dark brown hair behind each ear and peeled off her sterile gloves before addressing Olivia. "If you need an official statement from me, Detective Watson, that was definitely a defensive knife wound. Something with a short, thin blade—or else we'd be in surgery reattaching tendons and ligaments instead of mending skin and muscle. I can send the official medical report for your files if you need them."

"I'd appreciate that, ma'am." Olivia quickly noted the information on her phone before reaching into the pocket behind her badge. "Here's my card."

The doctor smiled as she tucked the business card into her lab coat. "I know the address. My husband and brother both work for KCPD."

A snort of derision turned her head to the man sorting through the bundle of clothing at the examination table. Was that aggravated huff a response to learning he was surrounded by KCPD fans? Or merely a frustrated testament to the stained jacket and one-sleeved shirt that had been cut apart to gain access to the wound?

Olivia turned back to Emilia, answering with a genuine smile to distract the other woman from Gabe's possible rudeness. "I know your brother A.J. He's a very well-respected leader at the Fourth Precinct."

"Thank you. My husband, Justin Grant, is on the bomb squad—"

A knock on the outer door stopped the conversation and a blond nurse peeked through the gap in the curtains. "Dr. Grant? We have a girl in Bay 2 who's having an allergic reaction to something she ate. She's breathing on her own, but the hives—"

"I'm on my way." She was already following the nurse to another ER bay when she glanced back to Gabe and Olivia. "Excuse me."

"Of course." Suddenly, Olivia was aware of how small this curtained-off area was—and that she was alone with the department's archenemy, Gabe Knight, a man who got under her skin and into her head far too easily for her peace of mind.

Several seconds of awkward silence passed before Gabe pulled on what was left of his white shirt. "Do I need to call a cab, or will you give me a ride back to the paper?"

"Can't wait to write an exposé about me letting the perp get away? Or allowing you to get hurt?"

The dark brow over his right eye arched, his cool demeanor easily deflecting the accusations. "I was thinking more along the lines of retrieving my car from the parking garage and driving home. I jogged over to Kober's building from the *Journal* as soon as the police bulletin came through. It was just a couple of blocks from my office."

"Do you check up on every cop in the neighborhood? Or did I just get lucky that you're my responsibility today?"

He inhaled deeply, drawing her attention to the expanding hills and hollows peeking through the open front of his shirt. Really? She couldn't maintain a polite distance, or a sneering disinterest in whatever testosterone he was exuding for even two seconds? This man was the enemy of KCPD. That made him her enemy, too. Right?

He pointed to the bandage wrapped around his left forearm. "*This* is on me. I thought that fool was going to hurt you. After seeing Dani the way I did, knowing I should have done something more, I…" The sharp angles of his cheeks and jaw softened with a wry grin. "Guess I had a caveman moment."

"Caveman?" As tempted to laugh at the apt description of his earlier interference as she'd been tempted to reach out to him when his eyes had darkened at the memory of his murdered fiancée, Olivia eased up on the self-recriminations and settled for smiling in return. That was probably as good an apology as she was going to get from him—and more of a concession than she'd expected. "Me no need Og's help," she teased. "Me carry big gun."

"You carry big attitude." No denying that. And then he extended his hand across the examination table. "Thank you."

"For what?" Although her instinct was to reach out to accept a proffered hand, her caution around this man left her fingers hovering in the air.

But there was no hesitation when Gabe closed the gap between them and wrapped his hand firmly around hers. Olivia's pulse leaped as if an electrical connection had just been completed. Instead of pulling away, her fingertips squeezed around the breadth of his palm. His skin was as warm as she'd imagined, and the heat of his grip seeped beneath her skin and lit a slow, easy fire that licked its way up her arm. "For listening to my side of the story. For not leaving me there in that alley to bleed. I know holding KCPD accountable hasn't made them my biggest fan."

"Any cop would have brought you to the hospital. We don't stop to evaluate whether or not we like you if you're threatened or hurt. If someone needs our help, we do our best to deliver."

"I'll remember that next time we meet." Gabe's gaze dropped to where they still held on to each other.

Next time? Olivia quickly pulled her hand away. Was that anxiety or anticipation crawling along her spine? She supposed another encounter with the bullying reporter was inevitable, since he'd made it clear he intended to dog the Cold Case Squad's investigation into his fiancée's murder. Didn't mean she had to cling to him as though…as though she liked touching him. Still, if he could make the effort to be a little more civil and respectful, then she would do the same.

Appreciating the unspoken truce, Olivia pulled her keys from her jacket pocket and headed for the door. "I'll drive. Finish buttoning things up and meet me out in the waiting room."

Olivia strode down the hallway, flexing her fingers down at her side to alleviate the tingling awareness that lingered, determined to leave Gabe Knight and his blue eyes, warm skin and bothersome words behind her. Whatever was out of whack with her libido this evening would surely go away once she got a good night's sleep. But she'd only inhaled a couple of cool, reviving breaths when she heard the commotion out at the information desk in the lobby. "Oh, no."

She recognized all five of those urgent, worried male voices. She turned the corner and her family shifted as one, like a flock of tall, robust birds, and hurried toward her.

"Livvy?" Her father's familiar limp led the charge, his arms outstretched toward her.

There must be a sign over her head today. *Trouble magnet.* Just because she *could* handle whatever the world threw her way didn't mean she wanted to. Thomas Watson's beefy arms wrapped her up in a bear hug that lifted her onto her toes. "What happened? How badly are you hurt? I heard you took a gun off a perp."

Olivia treasured a few snug moments against her dad's chest before dropping back onto her heels and stepping away. But that only allowed space for her brothers and grandfather to circle around her. One palmed the back of her head. Another squeezed her shoulder. "It's not what you think, Dad."

Her second-oldest brother, the one with the glasses and the medical degree, brushed her bangs off her forehead and hunched down to study her eyes. "Tell me exactly what your physician said."

"You're a doctor for dead people," she groaned, referring to his position as a medical examiner with the crime lab. She swatted his hand away. "I'm not the patient, Niall. I'm fine."

Her oldest brother, Duff, wasn't buying it. "The radio report said that *you* were headed to the ER."

"Damn it, guys. If you're going to eavesdrop on the police scanner, make sure you've got your information right. I brought in a…" What exactly was Gabriel Knight? A suspect? A lead on a murder investigation?

A not-so-innocent bystander? "I brought in a person of interest who is…helping with a case. He got injured at a crime scene late this afternoon."

Her father propped his hands at his waist and shook his head, needing a little more convincing for the fear to dissipate. "But you're okay? You missed dinner. Dad made his Guinness bread and stew. You never miss that."

"Oh." She smiled at the silver-haired gentleman beside her father. "Sorry, Grandpa. I lost track of the time. Did you save me a slice?"

Seamus Watson released his double grip on his cane and squeezed her hand. "Of course, sweetie."

Keir, the brother closest in age to her, loosened the knot of his tie. "I heard you were in pursuit of an armed suspect. Are you sure you're okay?"

"A couple of bruises and a wounded ego for letting the guy I was chasing get away. But I'm fine." She beamed a reassuring smile to each member of her close-knit family before reaching up to smooth the rumpled collar of her father's blue chambray shirt. "Now you want to get the gang out of here? I'm sure somebody in this family besides me has to work in the morning. I don't know about any of you, but I'm exhausted. Let's all go to our respective homes, and I promise I'll swing by the house tomorrow morning." She winked to the eighty-year-old sweetheart beside her dad. Seamus had always been her go-to guy when she needed someone in the family to listen to her. "A toasty piece of Grandpa's bread and an over-easy egg to dip it in is my favorite breakfast."

"I'm glad it was just a misunderstanding and that you're all right." His old-country lilt was as softly reassuring as the sweet peck on the cheek he gave her. "I'll have breakfast hot and ready for you. Good night, Livvy."

"Good night, Grandpa."

They were in the midst of hugs and good-nights and going on their way when her father puffed up to his full height and glared over Olivia's shoulder. "This SOB is your person of interest?"

Olivia didn't have to turn to know that Gabe had come up behind her. She was learning to recognize him by the size of his shadow and the subtle scent that was a mix of soap and starch and now a tinge of antiseptic. And that deep-pitched voice with the cynical undertones was unmistakable.

"Is this the rest of your family, Detective?"

The *rest* of her family? Although the question didn't quite make sense, Olivia nodded. Every loud, overprotective, stubborn Irish man belonged to her. "These are my guys."

Gabe stepped up beside her, his gaze sweeping the circle of her family. "Let me guess, you're *all* cops?"

"Kansas City's Finest." Her father's shoulders came back proudly as he made the claim. "Not that you'd care."

Of course, they'd recognize the department's harshest critic—and be less than pleased to learn he was the man she'd brought to the ER. She didn't suppose introductions would alleviate the tension rising around her, but it couldn't hurt to turn the rumored enemy into an actual person with a name and a stitched-up arm—or to let Gabe know just how proud she was of her family and their accomplishments.

"Dad, this is Gabriel Knight. You probably recognize his name from the *Kansas City Journal*. My father, Thomas Watson. Dad retired a senior detective from the department a couple years ago. This is my grandfather, Seamus, a longtime desk sergeant, also KCPD, retired." There was no sense adding a title to the other introductions—they all wore the badges and ME card from their respective departments proudly on display. "My brothers, Duff, Niall and Keir."

If anything, the animosity in the air thickened. Her father looked as grim as she'd ever seen him. "Introductions aren't necessary, Livvy. We've met."

She swiveled her gaze up to Gabe. He wasn't smiling, either. He nodded, confirming her dad's icy statement. "Watson. When I met your daughter, I wasn't expecting to run into you. Maybe I just didn't want to."

"How do you two know each other?" Olivia asked.

"Your father was the cop who investigated Dani's murder."

Chapter Four

"What were you thinking?"

The fidgety young man sitting in the plush chair on the other side of the desk was crawling out of his skin as he listened to the calmer voice.

"You could have ruined everything. I told you I'd take care of it."

"I had to do something," the young man argued.

"No, you didn't. If you'd been caught, your actions would have jeopardized everything we've worked for."

"Are you angry with me?"

"Surprised. Maybe a little disappointed." That sucked the nervous energy right out of him. "I thought you trusted me."

"I do. But I can't go to prison." The young man scratched at the marks on the back of his hand. He needed a shave, some sleep, and most likely, a fix. "I don't think I could handle that. What if Mr. Kober talked?"

"He won't now, will he? And he wouldn't have. As I said, everything is as it should be, according to my plan. I'm taking care of the situation, just as I'm taking care of you." The host unlocked the top right drawer of the desk and reached inside to pull out a small envelope filled with cash. The young man's eyes rounded like saucers and he nearly licked his chapped lips in anticipation. "You know I shouldn't give you this. It's not much, just enough to tide you over for a few days."

The young man leaned forward in his chair. "I can't get any money right now. It's all tied up."

"I'm sure you feel frustrated about that."

"Helpless is more like it. When I saw on TV that Senator McCoy was running for reelection, and that Mr. Kober was being investigated, I had to do something. He knew about that woman. What if he knew about me, too?" The nerves were kicking in again. "I could lose what little I have left. If the truth comes out…"

This misguided, troubled young man had no real understanding of the truth. "You wouldn't want your family to find out what you've done, would you?"

His chair rattled against the floor as he visibly shook. "No."

"Then trust me. Just like you have all along. I've taken good care of you, haven't I? I've helped you."

His brown eyes fixated on the envelope. "Yeah."

"When you listen to me and do as I suggest, everything is fine?"

The young man nodded.

"Then listen to me now." The host slipped the envelope across the desk and the young man snatched it up and stuffed it inside his jacket. "It's more important than ever that you don't draw any attention to yourself. Go home to your family. Clean yourself up. Get back to your work and leave everything to me. I've got it all under control—"

"*I* want to be in control." Angry tears dotted his cheeks as the young man pounded his fist on top of the desk. "I'm not in control of my own life, anymore."

The host inhaled a deep breath and exhaled the irritation this visitor was causing. "That will come in time. I promise you. We can't solve all your problems in one day."

"I'm trying to do the right thing."

"I know. But until you learn to make the best choices for yourself, you need to listen to me. Do what I tell you and everything will be fine. Do you understand that?"

The young man's head jerked with a nod.

"Good."

OLIVIA TILTED HER EYES to the rearview mirror and drummed her fingers on the Explorer's steering wheel. It was still there.

The low-slung muscle car with the tinted windows sat two vehicles behind her, waiting at the same stoplight. Normally, she would have dismissed several sightings of the same car on the way to work as a comrade in arms, battling rush-hour traffic en route to his or her job in downtown Kansas City.

But she didn't like not being able to get some description of the driver—gender, age, ethnicity. She didn't like having her vision so obscured by traffic that she couldn't get a license plate number. She especially didn't like spotting the same car cruising past her father's house long before she'd pulled onto the Interstate to merge with the thousands of other cars swarming into the city this morning. And seeing the same black car pull off on the same exit to enter the heart of downtown raised every hackle at the nape of her neck.

Someone was following her.

At least, that's what every instinct that had been on hyperalert since yesterday afternoon was trying to tell her.

Yesterday, she'd made a mental note of the silver SUV

Gabe Knight drove when she dropped him off. Although her goodbye and *Don't call me, I'll call you* had been firm and to the point, she wouldn't put it past him to tail her, in hopes of finding out information on his fiancée's murder. But why switch vehicles? She knew he had an obsessive interest in the case. But other than not sharing the connection he had to her father, he'd seemed like a straightforward kind of guy. This had to be something else, right?

But she'd been wrong about Ron Kober's murder being a wasted errand for her and Jim. She'd been wrong about the man in the stairwell intending no harm. She might even have been wrong about Gabriel Knight being the coldhearted villain the rest of the department believed him to be.

Maybe yesterday hadn't been a fluke, and her people-reading radar was on the fritz. She could be wrong about Mr. Muscle Car back there, too. But just to test a theory...

As soon as the light changed, Olivia nosed her Explorer into the turn lane and made a sharp left without signaling. She raised an apologetic hand at the honks of protest and cruised on through the intersection. Good. The driver in the black car wasn't laying on the horn or making any sudden moves to turn the corner after her.

Huffing out the breath she must have been holding, Olivia relaxed her grip around the steering wheel and merged into traffic to double back to her original route. So maybe the car wasn't following her. If it showed up again between here and the KCPD parking garage, she could always stick the siren on her roof and swing around to make a traffic stop and get her questions answered. But for now, she could drop her guard.

Olivia drove the last six blocks without another sighting of the black car. Not Gabe Knight. Not a threat. Her suspicion eased enough to chalk up the notion she was being followed to coincidence. Either a car dealer had made a fortune selling more than one customized car, or the driver was simply traveling the same route that she was. Stranger things had happened.

With a little rational thought, Olivia had her emotional armor firmly back in place as she pulled into the KCPD parking garage. She locked up her SUV and headed down the stairs, joining the migration of personnel reporting in for morning duty.

The sun in the east was warm, peeking between the tall buildings of downtown Kansas City. The newly planted dogwood trees in front of the limestone building that served as both Fourth Precinct and administrative headquarters were budding out. Her tummy was full of Grandpa Seamus's good cooking. Her dad had tolerated her questions about Dani Reese's murder—even though any mention of Gabe Knight still seemed to get him hot under the collar. The irksome conflicts that had messed up yesterday for her were just that—yesterday's business. She was nothing if not resilient. Feeling stronger and smarter and more sure of herself this morning, Olivia looked forward to seeing friends and getting some solid investigative work done.

The building's public facade was feeling more familiar, too, with several months of construction and re-installation and upgrades to the security system finally complete. The entryway at the top of the gray granite steps had been rebuilt after a tornado the previous summer had toppled stately pine trees and tossed a vehicle through the front doors. There were new benches out front, new shine to the steel framing the double doors, manufacturer stickers still stuck to the glass that had recently been replaced. But despite the torn-up landscaping, shattered windows and damaged antennae and satellite dishes on the roof that had been repaired or replaced, the concrete-and-steel heart of the ninety-year-old building remained intact.

Olivia wished the officer she'd been chatting with a good day and took a detour to one of the benches. Another departmental fixture that hadn't changed much was Max Krolikowski. Olivia grinned at the burly blond detective in the black leather blazer reclining against the back of the bench, with one foot propped up on the opposite knee and a Churchill-style cigar pinched between his lips. The uniform had changed as he'd moved from assignment to assignment, but now that the two were both working in the cold case unit, she'd learned that the former army sergeant wasn't as antisocial and bad for the department's public image as he'd like most people to believe.

He muttered a curse that made her smile when he saw her approach, sat up straight and pulled the flattened tip of the cigar from his mouth. "Here it comes," he growled.

Olivia sat on the bench beside him. "I thought you gave up smoking."

Although he wasn't any older than her brother Duff, Max had his grumpy-old-man shtick down to an art form. "Do you see a match or lighter on me?"

"Well, I can't imagine eating that stogie is any better for you." She eyed the trash can beside him. "Why don't you just throw it away?"

"Mind your own business, Liv." He flicked the cigar into the trash, then pulled two more wrapped smokes from his chest pocket to show her how ornery he could be. "I'm not one of your brothers. You don't have to take care of me."

Uh-huh. That's why there was a stain from breakfast,

or maybe even last night's dinner, peeking from behind the badge hanging at the front of his shirt.

Olivia checked her watch and stood. "You know I only nag because I care about you."

"Bite me."

Olivia laughed. "Come on. Roll call is about to start. Then we have our briefing with Lieutenant Rafferty-Taylor. I've got a six-year-old murder case I want to take another look at."

He tucked the cigars inside the front of his jacket and dropped his work-booted foot to the pavement. "Sounds like reason enough to start my day."

A shadow fell over Olivia and she shivered. But that rush of anticipation at the idea of butting heads with Gabriel Knight again quickly died when she faced familiar cocoa-brown eyes that had once made her heart skip a beat. Marcus Brower's perfect white smile lit up his face with a grin. "Hey, look, it's Beauty and the Beast."

Her heart still skipped a beat. But it was a jolt of surprise, of not being prepared to fend off the inevitable suspicion and remembered humiliation pounding through her veins. Even if the pain wasn't as intense as it had once been, it took Olivia a deep breath and a needless adjusting of the zippers on her teal leather jacket to paste a wry smile on her own face and answer. "Good morning, Marcus."

He winked. "Morning, babe."

What Max Krolikowski lacked in manners, he made up for in loyalty. While Olivia bristled at the endearment, her grousing coworker stood up beside her. "We were just leaving."

But Marcus's hand on her arm stopped her. "Hey, Liv. We see each other every day, but we never talk. Can we? Are you free for lunch?"

"No."

"Dinner?"

She shook her head. "I'm busy."

"Don't blow me off. I know you're not seeing anyone."

"That doesn't mean I don't have a life." She jerked her arm from his grasp. "I've got plans." And by dinner tonight, she hoped that pathetic little lie would be the truth.

"Okay, so you're not purposely avoiding me." A dimple appeared at the corner of his mouth as the charming smile reappeared. "Morning, noon or night—you tell me when, and I'll be there. I don't like the way we left things."

An image of a naked Marcus rolling around on *their* bed with the receptionist from his dentist's office or the gym or wherever he'd picked up that latest conquest blipped through her mind. Olivia resolutely slammed the door on that memory and backed up a step to follow Max. "There's nothing more to say. You made your choice."

He caught the tips of her fingers with his, lightly hanging on. "We were good friends—partners—before I screwed up. I miss the way we used to be. I made a mistake. I want to fix that."

Max leveled his icy gaze over Olivia's shoulder. "We've got meetings to get to, sunshine. So do you."

The charm bled from Marcus's tone. "Was I talking to you, Krolikowski? Bug off."

Olivia extricated her fingers from Marcus's pseudo-grasp and pushed Max on up the stairs before a real argument with an unwanted audience could start. "Let's go."

"I'm not giving up on this, Liv," Marcus called after

her. "I was a better person when I was with you. I owe you an explanation."

A spurt of her own temper rose like bile in her throat. The explanation was simple. Marcus was a player. His ability to say no to any flirtatious come-on when they'd been together wasn't any stronger than his ability to grasp the meaning of the word right now. Yes, she'd been good for him—but the reverse wasn't true. She didn't need a private heart-to-heart to understand that.

She spun around to let Marcus know exactly when she'd be willing to listen to any excuse he had to say. Never. "You don't owe me any..."

But the snarky rebuttal died on her lips. Her new partner, Jim Parker, had come up behind Marcus. "Is there a problem here?"

"No." Great. Just what she needed—her new partner discovering what a naive idiot she'd been with her old one. Olivia quickly excused herself, pushing past Max to shove open the front door. "I'm going to work, even if no one else is."

A look from Max and Jim wisely kept Marcus from joining them on the elevator up to the third floor. Olivia pushed the button and pretended the number three lighting up was the most interesting thing in the world. Max snorted and drifted to the back of the elevator to lean against the railing. "Does anything ever come out of that guy's mouth that isn't loaded with lies?"

When she didn't respond, Jim turned to Max. "Is there an issue with Detective Brower I should know about?"

"Liv used to be his partner over in Vice until Lieutenant Rafferty-Taylor recruited her for the Cold Case Squad."

Olivia was only partially aware of being the topic

of conversation as she pulled her hand away from the panel. She curled her fingers into her palm, caught off guard by a remembered touch. But it wasn't that cutesy little coupling of fingertips outside when Marcus had stopped her—or even the brush of his lover's hand across her body months earlier. She was remembering a firmer touch—a handshake, of all things—with Gabriel Knight. An unapologetic stamp of skin on skin. Strong. Warm. Lingering.

She trembled with a curious awareness that felt as vivid now as it had last night at the hospital.

"Is there bad blood between you two?" Jim asked.

Instead of answering, Olivia flattened her palm against the cool leather of her jacket and rubbed the back of her knuckles as if her right hand had somehow betrayed her. Oh, man. She was in trouble. Despite the stress Gabe Knight had caused, he'd somehow awakened hormones she thought had been in a permanent coma after tossing Marcus out of her life. She was totally screwed with both her family and her coworkers if she even hinted that she might be attracted to the reporter.

And Max was already feeling too chatty about her last relationship disaster to risk getting razzed about Gabriel Knight. "That's right." Max snapped his fingers at Jim. "You were working with the bureau task force for a while there. You're out of the loop. Brower and Liv used to be an item. For a few months. Pretty hot and heavy before she transferred."

"Shut up, Max."

But she couldn't get the hint through Max's thick skull. "I'm glad she wised up and ended it. You know, for a while there, I thought I was going to have to rent a monkey suit and go to a wedding."

She turned and glared.

Max had the good sense to raise a placating hand in apology as the elevator slowed. "Shutting up now." But not really. He leaned his head confidentially toward Jim. "You know, people think I'm the one you have to watch out for on our squad since I've been around so long and I've seen everything. Or they worry about Dixon because he's got that big, bad tough-guy thing going on." Max pointed a finger at her. "*She's* the one who'll break you in two if you cross her. I recommend staying on her good side."

"Good to know." Jim gave a hesitant agreement, looking from one detective to the other.

Olivia turned away, rubbing at the seed of a headache throbbing in her temple. "Take your own advice, Max."

The burly detective chuckled. "You know I love ya, Liv."

The elevator bell dinged, announcing their arrival on the third floor. "Thank God."

Olivia dashed out, leaving the gossip and that uncomfortable fascination with Gabe Knight behind her. She headed straight for a cup of coffee in the break room, hoping to claim a few minutes of peace and quiet, but she couldn't shake Max and Jim, their questions or teasing until the roll call meeting was called to order.

After the half-hour meeting to discuss cases of department-wide concern, announce BOLOs and sign-ups for the upcoming annual baseball game against the fire department, Olivia, Jim, Max and Trent Dixon, the fourth detective assigned to their unit, filed into Ginny Rafferty-Taylor's office. Lieutenant Rafferty-Taylor had recently been promoted from her work as a homicide detective. But the petite blonde had slipped right into command of the cold case unit with an intelligence and air of authority that Olivia not only respected, but aspired to in her own law-enforcement career.

In contrast to the senior officer's professional, no-nonsense demeanor, Lieutenant Rafferty-Taylor's office was decorated with framed artwork painted by her kids. A trifold picture frame on the shelf behind her showed a photo of her and her husband, Brett, a big, beefy man whose hair was as dark as hers was silvery-blonde, along with individual pictures of their daughter and son, who were carbon copies of their mother and father, respectively.

Somehow the lieutenant had found that equanimity between being a decorated career officer and being a woman with a life outside of work. Olivia had yet to figure out that balance for herself. And after her foolish affair with Marcus, she had a feeling she was further than ever from finding that happily ever after. So she concentrated on the part of her life that she knew she was good at—being an investigator who could ferret out the truth when others around her could not.

After listening to updates on other cases the team was working, Olivia briefed the team on the events of yesterday afternoon surrounding Ron Kober's murder.

"Wait a minute." Max's partner, Trent Dixon, a former college football player, picked up the newspaper he'd set aside and unfolded it on top of the small conference table. He tapped the article he'd been looking for and Olivia leaned over to read it. "Gabe Knight's column says that Ron Kober was subpoenaed to testify before the State Senate Ethics Commission regarding potential campaign fraud during Senator McCoy's last run for election. Do we think his killer wanted to shut him up?"

Information Specialist Katie Rinaldi sat at the end of the table with her laptop, going back and forth between typing notes and the ongoing project of inputting updates on the unsolved case records she was transferring from paper files into the computer database. She tucked the shoulder-length strands of her chestnut hair behind her ears. "Should I be copying Detectives Kincaid and Hendricks on our discussion if they're working Mr. Kober's murder?"

"Not yet." Lieutenant Rafferty-Taylor sat at the opposite end of the table. "If we find anything substantive, we will. But until then, Kober isn't our case. Jim, I see you pulled the file on the Danielle Reese murder from six years back. Did we get a new lead there?"

"That was my request, ma'am," Olivia answered. "I've got a lead that suggests Ron Kober had a connection to the story Dani Reese was writing at the time of her murder. I can't say that he's her killer, but I'd like to follow up on it."

"Katie, is Ms. Reese's file in the system yet?" Ginny asked.

"Yes, ma'am."

"Pull it up." Ginny typed a note on her own laptop before raising her gaze. "What's your lead?"

Olivia picked up the folded newspaper and pointed to the byline. "Gabriel Knight. He claims that Dani was getting inside information about a link between Leland Asher and Senator McCoy's election for an article she was writing. Kober was McCoy's campaign manager at the time of her murder. If anyone had inside information on a crime boss's support of a candidate, it'd be Kober."

"And how does Mr. Knight know this?"

"Well, he suspects." Olivia left out the fiancée part and stuck to the more important facts. "Dani Reese was a junior reporter at the *Kansas City Journal*. He was mentoring her, and read some of her notes on the story before she died."

Max sat forward in his chair across the table, looking dubious about the reporter's cooperation. "Can we get those notes?"

"I hope so. I know Mr. Knight isn't a fan of the department, but this case is important to him. I intend to ask him."

Lieutenant Rafferty-Taylor nodded, approving the reopening of the case. "I'm all for anything we can pin on Asher to put him away. And some good press from Mr. Knight can't hurt any of us. Let's talk it out."

Katie's work on entering data on cold cases dating back to the 1800s made it easier to cross-reference information from different investigations. She'd started, of course, with the most recent cases, so everything the department had on Danielle Reese's murder was there to access. But she pulled her bottom lip between her teeth and frowned as she skimmed the screen. "There's not much here. The ME's report. Witness statements from the men who found her. According to the ballistics, the gun used to kill her was a .25 caliber semiautomatic. But no murder weapon was ever recovered."

Jim skimmed the same information in the paper file he'd picked up yesterday. "No wonder the UNSUB had to shoot her three times. A little gun like that doesn't carry a big punch. Unless he wanted her to suffer."

"Maybe she knew her killer," Trent suggested. "And he didn't want her to die fast."

Max leaned back in his chair. "Or Asher told his man to stage the scene so it wouldn't look like a hit. Maybe Senator McCoy hired someone to silence her."

The lieutenant reminded them of the original investigation. "In that part of town, it very well could have been a robbery. If she struggled with her assailant, he might have panicked. But these are all just theories. I won't go to the DA unless we have a viable suspect and real proof."

Katie raised her eyebrows. "Yeah, Uncle Dwight is a stickler for that kind of thing," she added as her fingers flew over the keyboard, referring to the man who had saved her life when she was a teenager and become her legal guardian after marrying Katie's aunt.

Olivia agreed that any of the three scenarios was plausible, yet unprovable at this point. "Do we still have anything in evidence?"

Katie read the short list off the screen. "Crime scene photos. Bullets the ME removed. The victim's clothes, purse and a few items from her glove compartment. The officers on the scene said the insurance cards, registration and other paperwork were missing—maybe to delay identifying the victim, maybe as part of the carjacking—or else they just blew away. The notes here say there was a thunderstorm the night of her death. She wasn't found until the next day, and the doors, trunk and glove box were all open."

Max muttered a curse. "The wind and rain probably compromised the majority of any circumstantial evidence that was there."

"Do we still have Ms. Reese's car?" Lieutenant Rafferty-Taylor asked.

Katie nodded. "It's in Impound."

"Wait a sec. Go back. We have her purse in evidence?" Olivia looked at the young single mom turned computer wiz. "Why would KCPD investigate her death as a robbery if her purse was still there? What else was missing?"

"Her wallet and phone weren't in her bag or pockets.

The investigator's report says she wasn't wearing any jewelry, but she had pierced ears. Marks from a ring and watch that were gone, too. They assumed the jewelry was stolen. No notation that any of it was ever recovered." Katie looked up from the screen, her blue eyes wide with curiosity. "Hey, Liv. Is this your dad's signature on the file?"

Olivia exhaled a reluctant sigh and nodded. She hoped the personal connection wouldn't put her in dutch with the lieutenant. "I didn't know this was his case until last night. We chatted some this morning. He said it was the only one he and his partner Al Junkert never solved. There just wasn't enough evidence to go on. And no one with discernible motive."

If Ginny Rafferty-Taylor was concerned about Olivia's objectivity, she didn't show it. "Was Gabriel Knight involved with the case back then? Did he tell your father his suspicions about Leland Asher and Senator McCoy?"

"Dad mentioned it." Her father had also said that exploring Gabe's suggestion had led to a dead end, including a blanket denial of even knowing Dani Reese from the senator's office, and an unpleasant run-in with one of Asher's men. But that had ended with nothing more than a disorderly conduct charge. "Dad said they couldn't match ballistics to any of the guns owned by Leland Asher and his crew. And they all had alibis Dad couldn't break. Either proof of being out of town, or a family wedding with video that put the rest of them, including Leland Asher, at the reception during the time of the murder."

"Any records of Asher making big withdrawals around the time of the murder?" Jim asked.

Olivia shook her head, knowing what he was getting at. "If he hired a hit man, there was no paper trail that Dad or Al could find."

Gabe Knight's claims were looking less credible by the minute. Maybe, as her father said, the collusion story and cover-up was nothing more than a grieving fiancé grasping at straws. Danielle Reese could very well have been the victim of a random carjacking. Although Gabe had seemed so certain that his fiancée's death was some kind of mob connection cover-up that Olivia had believed him enough to bring Dani's case to the team.

And, maybe there was a little bit of Irish vindication running through her veins. If she could solve this case for her dad, it might make his forced retirement after a career-ending injury a little easier to enjoy.

"Are we a go on reopening Dani Reese's murder?" Olivia asked, watching her supervisor's gray-blue eyes for approval.

The lieutenant closed her laptop, signaling that the meeting was winding down. "Sounds like our type of investigation. Olivia, you take the lead. Reinterview any suspects and the men who found her, look at the crime scene, nail down the motive—you know the drill."

"Yes, ma'am." Olivia rose and pulled her jacket off the back of her chair. "I can follow up with Dad—see if he's got any insights that might not be in the records."

Jim jotted a line on his notepad and closed it. "I'll go over to storage and pull the evidence box. We can look at everything with fresh eyes. If there are any trace samples, I'll find out if there are new tests the lab can run on them."

Ginny Rafferty-Taylor shrugged into her sky-blue blazer. "If this was a robbery, let's prove it. If not, our best lead is to talk to the man who knew our victim best.

See if we can put our hands on those notes she allegedly kept and find a motive there."

"Best lead, as in Gabriel Knight?"

The lieutenant nodded. "You've already established a rapport. Talk to him. Let's make him KCPD's friend again. We need to get a look at the story Dani Reese was writing."

Olivia adjusted her jacket over the white blouse she wore before answering. Her fingers hadn't just started tingling at the mention of Gabe's name, had they?

Thankfully, no one seemed to notice her hesitation. There was a chorus of *yes*, *ma'am*s as they shut down computers and pushed away from the table.

"I expect regular updates," Ginny reminded them. "Keep in touch."

"Trent?" Katie set her laptop on the table and hurried past Olivia to reach the dark-haired muscle man before he left the room. "Tyler has Little League tryouts this weekend. I was wondering if you could help him with his swing? This is his first year playing regular ball instead of hitting off the tee. I'll throw in a home-cooked meal for your trouble."

"Baseball's not my sport," the big man conceded. But he smiled at the mention of Katie's son. "You know how much I like hanging out with the little guy, though. I'll give it a shot. Saturday okay?"

While the computer genius and the detective worked out the details of their weekend afternoon, Jim circled around the table to speak to Olivia. "I've picked up that Knight isn't your favorite person. Want me to go with you?"

Adjusting the cuffs and collar of her blouse, Olivia frowned. "I thought you and Natalie had an appointment with a Realtor about making an offer on that house you two saw yesterday."

"I'll postpone the meeting."

"Don't be ridiculous. I can handle Gabe Knight on my own." She tugged on the badge hanging around her neck. "The day I can't conduct an interview is the day I need to turn this in."

"You sure you're not just trying to go solo without me again? You can't break me in if we don't spend time working together." Although there was a teasing smile in his green eyes, she had a feeling he was half serious.

"That's not it." Still, Jim was right—they hadn't quite found their investigative rhythm yet. And she didn't want to be distracted with working a new partner into the equation when she met with Gabe Knight. "Like Ginny said, I've developed a rapport with him. He may not like any of us, but I think he'll talk to me." If Gabe's willingness to work with her meant the difference in solving the crime, then she'd deal with his stubbornness, her family's reservations against the man—even those illogical frissons of awareness he'd awakened in her—and make him her best friend. "If Knight gives me any grief, Max said I'm scary enough to take him down if I have to."

The grumpy detective chuckled as he followed them out the door. "You got that right."

Olivia smiled. Max was too much of a teddy bear beneath the grizzly exterior to stay mad at him for long. Jim was starting to grow on her, too. "Besides, if I need you, I've got your number."

Jim paused before heading over to the bank of elevators. "Use it. I'm here to back you up."

Maybe if he kept saying that, she might actually learn to believe in a partner again. "Thanks, Jim. Let me know what you find in the evidence box. Good luck with the house."

Max folded his arms across his barrel chest, blocking her path as he scratched at the pale stubble on his chin. "You want me to go with you? I'm not afraid of Knight."

Even though she could tell that his offer of support was sincere, Olivia let him off the hook with a teasing punch to the arm. "You're not one of my brothers, remember? I don't need you lookin' out for me. Go eat a cigar."

"Sounds yummy." Trent came out of the lieutenant's office with a sarcastic drawl and clapped Max on the shoulder. "You and me are taking a trip to Impound."

"Yippee," Max answered in a monotone. "We get the stinky old car." But he walked backward, following his partner's exit without further complaint. "Brower was a butthead for cheating on you, Liv."

"I know."

"I only told Jim because he needs to have your back in case Brower is dumb enough to think he can talk you into forgiving him or something."

"I know that, too. Get to work."

With Katie Rinaldi and Ginny Rafferty-Taylor going over data in the lieutenant's office, and the guys on the team out pursuing their assignments, Olivia finally got her peace and quiet. For a few moments. Then the cacophony of the Fourth Precinct's third-floor Detectives Division registered. Dozens of conversations, phones ringing, keyboards clicking and printers and other machines whirring as they spit out information filled her ears and wore at her nerves.

But, since running home for a hot bubble bath or a primal scream in the middle of the room probably weren't the best strategies for coping with this morning's stress, Olivia inhaled a deep breath and marched past the cubicle where her desk faced Jim's and pushed open the door to the now empty conference room. She exhaled the calming breath and rallied her patience. The last thing she needed was to lose her focus when she talked to Gabriel Knight.

Turning to keep watch through the glass windows on either side of the door, Olivia pulled up the number she'd programmed in yesterday and called Gabe.

A terse, low-pitched voice answered. "Knight."

Sucker. Her nostrils flared with a quick breath. Why couldn't she shake this skittish, way-too-feminine-for-her-liking thing about the man? She must have some kind of masochistic streak to be attracted to men who were trouble for her.

Olivia ignored the deep voice that skittered against her eardrums and focused on the muffled noises of a busy metropolitan newspaper office in the background. "Good morning, Mr. Knight. This is Detective Watson, KCPD. I need to speak to you. In person. Are you at work? I could meet you at your office or you could come to the station."

He answered with a long pause that made her wonder if he'd been interrupted at his end of the call. Then the noise in the background went silent and she suspected he'd closed the door to his office, turning this into a private conversation. "Are you reopening Dani's murder?"

Before she could answer, broad shoulders and dark hair appeared in the window. Marcus flashed his dimpled smile and rapped on the glass. "You free?"

Olivia frowned, hating the interruption, and frankly, hating him at that moment. She pointed to the phone. "No."

"Excuse me?" a deep voice challenged in her ear.

Oh, damn.

"Sorry, I…" She turned the lock on the doorknob and turned her back on Marcus. "That was for someone here. Yes, we're reopening the case. I need to ask you some questions—go over everything you know about your fiancée's murder."

"Two things, Olivia." She could feel Marcus's dark eyes drilling her through the glass, and suspected his cajoling smile had disappeared. But, for some reason, her ex's frustration with her didn't bother her as much as the displeasure tingeing the man's voice on the phone. "One, it's Gabe. And two? You'd better be bringing your *A* game to this investigation. I'll see you when you get here."

Chapter Five

Gabe spotted the rich blue-green jacket from the corner of his eye. He looked up from the article he was typing on his computer and watched Olivia Watson through the windows of his office. She said something to the receptionist who pointed in his direction, toward the line of private rooms surrounding the *Journal*'s news and editorial department's main floor, and raised her mysterious eyes to meet his.

When their gazes met, she gave him a slight nod before clipping the badge she'd shown the receptionist back onto the chain she wore. Olivia shot her fingers through that sexy crop of short, dark hair, steeled her shoulders and strode through the jungle of desks, reporters, columnists, runners and techs with a certainty of purpose that was at once professionally confident and surprisingly hot. At least, that jump in his pulse seemed to think so.

"I'm finally getting you justice, Dani," he whispered to the ghosts of the past that filled the air around him. "One way or another." After saving his story and clearing the computer screen, Gabe stood, smoothing the shirt sleeves he'd rolled up to his elbows. When the leggy detective paused in the open doorway, he extended his hand and circled around the desk to greet her. "Olivia."

"Gabe." She folded her firm grip into his. He liked

that she used his name the way he'd asked without making a big deal out of it. "This is a noisy place."

"Hence, the private office."

"You made it sound as though stopping by anytime was okay. So here I am."

"Now is fine. We already put tomorrow morning's paper to bed and I'm working ahead." Here they stood, sharing another handshake. Another linger. His thumb grazed over the soft bump of her knuckles. Olivia's skin was smooth, warm. Her eyes this afternoon were a muted shade of gray dotted with green-and-gold specks that darkened the longer he held on to her.

So let go already. This is a business meeting, not a blind date.

"How's the arm?" Olivia asked, showing more sense than he had by pulling away and stepping into his office.

He kept his back to her, needing a few seconds to compartmentalize this potent interest in the lady detective and concentrate on the reason he'd agreed to see her in the first place—getting to the truth about Dani's killer. Only then did he turn, waving his fingers in the air to prove their dexterity, despite the bandage wrapped around his forearm. "A little sore. But as long as I can type, I'm good." He pointed to her left wrist, indicating the violet bruise peeking out beneath the cuff of her white blouse. "Looks like you got a little banged up, too."

"I'll live."

"Coffee?" he offered.

"Sure. With cream if you have it." He pointed to one of the guest chairs and invited her to sit while he headed out to the break room.

By the time he returned with two insulated cups, Gabe had let enough of his cynicism and doubt creep back into his thoughts to temper his libido. He closed the door with his foot to block out the noise from the main room and handed Olivia her drink. "So where do we start?"

Gabe resumed his seat behind his desk while Olivia popped open her lid to swirl the coffee and creamer together and allow some of the steam to escape. "At the beginning. When we don't have a clear lead, we usually look at the victim. What can you tell me about Danielle Reese?"

"Looked like an angel. She liked baking and knitting and having fresh flowers around the condo. But that was more about being an overachiever than a homebody. She never could sit still. She came from a small town in Kansas—Cottonwood Falls. Got her journalism degree at the University of Missouri and moved to the big city, determined to be a success and never have to go back to where she came from. She loved her parents, but the pace of a small town bored her. She wanted the diversity and excitement of the city and the job. She wanted a Pulitzer. She wanted to make a difference."

Olivia pressed the lid back onto her coffee and took a sip. "Did she normally investigate suspected connections between organized crime and politics?"

Gabe shook his head, remembering the first time he'd seen the dewy-faced blonde lugging an armload of boxes to her desk in the middle of the reporters' pool. "She was willing to learn her craft, build her reputation. She took every assignment from covering wedding announcements to interviewing local human interest stories. But she always wanted to get into hard news."

"That's when you started mentoring her?"

"Yeah. I let her tag along on some of the tamer assignments I had—reporting on school bond debates, weather stories like the floods we had a few years back.

She'd draft a story and I'd read it, tweak it. I shared a couple of bylines with her." Dani's eagerness to learn and excel, her youthful energy and attentiveness had been an aphrodisiac to his ego. "Pretty soon she didn't need me to get the story or write it. By then, things had gotten personal between us. I proposed. She accepted."

Olivia set her cup on the edge of the desk and pulled her phone from her pocket, ostensibly to type in details of their conversation. "So you moved in together and continued your Svengali relationship with her. On the sly. You said you had to sneak a look at her notes? That she was keeping that last investigation a secret? Even from you?" She paused in her typing to meet his gaze.

He resented the Svengali allusion. Sure, maybe their relationship had started out like that, but once they became a couple, he and Dani had been equal partners. There'd been nothing more he could teach her. It wasn't until the late nights and the missed dinners and the calls that went straight to voice mail that he'd gotten worried enough to find out what she was keeping from him. And then he realized he hadn't taught her nearly enough about surviving a dangerous investigation.

Gabe took a drink that scalded the guilt from his throat. "Do you even know what she looked like?"

Olivia shook her head. "Just the crime scene photos. And those…are pretty rough."

That was an understatement. She needed to see the face of the woman he wanted her to fight for. Gabe set down his cup and crossed to the row of gray metal filing cabinets along the east side of his office. Without being asked, Olivia followed him to the top left drawer. "Here." He pulled out the framed photo that had once sat on the corner of his desk and handed it to her. "This was our engagement picture, taken about five months before Dani died."

"She's beautiful," Olivia whispered on a sigh that was almost reverent.

The kindness of hearing someone else mourn the tragedy of Dani's death soothed the wounds inside him. But just when he should have been remembering the sweet vanilla scent that had been Dani's, his nose filled with the citrusy freshness emanating from Olivia's short hair. There was something electric about this woman, an excitement at noticing the feminine details behind the gun and badge, an anticipation of trading words and opinions—an unexpected jolt of purely male interest that hit him every time they were together. The visceral impact of these encounters which heated his blood and stirred things behind his zipper reminded Gabe that he'd moved beyond the grief he'd felt with Dani's death.

But he curled his fingers into a fist behind Olivia's back and dropped it to his side before he gave in to the impulse to touch that sable-colored hair. His grief might have abated, but the guilt sure as hell was still there. "Yeah. She was."

Olivia touched a fingertip to the glass. "Is this the engagement ring that was stolen?"

He nodded, forcing himself to forget the untimely attraction and remain as focused on the investigation as she was. "That, some gold hoop earrings and a wristwatch from a discount store."

"Was the jewelry expensive?"

"Not enough to give the Rockefellers a run for their money, but probably enough to feed a junkie's fix for a few weeks." Gabe plucked the picture from Olivia's fingers to put it back in its drawer. "I know what you're thinking—Dani wasn't murdered for the diamond she was wearing—"

"I have to consider every possibility."

Gabe closed the drawer. "You only have to consider the right one."

"The right one?" Olivia planted her hands at her hips and tipped her face to his. "Just because it's *your* theory, that makes it right?"

He mirrored her stance, watching the green fire of temper take over the color in her eyes. "Factually, I know you have to explore every possible motive and suspect— but what do you think I've been doing for six years? Your father and his partner never found the thief they were looking for because he didn't exist. Dani was killed to cover up a story."

"That's only one possibility. I have to revisit and rule out any other—"

A soft knock and the door opening ended the argument. A platinum blonde, wearing a designer suit that cost as much as his monthly salary, entered with a friendly smile that faded when she saw the two of them together. "Gabe, I... Sorry. Didn't know you had company." Gabe's boss, the slightly older woman who'd inherited the newspaper, but earned her CEO status and his respect with her business and management skills, tucked the small box she carried under one arm and walked right up to Olivia. "Hi. I'm Mara Boyd, publisher of the *Journal.*"

The two women shook hands. "Detective Olivia Watson."

"Detective? Has something happened?" Mara tipped her bright blue eyes to his. "Has there been a break on Dani's murder? You know I want that story. She was our girl. Nobody gets to scoop us. Will you be able to write it? You deserve to have that vindication, but if it'll be too much, I'll assign it to someone else."

Olivia stepped in front of him, as though she meant to protect him from the verbal barrage. "Let's solve it first."

"Of course." Mara's gaze dropped back to Olivia. "But you being here is good news, right?"

"I hope so."

"Yes." Gabe closed his hands around Olivia's shoulders and scooted her to the side. He could fight his own battles. Not that talking business with Mara—or even something so personal as Dani's murder—was ever an issue. "Detective Watson is exploring the possibility of a link between Dani's murder and a death that occurred yesterday."

"Are you talking about Ron Kober's murder?" Mara asked.

Olivia subtly pulled away from the grasp of his fingers. "Did you know Mr. Kober?"

"Of course." Mara hugged the box she was carrying in front of her. "Ron delivered all kinds of press releases when he worked for Senator McCoy. I've met him at fund-raisers, and the paper did an article on him when he built the Kober Building and opened his private PR firm."

"Do you know of any dealings he might have had with Danielle Reese?" Olivia pressed.

"Dani and Ron?" Mara shook her head. "Dani was a cub reporter. They ran in different social circles. She wouldn't have been covering anything he was involved with."

Great. Just what Gabe didn't need—his boss contradicting his assertion that Dani and Kober had been working together. He stepped away from Olivia and escorted Mara back to the door. "Did you need something?"

Mara's smile was back. "I just wanted to remind you that you're covering the mayor's cocktail reception for party members and the press at the art gallery tomorrow night. And give you this." She placed the small, narrow box in his hands. "I didn't know if you had one of your own. I rarely see you wear them."

Gabe lifted the lid and arched an eyebrow at the black silk. "A tie?"

"I reserved the tux that goes with it at the rental place on the card inside. Plus, it's an election year, so you know there'll be a photo op. Madam Mayor may even be looking for our endorsement, but I'd like to hear her answers to some hard questions before I put the *Journal*'s name behind her. You know I'd go myself but, um…"

"I'll be there." Gabe knew firsthand about his boss's recent reticence to attend anything resembling a public society event. "I may even wear the stupid bow tie. Thanks."

"You're welcome. Keep me in the loop on any new developments with Dani's murder." Mara's smile included Olivia. "I'll let you two get back to work."

Gabe closed the door and tossed the tie box on top of his desk. "Where were we?"

Oh, right. Sniffing Olivia's hair, failing to keep his hands to himself, verbally duking it out with her and enjoying it all more than he should, considering Olivia represented the enemy he had to bring over to his side of the investigation.

"Your boss likes you."

"Because she knows I'll give her an honest opinion about what's really going on behind the mayor's party line."

"No, I mean she *likes* you." Olivia picked up her

coffee and drank a couple of swallows, using the cup to mask her assessment of his reaction.

She wasn't getting one. "The woman gave me a tie, not the key to her apartment."

"Have you two gone out?"

"We're friends. A couple of times she's needed an escort and I've obliged her so she doesn't have to mess with the whole dating-after-forty scene."

Olivia's eyes widened with mock surprise. "You date?"

Gabe circled around his desk opposite her. "Not every woman finds me to be—how did you put it?—*too damn arrogant* to spend time with."

When she lowered her cup, he was surprised to see that the cop could blush. "You *do* pay attention to details, don't you. Still, in the interest of the investigation, Ms. Boyd wouldn't happen to have a jealous streak, would she?"

He turned his chair toward her and sat. "Jealous of Dani? Mara hired her."

"To write for her newspaper—not to marry her star reporter."

Gabe considered the possibility for about two seconds, then shook his head. "Mara was married when I was with Dani."

"Some women want their cake…and everybody else's."

That wasn't the boss he knew. "I don't think so. Mara didn't have a good marriage. Her husband was Brian Elliot."

"The Rose Red Rapist?" Olivia's eyes widened at the mention of the serial rapist the department had put away a couple years earlier. Although, in Gabe's way of thinking, it had taken them far too long and far too many victims to identify Elliot and make the arrest.

"One and the same. Mara knew he wasn't right in the head, and shut down her feelings long before she got divorced. There was never any jealousy there. No strong emotion of any kind. The only thing she feels a passion for is this paper." Olivia set her coffee on the edge of the desk and started typing on her phone again. "You're not putting her down as a suspect, are you? Mara doesn't have it in her to kill anybody."

"But she'd have the money to hire someone to do it for her."

He pushed to his feet. "Olivia—"

"Fine. I'll move her to the bottom of my list."

"This isn't about jealousy." Gabe poked the desktop with each and every point. "We should be talking to Leland Asher. Or even Adrian McCoy and his people. We should find out if there was any recent contact between the three of them."

"*We* aren't going to do anything." Olivia lowered her phone, moving a step closer with every reply. "I'm the cop. I contact persons of interest and ask the questions."

"I'm a part of this investigation."

"You're going caveman on me again."

"Cave..." Gabe scrubbed his palm over his face and looked away, swearing at the apt description he'd given himself last night. But he wasn't about to back down from what he knew was right. He tapped his finger against his temple and settled back into his chair. "You need what I have in here to solve the case."

"Then how about a little information from that head of yours? Do you still have the story Dani was writing? Copies of her notes? Those would be more helpful than arguing with you."

Gabe clicked the mouse to bring icons back on his computer screen. "Dani kept her stories on a flash drive that she carried on her key chain. Had it with her all the time. I never saw what was on it." Olivia searched her phone again, while he brought up the different files of research he'd put together. "She made a few notes on her desk calendar—dates, times, code names—that I scanned. She called the source she was meeting with—"

"The source you believe to be Ron Kober?"

"Yes. She called him BB. Big Break. As in big break on the story she was writing—"

"Or the big break in her career." She held up her phone, although he couldn't read the text. "There was no flash drive collected as evidence. And her keys were still in the car at the scene. Do you still have it?"

"No. That proves somebody took it." Adrenaline rushed through Gabe's blood the same way it did when he broke a story. "You find out who has that flash drive and you'll have your killer."

"All it means is that we haven't found it yet. I texted a couple of detectives I work with who are at the impound lot to tear her car apart and see if she hid a flash drive somewhere that the crime scene techs never discovered." Olivia moved in beside him, reading the screen over his shoulder. "It also means I have to rely on you to tell me what was on that flash drive."

One step forward and two steps back. Gabe tempered his hope at finally getting through to KCPD with a good dose of cynicism. "Over the years, I've recreated as much of what I could remember from the notes Dani kept."

"But you don't have any of the actual notes or the article she was writing?"

"When we argued that night, she downloaded all the

files I'd read onto her flash drive and deleted them from her laptop."

Gabe felt Olivia's hand on the back of his chair. "Do you still have the laptop? Our tech guys can recover all kinds of data, sometimes even from corrupted files."

"She took it with her. Accused me of spying on her, not believing in her. Said she wasn't going to be treated like a rookie reporter anymore."

When the detective didn't immediately berate him for not having actual admissible evidence to share, he sought out her reflection on the monitor beside him. "That's a lot of guilt to carry with you, isn't it?" He watched her force the wistfulness from her expression before she patted his shoulder. "I'm sure the two of you would have made up, maybe even traded a laugh or a kiss, if she'd come back home that night."

Gabe reached up to capture her hand. The eyes weren't the only mystery he had yet to solve about this woman. "Sounds as though you know about that kind of guilt. What happened?"

But the quiet moment of a shared understanding didn't last. "What I know is that cold cases rely on plenty of circumstantial evidence to make a conviction. But so far all I have are bad guys with alibis, a missing flash drive and a lot of hearsay from you. A few tangible facts wouldn't hurt."

"So you get to ask questions, but I don't?"

Apparently not. Olivia pulled away with a determined huff and moved around the room, inspecting his office. Allowing his curiosity to simmer, he went back to pulling up files on the computer. "Did you know I was Thomas Watson's daughter when we met yesterday?" she asked. "Is that why you requested Jim and me from the Cold Case Squad?"

Gabe glanced up to find her oddly fascinated with a Missouri Press Corps certificate framed on the wall. "Not at first. I called Chief Taylor and made the request when I heard about Kober's murder. I didn't know he'd be sending you."

"Do you want someone else running this investigation?"

"Will you solve it?" he challenged. "Will you find Dani's killer?"

Her shoulders stiffened and her chin came up before she turned. Her eyes, all green and gold now, locked onto his as she came back to sit on the edge of the desk beside him, facing him. "Yes."

As much as her confidence intrigued him, six years was a long time to wait for the action and satisfaction he'd yet to see. "Do we bet money on this now, or what?"

"No bets. Just a promise that I'm going to do my job." His sarcasm hadn't fazed her a bit. She was dead serious, expecting him to take her at her word. "My father would have eventually solved the case, too, if he hadn't been injured and forced to retire. It always troubled him— haunted him, even—that he never found Dani's killer."

"Not as much as it has haunted me." But there was more regret than sneer in his tone. If he hadn't been such a self-righteous jerk back then, warning Dani she was going to crash and burn with her story—that she was playing way out of her league—she might still be alive. If only he'd done more than preach at her that night. If only he'd stopped her. Gone with her. Done anything besides let her go off and confront a killer alone. He needed to change the subject. "How did your father get injured?"

"High-speed car chase. His partner lost control of the car and they ran off the road." Finally, a question she would answer for him—although, interestingly, the question hadn't been about her. "They were both lucky they survived the wreck, but at the time, Dad was more worried about whether or not the perp got away."

"Did he?"

"No. He got caught in the accident, too. He's serving his sentence in Jefferson City." She moved some papers and brushed the dust off a trophy on top of the filing cabinets. "Dad and Al solved a lot of cases together, but neither one could return to regular duty after that. Dad works as a consultant for a security company now, but he hated having to retire from KCPD with an un-solved case."

"Dani's."

Olivia nodded.

"Is that why you're doing this? To avenge your father? To complete his service record?"

"Maybe a little." She traced the plastic lid on her cof-fee before picking up the cup and finishing it off. "I'm doing this because solving crimes is the job I'm trained to do. The job I swore an oath to do to the best of my ability. I know you don't have any appreciation for cops, Gabe. But I do. I take a lot of pride in protecting Kansas City, a lot of pride in being a detective. I do it because Dani and her family—and you—deserve justice."

He tilted his gaze to hers in a hard stare, assessing her sincerity and ability to make good on her words. "This isn't merely a personal quest for me, either. I'm just as committed to finding the truth as you are. It's what a good reporter does."

Refusing to look away from the challenge in his eyes, she returned to his desk. "So, if we're done trading phi-losophies, I'd like to get back to work. I have a feeling the only way I'm going to earn your respect, and redeem your opinion of my father and the rest of the department, is to show you how we get the job done."

Gabe stood to face her. "My beef with KCPD doesn't include you, Olivia."

She tipped her chin to keep their gazes locked. "You disrespect the department, you disrespect me."

"Fair enough. Prove me wrong about KCPD."

She inched a step closer. "Prove me wrong about reporters."

The beginnings of a smile tugged at the corner of his mouth and Gabe nodded. Despite the glimpses of some secret vulnerability, he hadn't run up against anyone in the department who was tougher than this lady right here. Maybe she was already halfway toward earning that respect.

He pulled out his chair for her to sit. "You can read what I've pieced together from Dani's report, along with the snippets I retrieved from her calendar and notebook. Then you'll know what I know."

Shaking her head, she pulled up the first file. "I'll know what you *suspect*," she corrected. "I'm still going to need witness corroboration or some other kind of proof before I can make an arrest."

"Are you and I ever going to agree on anything, Detective?"

She picked up her empty cup and held it out to him. "I like coffee. Do you?"

Gabe gave in to the urge to laugh before snatching her cup and heading for the door. "Keep reading. I'll go get us another cup."

Chapter Six

Olivia shifted her Explorer into Park and killed the engine before looking past Gabe to assess the rusting, swaybacked shell of Morton & Sons Tile Works.

Despite the puffy white clouds in the late-afternoon sky overhead, there wasn't anything cheery about this derelict block of condemned buildings. The pediment above the front doors with 1903 carved into it was one of the few bits of the brick-and-mortar facade not crumbling away from the rusting iron and chewed-up timber structure underneath. Olivia could smell the river on the other side of the warehouse, smell the faint stink of garbage or something else rotten that she wasn't in real favor of identifying. Boarded-up windows that had been used for target practice, and a building code warning sticker beside the front doors completed the feeling of death and decay about the old storage facility. "I don't much like the look of this place in the daylight. I can't imagine your fiancée coming to this part of town in the middle of the night."

Gabe drummed his fingers against the top of the rolled-down window—the only outward indication that being on the same street, in front of the same abandoned warehouse where Danielle Reese's body had been found, bothered him. "This is a hell of a lonely place to die. I wonder how many times Dani came here to meet her informant before I realized what she was doing and warned her it was too dangerous. The only people who come to this neighborhood are gangbangers, druggies and the homeless. Any reputable businesses have closed or moved to a better location. If Leland Asher or one of his men found her here…" He shook his head and turned back to Olivia. "Even if there was someone around to see what happened, this isn't a neighborhood where people like to talk to the police."

Olivia agreed. The only witness statements had come from the men who'd checked out the abandoned car and found Dani's body on their way to work the next morning. There wasn't anybody around that she could see, although it was hard to shake the feeling that there were eyes on them right now.

Glancing around at the broken windows and shadowed doorways across the street from the warehouse, she half expected to see two glowing, Halloween-like eyes staring back at her. But there was no one, of course. Nothing but some bits of trash and clouds of dust blowing along the empty street. Just a few blocks away, similar historic structures had been saved and remodeled to become a shopping district, apartments and restaurants. But there was no kind of care or redemption like that here. "I'm sure this is hard for you. I'd be happy to take you to a restaurant or coffee shop to wait until I'm done here."

Gabe's blue eyes stopped their scan of the neighborhood. "I'm not leaving you in this place by yourself. The last woman I knew who came here—"

"I'm not Dani. I've been trained for working in a questionable environment, and I'm certain I'm carrying more weapons than she did. Besides, I'm not here to roust out any witnesses or trap a suspect. All I'm doing is walking through an old crime scene, trying to visualize what happened that night. I'm not worried." Even though the prickle of awareness at the nape of her neck tried to tell her otherwise.

"All Dani had was a can of pepper spray. She shouldn't have come to this place alone. I should have protected her."

"You tried. You offered her your experience and wisdom and she ignored it. Maybe she thought she had something to prove."

"To whom?"

"To you." Gabe's blue eyes darkened like cobalt and fixed on her. Olivia didn't shy away from her point. Could he really not see the similarities here? "You seem to bring that out in people. You demand a high standard of excellence. Do the job now. Do it right. No mistakes allowed. If someone wants the mighty Gabe Knight's approval, then he or she has to go above and beyond normal expectations."

His drumming fingers stilled and tightened into a fist. "Am I really such a bastard?"

Pinching her thumb and forefinger together in the air between them, Olivia winked. "Little bit."

A low-pitched laugh rumbled through his chest, softening the hard lines of his face and alleviating some of the tension between them. "I'll try to work on that."

The rare gift of his laughter made her smile. "No, you won't."

"Probably not." The laughter ended on a resolute sigh as Gabe pushed open the car door and climbed out. "Come on. Let's get this over with."

Olivia grabbed the manila envelope from the seat behind her and got out of the Explorer. She made a sweep of their surroundings, still looking for those hidden eyes, before crossing the street and joining him on the sidewalk in front of the old Tile Works building. "Would you feel better if I called for backup?"

"Tremendously," he admitted in that sardonic grinching of his. "But we're here, and I don't want to be any longer than we have to." He, too, seemed to be scanning the area for any signs of life besides them. "What exactly are you looking for?"

She opened the envelope to pull out the pictures from six years ago, along with her father's crime scene report, making a point to keep the most graphic photos at the bottom of the pile where Gabe wouldn't see his fiancée's body or the pool of blood beneath it. "I want to re-create what we know about the crime. Visualizing what went down here may give us a clearer direction with our investigation. If we understand the how, then the why and the who might become more apparent."

Gabe held the envelope while Olivia lined up the images with their current surroundings. "Not much has changed except for the crime scene tape." Looking over her shoulder, he pointed to the rusted hinges on the front doors. "Other than that new padlock, it looks as though this place hasn't been disturbed in six years."

Olivia nodded, matching the double iron doors of the warehouse entrance with the background of the photo. He was right. There was no padlock back then. "Dani's car was parked against the curb here, and she was found on the sidewalk beside it, hidden from view from the street. There weren't any signs of a struggle inside the car, and no blood there, so she was already outside when she was shot. Probably talking to her informant, BB, someone she expected to see, someone she trusted enough to get out to talk to in this neighborhood in the middle of the night."

Gabe looked up and down the street. "There are plenty of places where her assailant could have hidden. Parked in a car in that alley. Up in one of those office buildings or warehouses across the street. He probably waited until her contact had left and ambushed her."

"If this was a carjacking, she'd have gotten out on the driver's side. I'm ruling that out." Olivia switched photos and knelt down where Dani Reese's body had lain, wondering why the woman would be trying to get into the passenger side of her car—or if there was some other reason why that door, instead of the driver's side, was open. She touched the spots on her back and chest where Dani had been shot. Once in the back when the shooter had surprised her, or she was running away. Once in the chest when he'd caught up to her. That shot had brought her down. "Even at night, she probably saw her shooter." Sinking back onto her haunches, Olivia looked up from the sidewalk where Dani had fallen, imagining a blank face where the killer would have stood over her. "With the small caliber of bullets that were used, he'd have to be fairly close."

When she touched her fingers to her face to note the kill shot, Gabe grabbed her hand, pulling it away. "Don't do that. Please."

With little more than a flare of his nostrils to reveal the emotions that must be reeling inside him at this re-enactment, Olivia switched her grip to squeeze his hand as she stood. "Sorry. Do you want to wait in the car?"

"Nope. Too far away." Gabe's grip tightened around hers before releasing her. "I want answers. But I'm not going to lose anyone else trying to find them. Understood?"

She reached up, obeying an impulse before really thinking it through, and brushed her fingertips along the firm line of his jaw. "I'll make it as quick as I can," she promised.

"Don't worry about me. I'm a crusty old bastard, remember? Just keep working. I'll be fine." He turned his face, tickling her fingers with a brush of soft stubble before pressing a quick kiss to her palm. "What's next?"

Little frissons of warmth tingled through the sensitive nerve-endings on her hand and she pulled away. It was just a thank-you kiss, an appreciation for the comfort she'd offered. It didn't mean anything more than that. There was no bond forming here.

With her brain misfiring on hormones and compassion, Olivia pulled up the next picture and forced herself to think about the murder. She looked at the picture in her hand, then down at the sidewalk where a few sturdy weeds were already turning green between the cracks.

There was one other difference in these photographs.

A different sort of electricity fired through her veins. She took two steps, three, four, away from the spot where Dani had died. Time and the elements had washed them away, but in the picture there were two tiny sprays of cast-off blood droplets, each one no bigger than a broccoli floret. Too small and too far away from the body to have come from the gunshots.

"Olivia?"

A six-year-old incident was starting to fall into place.

She went back to the curb where Dani's car had been parked and walked through what she was pretty certain had occurred that night. "Dani didn't open the passenger-side door that night. The killer did."

Gabe followed her path. "Why?"

She mimicked reaching inside the car. "To check the glove compartment. He was searching for something."

"The flash drive."

"Or proof of death. Sometimes with a hit, the killer has to bring the victim's ID to whoever hired him to prove the job is done." Gabe backed away when she turned and looked down at her feet, imagining Danielle Reese and a growing pool of blood there. "Our guy wasn't an experienced killer. He didn't want to touch the body if he didn't have to. That's why he shot her in the back first—from a distance. But he couldn't find what he needed in the car, so he went through her purse." She pulled out the previous photo. Dani's bag had a long strap that she wore across her body, from one shoulder to the opposite hip. Olivia knelt down, imagining how a man, anxious to get away as quickly as possible, would have gotten into the purse that was anchored beneath his victim. "He couldn't have pulled Dani's purse off her shoulder unless he moved her. That may have given him the idea to make it look like a robbery, if that wasn't his instruction in the first place."

She pretended to tug at the purse on the ground and rifle through the contents. Then she removed imaginary jewelry and stood. She stepped over the space where Dani had lain and walked toward the errant blood drops. Holding up her hand, Olivia looked at fingers that would have been wet with blood. "The report said this was Dani's blood, but she wasn't shot over here." She made the movements of flicking her hand. Twice. "He got blood on him, and it was freaking him out." Olivia lifted her gaze to the iron doors. "She didn't go into that warehouse. He did."

Gabe pointed to one of the photos he still held. "There was no padlock on the door six years ago." Olivia nodded and hurried back to her car. Gabe jogged behind her. "What are we doing?"

"Going inside that warehouse." She opened the back and put the photos inside before pulling the toolbox her father insisted she carry to the rear bumper. Between the clank of the tools shifting in the metal box and the drumbeat of anticipation pounding in her ears at the potential new lead on the case, Olivia hadn't been as alert to her surroundings as she should have been. But in the next moment of silence, she detected a low humming noise—like the sound of a car or machine engine idling in the distance. Olivia turned her head to the nearby cross street. "Do you hear that?"

"The traffic?" Gabe had turned to scan the abandoned buildings up and down the street the moment she did. Olivia tuned in to the stop-and-go sounds of vehicles in a residential area just a few blocks to the south. "There still may be some sump pumps working in the area since we're so close to the water."

"No, it's…" With a cooling breeze stirring up the hint of an evening rain shower, she was also more aware of the whoosh of the Missouri River current on the north side of the buildings as the water slapped against rocks on the shore and the pylons of old loading docks. She couldn't hear the sound of the engine at all, anymore. Maybe she'd imagined it. Or maybe, as Gabe had suggested, the sound had simply moved on with the flow of traffic. "It's nothing."

Time to scrap that fanciful flight of imagination. The watching eyes hadn't been there, either. She must still be a little off her game since that night when Marcus's infidelity made her question whether or not she could trust her own judgment. But she wasn't about to let Gabe

Knight see any hint of incompetence while she was on the job.

With a renewed sense of focus, Olivia handed Gabe a pry bar and pulled out a flashlight for herself. "Here, caveman. Make yourself useful."

"Really?" he mocked, dutifully taking the pry bar and closing the hatch for her. "Is that going to be a thing?"

"Well, there are other names I could call you," she teased right back. Joining in his low-pitched laughter, Olivia locked the Explorer and crossed the street to the iron doors of the Tile Works.

The steel padlock didn't immediately budge for Gabe, but with an extra oomph of muscle and a screeching surrender, the rusted bolts holding the hasp in place snapped in two. Olivia pulled at the outer door, but ended up having to put her shoulder into it and accept Gabe's help there, as well. The iron door itself was heavy, the hinges were rusty, and with the slight caving of the exterior wall, the tendency for it to swing shut again made it feel like pushing a dead car up a hill.

"I bet that hasn't been opened in six years." Olivia brushed the grime and dust off her hands and jacket before stepping inside the cavernous interior and turning on her flashlight. The sudden beam of light chased a band of small rodents and big bugs back into the shadows. "I love what they've done with the place."

"Wait. Unless you're going to arrest me for vandalism?" Olivia shook her head as Gabe pried off a piece of the framing from the inside of the door. It snapped off easily, indicating the wood was dry and rotten. "I don't think I'd lean against anything," Gabe warned, wedging the one-by-one between the door and the frame to prop it open. "I doubt it would hold up." Then he stood beside her, pulling back the front of his tweed jacket and propping his hands on his hips, heedless of the transfer of dirt and rust to his jeans. "Talk about a needle in a haystack. How do we find something the size of my little finger in here?"

"You mean the flash drive?" She swung her light up to the cobwebs hanging like Spanish moss from the second-story catwalk and stair railings, and the triangular ceiling joists holding up most of the roof. "I'm not sure what we're looking for. Hopefully, something here will tell us why the killer came in. Or better yet, who the killer is."

Gabe nodded beside her. "So where do we start?"

Windows on both levels had been boarded up. Some of the glass was intact, some had been broken by vandals using them for target practice, some had receded from their desiccated putty and fallen from their frames to shatter into dusty bits of shine on the concrete floor. The weight of a giant iron hook and heavy chains hanging from a winch near the dockside doors had pulled support timbers from the roof and peeled open several holes in the corrugated metal overhead. The openings in the roof let in enough sunlight to reflect off the dust motes floating through the stale air, and cast the interior in dim shadows. Olivia swung her light around at ground level, the extra illumination transforming hulking blobs in the corners into piles of wood pallets and cube-shaped stacks of old boxes.

"We start closest to the door. If our perp came in here to hide, he'd be looking for the first spot he could find." They went to the first pallet, where several rows of dust-shrouded cardboard boxes were stacked like bricks.

Gabe wiped off the top layer of dust to reveal the faded blue logo of Morton & Sons Tile. He lifted a box from the top to get a closer look, but the cardboard collapsed in his hands. He held it away from his body as sand and chips of broken tiles poured out onto the floor, sending a fresh plume of dust into the air that they both had to turn their eyes and noses from. Once the box was empty, he tossed it onto the pile of tile and grit. "Looks like old stock left over from when Morton & Sons went out of business. Age and moisture have turned the clay back to dust."

"Gabe." Olivia's attention had already moved on to the next pallet. Although the second stack of tiles was as perfectly cube shaped as the first one, something was out of place. "Look at that. Everything else is symmetrical here. Why is there an extra box sitting on top?"

Reaching over the top of the stack beside her, Gabe touched his fingers to a depression there. "This looks like a sinkhole. The boxes underneath must be caving in."

"Why?" she whispered, feeling that spark of anticipation again. She was on the verge of finding answers.

The urgency in Gabe's voice meant he could sense it, too. "Because there's an empty space beneath it."

"Where that box used to be." Retreating a step, Olivia ran her light over the stack again, stopping at a box three down from the top, about waist-high for her. "It's backward. The logo doesn't match up with the rest of the boxes in this stack." An idea, just as clear as a crime scene marker, flashed through her head. "Hold this."

After handing off the flashlight, she snapped a picture of the boxes with her phone. Then she hunched down to work her fingers into the seams between the boxes and pull the backward one out of the pile, as though removing a plank from a Jenga puzzle. Only, she was certain whatever she was about to find wasn't any game.

She waited for a line of sandy grit to stop spilling through the seam in the bottom before turning the box around. "Look."

Faint brown spots, five in the pattern of fingertips gripping the box to pull it from the stack, peeked out beneath the layers of dust.

"Is that blood?"

Olivia nodded and set the remnants of the box on top, snapping another photo. "I'll take that to the lab for analysis."

"So our killer who couldn't get Dani's blood off his hand pulled that box out. Why?"

"Your sink hole." Olivia tugged the sleeves of her jacket and blouse up her arm and flexed her fingers at the opening. "If anything in the rodent family runs up my arm, I *will* be screaming, and I'll have to shoot you if you tell anyone."

Gabe moved behind her to shine the flashlight into the empty cavity. "Good to know you have a weakness, Detective. Your secret's safe with me."

Slowly, she thrust her hand into the void. Up to her wrist. Up to her elbow. She stretched her fingers, hoping she'd find anything except a clump of fur and a worm-like tail. "You're sure it won't show up on the front page of the *Journal?* Do you have any idea how many mice and creepy-crawly things three brothers can find and bring into the—"

The iron door slammed shut and Olivia yelped. She jerked her hand back as if she'd been bitten.

"Easy." Gabe's firm hand closed over her shoulder, steadying her as the light in the warehouse dimmed and he looked across to the doors. "I don't think a rat did that. I wasn't sure that wood was going to hold, anyway.

Do you want me to find something sturdier to prop the door open with?"

"That's okay. There's still enough light in here."

The warmth of Gabe's hand remained on her shoulder as she reached inside the empty cavity again. But her startled heart rate didn't seem to be slowing any as her fingertips brushed against stiff, nubby material. "I've got something." She stretched half an inch farther and felt several hard, small items poke her through the dusty cloth. "If I could just reach… Got it."

Olivia closed her fingertips around a bunch of long threads and pulled out the hidden treasure. The threads turned out to be the fringe on a long green scarf. A cloud of dust stung her eyes and made them water when it plopped into her hand. She coughed the irritation from her throat and set the wad of material on top of the boxes to unfold it. "Is this Dani's?"

Gabe's shoulder brushed against hers as he moved in beside her to shine the light on their newly discovered treasure. "She liked to wear scarves. And I know she had one on that night. But I couldn't say for sure."

Olivia tugged at the material, stiff with mold and damp clay, untying several knots. "There's something tied up inside."

The flashlight beam wavered. "Did you hear that?"

She hadn't heard a thing beyond the rattle of whatever was inside the scarf clinking together. "Probably the building settling or some critter I don't want to know about running up the stairs." She blew a cloud of dust off the material and coughed again. "I need the light."

Gabe's focus was on their prize again. "Looks like more blood."

"The killer probably wiped his hands on it before stashing it in its hiding place." Olivia hesitated, glancing up at the grim shadows on Gabe's expression. "Maybe you shouldn't be here. I'm looking at things objectively, but it's all personal for you, isn't it?"

"I'm okay. Open it. I want to see what he took from her."

After loosening the last knot, Olivia flipped back the material. The light glinted off the sparkle of diamond facets and polished gold.

Gabe swore a guttural curse. "That's the ring I gave Dani."

"I recognize it from the photo." She pushed his hand away when he reached for the marquise solitaire. "I'm sorry. In case there's any kind of print or DNA left on it."

He shrugged off her sympathy. "What else is there?"

She took one more picture before pulling an ink pen from her pocket to scoot aside the other items that had been bundled up for six years. "Earrings and a watch. No sign of a billfold or ID." His gasp of hope deflated along with her own. "And no flash drive. I suppose that would be too easy. Wait a sec." Gripping the pen between her fingers, she stuck her arm back inside the opening, extending her reach. "I felt something else in there."

"Olivia?" The wary suspicion in Gabe's tone barely registered as her pen tapped against something hard.

With her cheek smooshed against the dusty boxes, she could barely hear him, anyway. "Maybe it's just a broken tile. I can touch it, but I can't grab it. Wait a minute. That's metal on metal. What if that's a gun? It could be the murder weapon." This cold case was heating up. But not if she couldn't retrieve the evidence. She pulled her hand back out. She slid the scarf to one side and lifted the box on top. "I'm going to have to dig it out."

"Olivia!"

She looked up at his sharp tone. Looked beyond him to the front doors where the beam of the flashlight danced off a gray, swirling haze that grew thicker by the second. "What is that?"

"Smoke."

Chapter Seven

A bright ball of flame bloomed at the base of the old timber beam beside the front door as though a giant matchstick had just been struck. The fire ebbed in its initial intensity, but the shower of sparks drifting through the smoke found purchase on the rotted wood. Each glowing ember ignited a tiny new fire of its own. In a matter of seconds, the flames branched out along the crosspieces above the door frame and climbed any available path toward the ceiling.

"We need to go," Gabe urged.

Olivia wrapped up the scarf and its contents and zipped it inside her jacket. The more the fire consumed, the brighter it burned and the faster it seemed to spread. But she wasn't going anywhere without that gun, if that was, indeed, what she suspected was hidden inside. She flipped the top box off the pallet and reached for the next one. "I need to retrieve everything in here."

Gabe's hand clamped over her arm, pulling her away. He thrust his arm inside the collapsing stack and pulled out the small caliber weapon along with a snowy cascade of dust and grit. "Ah, hell. Do you think this…?"

He didn't need to finish that choked-off question. Yes. Chances were that was the gun that had killed his fiancée.

Olivia plucked the small semiautomatic from his hand and stuffed it into the back of her belt. With flames shooting up to the second story now, there wasn't time to worry about trading compassion or compromising potential evidence. She grabbed the box with the bloody fingerprints and tucked it beneath her arm. "We need to go *now*."

With a curt nod, Gabe fell into stride beside her and they ran to the iron doors. By the time they reached them, she'd dialed 9-1-1.

"This is Detective Olivia Watson. I'm reporting a structure fire at the old Morton & Sons Tile Works on—"

"Wait!" Gabe shot his arm out in front of her and stopped her from touching the iron door. He held his hand out about five inches from their only unlocked, unbarricaded exit before quickly snatching it back. Then he leaned forward and spit on the door. Even through the mask of smoke, she could hear the moisture sizzling on the hot iron surface and they both retreated. "It's too hot. We need to find another way out."

"We must have created a spark when the door slammed shut."

"I don't think so." He nudged the one-by-one on the floor with his shoe. It had a swirl of char marks at one end while the rest of the wood glowed like an ember and was turning to ash. "That's a pour pattern from an accelerant. I saw that at a trio of arson fires I covered a few years back."

"This was deliberate? Why? A stupid prank? Do you think they knew we were in here?" Olivia blinked at the gritty air irritating her eyes and sinuses, and followed the swing of Gabe's flashlight as he searched for another exit. She finished her call to Dispatch, warning them of the two people inside and possible arson before giving up on escaping through the fire and smoke and scalding temperature at the front doors.

"We answer questions later, Liv. Come on." Gabe slapped his hand into hers and pulled her into a run beside him. The flames seemed to chase them across the ceiling joists overhead. When they reached the back iron doors that opened onto the loading dock and river below, he released her hand, tossed her the flashlight and pulled the pry bar from the rear pocket of his jeans. He wedged the tip between the double iron doors.

But even with Olivia setting down the box and pushing her shoulder to the door, and Gabe putting his full weight on the pry bar, they couldn't open more than a crack between them. Matching guttural roars marked the physical exertion and frustration that could quickly give way to fear. A glimpse of shiny silver through the centimeter-wide opening gave them the bad news. "It's padlocked from the outside."

Gabe didn't waste time maneuvering to find an impossible angle to pop the hasp the way he had the front door. Instead, he hurried to the window at the right side of the door. With more shared muscle they pushed it open and attacked the boards nailed to the outside. But the splashes below warned them that this avenue of escape wasn't much more promising.

The exposed timbers behind them popped and crackled, cheering at the new source of oxygen they'd let in. Gabe started out the window, but dropped back to his feet. His mouth hung open as he fought to breathe in a gasp of fresh air. But his eyes were hard. "Can you swim?"

Brushing away the tears of irritation that dribbled over her cheeks, Olivia stuck her head out the window and looked straight down two stories to the river. The dock had been built up for boats to unload their goods, but the only thing below their position was a few feet of rocky bank and the muddy green of the Missouri. Full with spring rains falling upriver, the water eddied and swelled and blustered on past the dock pylons.

"Not that well. But I can try." She just prayed they missed the rocks, hit deep enough water and didn't get caught in any currents that would drown them before they ever made it to shore.

Olivia inhaled one breath, two, psyching herself up for the long, dangerous plunge. On the third breath, the toxic air scraped her throat and she coughed. "We have to…" She braced her hands on her knees as the coughing fit worsened. "We have to go," she wheezed.

"Easy." Gabe splayed a warm, soothing hand against her back. "We can do this."

"Of course I can do this."

"I didn't say I. I said we. We're a team now, remember?"

The massage and the urge to argue stopped at the yawing sound of metal heating and stretching. The noise skittered up her spine like the scurrying steps of unseen vermin scattered through the walls. Instinctively, Olivia moved closer to Gabe, curling her fingers into the lapel of his jacket as they both lifted their gaze. The crossbeams linking the outer walls were bowing. Flames crawled above their heads toward the heavy winch and hook anchored above them. That contraption could crush them or bring down the entire roof if it fell.

Gabe swore against her ear. "I know why they condemned this place."

But looking up had given Olivia an idea.

She pushed away, grabbing the box with the bloody

prints as she pointed the flashlight into the rafters. "Up there!"

Spotting the chipped red-and-white exit sign beside an oversize window on the catwalk level, they moved at a crouching run to the grated metal stairs and climbed toward the second-floor fire escape. Each step took them into heavier smoke and hotter air, making it more difficult to breathe and see. Each step made Olivia more and more aware of just how brittle this aging structure had become. The stairs shifted and sagged the higher they climbed, unused to any weight, and weakened by the rising temperature, perhaps.

Olivia's boot hit the next step and the whole stairwell lurched, taking a thirty-degree tilt to the right. Her leg slid from beneath her and she clutched at the left railing. She lost her grip on the box and flashlight and they plunged into the pallets burning below her. With her balance off-center, her palm slipped and she tumbled beneath the right railing toward the fiery abyss.

But the long, strong fingers of a sure hand clamped over her wrist, catching her as she fell over the side. "Olivia!"

Pain snapped through her shoulder and rib muscles at the abrupt stop to her momentum. Her jacket slid up her torso as she swung out, and the knotted scarf dropped from its cache and plummeted into the fire.

"The evidence!"

"Forget it! It doesn't do us any good if we don't get out of here. Grab on!" Gabe shouted, his voice hoarse with smoke. "I've got you."

The ache in her side robbed her of breath but also renewed her will to escape and survive. When she swung back like a pendulum, she caught the edge of the stair with her right hand, curling her fingers through the grate and hanging on. With one hand on the left railing and his feet braced on the wonky stairs, Gabe pulled at her sore arm, lifting her inch by inch until she could latch on to the metal with both hands. He shifted his grasp to her belt and pulled her onto the stairs and onto her feet before pushing her up the last few steps to the catwalk.

"We're almost there," he gasped against her ear. With his hands on her waist, he was half lifting, half guiding her along the catwalk.

Although her vision was blurred and her breathing was shallow, Olivia could feel the metal vibrating beneath her feet. The strain of the broken steps pulling at it, combined with the heat making the metal expand, meant they had only minutes, seconds, perhaps, before the whole structure collapsed. "We have to hurry."

"I know. Stay put."

When he tried to lean her against the brick wall beside the window, she swatted his hands away. "I'm all right," she lied, clutching her arm to her side. She was light-headed and coughing again, and the wrench of muscles from that fall made every breath a sharp stab in her side. But she was damned if she was going to play the little woman needing to be rescued. She pulled the pry bar from Gabe's back pocket. "Just break the glass."

"Turn your head away," he warned, bringing the heavy metal tool back and smashing the window glass.

The building moaned, as if the new influx of oxygen was more than it could take. The catwalk trembled in earnest. Billowing black smoke snaked toward them and up through the holes in the roof, gathering like a storm cloud in the rafters because it couldn't get free quickly enough.

As Olivia broke off shards of glass at the base of the window, Gabe pried off one board, then two. After he'd shoved the third board off onto the top of the fire escape, he tossed the pry bar through the window and his hands were at her waist again. "Can you get through?"

With a nod and a boost, Olivia climbed onto the sash and crawled outside. Gabe's shoulders and chest were a tighter fit. She tugged at the next board and then at the collar of his jacket to help pull him through.

With Olivia on her rump and Gabe on his hands and knees atop the metal grating of the fire escape, they spared a few precious seconds to cough soot from their lungs and breathe in fresh air. But the smoke pouring out behind him was a reminder that they weren't out of danger yet.

"I'm sorry about losing the engagement ring and scarf," she apologized. "Even if we recover it later, the fire will have destroyed any DNA or trace. And that box with the fingerprints is already toast."

Gabe shook his head, pushing to his feet. "I don't care."

"I thought that was going to be our big break on the case." She patted the gun wedged behind her back. "At least I've still got this. And the pictures on my phone. We can go back in after the firefighters clear—"

"I said I don't care," he snapped at her. He thrust a sooty, grimy, nicked-up hand in front of her face. "This place took Dani from me. I'm not about to let it take you, too."

Olivia tilted her stinging eyes to his hard, unreadable gaze and let him pull her to her feet. "I'm not going anywhere."

As if a fire in an old deathtrap or his blunt opinions could make her quit this case.

The standoff ended with the warning pop of rivets separating the fire escape from the crumbling brickwork. They both turned their heads at the frighteningly familiar vibration of old metal battling to endure beneath unexpected weight and the forces of the infrastructure shifting on the other side of that wall.

They both swore a choice word and raced down to the first-floor platform. When they tried to release that ladder, though, it wouldn't budge. "Looks like it's been soldered together so trespassers won't climb on it." Olivia shook the stationary ladder in frustration, instantly regretting the flash of temper when it aggravated the pulled muscles in her side. She hugged her elbow to her ribs once more. "That's another twelve feet or more to the ground."

"It's not that far for me." Gabe wasted no time swinging his leg over the edge of the railing and hanging from the bottom rung of the ladder before dropping the last few feet to the sidewalk below. He stretched his arms up toward her. "Jump." Sparks sailed out the window above and drifted through the air around them. Another bolt broke free of the mortar and the whole thing jerked. Olivia cried out, startled, but Gabe stood his ground beneath her. "I'm not going anywhere, either, Liv. You have to trust me."

"No, I don't." Going back into that fire would be easier than giving another man her blind trust. But little these past few months and days had been easy. "I hate when people say that," she muttered as she climbed over the edge of the railing. "Trust shouldn't be automatic—"

"Jump, Detective!" he ordered.

Bracing for the jolt through sore muscles, Olivia released her grip. She slammed into Gabe's chest, knocking him off his feet. Strong arms circled around her as they tumbled to the ground. A sheltering hand cradled her head against his neck as the impact jolted through both of them, and they rolled several feet to avoid the chips of brick and mortar pinging down around them.

Gabe and Olivia came to a stop in a side lot, lying side by side, their legs tangled together, her arms clutched between them. By unspoken mutual consent, they each exhaled an exhausted breath and lay there for several seconds without moving.

Olivia appreciated the cool surface of the shaded concrete more than she expected, and relished not having to come up with any more strength or resolve or courage for the moment. They lay there, beyond the reach of falling debris, long enough for all the aches and bruises on her battered body to register. The shallow, slowing puffs of Gabe's breath stirring her hair, along with the low-pitched rumble of laughter in his chest beneath her ear registered, too.

"Is every day always this exciting with you?" he wheezed against her ear, his sarcasm as evident as the muscular thigh wedged between hers.

Olivia's fingers tangled in the collar of his shirt and a breathless laugh of her own joined his. "I thought it was your fault."

Gabe's hold on her shifted and he rolled onto his back, bringing her halfway on top of him. "You are one tough lady, aren't you."

Olivia raised up on her elbow as his strong hands that had saved her more than once today framed her cheeks and jaw. She was ensnared by cobalt eyes that studied her face, then widened, as if he'd discovered her real secret.

Not so tough, Mr. Knight. Olivia brushed her fingers over the dark stubble above his mouth, wiping away the soot that clung there. She hadn't been held for a long time. She hadn't wanted a man to hold her since Marcus.

That this man who should be her enemy could make her want like this, could make her feel a little less like a cop and a little more like a woman...

As if hearing her unspoken thoughts, Gabe raised his head and touched his lips to hers in a tentative kiss. It was a simple meeting of one mouth touching another, testing the welcome, getting acquainted.

The second kiss was a little less gentle, a little more potent, a lot more purposeful in the way his fingertips tightened against her scalp and his tongue slipped between the seam of her lips to demand and find a response. A moan of something like satisfaction echoed in Gabe's chest and resonated within her own.

Olivia curled her grubby fingers into his collar and held on, matching each foray of his tongue, each caress of that hard, sensuous mouth. This kiss was a mix of *hooray, we made it,* and that undercurrent of electricity that had been buzzing between her and Gabe from the moment they'd met. She'd expected him to taste like the dark, hearty coffee she'd seen him drink, and that flavor of richness was there in the background. But his mouth was ashy from the smoke, hot from exertion and so leisurely thorough and gentle on her lips and tongue that Olivia was at once grateful for his patience and frustrated by the very same. She stretched herself against Gabe's muscled chest, urging him to deepen this exploratory kiss and unleash the desire she could sense he was holding back.

But this unplanned meeting of two wary hearts, exposed by the challenge of their very survival, didn't last.

The roar of a powerful engine revving up to speed tore Olivia's attention from the soulful heat of Gabe's embrace. The noise was a jarring reentry into the real world of bad guys and danger and knowing the handful of people she trusted in this world didn't include the man on the sidewalk beneath her. Olivia raised her eyes to the street in front of the warehouse and pushed away, her cop's training reacting when her own self-defense mechanism had shorted out.

Gabe, too, rolled to his hands and knees as she scrambled to her feet and ran toward the screech of rubber spinning across the pavement, screaming for traction as the vehicle made a sharp turn.

But the chase was short-lived. By the time Olivia reached the front of the burning warehouse, there was no adrenaline left to call on. Her legs wobbled with exhaustion, she was winded and that all-too-familiar car was nothing more than a black shadow disappearing around the corner. Olivia bent forward, bracing her hands on her knees as another coughing fit wracked her sore body. "Who are you, you son of a bitch?"

She could hear the sirens now, over the pulse hammering in her ears, and knew that help was on the way.

"Did you see that?" she asked Gabe, certain that was the same car that had followed her that morning. She hated that she'd missed getting a look at the driver again—hated that a stranger had the advantage of that kind of knowledge over her.

A blur of brown tweed and denim moved past her. "Black car. I only caught the taillights. He probably stopped to gawk at the fire."

"Did you get a license?" He gave no response, so she assumed that was a no. "Me, neither."

"Olivia."

She straightened at the grim tone of Gabe's voice and turned toward the warehouse. His attention had moved on to something besides a speeding car and an untimely kiss, as though neither of them mattered, and she forced herself to do the same.

Flakes of ash floated along with the glowing bits of wood and debris in the air like some devilish version of snowfall. Olivia raised her arm in front of her face to shield herself from the burning heat emanating from the building, and walked toward Gabe. He was standing in front of the double iron doors again. Well, as close as he could get with the ovenlike temperature coming off the warping metal. He snapped a picture with his phone.

"What is it?"

They both jumped at the loud crash inside as the heavy winch fell. The concrete shook beneath their feet. Flames shot through the roof. Windows shattered against their barricades and joined the debris raining down around them. Gabe backed them both across the street to stand behind her SUV, away from the fire. "I think somebody's trying to make a point."

If it wasn't made of brick or metal, it was burning now. The smoke and flames eating away at the building now made it difficult to see. But the picture on Gabe's phone was clear.

Sabotage.

Olivia's blood chilled despite the heat and she hugged her good arm over the one she had injured. Just as with the board Gabe had shown her inside, the charred black marks of an accelerant poured over the doors and sidewalk out front meant that this fire was no accident.

And whoever set it—the driver of that black car, perhaps—hadn't wanted them to come out alive.

GABE SAT ON the rear bumper of the ambulance, dutifully holding the oxygen mask to his nose and mouth while the paramedic cleaned and doctored the cuts on his hand. He'd sat here more than an hour now, watching the organized chaos of first responders and follow-up personnel.

Three fire engines had been called to the scene, along with two ambulances and enough black-and-white and unmarked police vehicles to line the block and two side streets. Either there was some historical significance to the roofless shell that had once been Morton & Sons Tile Works he didn't know about, Olivia was a relative or friend to half the department or they'd all come to see for themselves if KCPD Enemy #1, Gabriel Knight, had perished in the blaze.

He'd seen the looks, caught some snippets of gossip about the trash-talking reporter who thought he could do their job better. And what the hell was Thomas Watson's daughter doing with him, anyway?

The fire had been contained. The scene was secure. He'd been questioned by an arson investigator with an artificial leg, and had given a statement to both a uniformed officer and a detective. He'd even chatted with some reporters and photographers he knew from the *Journal* and other media outlets. Night had fallen and various headlights and spotlights added brightness and created shadows. And while there seemed to be just as many spectators as there were professionals on the scene, his attention remained focused on the short-haired detective with her left arm in a sling and her beautiful eyes fixed in an expression of weary patience.

He'd watched a buff, dark-haired cop pull up and try to start a conversation with Olivia. But her touch-me-not body language and the arrival of her father and two of her brothers had sent him away.

Although she'd reassured her family enough to convince them to leave, the other members of her cold case team remained on the scene. Olivia was leaning against her car now, maybe twenty yards from his position, close enough that he could make out parts of their conversation through the noise around him. A big blond guy who needed a shave, and an even bigger, clean-cut guy who ought to be playing the offensive line for the Chiefs, each gave her a brotherly squeeze on her good shoulder before apologizing about a car they'd searched being "Clean as a whistle." From the gist of the conversation, Gabe figured out that they were the ones who'd gone through Dani's car, looking for any sign of the missing flash drive.

A third detective in a suit and tie had brought his wife to the scene. Gabe's guess was that they'd been on a date or to some function—but they cared enough about Dani's murder—or the lead detective on the case, at any rate—to interrupt their evening and be here to check on Olivia and the new developments she'd found. And while his dark-haired wife waited at their pickup truck, chatting with friends she knew on the scene, the blond detective bagged the gun Gabe had pulled from the hiding place Olivia had found inside the warehouse. Now the man was jotting notes while she talked.

"I'm done, sir." A voice from right beside him interrupted Gabe's observations. Gabe pulled off his oxygen mask and the paramedic with the blue gloves handed him a card. "If you develop any of these secondary symptoms from smoke inhalation, get to an ER immediately. Otherwise, you're already on antibiotics that'll help these cuts, and your lungs and sinuses look clear. Just get some rest."

"Thanks." Gabe handed off the gear, pocketed the card and picked up his smoke-filled jacket before making a beeline for Olivia. He didn't like this distance between them, didn't like not knowing all the details her team was discussing about Dani's case, didn't like the protective impulses firing inside him each time she rubbed her temple or reaffixed that "I'm okay" smile on her face.

He no longer had any doubts that Olivia Watson was good at her job. She was as dedicated and smart as he'd want any cop to be. But he wondered if anyone else was aware of her fatigue, her pain or those glimpses of frustration and vulnerability that cowed her posture or flattened her smile for a split second when no one was looking. Maybe it was just his eye for detail that noticed those tiny chinks in her armor and wanted to make sure that no one took advantage of them. She was his strongest ally in solving Dani's murder, after all.

Plus, he was seeing a painfully familiar parallel between the dangers Dani had faced during her investigation and the two life-threatening events he'd been through with Olivia. Someone in Leland Asher's organization or on Senator McCoy's team, or a third party they had yet to uncover, was working very hard to keep old secrets buried. They'd killed a naively ambitious young reporter, and now they seemed to be targeting the sexy lady detective.

He had to finish Dani's story. He had to find the truth.

But he couldn't go through the pain of losing someone he felt responsible for twice. Whatever he could do, whatever the task required of him, he would see that Olivia didn't end up the same way Dani had.

As he approached Olivia's car, Gabe could make out more of the conversation with the cop in the suit. Olivia was giving him a vague description of the black car they'd seen speeding away after their escape. "I didn't get a good look at it. I have no idea if it's connected to the fire or even my investigation. But I've seen it before."

"Do you think the driver has been following you?"

"Possibly," she admitted. Gabe didn't like the sound of that. Had he put her in more danger than he thought?

"That's not a lot to go on, but I'll make it my first priority."

"Thanks, Jim."

The male detective put away his pen and paper. "You going to the hospital or home?"

"Home. The medics cleared me. I just need a long, hot shower."

Really? An image of those long, lean curves naked and glistening under a spray of steam and water should not be the first thing that popped to mind, given the seriousness of the conversation and Gabe's intent for joining them. The leap in his pulse and the interest stirring behind his zipper fought to keep hold of the wish he forced from his mind.

"Good. I'll call you as soon as I find out anything." The blond picked up the paper bag with the gun they'd recovered off the hood of Olivia's SUV. "I'll get this over to the lab." He waved an almost done to his wife before turning back to Olivia. "What about Knight? Have you had your fill of him? You want us to drive him home?"

Olivia's head turned, hearing Gabe's footsteps as he joined them on the sidewalk.

"Knight can take care of himself if Detective Watson needs to get home right away," Gabe announced. He didn't stop until he stood beside her, facing the male detective. "I saw the black car, too. Got a glimpse of it, anyway. It was a newer model. Six or eight cylinders under the hood, judging by the sound of the engine. Not manufacturer issue. Could have been a souped-up Charger or Challenger."

Olivia straightened away from the car, cradling her

arm in the sling, or maybe just hugging a protective shield around herself. "Gabe, this is my partner, Jim Parker. Gabriel Knight. He's a reporter with the *Journal*."

Detective Parker stepped forward to shake hands, his expression polite but wary. "I've read your articles."

"No doubt."

"Olivia? You want me to stay?" Her partner wasn't budging until she gave him the all clear. Good. She wasn't as alone against this chaos as he'd imagined her to be.

She shook her head. "I got it. Keep me posted on anything the lab says. Thanks, Jim."

"See you in the morning at roll call?"

Olivia nodded. Jim rejoined his wife in their pickup truck and drove away.

"Come on, caveman." Her gaze tipped up to his for a brief moment, revealing surprise, embarrassment and ultimately regret before she raised a placating hand and turned toward the car. "Sorry."

Okay, so it wasn't the most flattering nickname a woman could give him. Yet Gabe liked the fact that Olivia Watson wasn't afraid to say what she thought, right to his face instead of behind his back. He headed around the car while she fished her keys from the pocket of her soot-stained khakis. "It's okay. Blame it on the long day and let's get out of here." He nodded toward the sling she wore around her left arm. "Unless you want me to drive?"

"I don't need a man to drive my car for me."

But she was clearly exhausted. When she dropped her keys and muttered a curse, Gabe beat her to the curb to retrieve them from underneath the car. "Switch."

She arched an eyebrow at the order. "You do realize

there's not a cop on this block who isn't watching us right now."

"I know. Does that bother you?"

"Doesn't it bother you?"

"I call things as I see them. I understand there will be hard feelings with that kind of honesty."

With a reluctant sigh, she walked around to the passenger door. "Everything's black and white with you, isn't it? Right or wrong. Good or bad. That seems like a cold, lonely way to live."

She had no idea. "I'm not always right, Liv. I don't get my facts wrong. But sometimes, I make mistakes about people. I made a mistake about you. I'm sorry I judged you against the standard of any other cop."

"Like my dad?"

Ouch. So defending the family honor was working on her, too. Gabe absorbed the rightful pang of guilt and opened his door. But he didn't get in. This needed to be said. "I thought your dad and Junkert should have solved the case. I didn't know about his accident or how he felt about leaving the force with unfinished business. I'm coming at this from the victim's side when I've criticized the department for dragging its feet on an investigation. Finding answers and hearing someone take responsibility for the wrong they've done is all we have to make up in some small way for the loss we've suffered."

"You think we don't know that?"

Gabe tapped his fist on top of the car, torn between his loyalty to one woman and his concern for another. "I've always believed that victims and their families need a voice. And I'm the SOB who's going to stand up and be that voice."

Her eyes were a deep storm green in the shadows. "Most of the time, we do our job right. We get the bad guys off the street and the victims and their families thank us for it. Why don't you print any of that?"

Because he'd been eaten up by guilt and pain for so long that it was hard to put a positive, hopeful spin on things when he hadn't felt much of that positivity and hope. Until now. Until Ron Kober's murder offered them a lead. Until Olivia Watson took over the case. "I'm sure your dad tried to find Dani's killer. If he's got half the determination you do, I know he tried. I didn't fully understand how determined Leland Asher and Senator McCoy were about keeping their collusion a secret. But I do now. I'll try to keep a more open mind about the department."

"You really do have a way with words, don't you." Why didn't that sound like a compliment? Olivia tipped her chin up to a nearby streetlamp, stretching her long neck before meeting his gaze over the roof of the Explorer. "How do you feel about no words at all? I'll trade ten minutes of not talking about the fire, not talking about the case, not talking about my family—not talking about anything—for that ride back to your car."

He braced his forearms on the door frame and leaned toward her. "Olivia, you know what we need to talk about."

That kiss. The way her hand felt in his. This unexpected emotional connection. The hungry urge simmering beneath the surface to kiss her again. To do it right this time—not on a concrete slab, not when they both reeked of smoke and fatigue. Not when she was locked down so tightly that he could see the muscle pulsing along her jaw.

She was no dummy. The blush on her cheeks indicated that she knew exactly what he was referring to. But she shook her head adamantly and opened her door.

"Ten minutes, Gabe. Please. I need some time to sort through things and regroup."

In ten minutes, she'd be dropping him off and driving away. "So we catalogue what happened between us with your phobia of small rodents? We keep it a secret, or else?"

Her voice was an angry whisper over the roof of the car. "I won't threaten to shoot you because you kissed me."

"You kissed me back."

"Ten minutes, Gabe." Her temper dimmed as quickly as it had flared. "Or you're walking. Deal?"

He wasn't going to add to her stress. As long as they solved Dani's murder, it would be enough. It should be enough. But it didn't feel like finishing a long-overdue job and then walking away could ever be enough with this woman.

Still, he'd been driven and obsessed and shut off from his heart for so long, he wasn't used to feeling anything but grief or guilt or anger. He'd be foolish to think whatever emotions he was feeling tonight meant anything to her—meant anything at all. Maybe he needed those ten minutes, too.

Gabe waited until she was buckled in before climbing in beside her. "Deal."

Chapter Eight

"I heard you've been spending time with Gabe Knight from the paper." Duff Watson pushed open the door into the Fourth Precinct lobby and cleared a path for Olivia to enter without anyone jostling her sore arm.

Rolling her eyes at the attention her volunteer chauffeur was drawing to the black sling she wore over her short gray jacket, she walked past her oldest brother. "He's a consultant on a case I'm working on. Danielle Reese's murder."

"Dad's old case?"

She nodded, stopping in the middle of the marble-tiled foyer. "You were at the hospital. You saw that Gabe and Dad knew each other."

"Yeah, but I figured that was a one-time thing." Duff muttered something under his breath. "I didn't know you two were going to be joined at the hip. Keir said he was at the scene of the fire with you last night. That the two of you escaped together."

"He knows more about that case than anyone." Duff had been a detective longer than she had. He knew that made Gabe her primary lead. "I'm hoping to kill several birds with one stone—take a killer who's gotten away with murder for six years off the streets, get Dad that perfect record he wants—and Lieutenant Rafferty-

Taylor wants me to try to mend some fences between Gabe and the department. Get us some positive press."

Duff, a younger, taller ringer for their stocky father, stuffed his hands in his jeans and drew in a deep breath. Maybe he was feigning surprise, and maybe he was just using his big silhouette to shield her from the officers and staff filing through the lobby. "That's a tall order."

"He's doing his job, Duff. The same way we do ours."

He nodded to some friends he knew from the drug task force he was currently assigned to before facing her again. "Yeah, but Knight has a way of putting things that makes it sound like he's got a personal vendetta against the department."

"Danielle Reese was his fiancée."

"That's rough." Duff rubbed his hand at the back of his neck, conceding that much.

"I try to put myself in his shoes and understand where he's coming from by remembering how we felt when Mom was killed." Olivia's gaze dropped to the KCPD logo on her brother's jacket, the only outward sign she allowed for the pain she could so vividly remember. "I was either crying all the time or angry at everyone." She pushed aside the memories and looked up again. "I said and did some things I regret—until Dad and Uncle Al caught that dopehead, and the healing started."

"You were only nine years old, kiddo. We all lashed out back then. Knight's a grown man."

"That doesn't make it any easier. I was scared that guy was going to come after me or one of you guys or Grandpa until I saw him in handcuffs on his way to prison." She shrugged, then winced as renewed ache in her shoulder ligaments made her wish she hadn't. "I don't think Gabe has any family here to worry about. But he's got friends, and the people of Kansas City he's speaking for. Maybe he takes us to task because he's worried his fiancée's killer is going to hurt somebody else—or already has."

"Whose side are you on?"

Olivia blew out a frustrated puff of air that lifted her bangs. Her words had echoed the speech Gabe had given her last night. They had more in common than she would have ever guessed, but her brother wouldn't understand this growing affinity she was feeling for the reporter. She wasn't sure she understood it herself. "I'm not on anybody's side. I'm just stating facts."

Duff reached out with a gentle finger to poke the strawberry scrape on her cheekbone. "The only fact that I'm interested in is that you seem to keep getting hurt around Knight."

"Technically, he's getting hurt because he's hanging out with me."

"All I see is you in a sling, sportin' those bruises on your face." Duff's fingers went back to his pockets. "I'm glad Dad called me."

"He shouldn't have." Apparently, showing up at the scene of the fire and a report from the EMT last night hadn't been enough to ease her father's concern. She shouldn't have been surprised to find her big brother at her front door this morning, waiting to drive her to her appointment at the clinic. "I pulled some muscles—nothing major. The doctor said I didn't even have to wear this if I take it easy, and then, only for a couple of days. If it weren't for Gabe, I'd have been fried to a crisp yesterday. He saved me."

"Now you're defending him? If Dad could hear you—"

"If Dad was here right now, I'd tell him the same thing." Olivia did a little poking of her own, right in the middle of her brother's chest. "Gabe wasn't the bad guy yesterday. It took both of us, working together, to get out of that warehouse. Trust me, somebody didn't want us to."

The lines beside Duff's green eyes crinkled with a teasing grin. "You got a thing for this guy?"

"What?" Olivia groaned and pushed him on his way. One kiss after a close call did not make her and Gabe a *thing*.

"Seriously." He waved his hands in front of her face, pointing out her tone and expression. "You've got that whole mama bear defending her territory thing going on right now."

Sometimes she wondered who the mature sibling really was in this family. "Get back to work. I have to get upstairs to roll call."

This conversation had already lasted too long and gotten too personal. But the big galoot wouldn't take the hint. "I'll be done with my shift at ten. You call me if you need a ride anywhere else today."

"That's exactly why I didn't want you to give me a ride here in the first place. You must be exhausted."

Although he scrubbed his palm over his end-of-shift stubble, Duff shook his head. "A cup of coffee and I'm good for another three or four hours. Dad said we needed to keep an eye on you. It was an easy way to help out."

"I can take care of myself. Or, I would have been able to, except now I'm without a vehicle."

"Your partner can drive you. Or call one of the bros. You know we're here for you, baby sister." He leaned down to kiss her cheek and started backing toward the doors.

"You do realize I'm twenty-nine years old. I'm not a *baby* anything, anymore."

Duff came back a step and dropped his square jaw into her personal space to whisper, "Teasing aside, you get hurt again, and Keir or I are going to start shadowing this investigation with you."

"No."

"And after what Brower did to you, if this Gabe Knight makes you feel something again, and then throws it back in your face, there *will* be a conversation with the man."

Great. He was dead serious.

"I don't need babysitters. And I really don't need romantic help from any of you confirmed bachelors. I am working my job and living my life just fine without—" But he wasn't listening. He was leaving. "Duff? Thomas Watson Junior, I am talking to you."

He tapped his thumb and fingers together like a quacking duck. "Blah, blah, blah. Big brothers never give up taking care of their little sister. See you at Sunday dinner. Love ya."

"Grrr." Olivia fisted her free hand down at her side, feeling smothered by just how much her family loved her at that moment.

She crossed over to the bank of elevators and jabbed the call button, softly chanting a reminder that wasn't easing her frustration one bit. "They mean well—you love them. They mean well—you love them. They mean…"

She stepped into the elevator and a man darted in behind her. She recognized his musky cologne before she turned to meet his dark eyes. "Oh, great. Good morning, Marcus."

"Good morning to you, too. Glad I caught you. I know you had a rough day yesterday." He reached in front of her to close the doors before anyone else could join them. "How are you feeling, babe?"

"Babe? Really?" This day was off to a freaking fabulous start. "Have you been lying in wait for me to show up this morning?"

"I wanted to see for myself that you were all right. You got trapped in a fire. You wouldn't talk to me last night. Can't a guy worry about you?"

"Thanks for asking. I'm fine." She punched the number three. With the unsettling and aggravating things Duff had said still stewing inside her, she'd pay good money to take this ride to the third floor in silence.

But that wasn't going to happen.

"You know I'd have gotten you out of there in one piece."

Somebody else did. Blue eyes, black hair and the most masculine hands on the planet had proved utterly reliable. "I *am* in one piece."

"Are you really?"

Marcus brushed his fingers around the shell of her ear and she lurched away from the touch she wanted about as much as that answering throb of pain in her side. "Do we have to do this again?" She tried to explain her revulsion in a way that could penetrate his thick skull. "We were partners. We're not, anymore. We were going to get married. We're not, anymore. You've got no claim on my life other than being a coworker I pass in the hallway."

But there was no getting through that ego she'd once mistaken as confidence. "Come on. Just because I screwed up doesn't mean I don't still have feelings for you. I want to take care of you. Especially when you're hurt like this." He opened his arms in a humble gesture. Did he really want a hug? "You said we could still be friends."

"No. That was your idea." She pointed at him, warning him to keep his distance. "I don't need you to take care of me."

"I saw Duff drop you off."

"Family's different." Annoying and overbearing, at times, but at least she could trust them.

"You're never going to forgive me, are you?"

"I've forgiven you, Marcus." Is that what he wanted? Absolution for breaking her heart?

She herself was the one she was having such a hard time forgiving. How could she have been so sad and stupid to think she could make a relationship with her partner—a man she knew to be a player, no less—work? She'd fallen for the charm and excitement he brought to her life, for the security he'd made her feel. But that had all been a sham.

She looked up into his dark brown eyes, willing him to understand. "Forgiveness is one thing. But I'm too smart to ever forget. I don't have the feelings we once shared. I'm not that naive about relationships anymore. I've moved on. You should, too."

"I can only apologize so many times, babe. We were so good together. We have to find a way to make this work."

They passed the second floor and Olivia turned on the man she'd once loved, determined to finish this conversation before they reached their destination. "The first thing you can do is stop calling me babe. You're damn lucky I don't file a sexual harassment suit. It's Detective or Olivia or even *Hey, you.* But it will never be *babe* again."

He had the gall to laugh, although the cutting undertones revealed a taunt, not amusement. "When did you get to be such an uptight virgin again? I know who you are. I know how you like it."

"What?" She sputtered on her anger. "You son of a bitch."

There was no charm in his voice now. "I've poured out my heart to you. I've groveled as much as a man can. I tell you, I'm not the same guy I used to be." When he stepped toward her, Olivia backed against the elevator's cold steel wall, not believing this wounded anger any more than she'd believed his altruistic concern. He slapped his hand on the wall beside her and she flinched. "I want to take care of you. I'm doing everything I can to win you back. And all you've got is that you want to sue me for harassment? It'll never fly with a review board, Liv. We were engaged."

"You're threatening *me?*" Olivia shoved him out of her space as the elevator slowed its ascent. *I'm doing everything I can to win you back.* The glimmer of an idea slipped in between two angry, defensive breaths. Just how did Marcus think he was going to win her back? "You want to take care of me?"

"Yeah. Like old times."

Could he have been following her? Hoping to rescue her from an emergency like yesterday's fire so that she'd be grateful enough to take him back? Un-uh. She couldn't handle games and lies like that again. "What kind of car do you drive?"

"You want to find out? It's got a backseat where we can relieve some of that tension."

She cursed his lack of an answer as much as the innuendo. "You seriously want to go on report, don't you?" She waved aside whatever smart remark he had in mind. "Forget it." She could run Marcus's plate numbers without prolonging this conversation. She jabbed the open door button. The air in the elevator had suddenly grown toxic. "Just stay away from me."

Olivia was on her way out before the doors fully opened. But Gabe Knight was standing right there in the waiting area. Jeans. Corduroy blazer. Taut features and black hair. The full package of cynicism and strength and blue eyes that never missed a detail.

She paused for a moment to meet the silent question in those eyes. But she had too many discomfiting emotions, too many unanswered questions of her own running through her head to be in a good place to deal with him right now. When Marcus bumped her on his way out of the elevator, she took off, too, wildly hoping that Gabe was getting on that elevator and leaving.

But she knew better.

Gabe followed her through the cubicle maze to her desk. "I came to see you," his deep, low voice announced. With that and a cheery good morning from Jim at his desk, Olivia changed course and headed for the long hallway and interview rooms on the far side of the third floor. "Chief Taylor said I could sit in on meetings and interviews related to Dani's case. Maybe share some insight on what your team has come up with. I promise I won't publish any details on the case until—"

She interrupted his explanation with a pleading hand. "I'm sorry, I'm glad you've got strings to pull, but I can't do this right now." She opened the first empty room and stepped inside.

But her efforts to shut out the rest of the world for a little while were thwarted by a big foot, a strong arm and the rest of Gabe Knight coming in after her. The businesslike timbre of his voice changed as he quietly closed the door behind him. "You okay?"

Great. Now she was cornered. Olivia whirled around. "I wish everyone would stop asking me that."

"Everyone?" He stepped toward her, his demeanor infuriatingly calm. "What's wrong?"

Olivia was either ready to blow, or to burst into tears, and she wasn't about to do either one in front of an audience. She hugged her right arm over her sling and faced the corner of the room, willing her Irish blood to simmer down. "Leave me alone."

That clean, starchy scent filled her nose when he closed the distance between them. "Is this about the case? Something that guy on the elevator said? I saw him try to talk to you last night. What's got you so upset?"

The firm grasp at her elbow felt like caring concern and burst the dam of emotions she'd struggled to hold in check.

"Upset?" Olivia turned on Gabe, nudging him back toward the door. "What makes you think I'm upset? What business is it of yours, anyway?" She meant to shove him right out the door. But her hand lingered on his chest, her fingers digging into pressed cotton and warm skin. "Someone tried to kill me yesterday. Tried to kill me and a civilian who shouldn't even be involved in a police investigation. I'm trying to solve a case that a mob boss or some other sociopath doesn't want me to. I lost potential evidence. I ruined my favorite jacket. My family wants to lock me up in an ivory tower and my stupid ex thinks he can…that I want him to…"

The grip of her fingertips pulsed against Gabe's chest, absorbing heat and muscle and the bold rhythm of his heart. Olivia snatched her hand away. Why was she telling him all that? *Way to go, Watson.* Add falling for a man she shouldn't even like to the list of conflicts she had to deal with before reporting for roll call this morning.

She splayed her fingers in the air. "Can't a woman have five minutes of peace and quiet for herself?"

"Is that what you need?"

"Yes!"

With a curt nod, Gabe reached behind him and opened the door. When he closed it behind him, Olivia curled her hand around the knob, ready to shut it in his face when he tried to come back in. She held her breath, gasped, pressed her lips together, then pressed them tighter when she felt the salty grit of tears stinging her sinuses. No way was she going to give him the blackmailable advantage of seeing her bawl like an out-of-control little girl when he came back in.

Only, he didn't.

The door stayed closed. The room stayed silent.

Olivia pulled her fingers from the knob, not quite trusting the reprieve. She glanced up at the camera in the corner, glad to see the power light wasn't glowing. Although without a suspect in interrogation, there was no reason for it to be on. Was she really alone? When the silence continued, she dropped her guard and gave in to one sniffling sob.

Not exactly a bawling schoolgirl. Still, she didn't feel quite right—not her usual self, by any means.

Raking her fingers through her hair, Olivia sank into a chair and tried to pinpoint exactly what had set her off. Or maybe it'd be easier to figure out what hadn't.

She hated that Marcus could get under her skin like that. Although, she had to admit there was more suspicion and indignation than any kind of hurt when she thought of her ex. What if he was the driver who'd been following her for several days now? What was his game?

Why torment her? Did he really think she had any interest whatsoever in taking him back? Even if she did still feel something for him, she was too smart to fall for his lines again. It would only be a matter of time before he lied or cheated and hurt her again.

And what was she going to do about her brothers and dad? She didn't want to worry them. But good grief, she was on the brink of thirty and they still thought they had to watch her every move and soothe every bruise or insult or…

A shuffle of footsteps and murmur of conversation got louder outside the door. Olivia swiped the wetness off her cheeks and turned her head, bracing for the intrusion.

"The room's occupied right now." That was Gabe warning someone away from the door. "Detective Watson is working on… She's working."

"Not a problem." The voices moved on. "Atticus, let's put him in room six."

Something shifted inside her at the protective gesture. It wasn't as physical as Duff clearing a path for her through the lobby. And it wasn't the fact that a man was standing guard outside that door. Gabriel Knight had listened to what she'd asked for—to what she'd practically screamed at him—and taken her at her word.

Olivia inhaled a deep breath, and felt the tension inside her relax. She wondered for a split second if there was an ulterior motive to Gabe giving her the time she needed to regroup. But she decided it didn't matter. He'd listened to her and respected her request. When was the last time her father or grandfather or big brothers or Marcus had done that without her having to put up any kind of fight? Or give some kind of reason or reassurance?

He'd simply given her what she needed.

She took another easy breath, and another, feeling more and more like the Olivia Watson she wanted to be with every passing second.

When Gabe knocked on the door—at five minutes on the dot—and asked, "Is it safe to come in?" Olivia was on her feet.

She opened the door, wrapped her hand around the lanyard that held his visitor's ID and press pass and pulled him inside. Once the door was closed, she gave another tug, pulling his head down to hers as she stretched up to kiss the corner of his mouth. His skin was smooth this time of the morning, his sculpted lips warm and firm beneath hers. "Thank you."

His lips chased hers as she sank back onto her heels and pulled away. Gabe's blue eyes darkened and an answering fire kindled low in her belly. Yeah. She wanted this, too. Olivia slid her fingers around his neck, sliding them into the silky thickness of his hair, pulling herself back to his mouth to resume the kiss.

Only this was no grateful peck. Gabe's mouth moved over hers, the softness of her lips giving way to the demanding pressure of his. A flick of the tongue and her lips parted, welcoming his heat and passion into her eager mouth. His hands skimmed beneath her jacket, finding the nip of her waist between her gun and the sling that cradled her arm. She felt the imprint of each hand on her skin through the blouse she wore. The heat of each palm, each grasping fingertip was a vivid reminder that she was a woman beneath the trappings of first aid and her job. Goose bumps prickled across her skin at the liquid heat he was stirring inside her and she pushed up onto her toes, taking more from the kiss.

And while she suckled his lower lip between hers, Gabe widened his stance and pulled her hips into his. But the resulting friction of denim rubbing against denim wasn't enough for either of them. With a garbled moan that was as deep-pitched as his sexy voice, he walked forward until the crease beneath her bottom was wedged against the table. She felt the imprint of his belt buckle at her stomach, and the thick desire of his own response pressing into the cradle of her thighs. The molten desire unleashed by his hands molding her against his harder body seemed to gather and build a ticklish sort of pressure in her most feminine parts.

And the kiss went on.

Gabe tugged the hem of her blouse from her belt and slid one hand beneath the material to splay like a fiery brand against the small of her back and pull her impossibly closer. The other hand came up to caress the fringe of hair at her nape. He angled her head back and skidded his lips along the line of her jaw. He nibbled at her earlobe around the sterling silver stud she wore there, then closed his mouth, hot and wet over the pulse beat throbbing in her neck. Olivia gasped at the sudden spark of heat that arced through her and blurred her mind to everything but what she was feeling with this man at this moment. She was floating. On fire. Powerful. Feeling right within her own skin again.

Olivia traced her fingertips over the angles of Gabe's cheeks and jaw, the strong column of his neck, beneath the crisp starch of his collar. He held her as close as the arm folded between them allowed, and for her it wasn't enough. Her nipples puckered and pushed against the lace of her bra and she wished his capable hands were there to soothe their needy distress.

But the moment the idea of Gabe Knight stripping off her clothes and joining her on top of this table popped into her hazy thoughts, she knew she had to end the embrace.

"Gabe." She offered him one last breathless kiss, then pushed her fingers between their lips. "Gabe, we have to stop."

"I know." With a throaty growl, he pulled away, dropping little kisses to her fingertips as he retreated. Their bodies were slower to disconnect. He pulled her away from the table, peeled his hips and thighs away from hers, removed his hands from beneath her blouse and hair. He stroked his finger over her swollen, kiss-stung lips before breaking contact entirely and leaning back against the wall across from her. "I know you're right. I don't like it. But you're right."

While she adjusted her jacket and relished the air between them cooling her skin and calming the disappointed nerve endings that were still firing with the need for some kind of release, Gabe propped his hands at his waist and took several deep breaths, in through his nose, out through his mouth.

Despite the rumpled coal-dark hair and the collar she'd wrinkled with her eager hand, his deep blue eyes were as clear and focused as ever. "So why did you kiss me? And yes, I know, it was a team effort. But I'm interested in your motives."

Motives? She hadn't thought that far ahead. Still trying to regulate her own breathing, Olivia ran her fingers through her own hair, dismissing the probing question. "Don't analyze it, okay? Just accept the thank-you."

"That was more than a thank-you."

And this was more of a conversation than she wanted to have at the moment. The instinct telling her she'd be safe with Gabe had to compete with her gun-shy reticence to get involved with another man—no matter how badly her hormones or emotions might want to. Maybe if she couldn't explain what she was feeling, she could at least explain why she didn't want to discuss it.

"I've wigged out on you twice now. I usually have a better grip on things than that." Straightening her clothes with only one hand and pulled muscles proved to be a more challenging task than she'd expected. She got the sleeves and collar right, but tucking in the tail of her blouse was giving her fits, and every time she thought she had it, the sling would catch the oxford cotton and pull it loose again. "I guess I'm a little tired, a little beat-up, a little frustrated by this case. I'm sorry I let things get out of hand."

"You're not scaring me off, Detective, if that's what you're apologizing for."

"I'm not apologizing. I'm just...cautious."

Her breath caught in a soft gasp when Gabe stepped forward and batted her fingers aside to take the oxford cloth, tug it straight and tuck it securely into the waistband of her jeans for her. His assistance was quick and methodical. And though his fingers brushed against her and she embarrassed herself with a quick intake of breath, he didn't linger. "I think I'm starting to figure you out, Detective Watson. Don't fix the problem for you—give you time to think it through so you can fix it yourself. Accept that you've got this emotional armor for a reason—and that you feel safer when it's in place." He was no longer touching her, but he hadn't moved away, either, forcing her to tip her chin to meet the fathomless depths of his deep blue eyes. "Believe me, that's something I understand. This connection between us—it's completely unexpected. And, frankly, a little unsettling."

"Thanks?" But the joke fell flat because she was feeling the same way, too.

"Somewhere in my brain I guess I thought there wasn't going to be anyone after Dani." He threaded his fingers through her bangs and brushed them off her forehead. "And then you walked into my crime scene."

"Technically, that was *my* crime scene. You're the consultant and I'm the cop, remember?" She curled her fingers into her palm, fighting the itch to straighten *his* hair and moved away. "You can't feel about me the way you felt for your fiancée. We don't know each other that well."

"You are no authority on what I do or do not feel."

How could she be when she couldn't label her own emotions? That spontaneous make out session seemed to indicate they were quickly becoming something more than acquaintances or coworkers. But that didn't mean they were falling in love. And he must have loved Danielle Reese with his whole heart to remain so obsessed with her murder six years after the fact. How could she compete with that?

Olivia plucked at an imaginary fleck on her jacket. "I thought we weren't talking about it."

"That's your call, not mine. You know it's my job to get to the heart of a story." Giving her the space she'd silently asked for, Gabe propped his hip against the table and sat. "Can we talk about that guy on the elevator, then?"

Olivia puffed out a disgusted breath that buzzed her lips. "Marcus Brower was a bad choice I made. Although he did teach me a whole lot about self-reliance and learning who you can and can't trust."

"Sounds like there's more to that story."

"He's a conversation for another time. We need to get to work." He stood as she walked past him and followed her to the door. She paused before opening it and reached back to squeeze his hand. "But I do appreciate you listening to me before. Maybe it comes from growing up in a noisy house with a bunch of men. Games, music, sports, arguments. Every now and then, I just need it to be quiet."

He squeezed back before releasing her. "I'll remember that."

"Come on." Smiling and sure of herself again, Olivia opened the door to the noisy bustle of the squad room. "I'll walk you into the meeting. I wouldn't want anyone to take a shot at you."

"Because you need me to solve this case for you."

"Not exactly."

But it was scary to think how easily she could simply need *him*.

Chapter Nine

Gabe stood in the corner of the small interview room, watching Detective Sawyer Kincaid and Olivia ask questions of Ron Kober's wife, Elaine, and her attorney.

Well, mostly he watched Olivia. He'd sat through their staff meeting this morning, listening to reports about ballistics saying the gun they'd found at the warehouse was the right caliber to be the weapon used in Dani's murder, but that damage done to the barrel itself made it difficult to match the actual bullets. Further tests would have to be run to find anything conclusive. The KCFD's preliminary report on the fire indicated arson—no surprise there—but it was too soon to have a chemical analysis on the accelerant used, much less a lead on its source.

The DNA lab had even gotten an ID on the man who'd cut Gabe in the stairwell of Kober's building. Stephen March was a repeat offender with a long list of petty crimes, mostly drug related. March had been brought in for questioning on another murder a few years back, but was quickly dismissed as a suspect because of an airtight alibi—he was in a lockdown room at a rehab clinic. Maybe the guy had a knack for being in the wrong place at the wrong time. Max Krolikowski and Trent Dixon, his partner, would work on tracking down Stephen March. They'd find out if March had witnessed anything at the building he'd broken into earlier in the week.

The Cold Case Squad's progress on finding Dani's killer was painstakingly slow—a rehash of facts he knew, with discussions on a few more details that would have to be explored and double-checked before a suspect could be brought in for questioning, much less arrested. A week ago, Gabe would have been typing up his next column about the square wheels of justice being stuck in a tar pit, and that victims and perpetrators alike might be dead by the time the department found their answers.

But today, watching Olivia in action, seeing the wheels of memory and intelligence in those intriguing eyes turning several steps ahead of the others at the table, Gabe found himself looking at KCPD a little differently. Maybe even with a seed of hope taking root in the cold morass of his cynical heart.

The other detectives and information tech at the meeting spoke and moved, but they were white noise and blurs of shape and color that sometimes blocked Gabe's view of the lady cop with the sleek curves and short, soft hair. Even now, Detective Kincaid, a soft-spoken giant of a man, the taciturn attorney and the weepy histrionics of Ron Kober's widow were a mere background to Gabe's study of Olivia.

Maybe if he hadn't kissed her. Maybe if he hadn't felt the warmth of her supple skin or heard those tremulous gasps of surprise and pleasure each time he touched her. Maybe if she didn't have that red mark on her cheek or that black sling over her arm which were direct results of the investigative path he'd set her on. Maybe if she hadn't awakened something more than these protective instincts inside him, he'd have been able to listen to the update and review of evidence and suspects with a more objective ear.

Logically, he knew whatever Elaine Kober was saying now could put him closer to finding Dani's killer—or at least confirm that her late husband had been Dani's information source, and had gone to meet her the night she died. But there was something disturbingly illogical about his fascination with the knowledgeable authority in Olivia's tone, and the way her eyes had cooled from that vivid green of anger and passion to the pale gray-green they were now.

It was Olivia's interruption to the questions about Ron Kober's friends and business associates that finally shifted Gabe's focus back to the interview. "Mrs. Kober, has your husband had a lot of affairs?"

The older woman with the silvering blond hair clutched the wad of tissues she held against her heart. Her bottom lip trembled and her red-rimmed eyes widened with shock, as if the question had caught her off guard, which was probably the intent. "Affairs?" More tears began to fall and Elaine dabbed at her cheeks. "Ms. Watson, I am burying my husband tomorrow—the man I loved. I hardly think that's an appropriate question."

Olivia's voice remained gently articulate, although she didn't back down from the line of questioning. "Earlier, you said he'd *gone through* several secretaries and administrative assistants. Since it appears he pays his top staff quite generously, that may mean disagreements of a more personal nature terminated their employment. Perhaps they accused him of harassment and he paid them off." Olivia glanced down at the reports on the table in front of her, as though checking her facts. Gabe knew that folder held the arson investigator's preliminary report of the fire, but it was all part of her fact-finding game. As volatile as she'd been this morning, now that she'd had her *five minutes of peace and quiet,* Olivia was one cool customer, playing the role of mildly curious backup to Sawyer Kincaid and manipulating this interview like a pro. "Has anyone ever tried to blackmail him over his indiscretions?"

"Ron and I were married for nearly thirty years." Elaine tipped her chin and puffed up, sliding a suspicious glance to the reporter in the corner before the tears flowed freely again. "My husband's reputation... *my* reputation... I couldn't. If word got out, our children..." Another sob sucked up her words. "My little grandchildren..."

Fine, so Mrs. High Society there knew he wasn't a cop. Maybe the crying show and lack of useful answers had been for his benefit. Maybe she was truly worried about bad press smearing her late husband's name. But he wasn't here as a reporter this afternoon. Gabe walked up behind Olivia's chair. "Your answers aren't going to show up in my paper, Mrs. Kober. But you *do* need to answer Detective Watson."

Elaine's glare softened on a stuttering sob and she leaned over to whisper something to her attorney. When he nodded, she dabbed the tissues to her nose and answered. "No. No blackmail that I'm aware of."

Meaning, yes, Ron Kober had had numerous affairs. Maybe that provided a different motive for his death, one that Kincaid and Hendricks would certainly explore, but Gabe was still looking for that connection to funneling information about illegal activities to Dani six years earlier.

He had to ask. "How good a friend was Leland Asher to your late husband, Mrs. Kober?"

The widow in the black suit stiffened, seeming to take

offense at the question. "They were business acquaintances. Ron knew Mr. Asher through campaign fundraisers and the like. What does Leland have to do with Ron's death, anyway?"

Suddenly, *Mr. Asher* had become *Leland?* Interesting. Mention of the affairs left Elaine Kober weeping and rambling. But asking about a *business acquaintance* of her husband's made her sit up straight and drop the hand with her tissues into her lap. The grieving widow had disappeared.

Olivia picked up on the woman's subtle change in attitude, as well. "Your husband hasn't worked on a political campaign since he started his own PR firm. Did he and Leland Asher still take meetings or run into each other socially?"

The attorney rose and pulled out Elaine's chair to help her stand. "I'm sorry, but you've upset Elaine terribly. This interview is over. I'm driving her home." His reprimanding look included Gabe as well as the detectives. "You may contact me if you have any further questions or developments to share in her husband's tragic death."

After the two of them had gone, Gabe tapped Sawyer Kincaid on the shoulder. "I'd follow up on her whereabouts during the time of the murder. Hell hath no fury like a woman cheated on."

Olivia dodged her gaze from Sawyer's quick glance, making Gabe wonder what that exchange was all about. But Olivia stood, still in work mode. "I'd check the affair angle with Kober's former staff, too," she suggested. "One of them may have been looking for retribution."

"Already on it." The oversize detective pushed back his chair and stood. "Joe's got Kober's latest assistant, Misty Harbison, the woman who found his body, in Interview 3. If she and Kober were seeing each other outside of work, we'll find out and let you know. And if she can link him to Leland Asher or your dead reporter, we'll keep you posted on that, too."

Olivia smiled. "Thanks for letting us sit in, Sawyer."

"Not a problem." He traded nods with Gabe before leaving. "Mr. Knight."

"Kincaid." Gabe knew better than to expect warm fuzzies from the department he'd once criticized for moving too slowly at solving cases. But he appreciated Sawyer Kincaid and the members of Olivia's team tolerating his presence. He glanced down at Olivia. "Elaine got ticked off when you asked…"

"Did you hear that slipup?" Olivia chimed in at the same time. They both grinned at the shared thought. "Somebody knows Leland Asher better than she wants us to believe. We need to find out how those two are connected. Either she's aware of Asher threatening her husband—maybe she's been threatened, too—or there's a personal connection we don't know about."

"Do we follow up on that or sit in on Miss Harbison's interview?"

"I think Sawyer and Joe have the affair angle covered." Olivia tucked the folder beneath her left arm and sling, and paused in front of the closed door.

For a split second, Gabe's pulse leaped with the anticipation of revisiting what had happened the last time they were alone in an interview room together. But he quickly put the brake on those thoughts. Olivia was thinking, moving puzzle pieces, intriguing him in an equally compelling way. "What is it?"

"I bet Miss Harbison could get us a look at Kober's appointment calendar for the past few months."

"See if he met with Leland Asher or one of his lieutenants?"

"And if she's worried about being called out on an affair, I'm guessing she'd be more cooperative than Mrs. Kober was." She pulled out her phone and texted a message. "I'll have Sawyer ask for a copy."

Gabe tapped the edge of her phone. "See if she can get us Mrs. Kober's appointment calendar, too."

"Smart man." Once the request was sent, she looked up at Gabe. "This is still speculation, of course," she reminded him.

"I know. Without Dani's flash drive we can't prove Kober was her informant. And without proving that, there's no motive for someone in Asher's or Senator McCoy's camp to kill him."

"We need to connect those two if we want any chance of proving that was the motive for Dani's murder. But until we get a clue to the location of that flash drive, this is a lead we can pursue." She pocketed her phone and opened the door. "I'll check Kober's social calendar, too. Even a casual conversation at a fund-raising event could have been an opportunity to threaten him about keeping mum regarding any links to McCoy's campaign."

"So we need guest lists."

Olivia grinned. "Paperwork is the best part of this job."

Even if the sarcasm wasn't so blatant, Gabe would have to disagree. He closed the door to the interview room and followed Olivia to her desk where she started making phone calls.

The best part of this job was watching Olivia Watson in action.

The host paced to the far side of the room and back again before taking a seat behind the large desk. "Are you nuts?"

"Don't say that to me." The young man stopped twisting his fingers together long enough to take offense. "You said that no one could ever suspect me."

"No one does."

But the gentle tone was no more soothing than the angry outburst had been. "That detective is figuring everything out. I could tell by the way she and that reporter were looking at pictures and breaking into things." He pawed at his own hands with a nervous mania again. "What if they found the gun?"

"Is it your gun?"

The young man shook his head. "You know you gave it to me."

"And you did what I told you to afterward, didn't you?"

He scraped his fingers through his dull hair and nodded. "I stuck a screwdriver into the barrel and scratched it all up. I wore gloves and I wiped it clean, just like you said." But he grabbed the desktop and pulled himself to the edge of his chair. "She's showed up where I am two times in two days. That's trouble for me, I can tell."

If this scheme unraveled because this stupid little tweaker couldn't curb his paranoia, then a more drastic means of ensuring his silence would have to be used. "I have professional friends who get paid a lot of money to take care of loose ends like Detective Watson and Gabriel Knight. I will deal with them." The host leaned forward, sheer proximity making the young man slink back into his chair. "Don't make me think you're becoming a loose end. Or I'll have to deal with you, too."

The young man was literally shaking with fear, or maybe crashing off his meth. "But you promised you'd help me."

"I have helped you, time and time again. All I've ever asked in exchange is that you listen to me, trust me."

He seemed to consider the advice, but ultimately rejected it and started pleading again. "I have to protect my family. That's the only reason I killed for you. You know that. If something happens to me—"

"Were my instructions completely clear?" The host stood, seizing the opportunity to drive the threat home.

"Yes."

"And you followed them to the letter?"

The cowering young man nodded.

"Thanks to me, you've gotten away with murder. Don't give in to these panic attacks. Leave the detective and her friend to me."

"But—"

"Go home. Keep your mouth shut. Do exactly as I say…or there won't be anyone around who can keep your family safe."

Chapter Ten

He'd served his time.

When the hands on his watch flipped to nine o'clock, Gabe swallowed the last of the tepid champagne he'd been nursing all evening, and set the flute on the next waiter's tray that went past. While he was happy to do this favor for Mara Boyd, and attend the elegant soiree along with hundreds of wealthy donors, state and local politicians and a cadre of reporters, he was more than ready to be done. He unhooked the button behind his bow tie and pulled out his cell phone, heading past mammoth oil paintings to the wide marble stairs that would take him out the Nelson-Atkins Museum of Art's original entrance into the covered walkway that led to the parking garage.

He was looking for a text or voice mail from Olivia, hoping she'd share whatever she found after he'd left her at the precinct office to get ready for tonight's black-tie gala. He wished he was with her instead of marking time at this see-and-be-seen social event, even if she was still glued to her desk and phone and endless mug of coffee. Working side by side with Olivia these past few days, Gabe had discovered a sense of drive and intellect that was his equal, if not his better, and he found that invigorating and as irresistible as the velvety waves of her hair.

He paused halfway down the steps and frowned at the blank screen on his phone.

Nothing. No word on whether they were getting the Kobers' appointment schedules or not, or if Misty Harbison had admitted to an affair. Nothing. He wondered if that meant she hadn't found anything or if she just didn't want to share the information with him. Then, not liking the instant internal debate as to which explanation bothered him more, Gabe tucked his phone into the chest pocket of his black tuxedo jacket and continued down to the ground floor.

Maybe she'd simply gotten tired and had gone out for a decent cup of coffee. Or the ache in her pulled muscles had gotten bad enough that she'd taken a pain pill and gone to bed. But if she had found something, and thought she was leaving him out of the loop on any part of this investigation, then she didn't know him at all. He'd call her as soon as he got to the privacy of his car and demand an update.

He'd made nice with the mayor and gotten a couple of good sound bites from her for his column tomorrow. He'd let his boss decide whether the standard promises to repair streets, grow the economy and bring more green space to KC's urban environment were compelling enough to earn the *Journal*'s endorsement. He'd chatted with his colleagues and listened to Adrian Mc-Coy's support the party speech. He was beginning to understand Olivia's aversion to an endless barrage of conversations and noise because right now, all he wanted was to be alone in the quiet confines of his car and get a hold of her.

Quickening his steps through the clusters of guests sharing conversations and admiring displays, Gabe headed through the museum's open bronze doors and turned down the ramp leading to the parking garage. But a bottleneck of people entering and leaving the museum gift shop near the exit stopped him. Craning his neck, he searched for the best path and excused his way through the crowd. But just when the bank of glass exit doors was in reach, Gabe halted.

The crowd filled in around him as his gaze landed on the stout man with dramatic silver sideburns and a pretty brunette on his arm—Leland Asher.

It had been some time since Gabe had met face-to-face with the alleged crime boss. His companion was different, a more mature woman than the bimbo he'd seen him with six years ago when Gabe had pressed the man for answers. The bodyguard lurking behind his shoulder was the same loyal hulk who'd prevented Gabe from getting too close to his boss at any time since. A young man Gabe didn't recognize completed the entourage. He was too short and skinny to offer much protection, so Gabe was guessing a nephew, or even an accountant or attorney on Asher's payroll.

But knowing that only a couple of people in the loitering crowd stood between him and the man whose illegal activities had inspired Dani's last story, and almost certainly sealed her fate, wasn't the most startling observation.

It was the fact that Adrian McCoy, the state senator Ron Kober had once worked for, the politician who'd taken money from Asher, according to the notes he'd read the night Dani had been murdered, was standing close enough to Leland Asher to shake hands. Had the two men been thrown together by the jostling of the other guests? Or was this "accidental" meeting no accident at all?

Whatever the two men were discussing, the din of

the crowd made it impossible to hear. Leland smiled. The senator nodded. Leland patted the senator on the shoulder and Adrian McCoy smiled.

Then one of Senator McCoy's handlers spotted Gabe zeroing in on them, and the entourage of aides and security quickly escorted the senator out the door.

Leland and his crew exited into the garage, too. But Gabe pushed through the remaining crowd and hurried out the door after them, catching the group at the valet stand. "Mr. Asher." He pointed to the car with the state flags pulling away toward the garage exit. "Care to comment on what just happened between you and Senator McCoy?"

The bodyguard put his hand on Gabe's chest and pushed him back a step, but Leland ordered his man to stand aside. "It's all right, Dominic. I'm not afraid of the press." The self-important lout smiled. "The senator and I exchanged pleasantries. I wished him well on his reelection campaign."

"Any idea why the senator and his team hustled him away from you as quickly as they could? Perhaps they want to distance their candidate from a man who's been investigated for making illegal campaign contributions in exchange for government contracts, tax breaks and other considerations."

"You're like a dog with a bone, aren't you, Knight?" His smile widened, but never reached his eyes. "As I recall, our fine police department cleared me of any charges of collusion. A fact which your paper printed."

"There's a difference between clearing your name and not having enough evidence yet to make a charge stick." Gabe kept the bodyguard in his line of sight and moved in closer. "I stand by my article— I never said you were innocent, only that KCPD wasn't able to make a case against you."

"Well, they've absolutely cleared my name of the murder of your fiancée that you keep trying to pin on me. As you well know, I was at my niece's wedding in Saint Louis on the night poor Miss Reese died."

"Leland…" The dark-haired woman rested her hand on her escort's arm, quietly diverting his attention. "Let's not ruin the evening by reopening old wounds."

"It's all right, Bev. This is business." He patted her hand with his thick fingers and directed her to the limousine that was pulling up. "You run along. I'll be quick. I promise." Leland leaned in to kiss Bev's cheek and handed her off to the young man.

But Gabe noted the older man wasn't willing to stand here and face him alone. He nodded for Dominic to wait right behind his shoulder.

"What game are you playing now, Asher?"

"No games, I assure you, Mr. Knight. If you have questions, ask them. I don't want you printing that I didn't cooperate with the press."

Gabe refused to back down from the subtle show of intimidation. "I saw you talking to Senator McCoy. Did Ron Kober's name come up? That's convenient for both of you to have him out of the picture."

"I may have extended condolences. But Mr. Kober was loyal to his former employer. He would never betray him by telling lies to some upstart reporter."

"You mean feeding information to Danielle Reese."

"That's where this interview is headed, isn't it? Don't they all come back to your accusations that I was somehow involved in your fiancée's death?" That big fake smile vanished. "I know you and your girlfriend are looking into my affairs. The lovely detective *is* your girlfriend, isn't she?"

Gabe bristled. The girlfriend part felt right, yet didn't feel big enough to describe the feelings for Olivia growing inside him. Still, that carefully worded statement got under his skin and put him more on guard than the hulking shadow behind Leland Asher did. "What do you know about Detective Watson?"

"I know she's Thomas Watson's daughter."

"You know her father?"

"We've had conversations over the years. Some less pleasant than others. He seems to think I know things."

"I'm sure your ignorance frustrated him."

"From what I hear, Ms. Watson is a bulldog like he was." Asher gave a mock fist pump. "Truth, justice and the Kansas City way. Determined to live on her own, determined to forge her own successful career, even after that embarrassing setback with her partner, Marcus Brower."

Right. The jerk on the elevator who'd set Olivia off this morning. Other than calling Brower her ex, Olivia had been closemouthed about her former partner. But with the look Sawyer Kincaid had given her when they'd discussed Ron Kober cheating on his wife, and the hints Leland Asher was dropping now, Gabe was beginning to piece together a relationship that had been more personal than professional. A relationship that had ended badly. The fact Asher seemed to know more about Olivia's past than he did stuck in his craw…yet reignited that protective urge that seemed to flare up whenever his thoughts turned to her. A reputed crime boss had no business knowing that much about a cop.

"Detective Watson is one of Kansas City's Finest," Gabe insisted. "If she's on your trail, you'd better be looking over your shoulder. No matter how long it takes, she and her team will solve Dani's murder."

"I don't know about that. I saw a picture of the two of you in the paper, with that story about last night's fire." The portly man clicked his tongue against his teeth in a pitying *tsk-tsk*. "You seem to be an exceptionally bad-luck charm for the women you get involved with. She might survive longer without you."

Gabe ignored the stab of guilt Asher had intended to inflict. "Is that a threat?"

"I wouldn't threaten a police officer." Asher touched the handkerchief in his chest pocket and sighed as if truly offended. "I don't know what kind of man you think I am, Mr. Knight."

"Off the record?" Gabe leaned in to whisper in his ear. "I think you're a greedy SOB who's taken advantage of this town and gotten away with murder, or, at least, murder for hire."

Asher was smiling again when Gabe backed away. "It's a good thing your opinion doesn't matter. I certainly won't be going to jail for a crime I did not commit. You and Ms. Watson be careful about pursuing this, or I'll be taking you both to court for harassment and defamation of character."

Gabe shook his head at the man's venom-laced charm. "You're responsible for Dani. And I'm guessing you're responsible for Ron Kober's murder, too."

"And I'm guessing that, after all this time, you still can't prove a damn thing. Neither will your cop girl-friend."

"I'll take that bet."

"I'm a tough businessman, Mr. Knight. I've made millions and I've made enemies. I don't apologize for that.

But I'm not this serial killer you seem to think I am. I never even met Miss Reese, and Ron Kober was a friend."

A line from Elaine Kober's curtailed interview this afternoon replayed in Gabe's head. "His wife seems to think you were just a business acquaintance."

Asher shrugged. "That's how we met, of course. But I've known Ron and Elaine for several years. I should call on her—I imagine she's struggling right now and could use the support. I hope you're not pestering her with these incessant questions."

"Then maybe you should start answering a few, so she doesn't have to."

"Blame me if you want for whatever difficulties Elaine is going through right now. Because, even though you've yet to prove anything, in your book, apparently, I'm guilty of every wrongdoing in this city." He twisted the signet ring on his left pinkie finger, then casually adjusted his cuffs and cufflinks. "Just think, if something was to happen to your detective friend right now, you'd probably accuse me of hurting her, too. But look…" He opened his arms, gesturing to the guests inside by the gift shop and filtering through the glass doors to the parking garage. "I have hundreds of people who can verify where I am, and that I had nothing to do with it…including you."

A chill ran down Gabe's spine. "Nothing to do with what?"

"Just giving an example of how wrong you are about me. This interview is over, Mr. Knight. Dominic?" Leland's bodyguard led the way to the limo and opened the back door for his boss. When Gabe caught a peek inside the tinted windows of the long black car, he saw the young man on his cell phone, staring right back at

Gabe as he relayed some kind of message to the caller at the other end of the line.

What the hell? Gabe read the threat between the lines—Asher's calm demeanor, the cryptic words, maybe even the twist of his ring—it all meant something. He didn't bother chasing Asher to his limo and demanding straight answers. For once, he didn't try to make sense of all the details. There was just one glaring fact that mattered. He and Olivia must be getting close to uncovering the truth.

So what were Asher and his cronies willing to do to stop them?

Gabe slapped the departing limousine out of his way and ran down the parking aisle to his SUV. He pulled out his phone and punched in Olivia's number before unlocking the door and getting inside to start the engine.

The number rang and rang. "What kind of cop doesn't answer her phone?" Gabe's stomach knotted as tightly as it had when he'd seen her plunge beneath that twisted stair railing toward the fire beneath them. But he couldn't just reach out and save her this time. "Come on, Liv. Pick up."

He glanced behind him, seeing the vehicles of departing guests starting to line up. He shifted the Chevy into Reverse and backed out of the parking stall, then sped as quickly as he dared toward the nearest exit before he got blocked behind traffic.

When the call finally went to voice mail, his warning was brief. "It's Gabe. Leland Asher is up to something. Be careful, love—Liv," he corrected before disconnecting the call and dropping the phone into the console beside him. He swung out into the street, flipped on his headlights and stepped on the gas. Let one of Kansas City's Finest try to stop him now.

What difference did it make if he'd let it slip that he had feelings for Olivia? If she was in danger and he couldn't reach her, what difference did anything he said or did make at all?

OLIVIA PUT HER PHONE on speaker mode and set it on top of the papers spread across her desk. Picking up Chinese takeout and changing into yoga pants, tennis shoes and an old flannel shirt she'd inherited from Duff were the only concessions she'd made to going off duty and relaxing at home. But the work hadn't stopped. Since she was taking a break from poring over Ron Kober's schedule for the past several months, she stood up beside the oak desk and did some of the stretches her physical therapist had recommended to speed the healing of the sprained muscles in her shoulder and side. "Hey, Niall. What's up?"

"Hey, Livvy." The least chatty of all her family, Olivia's middle brother skipped any small talk and got straight to his reason for calling. "I finished my autopsy on Ron Kober. I've sent a copy of the report to Detectives Kincaid and Hendricks, but I know you were curious about a couple of things, too."

Olivia smiled when she heard that he'd remembered her request. "Cause of death?"

"Blunt force trauma to the head. Blood and brain matter on the trophy the CSIs brought in confirm it as the murder weapon." Her smile became a grimace of *eeuw* at the details her brother discussed so casually. "I'm not the one who pieces together the clues, but it couldn't look any less like a professional hit."

Feeling a combination of gross-out and disappointment, Olivia gave up on the multitasking and sank onto the leather desk chair. She hugged her knees to her chest.

"So you believe his death was a crime of passion, not anything planned or carried out professionally?"

"Like I said—I just look at what the body tells me. He had bruising on his knuckles, too, so there may have been some sort of struggle." What struggle? Kober's office had been as neat as a magazine picture, other than the body, the murder weapon and the bloodstains beneath him. "The killer probably grabbed the trophy as a weapon of opportunity to defend herself."

"Well, somebody had time to clean up. What do you estimate as the time of death?"

"Somewhere between nine and eleven that morning."

Olivia shuffled through the papers on top of her desk to find Sawyer's initial report. Kober's secretary, Misty Harbison, had called 9-1-1 shortly after one that afternoon saying she'd discovered his body. The police had arrived by one-fifteen. Three or four hours was plenty of time to set the private office to rights. But why hadn't anyone seen or heard an argument? And why would Leland Asher, or anyone he might hire, create such a messy crime scene, and then have to spend time there cleaning it up? The risk of being discovered was too great.

"Wait a minute." Olivia dropped her feet to the floor and leaned closer to the phone. "You said *herself?*"

Niall chuckled. "I wondered if you picked up on that. Don't worry. I've already passed on the UNSUB details to Detective Kincaid. Mr. Kober was struck three times. The first blow might have made him dizzy, but wouldn't have rendered him unconscious. He was still fighting. The second blow took him down, and the third finished him off. Whoever was swinging that trophy didn't have the upper body strength to deal a single killing blow. Plus, the angle of the first two wounds indicates Kober's assailant was slightly shorter than he was."

Olivia thought of the young man in the gray hoodie who'd been so desperate to sneak out of that building and avoid the cops. What was his name? She flipped to another page in another report. Stephen March. "Niall, could his killer have been a short, slightly built man?"

"It's possible. But even wiry guys, unless they have some kind of handicap, would be stronger than these blows indicate."

She thought of the knife wound on Gabe's forearm. Although the wound had been deep enough to require stitches, the ER doctor had said it could have been much worse. Olivia had dismissed Stephen March as a hesitant attacker, a man more interested in getting away than in inflicting harm. But could March have some kind of physical impairment that weakened his strength? She flipped to a clean sheet of her notepad and jotted a reminder to do a medical background check before Max and Trent brought March in for his interview tomorrow.

"You still there, Livvy?" Niall asked. "Or are you putting a puzzle together?"

"You know me." Although she suspected Niall's autopsy report would be of more use to Kincaid and Hendricks in solving Ron Kober's murder, she wasn't giving up on the idea that this crime would lead her to answers on Danielle Reese's murder. Gabe was so certain the two deaths were related that somewhere along the way he'd convinced her, too. "What about the other thing I asked you to check?"

"You were right. I did find a small wad of torn-up gray paper in the victim's stomach." She heard a few clicks on a keyboard and suspected Niall was calling up the information on his computer. "I didn't find signs of trauma to the mouth or throat, so I'm guessing he ate it voluntarily."

Probably an impromptu effort to hide the note from his attacker. "I don't need any gross details about the acidic properties of stomach contents, but was there any message on the note?"

"The only thing I could make out on the paper was a name. 'E. Zeiss.'" She copied down the name Niall spelled for her. "They were on two separate strips of paper, with one fitting above the other, so there may have been more to the *E* and the rest of the message, but that's all I could recover." Niall's sigh was either a yawn or a stretch, an indicator that his workday had been as long as hers. "Is that enough information to keep you busy for the rest of the night?"

He knew her far too well. "Thanks, Dr. Watson," she teased.

"Not a problem, Sherlock. Are you feeling better today?"

"I am after talking to my favorite brother."

Niall laughed. "You say that to all of us, don't you."

She laughed along with him. "Maybe."

"Love ya, kiddo."

"Love you."

Olivia hung up to find she had a missed call and message from Gabe. And though the idea of hearing that deep, sexy voice stirred a warm flutter of anticipation inside that no longer made her feel as defensive as it did even a few days ago, she wanted to finish compiling the circumstantial and forensic evidence she'd gathered. She wanted to be prepared with answers to the follow-up questions she was certain he'd ask when she called back to share these new developments on the investigation.

She went back to the photocopies of Ron Kober's appointments the morning of his death. It looked as though two appointments and a staff meeting had been canceled.

Plus, he'd given Misty, his assistant, the morning off. The man had cleared his schedule, cleared his entire office that morning except for the appointment penciled in at nine o'clock.

"Zeiss." Olivia read the word out loud, then turned on another lamp over her desk and pulled the phone book from the top drawer. "Z, Z, Zeiss. Hmm."

There were only two Zeisses in the Kansas City directory, but neither one had a first name that started with an *E*. Avoiding a random search through the yellow pages, Olivia picked up her phone to run an online search.

"Zeiss Security." Now that was interesting. Based in the KC area, the Zeiss Security website offered private security and investigation services. "An empty private office with no chance of being interrupted." And Kober's building already had a team of security guards.

Ron Kober had hired a private investigator. But who or what was he investigating? Whatever he'd learned at that meeting might have been the thing that had gotten him killed. Whoever met with Kober should at least be questioned as a potential suspect or witness. She wrote down the company's phone number and made a mental note to call them as soon as they were open for business in the morning. Since their client was dead, they might ignore any confidentiality agreement and share their information without having to get a subpoena.

With a buzz of renewed excitement humming through her veins at the forward progress she was making on the case, Olivia called her voice mail and put Gabe's message on speaker phone while she straightened all the paperwork on her desk. Way to kill the buzz.

"Leland Asher?" Had Gabe had a run-in with the reputed crime boss?

"Be careful, love—Liv."

"*You* be careful," she warned the inanimate phone. But was it Gabe's urgent tone or the slip of the tongue endearment that made her emotions snap?

Olivia scooped up her phone to call Gabe back and remind him he had neither the authority, the proof nor the secure backup to accuse Leland Asher of anything. What was that stubborn, determined man thinking? By reopening the investigation, they were bound to stir up old secrets and make a murderer who'd been living free for six years decidedly uncomfortable and therefore unpredictable. If Asher was up to something, shouldn't the man who'd been accusing him of murder for six years be the one who should be worried about some kind of retribution?

Olivia pulled up Gabe's number, grateful for his concern, yet frightened that he didn't seem to practice the same caution about his own safety. "If you don't answer this phone, Gabe Knight, I'm going to—"

A thump against her front window stopped the complaint and the call. Olivia turned toward the picture window behind her couch, catching her breath and going on alert when she saw a blur of a shadow dancing across the sheer curtains there. She might have dismissed it as the streetlamp across the street shining through the branches of the sugar maple in her front yard. A breeze could have stirred the branches and startled her.

But the lamp and the tree were permanent fixtures, and that shadow had disappeared.

The hackles at the back of her neck shivered with a clear warning.

Someone had moved past her window.

With the lamps on over her desk, the peeping Tom would have been able to see her in here working. He'd have at least been able to see her silhouette in front of the desk and track her movements. Was that the threat Gabe had been so cryptic about? Did he think Leland Asher was coming after her?

Without wasting a moment to think of all the possible motives for being spied on, Olivia leaned over the desk and killed the lights. She dropped her phone into the chest pocket of her shirt, picked up her keys and headed through the dark house to her bedroom where she opened the closet and pulled the lockbox that held her gun and ammo off the shelf.

Once the box was unlocked and she was armed, she pressed the safety off her Glock and crept through the remodeled 1950s bungalow, scanning each window for signs of curious eyes until she ended up back in the living room. When she peeked behind the edge of the curtain, there was no one outside. She knew she hadn't imagined that shadow. Maybe the pervert had startled himself when he'd hit the window and run away.

"That's right, pal," she whispered, moving toward the front door. She knew she wouldn't be able to drop her guard and rest until she saw with her own eyes that the threat had vanished or been neutralized. "You picked the wrong lady to spy on."

After unhooking the security chain and dead bolt, Olivia slipped out onto the porch. Keeping her ears alert to the sounds of running footsteps or a car speeding away, she moved down the steps and across the yard, with her gun firmly gripped between both hands. The neighborhood was quiet. Other than the two streetlamps on the block, and the glow of a few late-night lights through curtains and closed doors, there wasn't anyone stirring inside or out. So either the peeping Tom had run away or he was still here somewhere, hiding in the shadows, holding his breath.

Olivia turned her back on the shadows for a cautious moment to squat down between the shrubs and her front window. She touched her fingertips to the impressions in the soft dirt there. Definitely not her imagination.

Those were footprints, man-size and deep enough to suspect that her spy had been there a long time. Watching. Waiting to see more than her silhouette through the drapery sheers. The flower buds broken off her forsythia bushes indicated he'd tripped over them in his haste to get away once discovered.

A shiver of uncomfortable awareness raised goose bumps across her skin and Olivia turned. Someone was *still* watching. But from where?

With her eyes adjusted to the dimness of the late spring night, she didn't bother retrieving a flashlight to aid in her search. With a quick look around the landscaping, and even up into the tree, she determined the yard was clear. But she couldn't account for every yard and every house or the smattering of cars parked along the curb. Keeping her gun pointed down at the concrete, Olivia quickly moved to the end of her driveway to gain an unobstructed view of the small suburban homes up and down the street. Other than the flickering lights of television sets through closed curtains, there was no activity at all. No trees or bushes stirring except with the rhythmic sway of the breeze. There were no neighbors out for a late-night walk with their dog, no teenager sneaking home from a party, no signs of movement at all except...

A shift in the shadows farther down the street darted past the corner of her eye. Trusting her instincts more than her vision right now, Olivia turned.

The black car.

"You son of a…" The engine turned over and roared to life. The driver knew he'd been spotted.

Forget stealth now. Besides, she was in the mood to let Marcus Brower have it for freaking her out like this.

"Marcus!" she shouted, raising her gun and walking into the middle of the street so he could see her and the Glock and know she meant business. "Get out of the—"

The headlights flashed on, straight to high beams, blinding her. Squinting her eyes against the painful shock to her retinas, she averted her gaze and fired up her temper.

"Damn you." She didn't have her badge, but no one could doubt her authority as she marched down the street. She aimed her gun at the closest headlight. "KCPD! Get out of the car right now." The motor revved and Olivia cursed the driver's defiance. She arced her path toward the opposite curb, still trying to get a bead on the man behind the wheel. But the lights were too bright. "Marcus, turn off the engine and get out. Now!"

But just as the loathsome man rolled down the tinted window to give her a glimpse at his face, she heard a shout. "Leave the dead alone!"

The powerful engine roared into overdrive. The car swung away from the curb and barreled toward her. Olivia braced her feet and aimed at the lights. But she was in a residential neighborhood, firing blind, so she lowered her weapon and backed away. But the lights grew large, like angry eyes, and the car chased her down like a giant predator charging its prey, forcing her to turn and run.

Olivia dove into the neighbor's yard across the street, tumbling over the sidewalk, wrenching her bruised shoulder. She heard the bang of the car jumping the curb and felt its heat bearing down on her.

She was on her knees, trying to regain her footing and find a target when the blare of long horn joined the attack. The black car shifted course, plowing up a ravine in the grass, tossing up clods of sod and gravel that pinged against her skin.

Porch lights popped on like fireworks going off. The horn kept honking. Since her feet weren't cooperating, Olivia rolled over onto her bottom and sat up, firing off a shot at the black car as it hopped the curb back into the street and sped away. She put out one taillight before it careened around the corner.

Ignoring the twinge in her arm, she pushed to her hands and knees. She instinctively recoiled from the screech of brakes in the street beside her and the second set of lights shining on her. She managed to stand, but swayed on her feet when she tried to run.

"Olivia!" Two strong arms grabbed her, pulling her against a wall of warmth and strength, trying to steady her. "Are you hurt?"

She knew the deep voice, knew the touch. But she pushed Gabe's arms away and stumbled back into the street as the black car's taillight disappeared beyond the houses in the next block. "He got away. That son of a bitch got away. Again."

"Come on." Gabe was on his phone, reporting the incident, following right behind her. His hand pressed into the small of her back, guiding her off the street as she pulled out her own phone. "You go back in the house while I move my SUV off the street."

"Damn you, Marcus Brower." Ignoring Gabe's order, Olivia planted her feet on the walkway in front of her porch and punched in a number she remembered far too well.

"Yep?"

"Marcus. Since when did you take up stalking?"

"Liv? What are you talking about? Are you all right?"

"Barely in one piece, no thanks to you. What kind of car do you drive?"

"I don't. Why do you keep asking that? I bought a red pickup after we split, and I still have that motorcycle we used to cruise on. Mmm. Hold that thought a sec."

"Excuse me?"

And then the background sounds registered. Soft music. Giggling. Moans. Not one indication of a speeding car or traffic. "Do you need a lift somewhere? I'm kind of busy at the moment."

She'd interrupted a make-out session. Yeah, he was real heartbroken over losing her. And she wasn't. Not anymore.

Olivia disconnected the call. All she felt was confusion. Marcus wasn't driving the black car. So who was following her? Who just tried to kill her? Or tried again, she suspected, thinking back to the fire. Who was the creeper getting in her head and messing with her life?

She clutched her arm to her side and slowly turned, looking around her for answers that wouldn't come. She recognized each of her neighbors, at their doors, on their porches, inspecting the damage done to their yard. No one was hurt. No one was a threat. She recognized the tall man on his cell phone striding toward her. The tuxedo Gabe wore didn't make any more sense than the rest of this.

Then she remembered an odd phrase and whispered, "Leave the dead alone."

"What did you say?" Gabe's hand was at her back

again. Warm. Supportive. A link to the reality just beyond her reach. The black car wasn't about an old relationship gone wrong. This was about a case. This was about Dani Reese's murder. "What's that?" Gabe was answering the dispatcher on his phone. "That's right. Black Challenger. The last three numbers were 487. I know it's only a partial, but I'm certain of the make."

Olivia was cradling her left arm at her side, rubbing her shoulder. Suddenly, the aches in her body lessened. She tipped her face up to his taut features. "You got a plate number?"

Gabe tucked his phone away and nodded. "I gave the description to 9-1-1. I've already talked to your partner, Jim. He's on his way. He'll take care of the neighbors and securing your place."

What else had she missed? "When did you call Jim?"

"On my way over. Jim's your partner. He's supposed to back you up, isn't he?" Olivia nodded. Yes. Trusting Jim Parker felt right. "I didn't know if your brothers or dad would stay on the line once they knew it was me. After my little chat with Leland Asher at the reception tonight, I needed someone to be with you. I didn't know if I'd get here in time."

"Do you think that was one of Asher's men? What kind of mob boss hires a peeping Tom?" She pointed at the window where the perp had hidden in the bushes. "I've been alone since dinner. He could have broken in at any time. But he was just…looking."

"You're not making me feel any better about what just happened… Ah, hell." Gabe pinched her chin between his thumb and forefinger and tilted her face toward the streetlamp. He pulled the pristine white handkerchief from his jacket pocket and pressed it against her cheek. She winced at the sting on her skin, but he didn't apologize. "You've opened that scrape again." When she took over holding the compress against her cheek, he dropped his gaze to her gun. "Is that thing secure?"

Olivia reset the safety. "It's safe."

He scanned over his shoulder at the neighbors. "You've got a lot of curious eyes on you right now. Should we go inside?"

She nodded, but didn't move.

"Olivia? Come on, love." That snapped her gaze up to his. He led her into the house and closed and locked the door behind him. She stood in the foyer watching him do the things she should have been doing. He flipped on the porch light and faced her again. "Do you need five minutes before police cars and an ambulance arrive?"

Alone? That was the last thing she wanted right now. Liv—love— He'd said it twice now, and she wasn't going to argue about the mix-up. "No." She set her gun down on the credenza beside the door, turned and walked into his chest. He was warm. He was solid. He was as real as a man could get. When his arms folded around her, she finally drew in a deep, calming breath. "I need you to hold me. Just hold me."

The arm behind her waist hugged her tightly against him. His other hand slid up to cup the cool skin at her nape. "Finally. I wasn't even sure you knew how worried I was about you."

Olivia slipped her hands beneath his jacket and turned her undamaged cheek into the pillow of his shoulder, burrowing into his warmth. "I hate it when I don't have the answers. When I can't settle my brain, I can't relax. I have all these pieces to the puzzle, but I can't make them fit together yet."

"Can I help?"

She tried to slow her racing thoughts to match the steady beat of his heart beneath her ear. "You are."

His fingers moved against her skin, massaging the tension there. "Tell me about the pieces that don't fit."

"Do you know an E. Zeiss?" Gabe shook his head. "Did Dani's notes indicate any reason why Ron Kober would hire a private detective?"

"No."

"I don't suppose the number thirty-six twenty means anything to you, either."

The massage at her nape stilled. "Thirty-six twenty?"

"It was on a shred of paper in Kober's office. He ate the rest of the note just before he…" Wait a second. The deep timbre of Gabe's tone had changed. Olivia leaned back against his arm and tilted her gaze to his. "You know what it means."

His nostrils flared with a resolute breath. With his arm at her back, he turned her to escort her into the hallway. "I want you to pack a bag."

If he had an answer, she needed it. Skipping a step ahead of him, she spun around and parked herself in his path. "Why? Where are we going?"

"I'm not leaving you here by yourself tonight. Even with your partner patrolling around outside, it doesn't feel safe." His blue eyes were dark like midnight, the careworn lines etched more deeply beside them. "I lost Dani because I wasn't paying attention to the details. I wasn't close enough to help save her."

That driving need to find answers abated beneath the compassionate tug on her heart. Olivia closed the distance between them, smoothing the lapels of his jacket and fiddling with the bow tie hanging loose from beneath his collar. Gabriel Knight was a confident man, as compulsive as she could be, sure of his goals and unafraid to pursue the truth. Yet there was this chink in his armor, this wounded place inside him where his love for Dani and his guilt over losing her still had a cruel grip on him.

Gabe Knight was a stunner in his tuxedo—sexy and sophisticated and maybe a little bit dangerous—but that wasn't what prompted Olivia's carefully worded invitation. "I know things have happened fast between us, and I like the idea of keeping an eye on each other. Maybe… you could stay here."

He threaded his fingers through her bangs and brushed them gently off her forehead before leaning in to kiss her. She felt the light touch of gratitude and apology before his lips moved over hers in a hard, sensuous kiss that gave her a brief taste of the desire arcing between. But before she could stretch up on tiptoe to answer that driving need, Gabe pulled away. He turned her down the hallway, swatted her rump and scooted her on her way. "Not if you want to find out what thirty-six twenty means. Pack your bag."

Chapter Eleven

"Thirty-six twenty." Olivia read the numbers spotlighted on the front of Gabe's building in downtown Kansas City as he pulled into the parking garage beside the remodeled textile factory that had been turned into condominiums.

Thirty-six twenty. The street address to Gabe's building.

"Ron Kober hired someone to find out where you live?"

"I've been thinking about that. I'm in the book. My name is in the newspaper. I'm easy to find." He parked his SUV and got out, circling around to her side as she climbed down. "But Dani never listed this place as her residence. She had an apartment over in Independence in her name that we were waiting for the lease to run out on. I'm guessing that finding a dead woman's old address might require a little research." When Olivia opened the back door to retrieve her overnight bag, Gabe was there first. "I've got it."

"I'm not an invalid."

He slipped the bag over his shoulder, away from her grasping fingers, and shut the car door. "Look, the caveman in me is screaming to lock you up someplace far away from KC to keep you safe. I'm at least going to carry your damn bag."

"I guess that *is* a thing with us now," she teased. But he wasn't laughing.

With her cheek bandaged and her left arm back in its sling, Olivia felt a bit like that little girl her father and brothers still wanted to protect. Gabe, at least, hadn't argued—much—about her taking the time to change into jeans so she could wear a belt to holster her gun before coming here. She could at least concede his concern and give him credit for respecting her need for independence.

As they walked out of the parking garage, she tucked her hand into the crook of his elbow and fell into step beside him. As soon as she made the contact, he exhaled a deep breath, the tight line of his mouth relaxed and they were a team again. "Why was Kober looking for Dani?" she speculated out loud. "If he was her informant, he'd already have contact information on her, wouldn't he?"

Gabe shrugged. "I guess we can't ask him, can we."

They strolled down the sidewalk, both of their gazes looking up and down and across the street, watching for signs of any other sort of danger lurking in the alleyways and shadows. "I'll call Zeiss Security first thing in the morning. Although I hate that I have to wait until tomorrow to move forward on the case."

She nodded to the two tanklike detectives pulling up in front of the building to keep an eye on things tonight. With Jim Parker taking reports from her neighbors and reassuring them that the speeding car and gunshots were a singular incident and that they were no longer in danger, Max and Trent had volunteered to follow them up to the City Market district where Gabe lived.

If nothing else, Olivia felt that her home was safe and that the perp in the black car wouldn't try anything else tonight. It felt good to have a team of coworkers she could rely on again. Men who made her feel like an equal, not an idiot. Intellectually, she'd known all along that they were supposed to have her back, but it was a special boost to her confidence to truly believe that her evolving relationship with the cold case team meant Jim and Max and Trent, and even Katie Rinaldi and Ginny Rafferty-Taylor, were becoming real friends. They cared that she'd been threatened, and like a family—like her family—they were there for her, without any questions asked, without any games to play, without any inappropriate feelings or harassment to make her second-guess their words or actions.

By the time Gabe had shown her into his spacious loft, Olivia was feeling a lot more like her old self, a lot more like the cop she'd been destined to be from the start. He seemed to be more in his element, too, more of that mature alpha male used to being in control of his domain. The industrial look of the condo suited Gabe, with its exposed brick walls and painted pipes running across the high ceiling. The dark wood floors led into the kitchen, bathroom and living area he showed her. There was no feminine touch anywhere, giving any indication that Danielle Reese had once lived here with him.

But then he led her into a bedroom and opened up the bottom drawer of a dresser where she saw a scrap of lace, a small stuffed bear and pastel-colored items that could only suit a woman's taste. "Maybe you don't have to wait until morning to work on the investigation." He paused for a moment, squatting down to finger the lace trim that looked as though it had come from a wedding veil or gown. "If Kober was coming here to retrieve something he gave Dani, or was looking for a clue to finding the flash drive, it'd be in here."

Olivia squeezed his shoulder beside her as he walked back through the memories he'd shared with the woman he'd loved and lost. She ignored the pang of jealousy that squeezed her heart. She was smart enough to know she couldn't compete with a dead woman for Gabe's affection, or presume to take Danielle's place. If there was going to be something between her and Gabe, Olivia would forge her own place in his life. Still, she couldn't help but be a little envious of the commitment Gabe still showed to his late fiancée. If Marcus had possessed even half of Gabe Knight's integrity and devotion, he wouldn't have followed his lusty roving eye and given up on their relationship quite so easily.

She pulled away to hug her arm around her middle. Okay, so maybe it did hurt to be this close to Gabe, to want him to love her as deeply and faithfully as he had Dani, to know he was exactly the man her heart needed—and worry that, once again, her love wouldn't be enough to make the relationship work. *She* wouldn't be enough.

Love? Her love? When had that happened? When had she given her heart to cynical Mr. Caveman there?

Olivia swallowed the surprising, fearful truth that suddenly stuck in her throat. She turned away and crossed the room, giving them both the space they needed. "You don't have to show me her things, Gabe."

Shaking his head, he pulled the drawer all the way out and carried it to the bed. "Maybe Leland Asher was putting pressure on Kober to ensure no trace of Dani's story could ever get out."

Right. Talk about work. Always a much safer topic than her emotions. "Or maybe he needed her story as insurance." She came back to the foot of the bed to stand beside him. "If he released it to the public or the authorities, Asher would be screwed."

"And Senator McCoy's campaign would be over."

"Kober could have wanted it for blackmail," she pointed out.

Pulling back the front of his jacket, Gabe propped his hands at his waist. "He'd still have to find it first."

"And now that he's dead, no one's looking."

"Except for us." Gabe glanced over the jut of his shoulder at her. "That's why Asher threatened you. He wants to stop the investigation."

The whole peeping Tom thing still didn't sit right with her. A man like Leland Asher was an in-your-face kind of threat guy. The man at her window who'd run away from both her gun and the fire didn't feel like the kind of thug Asher would hire to intimidate her. Setting that conundrum aside for now, Olivia concentrated on the private investigator angle. "And you have no clue where Dani would have hidden that flash drive or any other copy of her story?"

"I've checked her jewelry box, her bank box, her desk and locker at the paper. I've asked her folks." With a weary sigh, Gabe scrubbed his hand over the late-night shadow on his cheeks and jaw before gesturing to the drawer. "This is all I've kept of her stuff. I sent the rest back to her parents. But they let me pick out a few things."

Olivia nudged aside the teddy bear to pick up the worn leather bound book beneath it. "Her diary?"

"Those entries are the last thing she ever wrote." Olivia traced the embossed name on the bottom corner of the front cover, suspecting that Gabe had given the book to Danielle Reese. "She talks about the wedding plans in there, so her mother thought I should have it."

Heavy sentimental stuff. "No notes on her story, though?"

"She never mentions a name in there except mine."

Olivia butted her shoulder against his in a sympathetic gesture. "I'm sorry."

"Don't be. I've moved beyond that part of Dani's and my story. I just need the truth." He leaned over to press a lingering kiss to her temple before pulling away and shaking off some unseen burden. "Look at anything in the drawer you want. If you can find something that helps crack this case, I don't care how personal it is, you won't hurt my feelings." He tugged the loose silk tie from beneath his collar and stuffed it into his chest pocket, dismissing himself. "Og needs to change out of this suit."

"Good," she teased, turning to watch him as he backed out the door, taking his cue to lighten the mood. "I was tired of you looking prettier than I do."

"Not possible." Those deep blue eyes that had such a talent for noticing details raked over her from head to toe and back, pausing long enough in a couple of places to make her wonder if the heat in his condo had suddenly kicked on. "The front door's bolted. The windows are locked. Your buddies are downstairs keeping an eye on things. Please don't leave this condo to chase any black cars or follow up any leads on your own while I'm in the shower."

"I won't."

Although his nod didn't look as if he was quite convinced she'd stay put, he walked out the door. "Then make yourself at home."

THE COLD SHOWER hadn't helped much.

Gabe's thoughts and his fears and his needs were full with the image of one woman…and it wasn't Dani.

He toweled his hair dry and stepped out of the master bath to pull a T-shirt on over his jeans. The clock beside his bed read well past midnight, but he wasn't tired. He was itchy inside his skin, eager to satisfy this hunger he felt around Olivia Watson that was emotional as much as it was physical. The guilt he felt at letting Dani die, at not being able to lay her memory to rest, didn't seem to affect this powerful draw he felt toward Olivia the way it had with other women he'd met since losing his fiancée.

He knew the symptoms. He was falling in love. But he was a different man than he'd been when he'd fallen for Dani. Olivia was a different woman. She was his equal in so many ways. He'd been the experienced one in his relationship with Dani. He'd tutored her in the ways of making love and breaking stories. But there wasn't anything about hard knocks and heartbreaks and digging for the truth and sharing passion he could teach Olivia. He just had to hang on for the ride and pray she wanted to be on it with him.

Gabe tossed his towel into the hamper and raked his fingers through his damp hair, debating for about two seconds before he marched out of the bedroom to seek her out.

His type-A personality wasn't going to give this a rest until he did something about it. Maybe he just needed another look at her. Maybe if he could see one more time that Leland Asher and his thugs hadn't found her, he'd be able to relax enough to get some sleep without worrying about where this relationship might or might not be going.

She hadn't moved much. Gabe paused in the open

doorway to the guest bedroom. He rubbed at the tension knotting the back of his neck, wondering if this gut-kick of reaction stirring inside his chest and behind his zipper whenever he got that first glimpse of her would go away if they did manage to stay together for a while after this case was solved. He wondered if Olivia did relationships anymore, after that idiot ex of hers had cheated on her. Hell, he wondered if he had any business trying to make something work with a KCPD cop.

Olivia was in the middle of the bed in a gray tank top and jeans. The lamps on either side of the bed bathed her skin in a golden glow and warmed the deep rich brown of her hair. She sat pretzel-style, with her sling, flannel shirt and running shoes tossed on the floor, and her gun, badge, phone and keys in a pile on the bedside table. But she'd placed the items from the drawer in a neat circle on the bed around her.

"You're staring."

"I'm enjoying the view." Her cheeks heated to a rosy pink as she refastened the back of the framed photograph she'd opened and laid it gently on the quilt beside her. "And I'm wondering if your shoulder hurts as bad as it looks."

She tugged the strap of her shirt aside to look at the fist-size bruise there. "I won't be doing push-ups for a while, but it doesn't hurt right now." Her gaze came up to meet his and she swallowed. Gabe followed the tiny ripple of movement along her creamy neck and felt his own mouth go dry. "Um. I hope this is okay." She touched the picture frame, apologizing. "I was checking to see if Dani had tucked a note inside or written on the back of the photo. You said to make myself at home. I haven't found anything useful yet."

While he appreciated her reverence to the mementos

from his past life, he was more concerned by the angry mark on her cheek and the shadows of fatigue beneath her beautiful eyes. "We can move these things out to the coffee table if you want to sleep in the guest room."

"Do you want me in the guest room?"

"I want you in my bed." His wry laugh jarred the quiet inside the room. "Is that too honest?"

Unwinding her long legs, Olivia dropped them over the edge of the bed and stood. "You can't be too honest with me, Gabe."

"But I don't want you thinking that's the only reason I brought you here." He watched her cross the room toward him. He gripped the door frame on either side to keep from reaching out to grab her and end this torment. "As long as I can see you or hold you and know you're safe—as long as you don't sneak out of here without me, you can sleep wherever you want."

But he'd forgotten the part about being equals, about Olivia being a woman with a definite mind of her own. Keeping her gaze locked onto his, she sidled right up to him, winding her arms around his waist and pressing the sleek line of her thighs and hips against his. "Is this close enough?"

Gabe's knuckles whitened on the door frame and he groaned as every male cell in his body jumped to attention at the warm friction between their bodies. "Close enough for what?"

"To keep an eye on me."

Surrendering to her game, Gabe released his grip on the door frame and stroked his fingers through the velvety softness of her hair, framing her face between them. He dipped his head and brushed a gentle kiss beside the scrape on her cheek. "No. It's not."

"How much closer can a woman get?" She stretched up to nip her teeth against his chin. "Closer?"

He turned his lips to meet hers briefly when she kissed the corner of his mouth. His heart pounded against his ribs in anticipation. "Are you sure about this?"

Her stuttering breath whispered across his lips. "I want to be closer to you, Gabe."

If they both wanted this, he wasn't going to say no. He drew his hands down her back and slipped them beneath her shirt, finding the hot, smooth skin that his hands wanted to touch. At her soft gasp, he greedily pulled her strong body against his. Her small, pert breasts pillowed against his harder chest, spearing him with twin beads of answering desire. He turned his hands, sliding his fingertips beneath the waistband of her jeans to tease the curve of her bottom. The bold minx mimicked the same action, sliding her hands inside his jeans and shorts to pull at his backside.

"Skin on skin. I like it." He dipped his mouth toward hers. "I'd like it better if it was skin inside skin."

Her breathless need mingled with his own. "Show me."

When Gabe claimed Olivia's mouth, she was right there with him. Her tongue slid against his in a feverish caress. Her lips welcomed, took, softening beneath the assault of his mouth, then demanding a firmer touch. She suckled his lower lip between hers, rubbed her silken skin against his rougher jaw. The moans in her throat matched the needy hum in his chest.

They broke apart for mere moments to peel off shirts and toss them aside. Their lips reunited first, hungry for more of each other's kisses. They shared a quick laugh when their hands reached for the snap of each other's jeans, and they each gasped at the brush of fingers against their sensitized skin. Gabe backed into the main room so they had more space to explore and touch and taste, and Olivia followed. His jeans were hanging from his hips, his erection tenting the front of his boxers when he heard an urgent, guttural excitement in her throat and moved his lips to the tempting spot.

Olivia's hands roamed over his chest and back, into his hair and over his rump, exciting every place she touched, setting his blood on fire. Gabe worked his lips against the bundle of nerves beneath her ear as he unhooked her bra.

He could barely catch his breath as he fondled her, and the proud tips strained against his palms. She tipped her head back and he kissed his way down her neck to the soft swell of her breast, teasing the tender skin with his beard, soothing it with his tongue. When he reached the pink, pebbled tip, he curled his tongue around it and drew it into his mouth, making her fingers clench against his scalp. He repeated the decadent feast on the other breast, her fingers digging through his hair, holding his mouth against her as she gasped beside his ear. "Gabe..."

"I know." His body primed to burst into flame, he scooped her up in his arms and carried her into his bedroom. He dumped her onto the dark gray bedspread, shucking off his jeans and reaching for hers as she bounced.

He paused with his hands on her hips, his chest expanding and contracting in deep, uneven breaths. "Too caveman?"

Olivia started kicking off her jeans herself, reaching for him. "No."

But Gabe pushed her back onto the pillows, loving the way the moonlight coming through the high windows caressed her bare skin, hating the way the shadows emphasized the marks on her face and shoulder. He sat on the edge of the bed, ignoring his own discomfort, and hooked one finger beneath the waistband of her pretty pink panties, sliding it back and forth across her belly, wanting to peel them off and put his mouth on her damp center yet holding back. "I don't want to hurt you, love."

"You're kidding me, right?" Her eyes, deep green with the passion that stung her lips and made her breasts dance with each needy breath, zeroed in on his. She sat up beside him, facing him. "Other than the fact I might die if you don't finish this, Gabriel Knight, I think I'm tough enough to see this through."

She wrapped her hand around the bulge in his shorts and Gabe lurched into her grip. How could he have forgotten, for even one moment, that Detective Olivia Watson was no shrinking violet.

Fine. He could make her crazy, too. He slipped his hand beneath her panties and palmed her moist, swollen heat. Her breathing switched to short, ragged gasps, but she held his gaze. Then he thrust a finger between her hot, wet folds and her eyes drifted shut. He moved a second finger inside her and her thighs clamped around his hand as she whimpered with pleasure.

"You're not so tough, Olivia Watson." He leaned in to kiss her bruised shoulder, promising tenderness as well as need. "But that can be our little secret."

Moments later, the last of their clothing was gone, Gabe had sheathed himself and settled between her legs. Sparks danced behind his eyes as he slowly entered her and filled her up. She raised her knees and hugged her arms around his shoulders, whispering against his ear. "Don't think for one moment that I don't want this, Gabe. That I don't want you." She hooked her heels behind his hips, inviting him to complete them both. "You are everything I need."

Gabe pulled partway out and slowly pushed inside her again. Her lips found his and he moved again, faster and faster. Together they found that timeless rhythm. Like tinder and flame, they stoked the fires of intimacy and desire. When they reached that flashpoint, Olivia buried her face against his neck and cried out his name. She exploded around him and the tremors of her climax caressed him until he could hold back no more. He roared with his release and emptied himself inside her.

Careful of her injuries, Gabe collapsed onto the bed beside her and gathered her into his arms. He pulled the cover from the edge of the bed and folded it over their sated, exhausted bodies. Within minutes, Olivia was dozing against his chest, her arm draped around his waist, their legs tangled together.

Gabe pressed a kiss to the crown of her hair and settled back against the pillow, watching the night sky through the window near the ceiling. Something cold and painful inside him unfurled and drifted away on the moonlight.

Now he felt she was safe. Now he could lay his love for Dani to rest. His heart had found new life, new desire, new hope in Olivia.

"Olivia!"

Olivia smiled at the deep-pitched bellow and hugged her knees up to her chest in the sunny warmth of the window seat where she'd been reading.

When Gabe came running out of the bedroom in nothing but his hastily pulled-on jeans, she smiled. "Good morning."

"I woke up and you weren't there. I thought…" He

raked his fingers through his coal-black hair that had already been rumpled by her hands and the deep sleep he'd finally fallen into after their second round of love-making. The shadow of his morning beard gave his angular cheeks and jaw a feral look. And that deep voice was a low lazy rumble now that the panic had dissipated. "Morning."

She tossed off the cream-colored afghan she'd covered up with to ward off the chill of the early morning, tucked a slip of paper into the diary as a bookmark and stood. She walked across the open loft to the kitchen area and set the book on the edge of the granite-top kitchen island. "I made coffee."

"I could use some."

But when she circled around to the counter where the coffeemaker steamed, he slipped his arm around her waist and pulled her up onto her toes for a firm kiss that was half passion left over from the night before and half reprimand for scaring him this morning. When her sock-covered feet hit the floor again, Olivia stroked her fingers along the stubbled line of his jaw in a soothing caress. The worry he'd felt when he'd awakened alone in bed still lingered in his eyes. "I'm okay. Sorry if you thought I'd left. I know you didn't get much sleep and I wanted to get to work." The fuzzy nap of her flannel shirt caught for a moment in the crisp curls of his dusky chest hair, as if telling her she needed to stay close to this man. Still, she made decisions with her brain, not some whimsical symbolism, and she moved away from his solid warmth to pour coffee into one of the mugs that she'd found in the cabinet. "Black, right?"

"Yeah."

She topped off her own mug and added a shot of milk

before pulling other breakfast items out of the fridge. "Eggs with your toast?"

"You cook?"

She swatted his arm when he joined her at the stove. "My grandpa taught me how. I actually enjoy it when I have the time." She cracked two eggs into the bubbling butter of the skillet and retrieved the spatula she'd used earlier from the sink. "Which reminds me, I called my dad and brothers this morning to let them know I'm still okay. Duff and Keir are on their way over to spell Max and Trent, so they can get some sleep."

That hadn't been the most pleasant of conversations. While her father was relieved to hear she hadn't been seriously injured by the driver who'd tried to run her down, he'd taken a long, fatherly pause when she told him she had stayed the night with Gabe. *Is he treating you all right, Livvy?*

A hundred percent better than Marcus ever did.

Well, he's no standard to measure a man by.

Dad, I think you'd like Gabe if you had the chance to get to know him without Danielle Reese's murder coming between you. She'd held her breath for a moment before adding, *The two of you are actually a lot alike.*

Uh-huh. He'd dismissed the possibility of him and Gabe ever burying the hatchet and getting along, and taken care of the business she'd asked about. *I'll call your brothers or come over myself if they can't make it. You don't go anywhere by yourself until we sort this out. Understand?*

I do. Thanks, Dad. I love you.

"Liv?"

She snapped her thoughts back to the present and quickly flipped the eggs before the yolks turned to rubber. "I just wanted to reassure you that there will be someone watching us 24/7 now. Until we get this case solved and find out who owns that black car."

"What did your family say when you told them where you were?"

"Um, well…" So he knew exactly where her thoughts had wandered off to. "You do get bonus points for helping me last night and wanting to keep me safe. But they made it clear that they're here to protect *me*. Not you."

Gabe lifted his mug in a toast. "I can live with that."

"Don't worry, Gabe." She pulled out a plate and dished up his breakfast. "If you get caught in the crossfire, I'll be watching your back."

"No. You're the one in danger."

"You were trapped in that fire, too. I don't think these people care who gets hurt as long as it isn't them."

"I'm not going to have you taking any extra risks because of me. If Asher's men come after me, good. Let 'em come. It'll take the focus off you."

"I'm not going to let anyone…" She caught her breath, stopping the argument before it went any further. Since neither of them would budge on protecting the other, she raised her hands in a silent truce and changed the topic. "I've been reading Dani's diary."

"I saw that." Gabe stood there, a handsome, rumpled, stubborn devil, eating his breakfast. Olivia crossed to the opposite side of the kitchen island and pulled out a stool to sit. He pointed his fork at the diary when she opened it. "I don't suppose you found anything. I didn't miss her naming her informant or exactly what dirt she had on Asher and McCoy?"

Olivia flipped through the pages, remembering some of the entries there. "No. It's filled with normal things a woman writes in her diary. Falling in love. Arguments.

Concerns. Things she was looking forward to." She glanced up at Gabe. "Things that frustrated her."

He made a face and went back to eating. "Did anything jump out at you? A fresh set of eyes usually sees something new."

Dani had been planning a simple, summery, outdoor wedding at her parents' home in Kansas, with a second reception slated for the tony Cattleman's Club here in the city. She wrote about how much she had learned from Gabe as a reporter, and the new places and life experiences he'd shared with her personally. But mostly, Dani had written about falling in love, and how, no matter what, she loved being with him. "She was a talented writer. Almost poetic at times."

Gabe nodded, swallowing the last forkful of eggs. "Yet she could be completely straightforward and lose the purple prose when it came to the articles she wrote."

Dani had mentioned that, too, how Gabe had taken her raw skills and turned her into a better writer. "Some of the things she says in here, the way she says them, reminded me that a woman thinks differently than a man."

He gave her a thumbs-up on the breakfast and drank a sip of coffee. "That's not news worth reporting, Detective."

"Dani was angry that night she left."

"Yes."

"She downloaded her story and file notes onto her flash drive so you couldn't spy on her and tell her what she was doing wrong or—"

"I didn't say she was wrong. Her story was legit. I wanted her to understand that the people she was about to expose would do whatever it took to stop her. She didn't have backup who knew to go looking for her if she didn't call in or show up at a certain time. She was meeting in a dangerous part of town. She didn't have the right kind of protection in place."

As the tension radiating off him increased, Olivia reached across the island to touch his hand to soothe him. "I get it. You were both upset."

Gabe nodded, understanding that this was about piecing together a puzzle, not placing blame. He squeezed her hand before taking his plate to the sink to rinse it and put it in the dishwasher. "Sorry. That's old news. I know you're leading up to something. What is it?"

"When a woman gets really emotional like that, she has a go-to plan, a habit she uses to regain her equilibrium. Especially if she has an important job or responsibilities she has to take care of."

Gabe picked up the pan and spatula to load them into the dishwasher, as well. "Like five minutes of peace and quiet."

"That's right. Some women go for a run. Others take a bubble bath. I like to be alone in a place that's calm and serene." Like spending an hour watching the sun come up over the city skyline from the secluded nook of Gabe's window seat. She hadn't just been reading the diary, she needed some time to process the emotional upheaval of sleeping together and realizing just how important he'd become to her in the short span of time they'd been together. But that was a discussion for another time. "Where did Dani go when you two had a fight?"

"We didn't fight that much."

Olivia waved aside his defensive argument. "When anything upset her or frustrated her, what was her go-to plan to cool off and compose herself?"

Gabe finished his task and closed the dishwasher, using the time to think before rejoining her at the island.

"She liked to go up onto the roof. She planted some flower boxes and a bunch of pots with herbs on the deck up there, bought some patio furniture and a grill. She kept saying one day when we stopped working we were going to have friends over and entertain up there."

"You probably hated the idea of not working."

"So did she." He smiled at the fond memory. "But she'd plug in some music and go up there to trim off dead blooms, put together bouquets and dig around in the dirt."

Dani had been murdered on a rainy autumn night. "Would she go up there even if the weather wasn't nice?"

Gabe nodded. "She built a snowman up there once."

"Are the pots and flower boxes still up there?"

"She went up there that night. I swear I could hear her cursing through the ceiling. She went down the fire escape and left without coming back in to say goodbye." Gabe's hands fisted on the cool granite. "And I was too proud or angry or whatever stupid emotion I was feeling to go up there and apologize. I thought she'd come back down and we'd have a civilized discussion about how to handle her story."

Blame and regret didn't matter right now. Olivia climbed down off the stool. "How do I get to the roof?"

Gabe's blue eyes locked onto hers and widened. "Are you saying finding that flash drive is that easy?"

Olivia hurried into the guest bedroom where she'd left her tennis shoes and shouted her answer. "Not exactly easy. We haven't actually found it yet. And it might not be there. Six years have passed. You and my dad searched in the places a man would think of. Logical places. This is just a hunch I have based on…"

When she came back out with her shoes on, Gabe had disappeared. Seconds later, he walked out of his room, buttoning a starched blue shirt over the T-shirt he'd put on. "I'd trust your hunches over most people's eyewitness testimony any day, Detective." He pulled on socks and shoes, grabbed his keys and reached for her hand. "Let's go look."

Six years with mostly Mother Nature to take care of the rooftop garden had turned the red paint on the deck railings and flower boxes brown. The only flowers that had survived since their last caretaker were a pair of overgrown rosebushes in two giant pots chained to the railing at the far end of the deck. Dani had chosen hardy plants because, even now, there were new green shoots pushing up through the dirt.

"I can see why she'd like it up here." Olivia squinted into the damp morning breeze that indicated they'd have rain later in the day. But the view up here was panoramic, with the tallest buildings of downtown KC far enough away that she could see for miles in almost any direction. She tried for a few moments to think like Dani would have that night. "Are there any lights up here?"

Gabe nodded. "She used to string party lights up here. But you have to turn them on…" He paused to unlock a small shed. "In here." He hit a switch, turning on a bare lightbulb hanging in the middle of the shed, as well as twin spotlights on the outside, angled over the deck area. "That's the light she would have had that night, plus a few twinklers hanging from the railings."

"It's not much." She followed him inside the shed after he moved aside a grill and deck chairs stored there, clearing a path.

"It would have been crowded like this in here, too," Gabe added, uncovering the grill and checking inside. "We packed everything up over Labor Day weekend."

"Then it needed to be a place she could get to quickly. She wasn't up here that long, right?"

"Maybe five minutes, tops."

"Are there any cabinets or storage boxes where she might have stashed the flash drive?" Olivia asked, drifting toward the wall display of a couple dozen colorful glazed pots that Gabe or someone had brought inside out of the elements.

"Just those open shelves and the stuff sitting around on the floor." He pulled out a galvanized bucket and set it on the floor beside her. "We can use this or the empty pots to dump the dirt into and sift through it if you think it's in one of those."

The dirt inside the pots was dry and cracked or had filtered through the disintegrating bases of some to form neat, pyramid-shaped piles on the floor and shelves. She picked up a turquoise pot to start the search. Wait. Not so neat. She recognized the tracks through the dirt where tiny feet and balancing tails had scurried through.

Her heart thumped rapidly in her chest as she stepped back. "Do you have mice in here?"

"I'm sure they come in during the wintertime. Do you want me to search in here and you take the flower boxes?"

"No." Inhaling a quieting breath, she turned the pot upside down and shook the globs of solidified potting soil into the bucket. "I'm a professional cop and a grown... Yes!" A tiny black mouse landed in the bucket and Olivia screamed. The turquoise pot shattered on the concrete floor as the vile little vermin froze for a moment, looking up to see who'd disturbed his hiding place. Then he darted away as fast as Olivia dashed back onto the deck.

"Easy, tough lady." Gabe caught her in the middle of the deck and pulled her into his arms. "Hey. You're shaking."

A dozen different curses went through Olivia's head. She hated this weakness. And though she wanted to be able to shake it off and deal with this on her own, she found herself clutching a handful of Gabe's shirt and leaning against his shoulder instead. "Dad said my mother was terrified of mice, too. I think it's a hereditary thing. Don't think my brothers didn't take advantage of that one." But the firm stroke of Gabe's fingers at the nape of her neck took the edge off her irrational fear, and allowed her to think and breathe normally again. If a kid with a knife and gun and a man in a speeding black car couldn't scare her away from this investigation, then no furry little rodent would, either. "I'm okay." She pressed a kiss to the edge of Gabe's jaw and pushed away. "I'm okay."

"I'm just glad you're not so independent you don't need me for something," he teased, although the humor didn't quite reach his eyes. He turned away and went back into the shed.

It was on the tip of her tongue to call him back and tell him that she needed him to make her whole again. She needed him to love her and teach her to believe in trust and her own judgment and happy futures again. She just needed him. Of all the crazy possibilities in the world, she needed Gabe Knight, the one man in all of KC who hadn't broken the law, who didn't like cops. She needed him.

She loved him.

"I'll face the beast in here. If I find something, I'll bring it out." When he stepped back outside a few seconds later, Olivia shook the distracting revelation from her head. He set a pair of women's gardening gloves and a small hand shovel in her hands. "Here. Take these if you're going to be digging through the dirt."

"Thanks."

Ignoring her troublesome thoughts and wary heart for now, Olivia pulled on the gloves and started poking through the dirt and peeking through the slats at her feet. Common sense sent her to the flower boxes on either side of the railing where they'd entered off the fire escape. If Dani hadn't had much time to hide the flash drive, she would have looked for the most convenient place—if she'd hidden it up here at all. Olivia scooted the dirt around and dug all the way down to the wood at the bottom. Nothing.

Olivia sighed in frustration, scanning the nearly empty deck. She'd thought she was onto something here. This place was secluded, had limited access to outsiders, and it was probably the place where Dani had felt the safest. It's where Olivia would have stashed the flash drive for safekeeping until she could retrieve it later. But would Dani have done the same?

Even with the overcast sky, the morning sun had masked the most obvious hiding place of all. Olivia looked at the spotlight on the shed, and looked again. Her pulse rate kicked up a notch, with a far more even, healthier excitement than the startle she'd gotten from her run-in with Mighty Mouse.

"Are you sentimental about any of these flowers?" she shouted to Gabe, following the beam of the right spotlight over to one of the potted rosebushes.

"No." He came to the door as she plunged her shovel into the pot, attacking the base of the bush to loosen up the soil. "Did you find something?"

"She was up here at night, for just a few minutes. She

needed to catch her breath, clear her mind and hide her story so that she could get to the appointment with her informant on time."

"That light shines right on this pot." He joined her, pulling away the dirt with his gloved hands, then grasping the stalks of the plant itself, tugging and twisting until the roots started to give way. "She wouldn't have had to take time to unlock the shed, and she would have been able to see what she was doing here."

A big chunk of the gnarled old bush pulled free, dumping a shower of dirt at their feet. Gabe dumped the plant onto the deck and reached in to pull the rest of it out. But there was no need. Olivia dug out clumps of the broken roots and sifted through the dirt and debris with her gloved fingers. Was that… She felt the crinkle of something nonorganic between the root ball and the side of the pot.

"Gabe?" She yanked the zipped-up plastic bag from its hiding place. "Gabe!"

"Is that what I think it is?"

She brushed six years of dirt and the elements off the bag and held it up to the spotlight. Olivia was almost giddy with relief when they saw what was inside.

A thumb-size flash drive attached to a silver key ring.

"That's Dani's," Gabe confirmed, pressing a kiss to Olivia's cheek. "You found it."

"If the weather hasn't destroyed it completely, our lab can do amazing things."

He pulled off their gloves and tossed them and the tool into the shed and locked the door. "What are we waiting for?"

Olivia nodded and hurried down the stairs ahead of him. "Who's waiting?"

Chapter Twelve

"I know who murdered Danielle Reese."

Olivia stood at the side of the table and looked around at her team. Other than Gabe, who'd been at the crime lab with her yesterday and had read the same files recovered from the flash drive they'd found, she was met with looks that ranged from mild surprise to disbelief.

Max leaned back in his chair, blurting out what the others must have been thinking. "Then why don't we have this guy in custody? What's the catch?"

It was a big one. "I'm not sure I can prove it."

Ginny Rafferty-Taylor quieted her office by simply raising her hand. "Maybe you'd better give us a little more explanation. We all know how rare it is to get a confession on a cold case. Do you have circumstantial evidence?"

"Yes, ma'am. A ton of it." Olivia turned her laptop around to pull up the list of files she'd copied from the flash drive. She put it up on the screen behind her for everyone to read. "Dani Reese was meticulous about documenting her research."

"If I may?" Gabe sat at the table now, too. He'd been accepted as an integral part of this investigation if not exactly welcomed as friend. "Dani kept photos of corroborating evidence and transcripts of interviews with her informant, as well as several drafts of the articles she was writing about Leland Asher making payoffs to Adrian McCoy's campaign in exchange for political favors such as rezoning property Asher wanted or adjusting funding programs that would benefit his legitimate businesses or cutting budgets so there would be fewer cops in the neighborhoods where he conducts his less legitimate enterprises."

"Money laundering. Drug trafficking. Racketeering," Trent added. "We know the list. That flash drive can prove Leland Asher is a crook?"

Olivia answered. "We found evidence of collusion, at least. Although we can't tie him directly to Dani Reese's murder."

Max frowned. "I thought you said he killed that poor lady."

Olivia was quick to clarify. "I didn't say it was Asher. But whether she intended to or not, Dani did tell us who shot her that night."

"So what did she say?" Max asked. "What secrets are on that flash drive?"

"Dani used an old-school reporting technique," Gabe jumped in, explaining the gold mine of information the crime lab had retrieved from his late fiancée's notes. "She documented activities before and after each meeting. Basically, she kept a logbook to record her research, make note of potential sidebars, keep track of all the details of who, what, when and where, in case it might be related to her main story." He gestured to Olivia, throwing their attention back to her. "That's where we picked up on the man Olivia is talking about."

Olivia opened one of the files. "He must have been stalking her for several days, if not weeks before the murder. She mentions him several times."

Lieutenant Rafferty-Taylor jotted a note on the pad in front of her. "Stalking? Did Ms. Reese have contact with him? Had he threatened her before that night?"

"Not directly." Olivia punched a button on her laptop to post an image up on the screen. "Here's an example of one entry." She read Dani's words out loud.

"He never talks to me. But today he followed me through the park when I was power walking with Lucy after lunch. I think he has a crush and is just too shy to approach me. I've seen him in line at the coffee shop, parked in his car at the grocery store, pumping gas when I filled up my tank yesterday. But I don't know his name. He just watches me. He sneaks closer when he thinks I'm not looking. This guy gives me the creeps."

Katie Rinaldi shivered. "It'd give me the creeps, too, to have some guy lurking around me like that." When Trent reached over to squeeze her shoulder, she smiled and went back to work. "Did she happen to give a name to this scumbag so I can put him in the case file and we can track him down?"

"No name, but she gave a good description of him in several different places in her reports. Reddish-brown hair. Slight build." Olivia posted a collage of candid photos. "She even gave us his picture."

Several of them, in fact. A skinny guy waiting for a table on the far side of a coffee shop, his face partly obscured by the crowd of patrons between them. The same man in a hooded sweatshirt, caught at an awkward angle as though Dani Reese had been trying to hide the fact she was taking a picture. A young man sitting in a beat-up car across the street from the *Journal*'s parking garage.

"According to the time stamp on the photos, these were all taken in the two weeks before she died."

Max sat up in his chair and snapped his fingers. "Hey. I know that guy."

Gabe pulled back his sleeve and raised his arm to point to the gauze bandage covering the stitches there. "We all do."

"You're talking about Stephen March." Max smacked Trent on the arm beside him. "Son of a gun. We had that kid in here yesterday. He was high as a kite. He's the one who left his DNA on Mr. Reporter there."

Jim Parker took his cue from Olivia's nod and passed out copies of Stephen March's DMV photo and vehicle registration. "Five bucks if anyone can guess what kind of car Stephen March drives now."

"Black Dodge Challenger?" Gabe drawled.

Jim nodded. "He's been following Liv the same way he followed Dani Reese—maybe learning her routine and looking for the opportunity to find her alone, maybe working up the nerve to strike again."

Gabe set the papers on the table. "That's the car I saw try to run down Olivia. The last three digits of the license plate number are the same."

"And I saw the same car speeding away from the warehouse fire." Olivia nodded to her partner to continue.

"I talked to March at his sister's house after leaving your place," Jim said. "Found the car there, too, parked out back. One of the taillights was missing and the hood was still warm so I know he hadn't been watching TV down in the basement like he claimed. His sister looked too much like the family-sedan type to have been racing around in that thing. He couldn't account for his whereabouts the night of the fire, either. 'Out looking for some friends' isn't much of an alibi."

"The sister wouldn't confirm his alibi?" the lieutenant asked.

Jim shook his head. "She said the basement apartment has a separate entrance, and she doesn't always know when he comes and goes. In fact, she didn't say much at all. She seemed so skittish about having a cop in the house with her that I did the interview out on the front porch."

"She sounds like a piece of work," Max grumbled.

"Nonetheless," Ginny interrupted, "we have a viable suspect. Where is Mr. March now?"

Max shoved his chair away from the table and stood. "Hell. I'm an idiot. He's in holding. Yesterday, we booked him for assault and illegal possession of a firearm. He probably thinks he dodged a bullet because we didn't mention murder. You want me to bring him up here for questioning?"

"Hold on, Max." The lieutenant looked up at Olivia, her keen blue eyes seeing that even her lead detective didn't think this was a slam-dunk case yet. "What else do we need to prove he's our guy?"

"Motive would be nice. Most stalkers know their victims. As far as I can tell, Stephen and Dani were only random acquaintances who frequented the same businesses for the last two weeks of her life. There's no evidence that he issued any kind of threat. And she never reported him to the police."

Ginny followed up with a question to Gabe. "And Ms. Reese never mentioned this alleged stalker to you?"

Olivia recognized the grim line of Gabe's mouth and the guilt it represented. He shook his head. "She didn't tell me anything about the story she was working on or anything about that…undercover part of her life. I didn't know what was going on until I read her notes." He raked his fingers through his hair, erasing some of the tension and leaving a sea of rumpled spikes in their wake. "Are you sure he wasn't working for Leland Asher?" Gabe proposed for the umpteenth time since they'd reviewed Dani's research together. "That this whole stalking setup isn't some kind of cover-up for Asher's involvement?"

Olivia wanted to believe that, too. Lord knew there was plenty of information on that flash drive that Asher wouldn't want the authorities to know about. "The evidence doesn't support that. We have no proof that the two men have ever even met. They certainly don't run in the same social circles or live in the same neighborhood. And there's no record anywhere of money changing hands between them. Unless March gives him up when we interview him, there's no way to link Asher to the actual murder."

Trent Dixon interjected another voice of reason. "According to his juvie record and stints in rehab, that kid has been doped out of his mind for half his life. If Ms. Reese smiled at him or shared a casual conversation, that might have been all it took for him to believe there was a connection between them. If he finally worked up the nerve to approach her that night, and she didn't reciprocate…"

Olivia agreed. Reluctantly. "I know that's happened before. I still think there has to be a connection between Asher and Dani Reese beyond her uncovering a story on him. But right now, all the circumstantial evidence points to Stephen March having acted alone."

"Don't worry, Liv," the lieutenant reassured her. "Leland Asher isn't going to walk away from this unscathed." She turned to the brunette taking notes on her computer. "Katie—I want you to copy this to your uncle in the DA's office, see if he agrees we've got enough to get an arrest warrant for Mr. Asher."

Katie nodded. "Detectives Hendricks and Kincaid, too?"

"Yes."

"Sawyer and Joe will want to reinterview Elaine Kober." Olivia tapped her own laptop, indicating Dani's files. "And Zeiss Security. The *E* on the note Mr. Kober tried to get rid of stood for Elaine. When I talked to their representative, he said Ron Kober hired them to investigate his wife's 'suspicious' activities. Apparently, he wanted a divorce so he could marry his assistant, Misty Harbison, but with his infidelity track record, he needed some ammunition or else he'd be paying Elaine big bucks."

Gabe had been as surprised as she was when they'd read the notations in Dani's files. "For years now, I assumed Ron Kober was BB, Dani's informant." He shook his head, admitting his mistake. "But it was Ron's wife. Dani's first draft of her story uses the feminine pronouns *she* and *her*. Later, she changed them to genderless references to protect her source. Elaine was at almost every public event and private party her husband was. She'd be privy to what went on behind the scenes."

Olivia opened another file and put it up on the screen. "Elaine Kober took these pictures and gave them to Dani." There was a photo of a check signed by Leland Asher, sitting on top of several stacks of cash in Ron Kober's office during his tenure working for Senator McCoy. The paperwork beside it showed the check had been counted as a campaign contribution, but not the cash. Another picture showed Asher whispering into McCoy's ear at a charity event, with her husband lurking in the background. "I think she was more interested in exposing her husband's criminal activities as payback for his continued infidelity than she was with any sense of civic duty."

"And he didn't find out about her betrayal until now?" Katie asked.

"Or, he overlooked it." Olivia had a theory about that seriously twisted relationship, too. "Their divorce would have been expensive and messy. If Ron Kober could find that missing flash drive, he could hand it over to Leland Asher and let his old 'business associate' take care of the problem one way or another. I'm guessing Elaine found out what he was up to, there was an ugly argument and it ended with her bashing him in the head."

Max let out a low whistle. "Sheesh. That's why I'm never getting married."

"You're never getting married because no smart woman would have you," Trent gibed. "When we interviewed Stephen March, he said he saw a blonde woman cleaning in Kober's office—that's why he didn't stay to rob the place. We can show him pictures, including Mrs. Kober's, and see if he picks her out of a lineup."

Max laughed, not minding being the butt of his partner's joke. "What a loser. He went there to kill Kober, but the wife beat him to it. No wonder he freaked out on you two."

Olivia slipped back into her chair, not feeling the morbid laughter in the room. "That's the part that doesn't sit right with me. If March was stalking Dani, and she rejected him or did something else to send him over the edge into violence, then what's his motive for going after Kober?" She shook her head. "Even if he was there for drugs or money like he claims, it's an awfully big coincidence for him to show up at the scene of two related murders six years apart." She met Gabe's gaze across the table. She knew he felt the same. They'd solved the case, had solved three crimes, in fact, by the time others in KCPD rounded up Leland Asher and Elaine Kober. But the puzzle wasn't complete yet. "I just feel like there's something more going on here."

"Let's not borrow trouble. We've got a solid case against March." Their team leader wasn't about to let a murderer go because Olivia's instincts were nagging at her. "The gun you took off March and the gun you found in the warehouse are both the same make and caliber. A Raven Arms MP25. I know it's not conclusive, but criminals do tend to repeat themselves. It certainly builds more and more of a circumstantial case against him." Ginny rose from her seat at the head of the table, making a command decision. "Let's bring March up here and lay our case on the table—see if he feels like talking."

While Max and Trent stood to put on jackets and gather their notepads and laptops, Katie read an email off her computer screen. "I've already got a reply from Detective Kincaid. He and his partner are on their way to visit Mrs. Kober now."

"Hold up, gentlemen." Lieutenant Rafferty-Taylor patted Olivia's shoulder. "This is your case. Why don't you go down to holding and tell Stephen March the good news—that in addition to assaulting you and Mr. Knight, we're booking him for Dani Reese's murder. Good work, everyone."

Olivia followed the older woman to her desk. "Is it all right if I call my father in, ma'am? He was the original detective on this case. I know he'd like to be there when we finally close it."

Even if there were some loose ends about this investigation that nagged at her, Olivia knew getting a murderer off the streets was always a good thing. Helping her father find closure on an otherwise stellar career he'd been forced to end before he was ready to was even better.

The lieutenant agreed. "Make the call."

"WHAT DO YOU MEAN he's not in his cell?" Olivia turned 360 degrees, taking in the seemingly normal chaos of the holding wing's long hallway, processing counter, barred gates and steel doors beyond, as well as her father's shaking head and Gabe's piercing glare. "Where is he?"

Max was at the sergeant's desk, cursing the ineptitude of paper pushers and the stupid luck of the world in general while Trent Dixon offered a saner explanation for why the man she was here to arrest had gone missing. "March collapsed in his cell. The guard said he was going through some serious withdrawal symptoms this morning. Don't know if it's his heart or his lungs or his stomach, but he just couldn't handle detoxing cold turkey. They took him in an ambulance to Saint Luke's about an hour ago."

"Is he still alive?"

"As far as I know."

"Is he still there? Is he under guard?"

"You know he is. We're not going to let this guy slip through our fingers again." Curling his mouth into a wry grin, Trent patted Olivia's shoulder and excused himself. "Why don't you go down to Saint Luke's and read him his rights yourself while I take care of Mr. Charm School over there before he gets put on report."

"Thanks, Trent."

The big man nodded. "We'll follow as soon as we can."

"Gabe? Dad? Jim? Let's go."

Jim dangled his keys in front of her and backed toward the exit. "I'll drive."

Jim put the siren on the roof of his extended cab pickup, and got them to the downtown hospital in a matter of minutes. But the deathly quiet from the back seat Gabe shared with her father made the ride seem to last an hour.

Still, smoothing over familial tensions and figuring out whether she and Gabe had any future beyond working together to solve this case had to be filed away and dealt with later. Right now, she had a murderer to track down and put into official custody. She and Jim flashed their badges to give their guns clearance, and all four of them quickly moved through the security checkpoint to get into the hospital.

With Trent feeding them information over the phone, they hurried through the multistory lobby, skipped the information desk and went straight to the elevators to get to the second floor. "Room 222. Thanks, Trent."

Olivia tucked her phone away in her pocket and led the way out of the elevator and around the corner into the second-floor corridor. But her steps slowed to an uneasy pace long before they reached the room at the end of the hallway. Suspicion pricked the hairs at the back of her neck. Something wasn't right.

Jim stopped beside her, sensing it, too. "I don't like this." He checked behind them, then swiveled his green-eyed gaze back along the empty corridor. "Where's the guard?"

The chair outside the door was there. But there was no one standing watch at Stephen March's room. Olivia pulled back her jacket and unsnapped her holster. Resting her hand on the butt of her weapon, she warned Gabe and her father to stay back. "Wait here."

Gabe took a step after her. "Olivia, be care—"

"Let me do my job, caveman."

With a fuming reluctance, Gabe nodded and ducked into the room next door with her father.

Nodding her readiness to Jim, they both pulled their guns and flanked the door to room 2022. Switching between guarding and taking point, they quickly cleared the room, closet and adjoining bathroom. The rumpled bed and IV tube, needle and tape still swinging from its solution bag indicated March hadn't been gone for long. The empty, unlocked ring of the handcuffs still attached to the bed's steel frame made her think he hadn't left on his own, either.

Olivia muttered one choice curse and pulled out her phone. "What is happening here? Who's helping him escape?"

Jim holstered his gun and hurried out the door. "I'll check the front desk."

"Livvy?" Thomas Watson limped out into the hallway after the all clear, with a KCPD badge in his hand. "We've got an unconscious man in here. His ID says Derek Logan. I'm guessing he's your guard."

"Pretty nasty blow to the back of the head," Gabe added. "I already called the hospital staff from the phone in the room. Told them he'd need assistance as soon as it was safe."

Olivia added the badge number to the report she was making to Dispatch. "That checks out. Whoever's helping March is going to be in street clothes or hospital gear," she added before hanging up. "Officer Logan is the guard assigned to March. So we don't know who the accomplice is. We have to look for March."

"I notified hospital security. They're sending someone to every exit point." Jim returned with a nurse who hurried into the room to attend to the injured officer. "The nurse there said she took March's vitals ten minutes ago and he was still showing signs of detox. Chills, shakes, headache. It'd be hard for him to walk out of here."

"That means he's in a wheelchair or on a gurney." That meant the elevators. Olivia cursed. "They were probably going down when we were heading up. If they get out to the parking lot before security locks this place down, we'll never catch them."

Gabe grabbed her arm and stopped her when she hurried past. Any instinct to argue fell silent when she saw the keen intelligence lighting his eyes. "If he's on a gurney or in a chair, then they'd have to take the staff elevators. The hospital staff would stop and question them if they tried to get on the public elevators."

Oh, how she loved that cool logic of his. "You're right. Max and Trent are on their way, too. But we need to find them now. Ten minutes isn't that much of a head start if they had to disable Officer Logan and sneak out of the room."

She pointed to Jim but he was already nodding, moving down the hallway, sharing the same idea. "Let's split up. I'll search this floor, make sure they're not hiding out, and you get on down to the first. Hopefully, we can at least contain him here before he reaches any of the exits."

Thomas Watson still had KCPD blue running through his veins. "Livvy, you take Knight with you. I'll stay and help Detective Parker."

"Dad, you're not armed." She glanced up at Gabe. "Neither one of you are."

"Olivia Mary, I love you to death, but if you let this guy get away…"

She winked at her father and nodded. "Yes, sir. Let's go."

Leaving her father to limp into the room across from Jim, Olivia dashed toward the staff elevators and cleared each car before running to the stairs. Gabe was already there, shoving open the door and following close behind as she charged down the empty stairs to the first floor. A quick glance down the first floor service corridor showed no men who resembled Stephen March's receding hairline and wiry build.

But Gabe's hand at the small of her back turned her attention to the orderly pushing a wheelchair out through a swinging door. The patient bundled in a blanket looked far too familiar. "They're heading out to the lobby."

"Stay behind me," she ordered, pulling her gun and breaking into a run. "Call Jim and tell him we've got them."

For once, Gabe obeyed a command. Sort of. As she paused at the swinging steel door and peeked through to make sure the path was clear, she could hear Gabe giving Jim a succinct explanation of the situation and location. But he was right on her heels as she pushed through the door. "We've got a lot of civilians down here," he added before hanging up.

"Oh, my God," Olivia whispered, lowering her weapon. The public lobby at Saint Luke's was as tricky to navigate as downtown rush hour. The carpeted area was a maze of chair groupings, sculptures and planters filled with trees and flowers—not to mention the gift shop, information desk and dozens of staff, visitors and volunteers crossing through and hanging out there. "Do you see them?"

She and Gabe stood back-to-back, turning, searching. Wrong color hair. Too tall. A woman in that wheelchair. No orderly with that one. There was still only one guard at the front glass doors.

She felt Gabe's firm grip on her elbow and turned. "There. That's him."

Olivia moved out in a quick walk, keeping the orderly wearing green scrubs in her line of sight as she darted from one chair to the next tree. The patient in the wheelchair was bundled up with blankets that masked most of his face, but the shaking hands holding the covers up to his nose were a dead giveaway. The pair headed for the glass doors away from the check-in station at a fast enough clip that the guard had noticed them, too.

She held up her badge and waved him back, angling her head toward the families and staff, hoping he understood her silent request to start moving people away from the doors and the potential confrontation.

And then she saw the bulge in the back of the green scrubs. March's accomplice was no orderly. He was carrying a gun.

"Gabe?" She glanced up, sharing her concern with the man who never seemed to miss a detail.

He saw it, too. He squeezed her arm and started moving toward a seating area where two children were putting together a puzzle. "I'll get as many people out of here as I can."

There was a matter of yards between her and the two escapees when a woman screamed. She'd seen Olivia's gun.

Stephen and the orderly both glanced over their shoulders. And then they were running.

"Ah, hell." Olivia planted her feet and raised her weapon and Gabe whisked the hysterical woman out of harm's way. "KCPD! Stephen March! You with the wheelchair! I order you to stop."

Stephen shoved the blankets off his chair and tried to rise, but the covers tangled with the spokes of the wheel and the chair tipped over, throwing him to the floor. The man with the gun leaped over him, muttering something like, "You're on your own."

But the guard had locked the doors and when the orderly slammed into them, he knew he was trapped.

Olivia advanced. "Stop where you are. Drop your weapon."

The woman shrieked again when the man pulled his gun and spun around. "Get back!" he yelled, waving the gun back and forth before settling on her as the biggest threat in the room. "You get back!"

"Not gonna happen." Olivia froze, leveled her gun at the middle of his chest. "Everybody get down!"

"Olivia!" Gabe's warning shout was the last thing she heard as she fingered the trigger.

The next few seconds passed by in a slow-motion blur.

Stephen March crawled out of the wreckage and lurched to his feet. Olivia saw the gunman's finger squeeze the trigger. An elderly woman rose from her chair, blocking Olivia's line of sight.

"Get down!" she warned, averting her weapon and praying the gunman was a lousy shot.

There were two loud bangs from off to her left. The glass behind the perp shattered and the gunman went down.

Olivia glanced over and saw Jim Parker lowering his steaming weapon. "Told you I had your back, partner." He jogged past her and knelt beside the assailant, picking up his gun and checking the man's neck for a pulse. He shook his head as she joined him. "This one's done." He was already waving her off as she backed toward the path Stephen March had taken. "Yours is getting away. Go."

"Thanks. Partner."

The world reverted to real time as she took off after March. Even in his unsteady condition, that tweaker could fly. He knocked a man in a suit and the nurse beside him out of his way and zigzagged toward the gift shop. Alert to the danger now, the other patrons and staff dodged out of Olivia's path. He'd reached the long hallway now, stretching the distance between them. Her lungs were burning and she pressed harder. Her shoulder ached and…

A metal-rimmed chair flew across the carpet, knocking the young man off his feet.

Olivia caught a glimpse of coal-black hair as she ran past and grinned.

The man who'd escaped from lockup at the hospital— the man who'd gotten away with murder for six years, who'd tarnished her father's career, who'd tried to kill her more than once—moaned as he tried to push himself to his feet.

But Stephen March didn't take one more step. Olivia holstered her gun, put her elbow to the back of his neck and took him right back down to the ground. He groaned and complained and muttered a nervous stream of words that didn't always make sense. Olivia's voice was breathless with exertion, but perfectly clear as she pulled the handcuffs off her belt. "Stephen March, you are under arrest for the murder of Danielle Reese."

"What? I swear I didn't mean… Ah, hell. What about Rosemary? My sister needs me. I'm so sorry. I didn't mean to." He writhed on the floor beneath her knee, fidgeting with his fingers almost as soon as she pulled his hands together behind his back. He repeated the same words over and over, almost crying in his manic state. "I didn't mean to. I'm sorry. I didn't mean to."

She felt the tall shadow coming up beside her, and

recognized the familiar starchy scent as Gabe knelt beside her. "You just couldn't stay out of the way, could you?" she chided. "You didn't think I was going to run him down this time?"

"I had no doubt you were going to catch him, but this idiot doesn't get to hurt the woman I love."

A few of those words tried to reach her heart, but Olivia had to finish the job first. "Is everybody in the lobby safe?"

"Yes. Scared, but fine." He reached out beside her, pinning March's flailing legs. "You got him yet?"

"I don't know who that guy was." March's rambling never ceased. "He said he had to help me. I had to kill that girl. I had to save my sister. I didn't mean to. I didn't want—"

Olivia could seriously use five minutes of peace and quiet right now. She slapped the first cuff on his wrist. "You have the right to remain silent."

Gabe added, "I recommend using that right."

"Anything you say…" Olivia paused, seeing her father's uneven gait as he walked up on the scene, flanked by Max Krolikowski, Trent Dixon and Jim Parker. She looked up and smiled at her friends, her partner and her father. All men she could depend on, men who'd shown her time and again that they believed in her skills, that they trusted her, that she could trust them. A feeling of warmth rose up inside her, a feeling a belonging, a certainty that the damage Marcus Brower had done to her was finally in the past and that she would never have to second-guess these relationships again.

She smiled her thanks to each of them, but paused when she met Thomas Watson's moss-green eyes. She held up the loose end of the handcuffs. "Dad. This is your collar. Go ahead and close your last case."

"I'm proud of you, sweetheart." He squatted down on the other side of Stephen March and closed the cuff around the other wrist. Then the two of them helped March to his feet and finished Mirandizing him. "Your mother would be, too."

"We'll take him." Trent nodded to Olivia and her father and pulled Stephen March between him and Max. They turned with Jim and walked down the hallway to return their prisoner to lockup.

A worrisome pang tainted the satisfied feeling of success that had made everything right in her world for a few moments. She tipped her face up to Gabe. This case had brought them together. But the hunt for the truth was over. He had his answers. She'd solved the case and captured his fiancée's killer. He could finally lay his guilt to rest. What happened now? "Thank you."

His deep, hushed voice resonated in her ears. "This never would have happened without you."

The next moment was filled with awkward silence.

Until her father's gruff voice interrupted. "Oh, for Pete's sake, you two—get in an empty room and say what you need to say."

Gabe didn't argue. He grabbed Olivia by the hand and pulled her into a vacant office, shutting the door behind them.

"Gabe, I—"

His mouth stopped up her words with a kiss. His hands came up to frame her face as he drove her back against the wall and staked a claim she was willing to answer. "Are you hurt?" He kissed her again. "I don't think I'll ever get used to seeing you in the line of fire like that." She caught his lips and assured him she was in one piece. "I know you're good at what you do. But a little part of me just wants to—"

Olivia kissed him soundly, tangling her fingers in his thick hair, holding him close for a moment before pushing him away to latch on to the lapels of his jacket and rest her hands against his chest. "Did you mean what you said back there? That you love me? We've only known each other a few days. It hasn't exactly been an ideal courtship."

A smile spread across his mouth, softening the chiseled angles of his face and lighting a spark in his handsome blue eyes. "If it's the right person, it doesn't take forever to fall in love."

She answered with a smile that reached deep into her heart. "You are a writer, aren't you? That's a good line."

"I'm a reporter. I tell the truth." He brushed her bangs off her forehead and gently touched his thumb to the skin beside her scraped cheek. "I don't want every week to be like this one—I don't know how many times my heart can handle seeing you get hurt. But being together suits us, don't you think? A couple of workaholics with plenty of emotional baggage. I think we have to dive in to happiness when it finds us."

Olivia nodded. "We both know how rare and fleeting it can be." She slipped her arms around his neck and pressed her body against the solid strength of his. "What about my family? I know they want me to be happy, but getting involved with the man who slammed the department in his newspaper? You're going to take some getting used to."

Gabe's arms settled around her waist. "I don't know. I think your dad and I can agree on one thing."

"What's that?"

"That you are the most special woman in the world—and all we want is for you to be happy and safe."

"You make me happy. And I keep myself safe."

"We'll work on that."

She stretched up on tiptoe and welcomed his kiss. But there was one last ghost between them. "What about you, Gabe? Have you really let Dani go? Is there a place for me in your heart?"

"She'll always be a part of me. But I've said goodbye. Thanks to you, I've finally done right by her—her story will be told and her killer will be in jail." Those piercing blue eyes looked down into hers and she knew his words were the truth. "She took on the world with such gusto that I'd be doing her a disservice if I didn't look to the future and live my life to the fullest. I want you in it. If you need time, if you need me to make peace with your dad, if you need me to not be so stubborn—"

"That's not going to happen." When she laughed, he joined her.

But when he stopped, he pulled her arms from his neck and captured her hands against the steady beat of his heart. "Please give us a chance."

"Promise you'll always be honest with me?"

"Always. Promise not to whack me over the head when I go all caveman on you?"

"Um…" She had to be honest. There was that whole independent spirit and temper of hers to consider. "I can promise to love you. With everything in me."

"I'll take that promise." He leaned down and captured her lips in a kiss that made her believe his word, a kiss that made her wish there was a lock on this door and an endless amount of time to explore all the wonderful ways this man's hands and mouth could make her go weak in the knees.

But that sentimental romancey stuff wasn't who they were. Knowing they would revisit this precious connection when the timing was right, maybe at his condo later that night, Olivia pulled away with a sigh of regret. "I have reports to fill out."

"I have a story to write."

"We'd better go."

With her hand held firmly in his, Gabe led her out the door. When they reached the end of the hallway, her father rose from the chair where he'd been sitting and blocked their path.

For one moment, a nervous breath locked up Olivia's chest.

Thomas Watson's stern paternal eyes looked straight at Gabe, who stood tall beside her. "If you're going to be spending time with my daughter, I'd like to get to know you better, Mr. Knight. We have a family dinner every Sunday afternoon. My dad grills burgers and brats. We watch baseball and root for the Royals when they're playing. It's football and the Chiefs in the fall."

Gabe didn't bat an eye. "I like a good ball game and a burger."

"Good. You can bring the beer." Olivia released the breath she'd been holding and hugged her father when he leaned in to kiss her cheek and whisper, "Don't let this one break your heart."

"He won't, Dad. I trust him."

Chapter Thirteen

Orange was a lousy color on any man. But with Stephen March's thinning hair and pale brown eyes, he looked especially pitiful. Of course, that helplessly doomed look might be more about the handcuffs and leg irons Stephen wore as he sat in the long Fourth Precinct hallway, awaiting transport to the county jail along with other prisoners due for arraignment tomorrow.

Stephen fidgeted in the plastic chair, clawing at his own hands as the host, ignoring the curious glances and outright stares of the others there, sat beside him.

"I'm disappointed in you, Stephen."

"Shut up." Really? This weak-willed addict who'd been saved from certain death on the street, who'd been so desperate to change his fate, thought copping an attitude with the one person who'd helped him the most was the smart way to go? Stephen rocked back and forth in his chair, refusing the guidance and friendship that had been offered so willingly for so long. "You should have let me kill her. Instead, she arrested me."

"Let you?" The host laughed at the absurdity, but spoke in a hushed whisper. "You barely accomplished the task when I sent you to kill Danielle Reese."

"You should have let me kill that detective, and

stopped her from poking around in my business. Then all this would have gone away." Stephen needed a fix so badly that his scratching fingers were drawing blood. "Now I'm going to prison and there's nobody to look after my sister."

Fear had always been an easy motivator—fear of not having any money, not having a home, not being able to afford a dime bag to keep his teeth from rattling out of his head—fear that the one person he'd always been able to count on would be taken from him. But that fear had given way to panic and desperation, two volatile emotions that were much harder to reason with and control.

"That's right, Stephen. You made a mistake, and now you're going to have to pay for it. Perhaps if you had listened to me, if you'd trusted my wisdom and experience, you'd still be a free man. I told you it was a perfect plan. But you strayed from it. I sent my friend to help you escape from the hospital, but once again, you wouldn't do as you were told. You hesitated when he told you to come with him. Now my friend is dead and look where you are." A glance up and down the hallway at the thieves, gangbangers and molesters set to make the same trip were warning enough. "I can make your stay in prison easier for you if you let me."

The chains rattled as Stephen shook his head and scooted to the far side of his chair. "It's not my fault your friend died. I'm not your puppet, anymore. You're not going to talk me into anything else."

True, they would no longer have easy access to each other. And their future meetings would be infrequent if they happened at all. But even through prison bars, there were ways to reach out to Stephen—to use him again if needed, or just to keep an eye on him to ensure his continued cooperation.

"I'm glad we could have this one last talk, then. Good luck. And remember, one word about our agreement, one mention of my name…just think how easy it will be to get to your sister with you stuck on the inside."

"Leave Rosemary alone." Stephen's wide, fearful eyes induced a rush of satisfaction. The rebellion had been brief.

And if, for some reason, Stephen March should grow a backbone and reveal anything more than his role in murdering Danielle Reese, there would be numerous ways, with enough money and the right persuasion, to reach out and silence him.

Permanently.

GABE LOOKED UP from his computer as Olivia walked into his office with two cups of coffee. He smiled. Her eyes were a pale gray-green, meaning she was content. No temper brewing. No overwhelming stress that required a private time-out. Or a shared time-out in a hot, steamy shower that started with a relaxing massage and ended up in the bed with damp sheets and her dozing on his chest.

Now he was really smiling. "So how's my favorite cop?"

She set the coffee on his desk and circled behind his chair. "You promised me lunch. And I believe you have proved yourself to be a man of your word."

Olivia hugged her arms around his shoulders and Gabe turned his head to kiss her.

"So what are you working on?" she asked.

"Making amends." He reached up to squeeze her

hand. "I finished my front-page article for the morning paper. What do you think of the headline, Detective?"

PRAISE FOR KCPD
6 YO MURDER SOLVED/KILLER BEHIND BARS

* * * * *

The mystery continues in the next
exciting installment of
THE PRECINCT: COLD CASE *miniseries*
by **USA TODAY** *bestselling author Julie Miller.*
Coming in August 2015.

"Braydon, I'm only going to tell you this once. I don't, and will not, blame you for the actions of a psychotic man. You did *nothing* wrong."

"But now I'm afraid he's after you." She may not have known Braydon long but she did know that the vulnerability he was showing now was rare. It pulled at her heartstrings.

"We don't know that for certain," she said.

"He wants to make me suffer. What better way than to use you."

"You care about this entire town and all of its people. He can use any of us." She said it to lighten the mood. They were skating around saying something significant again. Sophia could feel it. She watched as the conflicted man next to her chose his words carefully.

"He knows you're different."

MANHUNT

BY
TYLER ANNE SNELL

Published in Great Britain 2015
by Mills & Boon, an imprint of Harlequin (UK) Limited,
Eton House, 18-24 Paradise Road, Richmond, Surrey, TW9 1SR

© 2015 Tyler Anne Snell

ISBN: 978-0-263-25302-3

46-0415

Tyler Anne Snell genuinely loves all genres of the written word. However, she's realized that she loves books filled with sexual tension and mysteries a little more than the rest. Her stories have a good dose of both. Tyler lives in Florida with her same-named husband and their mini "lions." When she isn't reading or writing, she's playing video games and working on her blog, *Almost There*. To follow her shenanigans, visit www.tylerannesnell.com.

This book is for my mother, Robin.
Who, against all odds, has never stopped believing that
I can do no wrong. Without her support and never-
faltering love, this book might still be a tangled
web caught in my head. I love you, Ma!

Chapter One

Detective Braydon Thatcher looked at the dock with an anger he had learned to contain burning in his chest. No matter the time that passed, that spot was his personal hell.

"I just don't understand! Amanda and I fight sometimes, but nothing so bad that she'd just leave."

Braydon tore his eyes away from the dock, no longer in the Bartlebee name but that of the Alcasters, and took in the rumpled Marina Alcaster. She was upwards of sixty but looked as frail as if she were pushing eighty. Her slumped frame and thin bones were deceiving at best. Everyone in Culpepper knew she had a temper that often boiled over and ran hotter than the Florida heat. Her screech could be heard like a car crash in the town square.

Which was why no one, not Braydon or his partner Tom Langdon, was surprised to hear that Amanda had gone. Though, her mama refused to entertain such a thought.

"When's the last time you two had it out?" Tom asked, sending Braydon a significant look when Marina hesitated. "Did y'all fight last night?"

Marina pursed her lips and shifted a hip out. "I wouldn't call it a fight...but we did have a conversation."

"A conversation?" Braydon raised his eyebrow as Tom wrote that one down. "What kind of conversation?"

Marina put a hand on her hip. "A loud one." She huffed.

"Was Amanda mad when this loud conversation ended?" Another hesitant look.

"Well, yeah. She got in her car and left." Before Braydon or Tom could point out that Marina had called to file a missing-persons report, she rushed on. "But she came back later! Look—" she pointed over her shoulder at a blue Honda "—that's her car!"

"And you haven't seen her since?"

"No, that's why I called you two." Marina's temper was starting to flare and Braydon didn't have the patience to deal with it today. Not with the dock looming in the distance with its invisible stain of agony. Tom, one of the only constant friends Braydon had kept since the incident eleven years ago, knew his partner was distracted by the closeness of it. He took down Marina's contact information and assured her they'd look into it.

"We'll give you a call when we find her," he called, already following Braydon to the truck. "I bet you thought after your promotion to detective you'd have a lot more interesting cases than dealing with a little Alcaster dispute, huh?"

Tom was trying to lighten the mood Braydon had fallen into—he smiled big, exposing teeth slightly stained by too much coffee. Braydon appreciated the gesture and shook himself as they pulled out of the driveway and took the winding dirt path back to the main road.

Tom was right, though. Braydon expected—and hoped—for more exciting work than looking for Amanda, who was twenty-six years old and probably at a friend's house waiting for her own anger to sizzle out. Not to mention, her being gone wasn't an actual case until she had been missing for forty-eight hours. The only reason they had driven out was due to a lull in between cases. Also, it wasn't wise to anger the elder Alcaster, which is exactly what would happen if they had told her to wait her daughter out. So out they had come, ready to help a member of the community. Though, again, trying to patch up a fight between mother and daughter hadn't been on Braydon's mind when he signed up for law enforcement. For the better part of his career, he had worked hard for the promotion to one of the two detectives in Culpepper. The town wasn't big by any means, and mostly sleepy, but there were still investigations that needed working and cases that needed solving.

Plus, it wasn't the promise of excitement that had pushed him into the profession—it was the pursuit of justice.

"Have you ever met Amanda?" Tom asked, facing ahead so the sun lit up his blond hair.

Braydon nodded. "I've been to a few parties with her but that was when we were in school," he answered. "I had to be about seventeen…maybe eighteen." That had been almost eleven years ago, Braydon calculated. Back when he was going through the wild and rebellious stages of being a teenager—drinking, partying and feeding hormonal impulses at every turn. He had been one of the undesirables then, on the wrong side of the law that he now tried to uphold. His mother had sent him to church every Sunday as if it would absolve whatever demon had possessed him, but there was nothing Pastor Smith could preach that would end Braydon's lust for the wicked.

That is, until one rainy night changed everything.

Tom seemed to realize the bad mood was relapsing. He shifted in his seat and turned up the radio. The cool sounds of 103.1's program of all things '80s pumped through the truck's speakers. Normalcy returned in the small cab.

The end of September had crept up on the town, though the Culpepper heat still radiated like it was August. Sweat pooled beneath Braydon's white polo shirt, adhering it against his suntanned skin. One of the perks of his promotion—shedding the uniform. Despite his reformed sensibilities, wearing the cop getup pricked against his inner rebel.

It was a twenty-minute trek from the Alcasters' back to the station at the heart of town. Braydon spent the rest of the drive watching the rural part of Culpepper transform into neighborhood turnoffs, industrial buildings, shopping boutiques and the few dilapidated structures littered in between.

This part of town had once been run-down—a meeting place for drug dealers, prostitutes and people who liked and used both. It wasn't until six years ago that Richard Vega had pumped life, and money, back into the four-block stretch. The New York City native had a business acumen to be reckoned with and enough funds to open Vega Consulting—a company of marketing strategists created to serve not only Culpepper, but all of North America.

Braydon didn't know the extent of how Vega Consulting operated, but he had to believe they were doing well. Richard Vega lived at the end of Loop Road with an electronic gate surrounding the five acres of land he had purchased without batting an eye.

The partners had fallen back into a comfortable silence the last few minutes of the drive. It was as though the growing distance from the dock was lifting a sour weight from Braydon's shoulders. When the police station came into view, the ill feelings had all but disappeared, though Braydon knew he wouldn't get any sleep tonight.

"Langdon," Tom answered after his phone did a vibrating dance.

Braydon pulled into the parking lot that butted up against the side of the station. The building dated back to the '50s and had been renovated at least three times. It was all brick, cracked tile and offices that were small enough to pull double duty as closets. When most officers, Tom included, complained about the state of the building, Braydon found he didn't share their sentiments. He never felt more at home than when he set his eyes on the place.

He turned off the truck and met the humidity with a deep breath. It was midmorning, and the heat was at its worst. The rain that had bathed the town hours earlier had done little to reduce the temperature. He smiled to himself. There wasn't a cloud in the sky. Despite all of the opportunities he'd had to leave his hometown, it was beautiful days when the sun was shining that reaffirmed his decision to stay. A person just couldn't beat a beautiful day in Florida.

"Okay, we're right outside now." Tom hung up the phone and followed Braydon around the building to the front double doors with Culpepper Police Department hung in rusting letters above them.

"There's a woman waiting in your office," he said, holding the door open. "And apparently she's not too happy."

Braydon quickly ran through the list of women he had been with in the past few years, trying to find a name that stuck to someone who might be pissed. Well, recently pissed. Angela had been the last woman he had been with but that had been two months ago. Surely, she wasn't the one in his office pitching a fit.

"She's from out of town," Tom offered, cutting off Braydon's line of thought. "Probably got a ticket from John and wants to complain to someone." John was a policeman who loved giving tickets to tourists passing through. Some people loved golf, John loved giving tickets. Braydon sighed.

"I'll deal with her," he said, feeling his nerves switch to annoyed. He'd never had much of a stomach for outsiders.

"Sounds good to me. I'm going to call around and see if I can't find Miss Alcaster."

They parted ways after walking through the lobby and into the largest room in the station. Rows of desks, computers, chairs and coffee cups filled the room. Some were occupied with Uniforms—a few colleagues Braydon didn't like and a few who didn't like him. John the Ticketer's chair was empty. He was probably writing someone up right now, Braydon mused. Along the far side of the room stood four doors that led to a break room, Tom's office, Braydon's office and the conference room. To the left, with the blinds always shut over the window in the door, was Captain Westin's domain.

A man was smart to avoid that office when the captain's temper was high.

Braydon walked across the room and let out a sigh as he saw his door was closed. Why they had left a stranger unsupervised was an issue he would bring up as soon as he ushered her out. Not only was it an invasion of privacy but also breaking regulation.

He reached out to grab the doorknob when the old oak slab flung open.

"It's about damn time!"

Braydon stepped back, caught off guard. He furrowed his brow at the woman standing before him. No one in Culpepper would believe she was anything but an outsider. Despite the heat and humidity, she was wrapped in a black pantsuit with a blazer that covered the length of her arms and a shirt that dipped low in a V. Although Braydon tried to keep his gaze up, he couldn't help noticing the suit hugged her chest and hips in a very attractive way. Her skin was creamy porcelain, another sign that Florida was not her home. It stood out like a shock against the glossy dark hair that was pulled high in a bun. Although her eyes were a deep shade of sage, there was no denying the fire that sparked behind them.

"I've been waiting in here for almost half an hour!" she fumed.

Braydon put up his hands. "Whoa, calm down. Why don't you take a seat and we'll get this all straightened out." He moved around her, catching a whiff of perfume. It filled his senses with its sweet aroma.

The woman hesitated, as if unable to immediately obey, before she dropped down into the seat across from his desk.

"Now, Mrs...."

She waved her hand through the air. "Miss," she corrected impatiently. "Sophia Hardwick." The name sounded vaguely familiar but Braydon couldn't quite place it. The red-lipped Sophia had scrambled his attention. "And like I told the man out there, I'm here about my sister." She was gearing up to explain, her hands intertwining on the top of the desk. The way she leaned forward a fraction, didn't improve the hold on his concentration.

Before she could start, Tom appeared in the door. His brow was furrowed. He didn't bother with knocking.

"Braydon, we need to talk." He tipped his head toward Sophia. "This will only take a minute, ma'am."

Sophia slammed her hands onto the desk. She stood with such speed that Braydon mimicked the act, hand flitting to his holster.

"Are you serious? You just got in here. I've only had time to tell you my name for heaven's sake! You will not put me off anymore," she said, looking between the men. "I'm here because my sister is missing and I need you idiots to do something about it." There was a pause as all of the air seemed to rush out of her. Color tinted her cheekbones, whether from the exertion or her makeup, Braydon didn't know.

"I didn't know Amanda had a sister," he said, lowering his hand but still on guard. Sophia may have been petite but her passion was seeping out of every pore.

"What? Who's Amanda?" she huffed. "I'm here about Lisa." Braydon looked at Tom, who had turned white as a sheet. Something must have happened as soon as Tom had gone to his office.

He looked down at a paper in his hands. "Lisa? Does she happen to go by Trixie?"

Sophia shook her head. A few strands of hair came loose at the movement. Tom's upbeat mood was gone—an issue that brought Braydon's nerves back to the edge.

"No. She goes by Lisa. Lisa Hardwick."

Tom's mouth set in a deep frown. Without explanation to Sophia he turned to Braydon. "We need to talk," he said. "Now."

"Unbelievable! I just tell you that my sister is missing and you just—"

"Ma'am. We will be with you in a second," Tom snapped. It was a rare occurrence to hear the shorter of the two men so tightly strung that Braydon didn't hesitate. He followed Tom into the conference room two doors over.

"What was that about?"

Braydon didn't know what answer to expect but it sure wasn't what came next.

"Cal Green, you know him?"

Braydon nodded. "The mechanic?"

"Yeah, well he left a message a few minutes ago. He says his secretary, Trixie Martin, hasn't shown up to work for two days. He got worried because she wasn't answering her phone and headed to her place. All the lights were on, the TV, too, and the front door was unlocked. He talked to the nearest neighbor but they didn't see or hear anything. Her car was even in the driveway." He didn't wait for Braydon to respond. "If that woman in your office is telling the truth, then that means—"

Braydon felt like he was waking up—all of his senses stood alert.

"That means that we have three missing women."

SOPHIA WAS FED UP with all of the interruptions Culpepper had to offer. From the moment she had stepped foot inside the police station it had been a stream of one after the other—keeping her from asking whole questions, let alone getting full answers.

She had been bounced from officer to officer only to be told to keep quiet and wait for the lead detective to come in from a call. So, there she had stayed, sans the quiet. The four-hour trip had strung out her already thin patience as she left voice mail after voice mail on Lisa's phone. It wasn't her fault that the Culpepper PD wasn't prepared for her volley of loud complaints.

Sophia smoothed out the invisible wrinkles in her slacks and tried to keep her temper in check as the min-

utes ticked by and the detective hadn't returned. On a
normal day she would have been more understanding,
perhaps more patient. She knew that if she were back
home in the city, the chances of her still waiting in the
department's lobby would be great. At least here she had
been ushered into an office. Small blessings and silver
linings.

Being alone was something Sophia had grown accus-
tomed to throughout the past few years, but she found the
lack of communication now was grinding into her anxiety. Lisa might fly by the seat of her pants 80 percent
of the time, but she had never been so irresponsible as
to leave without saying a word. Their relationship may
have become strained lately, but it wasn't that strained.

"Sorry to step out like that." Detective Thatcher
walked back into the office with a notebook under his
arm. Instead of sitting behind the desk, he leaned on its
corner and tilted his head down to meet her gaze. His
eyes were the color of the sea—swirls of aquamarine.
They were the kind of eyes that captured a person, making them want nothing more than to get lost within the
bright pools. Sophia hadn't noticed their allure until he
was so close.

He had a swimmer's build—tall, lean, but with muscles that peeked through his clothes. His shirt was pulled
taut over broad shoulders, while his sun-kissed skin was
a rich bronze—a shade she hadn't been able to achieve
in the muck of Atlanta. In contrast to his partner's thinning blond hair, Thatcher had a mass of dark brown locks
that were mussed to mimic what she thought would be
his bed hair.

Sophia realized she had been staring. She needed to
pull it together for Lisa. She cleared her throat and pushed
her back straight.

"Now, if you would start from the beginning," he prompted. His long, and ringless, fingers wrapped around the pen. He wrote with controlled precision as she spoke.

"My birthday was four days ago, on Sunday," Sophia started.

"Happy belated birthday, then."

She waved her hand dismissively but said thanks. Turning twenty-six hadn't felt any different than turning twenty-five. "Lisa was supposed to come celebrate and she didn't. And before you come up with a bunch of excuses as to why she didn't show, let me stop you. My sister is an intelligent woman who, despite her occasional bout of forgetfulness, is one of the most responsible women I know. I've been trying to get a hold of her since yesterday. I called her cell phone, her house and even her work."

"Have you been to her residence?" Thatcher asked, his eyes piercing. Sophia shifted, suddenly uncomfortable.

"Yes, she obviously wasn't there."

"Was there any kind of disturbance? Did it look like someone had been there recently?"

"No, but that doesn't really surprise me. From what I've heard she practically lives with her boyfriend." Thatcher raised an eyebrow, this quiet gesture asking more than any verbal question would. "She isn't at his place, either. He's the one who called me yesterday asking where she was."

"Wait, didn't you say she missed your birthday was four days ago? Why did you wait until yesterday to try to contact her?"

"We haven't really been on the best of terms this past year." Sophia's face heated. "I assumed she didn't come because she didn't want to. It wasn't until Rich-

ard called that we realized she had been missing for two
full days already."

"And Richard is the boyfriend?"

She nodded. "Richard Vega, I think he owns a company in town."

Thatcher's expression sharpened, his brow furrowing
together as he paused writing.

"Your sister is dating Richard Vega? As in Richard
Vega of Vega Consulting?"

Sophia nodded, more hair fell away from the bun atop
her head. Whatever Thatcher was thinking, it wasn't
showing in his expression. His calm demeanor had turned
utterly blank.

"And why didn't he file a missing persons?"

Sophia felt her eyes widen. "You mean he didn't?"

Thatcher stood and beckoned his partner from the
other room.

"Did Richard Vega file a missing report a few days
ago?" The blond man didn't leave to go check. He instantly said no.

"We would have heard if Vega came here."

Thatcher scratched his chin. It was smooth—void of
facial hair that would hide the perfection that outlined
his face. How kissable it looked, Sophia would have
thought, had anger, fear and suspicion not been vying
for the top emotional spot. Richard had called her with a
voice drenched in worry. When she admitted she had no
idea where Lisa was, he had assured her he would have
it taken care of—that he would take all of the necessary
steps to find her sister. Sophia had assumed that meant
talking to the police.

"Why wouldn't he have talked to you?" she asked.

"That's a good question," Thatcher said before lev-
eling his gaze. There was a look she couldn't decipher

behind the eyes of the detective. All she knew was that it comforted and scared her at the same time. "That's a very good question."

Chapter Two

Detective Thatcher's cool expression returned as he ordered Sophia to stay in his office. He sent in one of the beat cops, Officer Whitfield, to take down an official statement with all of the contact information between her sister and her. Whether he sent in a woman thinking it would make her more cooperative, she didn't know.

Cara, as she was told to call the woman, was curt but kind and even though her gender didn't affect Sophia's mood, she managed to dot all the i's and cross all the t's.

"Don't worry too much," Cara said with a smile that contrasted her darker skin. "Detective Thatcher is one dedicated man. He'll locate your sister and bring her back, no problem." She went as far as to pat Sophia's knee. "I'm sure she's just lost track of time or is staying with a friend."

Sophia resisted the urge to disagree and instead pasted on a smile. Maybe the woman had softened her attitude a bit, but that was only patching one spot in a dam that was ready to burst. If she didn't get some answers soon, there would be no man or woman in the whole town who could keep her from exploding.

"Thank you for waiting," Detective Thatcher greeted when he came back in. He nodded to Officer Whitfield as she collected her things and exited.

"Well, I seem to be doing that a lot here."

Thatcher ignored the pointed response and leveled his gaze at her.

"Miss Hardwick, do you know any women by the names of Trixie Martin or Amanda Alcaster?"

Sophia didn't have to think about that long. She shook her head. "No."

"Those names don't ring a bell at all? Maybe your sister, Lisa, has mentioned them?"

She crossed her arms across her chest. "No, I don't recall her talking about them. As I stated before, Lisa and I haven't been on the best of terms recently. There's a chance she may know them, but I couldn't help you with that," she answered honestly. "What does that have to do with Lisa being missing? Do you think they took her?" She compiled a quick list of why someone would kidnap Lisa. For one, she was beautiful—long legs, big bust, thick black, tangle-free hair and a pair of lips that drew men's attentions from a mile away. Lisa was also annoyingly perfect when it came to socializing. She knew how to command a room and entertain an audience. She also seemed to be dating a man who carried a lot of weight in town. Surely any or all of those reasons could make a few women jealous.

Detective Thatcher scratched at his chin, staring through her as he thought. When he realized she needed an answer, he straightened.

"I don't think so." His answer was made to put her at ease, but it wasn't as concrete as she would have liked.

"Then why are we talking about them and not about Richard and the fact that he *did not* report my sister missing?"

"I'm about to go question him myself," Thatcher said, pushing off the desk. He handed her a piece of paper.

"That's my office number and my cell number along with Detective Langdon's numbers."

Sophia raised her eyebrow. "And you're giving this to me why?" It was his turn to look confused.

"So you can contact us if you hear from Lisa or think of anything else that could help this investigation."

"But you just said you're going to go talk to Richard, right?"

"Yes, I certainly am."

"I'm coming with you, then." Sophia stood and pushed her bag up her shoulder. Detective Thatcher looked less than pleased but she didn't care. She had up and left her job as an office manager at Jones Office Supply, traveled from the big city to a town that in comparison would barely fit in a shoe box, all while being submerged in a pool of worry. She didn't want answers—she needed them.

"We'd like it if you would stay here and answer a few questions to help us, Miss Hardwick. Don't worry, I'll ask Richard all of the important questions."

"I can answer questions later, *Detective.* Right now I want to go see what Richard has to say." She crossed her arms over her chest. She was glad she hadn't changed her outfit since work that morning. The heels gave her the height to feel intimidating.

Thatcher mirrored her stance, crossing his arms over his chest. The biceps that flexed at the movement didn't lie about his workout habits.

"Listen, you've made it pretty clear that you don't know much about your sister's boyfriend or this town, so let me enlighten you on a few things." He made sure she was focusing on what he said next. "Richard Vega is the wealthiest man in Culpepper. He is also one of the most loved residents. Pissing him off and yelling at him won't get you any answers. At least, no truthful ones. If you want to come with me you need to calm down and try to keep a level head. Got it?"

Sophia nodded, slightly offended. It was true that she wasn't the best with confrontation but why Richard didn't report Lisa missing was a big question she was more than capable of asking. Unless Thatcher was arresting her for something, there was no way he could stop her regardless. She knew how to work the GPS on her phone—she could get to Richard's by herself. Sophia would go over the detective's head or behind his back if necessary. He must have guessed as much. After a tense moment he let out a long sigh.

"You're riding with me, then," he said, not trying to hide his annoyance.

"I have my own car, thank you."

"Listen, if you want to come along, you're riding with me."

"Why?" she asked, voice raised. Was this some kind of cop-civilian power trip? She wasn't afraid to start yelling again.

"Because I want to make sure you come back to answer those questions." He took his keys out of his desk and motioned for her to go through the door. "I have a feeling you aren't a person who respects any kind of rules."

Sophia tried not to blush as she struggled to get into the cab of the detective's truck. Her heels, now more cumbersome than intimidating, snagged on the small step up making her look like a drunken fool as she stumbled inside. At least Thatcher kept his mouth shut and pretended not to notice. If she had been Lisa, the movement would have been effortless and graceful.

"How far is it to Richard's?" Sophia asked as they turned out of the station's parking lot.

"You've never been there?" he asked.

"No, I haven't." She shifted uncomfortably in her seat, guilt starting to move through her stomach. "I've never met the man, either."

"And how long have Richard and your sister been dating?"

Sophia rolled her eyes. "Over a year now." She set her jaw and mentally dared him to ask why she hadn't met him. He must have picked up on her body language—he shut his mouth and they rode in silence until he finally answered her.

"Richard Vega lives on Loop Road. We have about ten more minutes until we get there. He lives on a large piece of land so it's farther from the town center."

She nodded. The anger she had felt toward the detective was lessening as she struggled to bat down her aversion to his authority.

"I do follow the rules, by the way," she said after a few minutes had passed. "I just—" She looked down at her hands. "Lisa is the only family I have left. Well, the only one who counts at least. So, I've been kind of high-strung lately." She felt her cheeks heat up again as she tried to apologize for her rude behavior without actually having to say it.

The detective glanced over before he sighed for the second time that day.

"It's okay. Situations like these are stressful." He hesitated before continuing. "We were late into the station because we were on a call about a woman named Amanda Alcaster who was reported missing. There's also another woman, named Trixie Martin, who was reported missing within minutes of us arriving."

Sophia sucked in a breath. She didn't know what to process first.

"I wanted to tell you so when I bring it up to Vega, you don't freak out," he continued. "This all could just be a misunderstanding or some women who want to escape their lives for a little while. But on the off chance that it isn't, I need to make sure I approach the only suspect we have with caution."

"I'll keep quiet, then," she said after a moment. "But I still want to be in the room."

"Deal."

IF THE DETECTIVE hadn't told Sophia that Richard was the wealthiest man in town, she would have known the moment she saw his house—if it could even be classified as something as typical as a house. It sat at the end of a small one-lane road and could only be accessed by being buzzed in at a gate just outside the large loop driveway. The more Sophia looked at the place, the more she wanted to classify it as a mansion. It was only two stories but it expanded wide on both sides, looking like an old plantation home. An expansive garage sat to the left of the main house and beautiful, meticulously groomed landscaping was placed in between as a testament to some gardener's handsomely paid green thumb. Large white columns lined the front porch a few feet from the driveway while the double, red, arched front doors were held open by someone who looked suspiciously like a butler.

"Who's that?" Sophia asked as Thatcher opened her door and helped her out. Normally, she wouldn't have accepted his help but she didn't want another awkward moment in front of such an impressive abode.

"I never remember his name, but that's Vega's assistant. He's a mousy fella, but you can't see Vega without getting through him." Sophia let Thatcher lead the way to the well-dressed man. She wondered if his boss bought him the suit that he wore despite the humidity which played havoc with her hair.

"Detective Thatcher," the man greeted, shaking his hand. He looked over his shoulder to Sophia. Recognition flared behind his mud-colored eyes. "Miss Hardwick, it's nice to finally meet you." On reflex she shook his hand.

"I'm sorry, but do I know you?"

The man laughed and shook his head. "No, but Lisa loves to show us pictures." Sophia had to roll her eyes again. That certainly sounded like Lisa.

"Mr. Vega is finishing up a meeting with some vendors. He shouldn't be long." He led them through the front door and immediately to a large open room to the left. Sophia was almost disappointed she couldn't take a tour of the house. Just from the front door she had seen a large, marble-white staircase with a banister worthy of being a makeshift slide. "Make yourselves at home. He'll be in here shortly." The assistant scurried off, shutting the door behind him.

They were obviously in what was used as a formal study. Built-ins lined the walls from floor to ceiling and were filled with matching sets of thick-spined books. A large, formidable desk faced the door, no doubt to keep an eye on those who might enter, while high windows were draped in translucent cloth. A rug the size of Sophia's living room cushioned the noise of her heels on the hardwood. She walked around the room, wondering if Lisa spent any time in it reading.

"I knew Richard had money, but I didn't realize how much," she admitted to the detective. He kept still in the middle of the room, looking as out of place as she felt. His jeans and plain shirt were a few leagues below the apparent dress code that Vega's staff employed on a regular basis.

"They say he works hard," Thatcher replied.

"They?"

"Like I said, this town loves Richard Vega." Sophia wanted to ask what *his* thoughts on the man were, when the door opened.

Richard Vega was all suit, hair product and posture. He walked into the room as if it had been his idea. As if *he* had been the one to invite Detective Thatcher into his home. Watching him make his way over, Sophia immediately understood why Lisa was so drawn to the man.

There was an undeniable overriding sense of confidence that rolled off of him in waves. Lisa had always been drawn to, not just strong, but powerful men. She had a track record of getting involved with the big dogs only to realize what they had in confidence they lacked in kindness. Lisa had assured Sophia that this man was different, that Richard Vega had a good heart, but now Sophia didn't know if she bought that assessment.

Although he was handsome—tall, blond and tanned, angled facial features—Sophia found herself thinking that the detective had him beat. A thought that made the color rise in her cheeks. She glanced at Thatcher from the corner of her eye. He was straight-backed and concentrated on the approaching man. She doubted he was thinking about how she might be more attractive than Officer Whitfield or any of the other women in the station.

"Detective," Richard said, extending his hand. Thatcher shook it, though there was a stiffness to it. "And you must be Sophia. Your pictures don't do you justice." They shook hands. "I'm sorry we had to meet under these circumstances."

"Yes, let's talk about those circumstances."

"Of course, let's sit." Richard was at least smart enough to know that sitting behind his desk while the two of them sat in chairs on the other side was not the best move. If this had been a business meeting, he would have been the man in charge, but this was an investigation and Detective Thatcher was the one calling the shots. Richard instead situated himself on one of two leather love seats at the far side of the room.

Sophia and Thatcher took the one opposite, the small furniture making their legs touch. She made a point not to look at him as he leaned forward, slipping into detective mode. She also tried to ignore how her heart sped up at his closeness. At the station she had been at the man's throat but now he was pulling at her concentration. She didn't need distractions right now. Lisa couldn't afford it.

"Let's jump right into this," Thatcher started. "You called Sophia Hardwick on Tuesday morning around six-thirty asking for the whereabouts of her sister, the woman you've been dating for over a year. Correct?"

"Correct."

"When she told you she didn't know, you told her you would take care of the situation. Again, is this correct?" Richard nodded. At each question his jawline tensed. "Sophia says that her sister never made it to see her. You found this out, so that puts Lisa Hardwick unaccounted for since Sunday morning. That's four days, not even including today, that Lisa has been missing." Slowly, Richard nodded. "So tell me, Mr. Vega, why the hell you didn't call us or file a missing-persons report?" There was no mistaking the anger in Thatcher's voice—nor the hidden accusation beneath his question. Having the whole situation recounted had a similar effect on Sophia. She wished she had as much experience as the detective at spotting a lie or pressing on a weak point to get the right information. Instead she kept her mouth shut and decided to follow whatever lead the man next to her would take.

Richard kept his face calm, not at all surprised at the question or its parallel series of thoughts. He leaned forward, elbows on his knees, and looked between them.

"I had a potential client come in Saturday night. It was a last-minute announcement but I wanted to show this person that I could be flexible and that I was very interested in taking on his business. If he agreed to work with me, then I could get him to participate in or donate to the Culpepper Fund-raiser this year."

"The what?" Sophia had to ask.

"It's a fund-raiser scheduled for next week. I started hosting them a year after I moved here. The town buys tickets while various organizations hold different auctions to raise money. It's also a banquet of sorts—champagne, food and music."

Sophia's eyes widened as she remembered where she had heard about that before.

"That's where Lisa met you."

"Yes, the first one she came to she picked it apart, saying the vendors had ripped me off and that she could do it better if she was in charge." He smiled. "I thought she was joking but Details did a great job last year."

It was Detective Thatcher's turn to raise his eyebrow. "Details? Why does that sound familiar?"

"It's an event-planning business Lisa started when she first moved to Culpepper," Sophia responded. It was also one of the reasons that they had drifted from each other.

"Got it. Now continue, Mr. Vega."

"Lisa helped me host a very small, informal gathering here in the house with said potential client and a few of my employees."

"And does this potential client have a name?" Thatcher asked with a raised eyebrow.

"I'd like to keep that confidential, if you don't mind. We don't want any rumors going around before anything is official."

"I do mind," the detective said with seriousness. "But we can get back to that later." Richard didn't miss a beat as he continued.

"We stayed up well into the next day. However, Lisa turned in early and left early. I, on the other hand, ashamedly slept in until almost noon. She had left me a note saying she was heading to the birthday party and would call when she made it. I turned my mind back to the potential client's entertainment needs as well as business and before I realized it, it was Monday." He balled up his fist. "I didn't question the fact that she never called until Monday night after my guest left. I called her and got her voice mail." He switched his gaze, now intense, to Sophia. When he spoke his anger was palpable. "I assumed you would have called if she hadn't shown up. I just thought the silence was the two of you doing some sisterly bonding thing and Lisa just forgot to call. Why didn't you call when she didn't show up?"

Sophia's face flushed red—a mix of embarrassment, guilt and anger.

"Lisa and I haven't been on the best of terms this past year," Sophia almost spat, trying to defend herself. "You should have known that. She didn't tell me she was coming, so when she didn't show up *I* assumed it was on purpose."

There was a heated silence, not at all like the thoughtful one she seemed to share with the detective when they were sorting through new information. This was weighted. This was bogged down with ill feelings and regret.

"Continue, Mr. Vega," Thatcher said, commanding the two of them to snap out of it. Richard looked back at the detective and let out a loud breath.

"When I still hadn't received any word by Tuesday morning, I decided it wasn't just Lisa's forgetfulness. The phone call with Miss Hardwick here just confirmed it. I left work and began looking for her, only to come up empty."

"Why didn't you call us?"

Richard sat up straighter. "At first I thought…" He paused, trying to find the right words. "I thought that Lisa had left me, using Sophia's party as an excuse to disappear."

"Why would she leave you?"

"Over the past year, I've grown to trust Lisa more than I've ever trusted anyone else. She has become not only a woman I care about, but a confidante." At this admission, Richard for the first time seemed uncomfortable with what he was saying.

"She knows secrets about you," Thatcher said.

"Not only personal, but professional. Secrets my competitors would pay big for. Secrets that could undo everything I've worked for my entire life. I've had much worse attempted by people who want my money or business before."

"Lisa wouldn't do that, though." Sophia spoke up with certainty. "From what I know, she has been very happy with you." Richard's intense expression softened at that.

"I couldn't rule it out entirely. So I called in a few favors and had her phone traced." He didn't bother acting sheepish. "I found it."

He shared a look with Detective Thatcher. It sent a chill through Sophia.

"And?" she prodded.

Richard stood and went to retrieve a box under his desk. He presented it to Thatcher. The contents made Thatcher's brow furrow. Sophia was almost afraid to look but she had to be strong. She had to be strong for Lisa.

Holding her breath she peeked in.

"Is that it?"

Richard nodded, frowning deeply while Thatcher pushed around the several pieces of what once was a cell phone. Sophia felt her stomach drop.

"Before it was smashed, I was able to follow it to the main road, just past Tipsy's Gas & Grill." Sophia looked at Thatcher questioningly.

"It's a family-owned gas station and mini-restaurant off of the main road," Thatcher explained. "Busiest gas station in town." He motioned to Richard to continue.

"When I went to where it last was turned on I found it scattered along the side of the road." He sent another significant look to Thatcher.

"I'm assuming you already tried to salvage the SIM card inside? To recover any pictures or—"

"None of it could be saved." Richard dropped back into his seat. "I couldn't even find the remnants of the card."

"So, what does that mean?" Sophia asked.

"It means," Richard began, running a hand through his hair, "that either Lisa doesn't want anyone to find her or someone doesn't want us to find Lisa."

THE AIR SEEMED to zip out of the room—leaving behind an unsettling silence. Braydon felt Sophia tense next to him. It was a response he was familiar with when bad news was flitting around.

"Did you find anything else?" Braydon asked. He

wanted to know if Richard was aware of the other missing women.

"I called the hospitals and even morgues in the neighboring cities looking for her or a Jane Doe who matched her description, but nothing came up." He pulled out a card and handed it to Braydon. "I even hired two PIs from this firm to search the cities."

"You hired out-of-town private investigators before you contacted your local PD?" Braydon said incredulously.

"I hired them to stay *out* of town to find her. Culpepper is small. I had faith, if she was here, that I'd run into her."

Braydon was fighting the urge to yell at the very rich, very pompous man in front of him. If he had just called the police when he first realized Lisa was missing, it could have made all the difference, but instead he wanted to handle it himself. He had as much pride as he did wealth.

"You still should have filed a report," Sophia barked out, breaking her silence. "Did you ever think 'What if she didn't run away?'" Braydon could tell her composure was cracking.

"Of course I did. I'm not an idiot."

"Well, you could have fooled me!" Under different circumstances, Braydon would have smiled at Sophia's brashness. She didn't bottle up her emotions—she let them pour out instead. The two of them would have kept on, but Braydon had had enough.

"Do you know Trixie Martin or Amanda Alcaster?" Braydon watched the man's facial expression closely. He could see wheels turning but there was no concrete recognition of either name.

"Not personally. The Alcaster name sounds familiar, but what has that got to do with Lisa?"

Braydon took a breath. Sophia's hands fidgeted across her lap. He wanted to hold them still, to keep her worries at bay. Personal experience had taught him that as long as a loved one was out there in trouble, no one, not even he, could quell all worries. That didn't mean he didn't want to, though. He cast another look at Sophia; the realization that he wanted to make sure she was okay was an odd one. He'd only known her for two hours at best and yet he empathized with her completely.

"They were reported missing today," he said, squaring his shoulders. Richard's brow furrowed, his frown deepened. Braydon balled his fists again, his body winding up. "This is why you let us know when something like this happens. This is why you call the police. It doesn't matter if you're taking time off of your job to locate Miss Hardwick because it's *my full-time job* to do that. I help people for a living, Richard." Braydon wasn't yelling. In fact, his voice had taken on an eerie calm. That calm voice indicated how furious he was that Richard had not reported the disappearance of Lisa. The missing woman who had a sibling drowning in a sea of worry— one beautiful woman desperate for answers. Professionalism was dialing his volume back but it wasn't diluting his intensity. "Now let me do my job and tell me everything else you found out or I'll arrest you for impeding an investigation."

It turned out that Richard was almost as clueless as they were. Apart from the cell phone, he hadn't found any evidence of blatant foul play or anything that pointed to Lisa running away. He had instead kept eyes and ears out for the woman he loved, hoping above all else that everything had been a misunderstanding. She hadn't run. She hadn't been taken. Braydon knew better than to cling to such false hope. If someone dropped off the face of the earth for four days, there was something wrong. Like kicking an addiction, admitting there was a problem was the first step.

Richard Vega hadn't handled that step well.

They wasted little time in unnecessary back-and-forth before Braydon told Richard he needed to see the exact place where the cell phone had been recovered. As far as they knew, it was the last place Lisa had been—tied by electronic tracking and hard evidence. If he could see it with his own eyes, then maybe he could see more of what had happened through hers.

"Am I riding with you or him?" Sophia asked as Richard pulled his car out of the garage. Like most houses on Loop Road it had more square footage than the resident had known what to do with.

"You can ride with either," Braydon said, watching Richard for any signs of fleeing. He didn't think the wealthy man would run, but he couldn't be too sure he wouldn't. Just because the whole town seemed to love the upstanding, well-groomed businessman, didn't mean Braydon was going to put his faith in Richard's good intentions. "We're all going to the same place."

Braydon walked over to the 370Z and inclined his head down to meet Richard's gaze.

"It should go without saying but if you try to leave or do anything suspicious, I'll find you and arrest you."

"I understand." He responded without hesitation. "I assure you that you now have my full cooperation."

"Good." Braydon patted the top of the car and went back to his truck. He was surprised to see Sophia already sitting in the cab with the air conditioner blasting. "How did you turn the car on?"

She remained still as she answered, her eyes closed in the cold air stream. "I used the key. You know, the things that people use to start cars?"

"Your sarcasm is noted, but what I meant was how did you get my keys?"

"You threw them on the dash here." She opened one eye, watching as he climbed into the driver's seat. "Not the best hiding place." He shifted into Drive and began following Richard out onto Loop Road.

"Tom says I have a nasty habit of doing that." Being a cop in Culpepper had seemed to activate an invisible barrier around the truck. No one wanted to steal or strip down his vehicle. The townspeople knew better. "That still doesn't give you the right to turn it on."

"Listen, it feels like it's over 100 degrees in this place. I needed some air and I needed it fast." She closed her eyes again and let the air conditioner push against her face. It was flushed from the heat, he could now tell. There were patches of red across her soft skin, though she was still attractive.

"That outfit isn't helping," he observed.

"And that is also noted."

They dove into a small silence. Sophia's perfume was slowly filling the space of the cab. He marveled at the contrast between its airy sweetness and her hard resolve.

"I'm surprised you didn't want to ride with Richard," Braydon admitted. "I thought you two would want to catch up." She had picked him, a stranger, over someone she knew of and who had close ties with her sister. Plus, that man had been Richard Vega. He could charm his way out of a jail cell faster than Braydon could lock the door. Another reason why he hadn't yet arrested the man. Though, he would in a heartbeat if he needed to.

Sophia snorted.

"Remember when I said Lisa and I weren't on the best terms this past year?" She motioned to the sports car in front. "Meet Richard Vega. He was the hammer to our nail."

Braydon glanced over at her. "What happened?"

Sophia turned her head so fast that her bun released the rest of her hair. "It's none of your business," she snapped.

"It is if you want me to find your sister, I need *all* of the details pertaining to her and Richard." Her anger seemed to fade.

"Why? Do you think Richard had something to do with her disappearance?"

Braydon thought about it before he answered. Richard certainly had the means to make a person fall off the radar but there had been an unmistakable concern that had covered every word and movement when he spoke of Lisa. "I personally think the only thing he's guilty of is being a prideful son of a bitch, but I don't want to rule him out, either. So, if there was a fight between all of you, there could potentially be a motive."

She went back to fidgeting with her hands.

"I really don't think that has anything to do with what's happening...."

"A good detective can't leave clues half-uncovered." He prodded with a gentler tone, "If we're going to find your sister, I need all of the information."

She put her hand up to the vent and quieted. The past wasn't a pleasant place to frequent, he knew that, but sometimes it was a necessity. He remained patient and watched as Richard turned off Loop Road and onto a connector that would get them to the main one. His red little car could easily outrun the truck. Braydon imag-

ined the only reason he was going the speed limit was
to avoid pissing him off any more.

Sophia sighed, touching her face with her now-cold
hand.

"It was over money," she started. "And we never really
had a fight. It was more of a buildup of things we *didn't*
say. My dad died when we were little and Mom worked
full-time while doing odd jobs along the way to support
us. The years went by and we could see her trying to not
blame us for her having to work so hard, but eventually
the resentment set in. Lisa and I picked up the slack and
looked out for one another—encouraged good grades,
gave each other rides to work and helped take care of
everything else. Lisa was my older sister, but she didn't
raise me—we raised each other." Her voice shook and
Braydon had to look to see if she was crying. Her head
was bent, her fingertips suddenly fascinating. "Lisa has
always been the prettier, more charming sister. As we got
older, she was handed more opportunities, but she never
really took them. That is until she started dating Richard.
He offered her a world on a gold platter and she just took
it. No questions asked. We spent years working so hard
to make something of ourselves and then it was like she
took the easy way out." Her voice softened. "We never
fought about it—I never said those exact words—but she
picked up on how I felt."

"And that was?"

"Anger…with a touch of resentment." Her face flushed
red. "Saying it out loud seems stupid, especially now
with everything going on. I should be happy for her, but
Richard was just a hard pill to swallow, I suppose. Still,
I don't think that has anything to do with her disappearance. The times we did talk this past year, she seemed
genuinely happy."

Again, Braydon was surprised by the woman next to him. Just like that she had not only told him a personal story, but she had admitted her true feelings about it. He understood her stubbornness; however, it was the ease at which she told the truth that made the younger Hardwick sister more and more intriguing.

"Does your mother know about Lisa, then?" He couldn't remember her bringing the woman up in detail before. Surely she would have been there.

"No." She didn't elaborate and Braydon didn't push her. The way her body tensed like the string on a bow, he knew he had hit a deep nerve. Her openness apparently had its limits.

"What about you, Detective? Any family drama to share?" Sophia said it as a joke, something to lighten the dark mood, but she couldn't have picked a worse topic. Years of experience saved his composure. He smiled and shook his head.

"Nothing worth talking about."

Chapter Three

Richard took them west on Highway 20, following the slight curve of the two-lane until they passed Tipsy's Gas & Grill on the left. Sophia was surprised at the appearance of "One of the Best Eats in Culpepper" gas station/eatery. It was bigger than she had imagined—the original convenience store attached to another building, twice its size. She didn't know if it was the city girl in her, but she hadn't expected it to look as cozy as it did. Her stomach growled at the idea of Tipsy's advertised fried shrimp. The last thing she had eaten was a granola bar the night before.

They drove a few miles past Tipsy's before Richard turned on his blinker and pulled to the shoulder. Thatcher followed, the moment of vulnerability on Sophia's part gone. Why had she given him so much detail about Lisa and herself? Why did he need to know about their childhood or the fact that a part of her had started to resent Lisa? Maybe it was sleep deprivation. She hadn't been able to sleep all that well since Richard had called.

That was it. She'd blame it on that and not the mysterious man next to her.

Richard pointed at the tall grass a few feet from the road. They followed him, examining the area around it for something he might have missed. There was nothing.

"I'm going to call over a car and have them sweep farther back." Thatcher walked to his truck and pulled out the radio to make the call. Sophia and Richard kept to the grass.

"I'm sorry," he said, using his foot to move some rocks around. If it was meant to make him look vulnerable, it wasn't working. "I should have kept you updated. I was too caught up in finding her."

"You should have called the cops."

"Sophia, just because I chose not to call them doesn't mean I didn't have people looking for her."

"You mean the private investigators?"

"They aren't the only ones."

Sophia gave him a questioning look.

"I'm a very wealthy man with a lot of friends. I have contacts that operate outside of the police purview." He turned his body so his back was facing the cars. "I know people who don't get stopped by red tape."

"What does that mean?"

"Cops sometimes slow down investigations."

"I don't understand what you're trying to tell me." Sophia crossed her arms over her chest. The tip of her heels sunk into the ground. "You don't want the cops looking for Lisa because you have 'friends'?"

He made a frustrated noise.

"I'm just saying, there are reasons why I didn't call the police in the first place."

"You said you didn't call because you thought she just ran off?" A feeling of alarm was starting to rise within her. "Are you saying you *knew* she didn't just leave?"

There was the underlying implication again. A man with that much money, good looks and charm—though she didn't see it—could get away with a lot. If he had "friends" like he claimed, couldn't he use them to help him... Help him what? Dispose of Lisa?

Just thinking it sent a chill through Sophia.

"No, it's just— We were so happy, Sophia. I didn't think she just left."

Sophia dropped down to a whisper, eyeing Thatcher's back as he talked to the dispatcher.

"You lied to us," she said in a rush.

"I didn't lie. There was a moment where I wondered if she had gone on her own accord but, you know your sister, she wouldn't do that." She felt her defenses flare—of course she knew her sister. Even though they had grown apart didn't mean she had forgotten her.

"So, who are these friends of yours? Where are they?"

"All you need to know is that they are doing whatever they need to do to find Lisa." He stopped there and didn't make any sign of elaborating other than maybe using the whole "I've already said too much" excuse for keeping silent. In his black suit, the sun shining bright around them, Richard Vega looked a lot more threatening than he had in his home. He was shorter than Thatcher but had a solid body frame with muscles hidden beneath his custom-made suit, a gift from his personal trainer no doubt. Sophia wasn't a string bean or anything. She had muscles, too. They were just a little harder to see. Work had become hectic in the past two years. Going to the gym had been low on her priority list. That didn't mean she was completely defenseless.

Now, standing so close to a man she hardly knew but was admitting freely that he had connections that didn't pay heed to law enforcement, she was second-guessing if she could really hold her own and defend herself if needed.

Maybe her face showed the new sense of trepidation she was feeling. Thatcher tilted his head slightly to the side when their eyes met. His own expression was heavily guarded.

"A car should be here soon. They'll sweep this area again and then go farther back, just to make sure," he said. "If there's anything out here, they'll find it."

He brought his gaze to Richard now. There was no mistaking he was in detective mode—his feet spread apart, his back straight as a board, determination seeping through his stance.

"Now," he went on, "I'm going to have to ask you to come down to the station, Mr. Vega."

Richard seemed taken aback. Anger flashed across his face.

"I've already told you everything. Shouldn't we be using our time more wisely?"

Thatcher crossed his arms. Sophia couldn't help but think about how handsome he was in that moment. No-nonsense, authoritative, and all wrapped within a rock-hard body. She would have liked to meet Braydon Thatcher under different circumstances.

"Richard, I'm not giving you a choice. You're coming to the station." Thatcher pointed to his sports car. "The only decision you have to make is which car you ride in to get there."

Sophia rode with Thatcher again as they went back to the station. Richard had opted to ride in his car, barely keeping his cursing below his breath, while the detective had spent a good five minutes once again warning him against fleeing.

"Are you going to arrest him?" Sophia asked as soon as we pulled onto the highway.

"Yes."

"Why? Can you do that?" Sophia asked, adjusting the

air so that it was blowing on her face again. Florida heat didn't agree with her. Thatcher's teeth ground together, his jaw muscles clenching. Whatever he had learned had upped his aggravation level exponentially.

"We just got word that a colleague of Vega's has been going around asking people about Lisa, using the man's name as an unofficial police badge." He turned to her, nostrils flared. "That's impeding an investigation."

Sophia jumped up and down in her seat once. It caught Thatcher off guard but she didn't care. She repeated her recent conversation with Vega. It didn't improve his mood. When they pulled into the station's parking lot, he turned to her with a silent ferocity.

"I want you to go in there and answer every question we have about your sister." Having been given the instruction made her want to run the other way, but she knew it had to be done. "And, Sophia." He grabbed her hand. "I swear to you that I'll find your sister and bring her back safely."

The station seemed to stand at attention when Richard Vega walked in with Thatcher close behind, watching with expressions of interest mixed with disbelief. Even Cara looked up from her computer as the two men marched into the interrogation room.

Sophia wanted to follow them but doubted Richard would say anything else without an attorney—one dressed to the nines and with a bank statement that would be too good for the town of Culpepper. She instead was guided into Thatcher's office where she sat with a sigh. Back to the drawing board, she thought, crossing her legs like the dignified woman she hoped she appeared to be.

"Give us a minute," Detective Langdon said, popping out of the room before she could object. It wasn't as if she had any pressing matters to deal with or anything.

Just because she had bonded with Thatcher during their field trip didn't mean her impatience would keep its head down. She waited for a few minutes, with tried calmness, until only Thatcher breezed in.

His thick eyebrows were furrowed—his lips thinned in contained anger. He sat down behind his desk and ran a hand through the dark mass of hair. The obvious frustration he was feeling put Sophia further on edge.

"Well?" she prompted. "What did Richard have to say?"

"That he won't say anything else until his attorney arrives." Well, she called that one. "But, I hadn't expected anything different. With the amount of money that man has, I'm surprised he even talked to us as much as he did." A sigh rumbled out.

"So, what now? Do you want me to go talk to him? I can try to—"

Thatcher held up his hand to silence her.

"Right now you need to answer some questions about your sister."

"Fine."

They were able to slip into the civil roles of detective and citizen as Thatcher asked a series of questions that would help him form a "psychological profile" on Lisa. Even though they believed Lisa hadn't disappeared on her own accord, Thatcher had to still get a feel for the woman's mental and emotional states as well as any health issues she might be experiencing. Sophia did her best to answer each question in an objective manner, but, the truth was, she couldn't be sure how happy Lisa had been before the disappearance. Nor could she tell the man in full confidence that her sister had been upset.

"In general Lisa has always been an optimist," she confessed. "She always smiled and had something nice to say growing up—compliments on the tip of her tongue at all times. It's part of the reason why she charms everyone she meets." Thatcher raised an eyebrow but lowered it before she continued. "Like I said before, the times I did talk with her she seemed genuinely happy while here in Culpepper."

"Was there a particular reason she moved to Culpepper?" Sophia sent him a questioning look. "I only ask because you said the two of you were very close until this past year."

A smile crept across her lips before she could stop it.

"Her moving to Culpepper had nothing to do with our relationship. Lisa and I were the best of friends—annoyingly inseparable." Sophia hesitated on the past tense and sobered. "But Lisa hated Atlanta. I couldn't blame her for leaving. She was passing through Culpepper on the way to a wedding almost two years ago when she said she fell in love with the town. She moved a few months later."

"And you didn't follow?"

"No, but she tried really hard to get me to." Lisa had in fact boxed up Sophia's room while she'd been at work. She'd just smiled when Sophia had started yelling.

I'm not moving, Lisa!

Why not? Your stuff is already packed! she'd reasoned. Sophia had found it annoying then, but now she couldn't stop the ache in her heart.

"I don't blame her," Thatcher said under his breath.

"Excuse me?"

"Sorry, I meant I don't blame her for not liking the city. I'm not a big fan, either," he said with conviction.

"It's not too bad," Sophia defended. "It can be lonely at times and the traffic leaves more to be desired, but the opportunities are great."

"Lonely, huh? I take it you aren't married, then." It

wasn't a question and his eyes stayed down on his notes. Sophia picked at invisible lint on her pant leg and tried to keep her voice even.

"Not that it matters to this investigation but, no, I'm single." A blush rose fast to her cheeks. Thatcher looked up. She had only meant to say she wasn't married, not divulge that she was single and had bouts of loneliness.

"What about you?" Sophia wanted to stick her head in the sand. She had blurted the question in an attempt to save face. She had to give it to the detective, he answered without skipping a beat.

"No, I'm not married. Now, are there any health issues Lisa has that we should be worried about?" The change in subjects left her speechless for a moment, but still able to feel the heat in her cheeks, she finished the rest of his questions without any more awkward outbursts.

"The other two women who are missing…" she started after he closed his notebook.

"Amanda and Trixie."

"Are their families being asked the same questions?" Thatcher nodded.

"Amanda's mother and Trixie's boss are in the other rooms with Tom and Cara." His cell phone started to vibrate against the desktop. The noise made Sophia jump. He didn't notice as he read the message.

"What happens now that I've answered your questions?"

"Now we are going to go to each missing woman's house and place of work." He stood and stretched, his biceps rippling at the motion.

"All right." She started to stand but he stopped her.

"By 'we' I mean Detective Langdon and myself. You can't come this time and that's final."

"Then what do you want me to do? Sit here and twiddle my thumbs?"

"We have an all-points bulletin out on all three women. We have good men and women on the job, Miss Hardwick. You need to stay out of Lisa's house until we're done with the search but after that you can go wherever you please. There's a diner down the road that has a great dinner special or you can stay here until we're done with each search. It's really up to you at this point."

Sophia chewed the inside of her lip. Thatcher took her silence as compliance.

"I'll let you know when we're done at Lisa's."

The detectives left soon after while Sophia remained behind. She wanted to snoop to fill the void of helplessness within her but decided against it—she was in a police station after all. Cara, as she was told once again to call the officer, showed her to the restroom and then the break room. Unlike the many cop-related clichés found on TV, there were no doughnuts or cream-filled pastries. Instead she walked a block over and ate a burger at Sal's Diner, all the while fighting the heat and humidity. Worry had taken her healthy eating habits and thrown them clear out the window. The walk back was more sluggish but she couldn't deny she felt better having eaten.

An unfamiliar car was parked two spots next to her own when she rounded the station, though it didn't take long for her to guess it belonged to Richard's attorney. The BMW was black and slick and probably worth more than she made in two years. She hurried inside to see the new suit but was stopped by another man she hadn't seen until now.

"Miss Hardwick," he said, extending his hand. "I'm Captain Jake Westin." They shook—his hands were rough and large.

"Nice to meet you, sir." The man wasn't much taller than Sophia, but he exuded authority through his uniform and impeccable posture. She placed his age in the upper fifties.

"I wanted to let you know that we're doing everything we can and we'll find your sister." His small smile wasn't charming but it was infused with confidence. She nodded and thanked him. "I'm afraid I can't talk long. I have a meeting with Mr. Vega and his attorney."

"I understand," she said before shaking his hand once more. Though his grip was solid, she couldn't help but compare it to Detective Thatcher's. "Let me know if I can do anything to help."

"Will do." He turned and then disappeared into the conference room—all blinds were closed over the windows. If Cara and another cop hadn't been in the room with her, Sophia would have pressed her ear against the door to listen.

The Florida sun raged on as the hours dwindled into night before Sophia finally left the station. She had stayed around to see what would happen with Richard, but Captain Westin hadn't come out of the room by the time Thatcher had called to give the okay to go back to Lisa's house. She had even waited another half hour but decided it was a lost cause for the moment. With Richard's attorney in there, the man had probably not even spoken yet. She said a quick goodbye to Cara and headed to her car.

Sophia's adrenaline from the day's events was also on the decline. She hadn't lost her drive to find Lisa, in fact it felt stronger than ever knowing even Captain Westin was personally involved, but she couldn't deny the weight of exhaustion settling on her shoulders.

She was practical enough to realize that she was no

help to her older sister if she was constantly battling the droop of her eyelids.

Lisa lived in Pebblebrook, a neighborhood on the outskirts of town. It was a community of nice brick houses, man-made ponds and flowers galore. There always seemed to be a mother and her children walking the seemingly unending sidewalks—geared up to lose weight and release toddler-induced stress. When Lisa had moved into the neighborhood two years before, she hadn't been able to hide her happiness. It was a giant leap above her last apartment.

Sophia drove on autopilot deeper into Pebblebrook's belly with the soft sounds of a local talk radio show in the background. Since she didn't have as much to contribute in the ways of police detection, she was already forming a proactive to-do list in her head.

Check Lisa's house more thoroughly.

Go to Lisa's work and search for a work schedule or appointment books.

Get an update from Detective Thatcher—

Her train of thought derailed. Thatcher's voice when he promised to find her sister blanketed the ever-present fear inside her, comforting Sophia for the moment. She believed his sincerity—it was strong and determined. His blue eyes had pierced her own with a ferocity to undo all of the bad and replace it with the good. The reaction had been a lot more than Sophia had expected from the small-town detective.

However, the fact remained, Lisa was *her* sister, not his. He hadn't grown up with her, cared for her, been there at the lowest points in life or the highest. He didn't know that her favorite movie was *The Little Mermaid* or that she was deathly afraid of owls. He didn't know about the scar across her ankle that she had gotten from falling off a swing set when she was nine or that, despite their rocky childhood, she had always been kind to their mother. Detective Thatcher didn't know Lisa, so he couldn't love her the way Sophia did.

No matter how dedicated he was to his job, he would never have the drive she had to make sure Lisa was found.

It was almost six by the time she pulled into 302 Grandview Court. The street was the farthest from the entrance to Pebblebrook, all houses backed up a thick stretch of woods, and all Sophia could hear were insects and frogs—the music of the South. The loud but subtle sound annoyed her, as it always had. In the city there were still the sounds of insects but car horns and loud neighbors drowned them out. Here, there were no such distractions.

Lisa lived in a single-family home that was a mix between contemporary and ranch-style. Alternating shades of beige and brown brick wrapped around the three-bedroom, two-bath home while a well-tended garden lined the entryway. Sophia didn't know how Lisa had kept the plants alive and healthy. If it had been her garden, there would be more weeds than flowers and a lot less color—she just didn't have enough patience to have a green thumb. The inside of the house, admittedly, made Sophia a little green with envy.

The entryway led past an open front room and into an open-floor-plan kitchen, dining area and living room. Off the kitchen was a hallway with the two guest bedrooms and a full bath; off the living room was the very large master bedroom and en suite. Plus a walk-in closet that was bigger than Sophia's bedroom in her apartment. It wasn't enough that the house was large, but it was also *upgraded.* Granite countertops, dark-wood cabinets, vaulted-and-tray ceilings with exposed wooden beams, and hardwood throughout. The house had been done to the nines. It was beautiful.

Sophia felt a stab of guilt as the green monster inside poked his nose up into the air. She should be happy that her sister lived in such a nice house—that she had such a nice life. However, Sophia couldn't swallow the lump that Richard had had a hand in securing the house. It would have been different if he also lived there but he stayed in his mansion on Loop Road. Sophia may have lived in a tiny apartment but it was a tiny apartment she had *earned,* not been handed. Lisa, although older, had always skirted the line of earning things versus being handed them—something made easier by her good looks and charm.

Sophia sighed.

This was an old fight between the Hardwick sisters, a useless, petty one now that Lisa was missing.

Sophia grabbed her duffel and changed into a striped tank top, blue jeans and a pair of Nikes. Relinquishing the heels and stuffy pantsuit was a welcomed feeling. There was no boss here that she was trying to impress, no promotion she was chasing with professional work wear and impeccable posture. She was in a safe zone—one lacking work-related worry yet lined with stress-induced questions about Lisa's future.

Packing had been quick and careless. She noticed the absence of her shampoo, razor and sleep clothes, though they hadn't seemed too important at the time. She wondered if it was a note about her character that she hadn't forgotten her work laptop. She rummaged through the bag until she found her cell phone charger. It wasn't like anyone was anxiously awaiting her to text or call but with Lisa out there, she wanted it to at least be fully charged.

She plugged the ancient phone into a wall socket before stretching wide.

Even though sleep had been a rational thought, Sophia couldn't bring herself to settle down. All notions of getting some rest had evaporated. Instead she found the coffee and thanked the high heavens that there was enough creamer left for one cup. One very large cup. With the silky goodness sliding down her throat and warming her belly, she decided to search the house again.

She went through each room much slower than when she had first blown into town, searching high and low for any clue that could peg a time frame or place Lisa had gone to. The detectives left the house in the same order they had found it, thankfully, and this time around she was able to note the details—the decorations that made the house innately Lisa's.

The front room had been set up as an office. A desk and bookcase lined one wall while a bright blue love seat sat opposite. From first glance there was nothing that screamed, "This is where I went and this is who took me!" There was also no laptop, just a pristine area of minimal clutter.

Sophia opened the desk drawers and searched its contents. She found coupons for a clothing store two cities over, enough sticky notes to create a note-taking army, and bundles of multicolored pens scattered throughout. Lisa had always loved what she called "nontraditional" pens.

"They dare to be different!" she would say after signing a check with electric-green ink or writing her name in a birthday card with an annoyingly loud shade of fuchsia. It was a habit she had picked up in grade school and hadn't been able to shake since. When Sophia was little she had been so angry with her sister that she'd replaced the colorful pens for a ten-pack of black and blues. To this day she had never seen Lisa so angry. The then-girl had turned such a bright shade of red, she would have probably liked to add it to her collection of odd inks.

Sophia took care to shut the drawers without snapping or pinching the writing utensils. If Lisa came back to find them busted open it would be another round of older-sibling rage.... She paused. *When* Lisa came back.

Picture frames and knickknacks lined the bookcase. From little elephant figurines to frozen scenes of Lisa, Sophia, friends she didn't know and even Richard. The two of them were pressed together in an intimate hug— both smiling, both happy. Another pang of jealousy twisted in her stomach. She physically tried to tamp it down with her hand. There was no time or reason for her to be envious again.

The guest bedrooms were also unhelpful. They both housed a bed and night tables but were neat and orderly— no one had stayed in them recently. The guest bathroom told the same story as well as the pantry and refrigerator. Both were barely stocked. She moved through the living room, warily eyeing the yellow sectional and glass coffee table that was decorated with neon-colored candles, and once again was met with the master suite.

If ever a room could capture the essence of Lisa Gale Hardwick, it was this room. The walls were a light pink that traveled up and across the double-tray ceiling while white trim lined the two windowsills on either side of the bed. That bed. It was a king-size, another luxury Sophia hadn't been able to experience yet, covered in a loud pink silk comforter with flowers of varying sizes sewn in. There were six fuzzy pillows piled high, all neon green, yellow, orange and pink. They were soft to the touch. Sophia smiled.

She remembered how annoyed she used to be at Lisa's love for pillows. Even though their bedroom was small and they each had a twin-size bed, there always seemed to be more pillows than bedroom. The older Hardwick would pile them high during the day only to throw them on the floor between their beds during the night. It had driven Sophia crazy.

But you'll sure thank me if you roll out of bed while you're asleep, she would say. If that didn't appease the younger, grumpier girl, Lisa would go as far as to demonstrate by rolling out of bed. She would laugh as the pillows cushioned the fall. *See? I'm kind of brilliant.* If this second attempt still didn't work, she would tug Sophia down with her. No matter her mood, this always did the trick. She would laugh and feel the sisterly bond that connected them. Over the years it became a skit between them—an inside joke. Sophia hadn't realized how much she missed those moments until now, staring at a much bigger bed, standing in a much bigger room.

Her lips went slack, the smile fading. She put the pillow back, wanting to stop the trip down memory lane and find the lost woman instead. If there were no clues to find in the house, she would just have to continue the search elsewhere.

The coffee was doing its wonderful job. It pumped energy throughout Sophia's body like water down a twisty slide. The heaviness in her eyelids had been replaced by an almost nervous twitch as she hopped into her car and drove down the road, fingers drumming against the steering wheel along with an alternative rock song she didn't quite know and her mind set on Details. Most of Culpepper were getting into bed, their heads heavy but hearts happy that Friday was only a deep sleep away.

The rest of the house search had been uneventful.

There were no hints or clues to where Lisa had gone or why, but Sophia hadn't been too surprised—the house looked barely lived in. If there was anything she had left behind it was either at her work or at Richard's house. She didn't know how either search would go considering Richard and his motley crew of "friends" had probably already gone through both, but she wanted to try. Once she went through Details, she would be giving Richard a call.

The sound of buzzing made Sophia swerve. Her heart thudded hard as she reached for her cell phone, expectations high. An unknown local number flashed on the screen.

"Hello?" she answered, hope pouring through the sound.

"Sophia Hardwick?" The hope that her sister was on the other end of the line evaporated as the man answered.

"This is she."

"It's Detective Braydon Thatcher, sorry to call so late." A new feeling of alarm followed.

"Have you found Lisa?" She wanted and didn't want an answer. What if they *had* found her and she was—

"No, but we're working hard on that." She let out a breath. "I wanted to—" There was a pause. Sophia pulled the phone out to make sure the call hadn't dropped. "I just wanted to check in. How are you doing?"

That caught her off guard. She answered honestly.

"Frustrated. I also went through Lisa's house but didn't find anything. I'm heading over to her work right now to see if I can find *something*."

"We already went through Details," he said.

"Well maybe you missed something only I would pick up on."

"You know, you aren't supposed to go over there. I've already had to section it off because so many people think they are cops." There was no mistaking the anger that lined his tone. Though Richard seemed to be popular among most of Culpepper, that didn't seem to count for much in Detective Thatcher's book. "I can arrest you for going, you know. For impeding a police investigation."

"But I'm her sister!" she said in a rival degree of anger. "I have more right to be there than you!"

"Not by law, ma'am."

"Don't you 'ma'am' me!" If Thatcher hadn't been in law enforcement she would have hung up the phone then. No one was going to tell her what she could and couldn't do when it came to finding Lisa and they certainly weren't going to do it while calling her ma'am.

Maybe Thatcher realized she was ready to have an all-out verbal phone fight. He waited a beat before the sound of a heavy sigh escaped on his end.

"Fine, but go through the back door so you don't break the tape. I'm assuming you have a key?"

"Yes, *sir*."

"Call me if you find anything, but don't get your hopes up. We already swept that area thoroughly."

She bit her lip. "Fine. I'll call if I see anything."

They ended the call and Sophia tried to ignore that continued thud of her heart.

Details was housed in a small, narrow building that had once been home to a florist's shop.

"It's the perfect fit, Sophy!" Lisa had exclaimed after the first walk-through. "I don't even have to change the colors!"

She sure was right about that. The outside brick concealed an inside of varying shades of blue and yellow that popped from natural light from the mostly glass front waiting room. Details was attached to a home decor store dedicated to everything wood. Lisa had told her that the couple who owned it were "more religious than God himself" but that information was neither here nor there for Sophia. She was on a mission to find something, anything that would help her locate her sister.

Like Detective Thatcher ordered, she pulled out her key and walked around back. She knew this building as well as she knew Lisa's house. It was the whole boyfriend area that she had missed out on. She moved through the building, checking the lobby, Lisa's office, the break room and the bathroom. It was ridiculously neat. If there were any colored pens they were hiding. What's more, she couldn't find anything that resembled a calendar or appointment book that could help peg where and when she had gone.

That seemed like a clue in itself but she refrained from calling Thatcher to tell him so. Instead, after an hour of searching high and low, she admitted defeat and drove back to Pebblebrook, yawning the entire way there. The cup of coffee had been big, but not big enough.

SOPHIA DIDN'T HAVE the heart to move the pillows aside when she decided she needed a few hours of sleep. Without her older sister's giggles or beaming smile as she threw one pillow after the other to the ground, it didn't seem worth the effort. She grabbed a blanket from the hall closet and made the couch her target instead.

She tried to sleep with all of her might, but worries plagued her thoughts. A few minutes of rolling around turned into an hour before she decided sleeping couldn't happen yet. What she needed was something to snack on but after going through the pantry and refrigerator again she came up empty. Another defeat to add to the growing list of disappointments.

"You don't even have some crackers, Lisa," she said aloud. "I would have been happy with only a few."

She stood back and patted her stomach, uncertain of her next move. The sound of the lock turning from the back door sounded like a bomb going off in the silent kitchen. She whirled around as hope sprung through her so violently that she stumbled backward. It had to be Lisa. It just had to be.

Before she could run to greet the long-haired beauty, the door opened to reveal a man Sophia didn't recognize. A grin split open his face. He shut the door behind him and flipped the lock.

Sophia may not have been perfect under pressure, but she had enough sense to grab a knife from the holder on the counter. She brandished it like a sword and tried not to scream.

Chapter Four

Sophia held the knife tight—both hands clasped around the grip. She didn't know if it was sharp but it sure didn't look dull. The blade was almost as long as her forearm. If this man came at her, he'd be the first to know how easily it could cut through skin.

"Who are you?" she asked, a noticeable tremor in her voice. "What are you doing in my house?"

The man walked into full view, a missing front tooth showing a dark, endless void.

"You aren't Lisa Hardwick," he stated. "This isn't your house."

"But I am her sister." Her grip was so tight on the knife, her hand hurt.

The man laughed, and thankfully kept his distance.

"I know who you are, Sophia. You put my employer in jail."

"Your employer?"

"Vega."

"You aren't the one who took Lisa?" His smile dropped. It was unnerving to see the stranger lose whatever humor he had.

"No, ma'am. I was hired to find her and bring her home safe."

Sophia eyed him warily.

"You can put the knife down. I have a gun in the back of my pants. If I wanted to kill you I would have done it by now." Sophia's stomach flip-flopped as he pulled the handgun out to show her before putting it back into the waist of his pants. "I was supposed to update Vega but seeing as he's in jail, I'm reporting to you."

That got Sophia's attention. She lowered her arm but kept the knife in hand.

"Do you know where she is?"

He shook his head. "But I found her car."

BRAYDON WAS STARING down into his never-ending cup of coffee. He'd already been getting bad sleep the past few days. Now time was starting to blur for him—he couldn't remember the last night he'd slept solidly. Tom and Officer Whitfield had stayed with him after all of the searches, going through phone records, financial reports, and trying to pinpoint where the women had last been before they'd disappeared. He was paying most attention to where Lisa had gone. He told himself it was because she had been the first to go missing, but a part of him knew the focus had been forged out of sympathy for Sophia Hardwick. No matter the motives behind the search, nothing was fitting together. No new evidence had popped up during the women's house searches or work searches. Aside from Richard's admission of tampering with potential crime scenes and withholding information, they didn't have any other leads.

Braydon took another long pull on his coffee. He knew he needed sleep—it would make him think better, but he couldn't bring himself to try. That would be valuable search time he would be wasting. Lisa, Trixie and Amanda couldn't afford for him to catch up on beauty sleep.

Sophia couldn't afford it, either.

Thinking of her, of her determination to find Lisa, was enough to push him into his third wind. He went over to the map of Culpepper stretched across the wall and looked at the locations of interest. All three women lived as far away from each other as possible. Lisa lived at the back end of Pebblebrook; Trixie lived on the opposite side of town in a house that was tucked away in the middle of some acreage; and Amanda lived with her mother in a house that backed up to the bay. His eyes stuck to the Alcaster tack on the map.

After all of these years, it was once again a part of an investigation. He just hoped this time it didn't involve a murder.

His concentration started to lose traction as he thought about Amelia—her vibrant smile, her infectious laugh... and her bloody corpse. It sent a familiar fire through him. If he had only been there sooner, if he had only protected her like he had promised when they were young, Terrance Williams wouldn't have had the chance to kill her.

He punched the top of his desk, his thoughts turning turbulent.

"Braydon." Tom knocked on the side of the opened office door. He craftily ignored the anger that was seeping out of his partner and waved with a phone in his hand. "You left this in the conference room. It's Sophia Hardwick."

"Thanks." He grabbed his phone and tried to tuck back into his normal self. He took a few breaths before answering. "Thatcher here."

"I know where Lisa's car is!" the woman all but screeched.

"What? How?"

"A man broke into the house and—"

"A man broke into the house? Are you okay? Is he still

there?" Braydon put his gun back into its holster, grabbed his keys and started to leave the station. He motioned to Tom to follow him.

"I'm fine. He's gone. He works for Richard. He was one of the 'friends' he told me about."

That relieved Braydon, but only a bit.

"Where's the car, then?"

"I'll tell you when you pick me up." There was that stubbornness weaving into her voice.

"Sophia," he warned.

"I promise I'll tell you when you get here. I don't want you to leave me behind, Detective. Now please hurry so we can go see if it's true."

"Fine, but lock yourself in a room and wait for us to get there."

"He's not coming back," she said. Braydon blew out an irritated breath.

"Sophia, three women in town have already disappeared. A man just broke into the house. Unless you have him chained up in the garage, I want you to go into a room and lock yourself inside. Do you understand me?"

There was a pause. He may not have known Sophia that well but he bet she was currently rolling her eyes. She finally sighed and said, "Okay."

Braydon had a patrol car closest to Pebblebrook search for a suspicious person while Tom followed behind to Lisa's. The heightened sense of urgency, he realized, wasn't for Lisa or the other missing women, but for Sophia. He didn't know how someone he barely knew had gotten so far under his skin, like a plant that had taken root years ago. He did, however, know that he had to protect her.

The drive to Lisa's would normally take ten minutes—Braydon got there in five.

"I'll secure the perimeter," Tom said as they met on the sidewalk. "You go check the house." They both pulled out their guns, Tom disappearing around the house, Braydon slowly opening the front door. He was going to go straight to the bedroom, thinking she would most likely hide there, when a crash from the kitchen snagged his attention. He rounded the corner with his gun raised.

"Sophia!" He found the woman standing over a broken glass. She jumped at his appearance.

"What are you pointing a gun at me for?" she said, face reddening.

"What are you doing in the kitchen? I thought I told you to lock yourself in a room. The front door wasn't even locked!"

"I was about to go to the bedroom but I was thirsty! And I left the front door unlocked so you could get in without breaking it down. Lisa would kill me if she came home and her door was destroyed." She put her hands on her hips. "Can you please put that thing away?" She motioned to the gun still raised in his hand. "It's not like I'm armed or anything." It was his turn to roll his eyes.

"You are a very maddening woman," he said. "Do you know that?"

"I've been told I'm difficult."

He put the gun back into its rightful place against his side. "Now stay here while I search the rest of the house." Braydon could tell she was about to argue, so he put up his hand to stop it. "Just let me do this."

She surrendered. "Fine by me."

The house was clean, he noted once again, as he searched each room and closet. It was also empty. There were no broken windows, doors or any signs of a break-in. The man hadn't used force to get in, that was for sure.

"All clear?" Sophia asked when he finished his round.

She put down a dustpan to get the remainders of the glass. Without thinking he crouched down to hold it. If the act surprised her like it did him, she didn't show it. Instead she swept the rest of the shards in without commenting.

"Were all the doors locked before he showed up?" he asked.

She nodded as he moved the pan back so she could get to the line of bits that never seemed to want to go in the first place. Braydon's house was all hardwood. He knew what a pain it was to sweep. "Of course I did. I doubled-checked all of the windows and doors. He either picked the lock or…" She stiffened a fraction.

"Or what?"

"I think he had a key."

Braydon stopped, the dustpan in his hand.

"A key?"

"It makes sense—I don't remember hearing anything weird like someone working on a lock. He unlocked it with ease. He *did* say that Richard hired him to find Lisa. I guess he gave him a way to get into the house."

That didn't sit right with Braydon. His brow furrowed. Sophia put the broom down and took the dustpan from his hand. Their fingers brushed. They paused in unison. Electricity coursed between their touching skin. Whether it was a desire to protect the black-haired beauty or something more sensual than that, he wasn't sure. She looked up at him through her long lashes. There was a feeling that flickered behind her deep green eyes, but he couldn't place what. Sophia cleared her throat and took a step away.

"But, I—that's not what we should be focusing on here," she said, emptying the pan into the trash can.

"I don't know about that, but we'll revisit this topic." Tom came in then and reported the lot was clear. He said a quick hello to Sophia before she led them into the living room. Barely veiled excitement propelled her forward—a bounce lining each step—the moment between them in the kitchen short-lived.

"The man, and before you ask he didn't give a name, went through Lisa's office and found something we all missed." She handed him a Post-it note. "He said it had fallen between the desk and the trash can. Do you know where this is?"

Braydon froze. It read Dolphin Lot.

He knew *exactly* where it was.

Chapter Five

Sophia didn't have to know the men all that well to know something was off. Instead of immediately jumping into the cars to go to Dolphin Lot, there was a mass hesitation. Tom was staring at Thatcher while he stared at the note. She didn't understand the cause of the silence attached, either. Lisa had been missing for five days—locating her car was a lead she was happy to have found…or rather, been given.

"So, you do know where the Dolphin Lot is?" she prodded when neither man answered her first question. Thatcher nodded. He didn't elaborate. Sophia looked to Tom for answers.

"Braydon and I were actually near there the morning you showed up."

"Well, great! Then we can go there now." Tom cast a quick look at Thatcher, concerned. Sophia didn't understand why everything had suddenly slowed down. This was the first real clue they had. She was about to say as much when Thatcher folded the note and put it in his pocket.

"I guess I can't get you to stay here," he said to her. His voice was flat, cold. It was such a drastic change from his earlier tone that she took an involuntary step back. Thatcher noticed the movement and tried on a small smile. Sophia wasn't buying it.

"No. For good or for bad I want to be there," she said. "I *need* to be there."

The detectives looked at each other, passing a message with their eyes, until Thatcher nodded. "Fine but only after you give us a brief description of the man who gave you this note."

Sophia held her temper and described the man's appearance to Tom as best she could.

"Are you going to arrest him? Shouldn't we have as many people as possible out there looking for these women?"

"What would be more helpful is if we were all on the same page," Thatcher was quick to answer. His jawline had set so hard that Sophia bet she could wield it as a weapon if she wanted.

Though, she couldn't disagree with the truth of what he said.

The detectives sent out the man's description to all of the on-duty cops. Sophia doubted they could catch the missing-tooth man. Even if he had a key, he had still caught her off guard. Plus, if Richard had hired him to "do whatever it takes" to find Lisa, then maybe it was better for everyone involved if he stayed elusive.

Sophia went through the familiar motions of getting into the passenger side of Thatcher's truck. She had ridden in it so much in the past twelve or so hours that she was met with the scent of her perfume as she sat down. She caught herself wondering if Thatcher liked it…and if the scent had attached to him, as well. If someone was close enough to him, would they smell it and think he was taken? Would the aroma act as a barrier to keep women from trying to hit on him?

Sophia quite liked that idea.

"So where is Dolphin Lot?" she asked. They pulled out of the driveway and drove into the night. Lisa's next-door neighbors peeked out from their windows as Tom reversed in his car and followed. "There seemed to be some tension at the mention of it."

Thatcher shifted in his seat. He kept his eyes straight ahead.

"It backs up to the bay on the outskirts of town. It's an undeveloped piece of land, maybe five acres in total. The closest house belongs to the Alcasters."

Sophia gasped. "Amanda Alcaster?"

"Technically her mother, Marina, owns the house, but, yes, Amanda lives there, too." Before Sophia could completely process that, he continued. "What's more is Dolphin Lot is owned by Marina, as well."

"That can't be a coincidence, can it?"

"I don't have all of the information to make a conclusion either way," he said before adding, "but, no, I wouldn't chalk it up to that."

The car filled with a pregnant silence. Sophia didn't know what to think now. Why had Lisa written down that address? Had Amanda called her over for help? Or maybe she had lured her in? Maybe it had nothing to do with the disappearances. Maybe it *was* just a coincidence. There were too many unknowns and she was starting to feel the lack of sleep drag her senses down.

Now that the small mystery of why the detectives had such a reaction to the address was solved, the more troublesome mystery started to settle in. What would they find once they got to Dolphin Lot?

THIS WAS ALL too familiar. The winding dirt road, the blanket of darkness, the feeling of growing anxiety...

He had done this before. He had traveled down the same road, hitting every bump and dip in the dirt path, hurtling toward an uncertain future with a gun at his side. He had been here before.

Eleven years ago.

The difference now was that he wasn't alone. Sophia sat with her shoulders squared, lips thinned and hands back to fidgeting in her lap. Although she was looking at where the truck's headlights fell, he doubted she was seeing anything there. The happiness at finding a solid lead had ebbed away. She was worrying about her sister and what they would find now. He couldn't blame her one bit.

"This road will take us through the entire lot until it stops at the bay toward the end of the property," Braydon said. They turned with the road and crossed what he knew was the property line. "Those trees—" he pointed out her window "—divide the property in half. Tom will take the road that cuts across the field on the other side of them. We'll drive through first to see if we see anything, then we'll go out on foot."

Sophia nodded.

"I guess we got lucky with the weather," she said. "If it was cloudy we wouldn't be able to see anything."

She was right about that. The moon wasn't full but it was bright enough to allow them to see most of the field on each side. What would have been better was if they had found the sticky note during the day and not after midnight. The fact that they technically hadn't found the clue at all was a nuisance to his detective pride—he should have found the Post-it, not one of Richard Vega's hired thugs. He didn't have time to dwell on it too much. He needed to stay focused. He looked to his left while Sophia kept watch on the right. He wanted to keep her spirits high, but was having a hard enough time trying to push the past out of his thoughts.

Eleven years had passed. Terrance Williams wouldn't be back here. This might be familiar but there was no way it was the same as when he was eighteen. Braydon was thinking of ghosts when he needed to be focusing on finding Lisa. She had written the lot down for a reason, most likely to meet someone. If they could find her or why she had potentially gone there, then they might be closer to finding Trixie and Amanda, as well. He was still having a hard time swallowing that each disappearance wasn't connected. Like he told Sophia, he didn't buy that they were all coincidences.

"Are there any houses or buildings back here?" Sophia asked.

"No."

"Why not? If it backs up to the bay, I'd imagine you could sell it for a good amount." She was nervous, trying to distract herself, but she was closing in on bad territory. He may not want to talk about it, but Braydon didn't want to lie to her, either.

"Marina is a very superstitious woman. There was an incident here a while back where a man died." He shrugged, hoping his composure stayed firm. "She bought the land from the previous owner because she didn't want someone to build near her house but she refuses to touch the lot. Afraid of spirits and the like." The man hadn't been a good one and that was why she wouldn't build. Braydon kept that detail out, however.

"Hmm…" She went back to searching her side and Braydon attempted to ignore the growing anxiety in his chest. In less than two miles they would pass the area where the incident that changed his life all those years ago had taken place.

If the dock was his personal hell, that spot in the Dolphin Lot field was his personal devil.

"Does anyone come out here usually?" Sophia asked after a minute or two had passed.

"The occasional fisherman but only if they clear it with Marina. She'll call us if someone drives out here that she doesn't know. Out-of-towners don't usually know about it."

"I'm just trying to figure out why Lisa would be out here. She isn't the most outdoorsy kind of woman. One time she—"

Sophia may have been the most interesting woman Braydon had met in a long time, but he stopped listening to her halfway through. He slowed the truck involuntarily. Last time he had been here he had been so young and so angry. Ready to do what needed to be done. Ready to end a life. Now, as they neared the area, he kept his eyes to the left.

That's when he saw it.

He stopped the truck and radioed Tom.

"I need you to get over here, now."

Sophia turned and saw it, too. She took in a breath. "That's Lisa's car!"

"Where are you?" Tom asked.

Braydon clenched his teeth. There was no way it was a coincidence that Lisa's car was *there*.

"Right where Terrance Williams died."

"STAY IN THE CAR, SOPHIA" is something Thatcher would have probably said had she not thrown open the truck door and taken off running toward the car. He hadn't even finished his conversation with Tom but she didn't care. After days of not knowing anything, she finally had an answer. Although, Sophia knew that whatever was in the car wouldn't be an answer she wanted.

There were really only two ways it could go: the car would be empty or the car wouldn't be empty. The second option terrified her to her very core. The bright smile of Lisa Hardwick danced across her vision. Somewhere in the back of her mind she realized she might never see it again.

Sophia pushed through the thigh-high grass. Her adrenaline had spiked and at each step closer her stomach knotted tighter. Thatcher was yelling behind her but she didn't care. She needed to see what was or wasn't in the little green car.

The moonlight made it hard to see the small details around the vehicle when Sophia reached her destination, but all of the doors were shut and the windows intact. She let out a shaky breath. The front seats were empty. Her eyes roamed to the backseat. Her heart dropped with shattering speed. Without thinking, she opened the door and was hit with a wave of stench. It made her stomach roll, but not as much as the body lying across the seats.

Sophia stumbled back just as Thatcher caught up to her. His presence did nothing to stop the scream that tore from her throat.

Chapter Six

"Oh, Sophia." Braydon pulled the woman into his arms, walking her backward farther away from the car. He didn't have to look into it to know there was a decaying body inside. He could smell it. "I'm sorry. I'm sorry."

"No!" she cried into his shirt.

"Sophia." He held her close, knowing her grief. Years had dulled his own but he would never forget the original pain, like a wound that never healed—a puckered red scar that only he could see.

"No!" she yelled again, fisting her hands into his shirt. He was prepared to stand there, holding her, trying to console her as best he could, until Tom came. Seeing her sister's body would spike her emotions and make her irrational. He didn't want her to go back and look again. "No. It isn't—it isn't Lisa."

"What?" he said. She looked up, tears streaking her face.

"The body. She has blond hair." He knew he shouldn't have felt the slight relief that filled him now. There was still a woman in there. That someone had a family—a Sophia who cared—and wouldn't see them again. There should be no relief for someone else's death. "Go," she said, taking a shaky step back. "I'm—I'm okay."

"Are you sure?" He titled her chin up so he could

look squarely into her eyes. They shone bright green beneath the tears. An overwhelming desire to protect this woman consumed him. He wouldn't leave her side unless he knew she was okay and even then… He shook his head to clear any thoughts of the future. Right now he had to deal with the grim present.

"Yeah," she answered.

He nodded and gave her arm one last squeeze. "Stay here while I take a look, okay?"

"No problem."

Braydon switched on his flashlight and moved over to the car. If driving down the road had been familiar, then walking up to the car was downright déjà vu. The car in the clearing, the body in the backseat, the blood splattered against the back windshield. Braydon was on autopilot as he swept the light across the body. His mind raced. His palms became slick with sweat. The details weren't just similar but almost exact.

He had seen this before.

The body on its back, the gun pressed against the temple, a hole through the head where the bullet had traveled… It was the scene of suicide and, even though this time it was a woman in the same position, all Braydon could see was Terrance Williams.

HE WATCHED AS Braydon Thatcher, golden boy of the Culpepper PD, walked up to the car. Before the new detective even shone his flashlight over the body, he could see the tension that lined the man's shoulders. Braydon wasn't stupid. He knew what he would find inside. The detective had enough reason to not believe in so many coincidences.

Just like he had planned, Braydon's face contorted into

terrifying realization when he saw poor Trixie Martin with a gun up to her head.

It all made him smile.

He put his beer bottle back into the built-in cup holder of his chair. There were empty bottles scattered at his feet from the previous days. Waiting for Braydon to find the car had been a true test of his patience. One he had been afraid he would fail if he'd had to wait any longer. He was extremely thankful for the dispatch he'd picked up ten minutes before. Without hearing that Braydon was on his way to Dolphin Lot, he would have missed the entire show.

That would have been a pity. If Braydon had never found the car, then all of this would have been for nothing. He had worked too hard for the setup to go unseen.

Braydon's movements became clipped and clumsy while his mind, no doubt, worked through what was in front of him. The part of the puzzle he was meant to understand was laid out and rotting in that car while the "who" was a short, yet unconfirmed list. Eventually the man would fill in the blanks, but right now he was trying to maintain a professional neutrality with the crime scene and the woman shaking behind him.

That woman. She must have been Lisa's little sister, Sophia. They shared the dark hair but varied in height and curves. Whereas Lisa was a long-legged conventional beauty, Sophia was small and, dare he think it, cute—like a child playing dress up in adult clothing. He couldn't see the tears that spilled down her face from this vantage point within the cover of the trees, but he knew she was crying—her body shook in the humid night air.

Even though finding Trixie's body had been the main interest, he found Braydon's attention kept moving toward the woman. How the detective looked at her, how he held her, how he tried to console her… He felt something for her. He cared. This was a new development.

He took another pull on his drink. A new addition to the plan was forming. Sophia Hardwick was about to be reunited with her sister, though not under the circumstances that she wanted.

The idea was a catalyst to the smile that stretched across his face. It was time Detective Thatcher suffered the way he had all those years ago. It was time to show him that not all was forgotten.

The thought of his brother only hardened his resolve. He finished his drink and grabbed his bag. Right now Braydon was going through emotional shock but when that dissolved and the cop part of him kicked in, he would get suspicious of his surroundings—he would start looking for the culprit. It would be a shame for the detective to see him now.

That time was quickly approaching. Trixie's body was the first domino. Now, all he had to do was introduce himself to the second Miss Hardwick.

It was time to show Braydon that his entire life could be undone as easily as Terrance's had.

Chapter Seven

Detective Langdon showed up shortly after, racing at the insistence of his partner. He jogged to the car from the road, passing Sophia who had taken a moment to get sick off to the side. He, too, understood that the positioning and circumstances of Trixie's death, everything, right down to the spot on Dolphin Lot, was mimicked. The way he kept cutting his eyes toward Braydon spoke volumes.

"Who is it?" Sophia called from a distance. Her voice reminded Braydon that he needed to get back to the present and do his job. He focused on the woman's face and hair.

It was the blue-eyed, blond-haired Trixie Martin. Missing woman number two. She wore a tank top, running shorts and tennis shoes. Apart from the gunshot wound, the rest of her body seemed unharmed.

"I'm going to go call this in and get some backup here," Tom said just low enough for Braydon to hear. "Do you want to take Sophia home?"

"No. I want to go over the scene." He paused, then lowered his voice. "It's just how I found him all those years ago. This can't be a coincidence. The crime scene wasn't public knowledge. At least, not all of the details. Only a few of us saw it and Trixie Martin was nowhere near involved in it." Tom didn't respond. He didn't need to. There were only a handful of people who could have copycatted the death of Terrance Williams with such detail. Braydon's jaw hardened and he shook himself. "But send a car over to take her home." Tom nodded and started to turn around. "And tell them to watch her house." He couldn't shake the growing feeling of unease within him.

"You got it, Partner."

Braydon took another look at the young woman in the car before retreating to Sophia's side. Her expression tore at his heart. She had stopped crying but the concern and fear radiated off her in waves. More than anything, he felt the need to hold her and tell her everything was going to be okay. He would figure it out, he would find Lisa and Amanda, and he would bring justice crashing down on whoever was doing this.

"Who is it?" she asked again.

"Trixie Martin," he answered. "It's Trixie Martin." Sophia sucked in a breath.

"And she killed herself? In my sister's car? But why?"

"Just because there's a gun to her head doesn't mean she's the one who pulled the trigger." He regretted it as soon as he said it. Sophia's eyes widened.

"You think she was killed?"

"We can't rule out the possibility yet." They stood there a moment, each caught in a web of dark thoughts. Dealing with a kidnapper was one thing. Dealing with a killer was another. "A cruiser is coming to take you back to Lisa's." She opened her mouth to complain but he kept on. "This isn't a discussion. If you want me to find your sister, you need to trust me. I have to do my job and this part will go faster with less people hanging around." He put his hand on her shoulder, hoping it provided some comfort. "I promised you I would find your sister and I will, okay?"

Sophia pursed her lips but nodded.

"And you'll call me as soon as you find something?" she asked.

"Of course." He dropped his hand from her shoulder. "I want you to call me or Tom if you need anything. Anything at all. Got it?"

She nodded again.

"And, Sophia? Do me a favor and lock the front door this time."

A CAVALRY OF PEOPLE showed up within the hour. The car and area around it had become a true crime scene buzzing with activity as everyone carried out specific jobs. Sophia was told to wait in the truck—away from all the action. She understood the delicacy that had to be taken with the body, fingerprints and any clues left behind, but that didn't stop her from feeling like an errant child told to go sit in time-out.

She wanted to help. Whether or not Trixie had killed herself or been killed, there were still two missing women out there and Sophia couldn't help but feel like time was running out.

She sighed—it almost felt painful. Her lack of patience was showing itself, though she doubted any normal person in her situation wouldn't be facing the same issues.

It was almost four in the morning by the time an officer came to collect Sophia. She wanted to stay and continue to watch Thatcher dissect the crime scene. The way he moved around it, the way his brow pulled together, the way his hands, now in gloves, moved across the surfaces of the scene, all had her enraptured. She had met men before who had taken their jobs seriously, but she had never seen Thatcher's kind of conviction in it. Then again, the men she was comparing him to had never had a dead body as part of their job description.

Officer Murphy, a man of few words, held the door open for her when she finally gave in—she couldn't deny the exhaustion that pushed against her body. Even an hour of sleep would be welcomed at this point.

Unlike the detectives or Officer Whitfield, the new cop was less than chatty on the ride to Lisa's. That was fine by her. They rode in silence for the fifteen-minute drive, giving her time to deal with the main reason she had broken down after seeing Trixie's body. If the second woman to go missing was already dead, then what chance did Lisa have?

It was a question that sliced through the hope she had been holding on to. The only reasons it hadn't completely disappeared was because of a tall man with dark hair and the most beautiful blue eyes. If anyone could find Lisa and Amanda, she had to believe it was Braydon Thatcher. Watching him work, his face set in unfailing concentration, Sophia knew he would keep his word. Or, at the very least, try with all that he had.

"This is it," Sophia told the officer as Lisa's house came into view. Instead of pulling into the driveway he parked in the road and opened the door. She threw him an inquisitive look.

"You stay here while I make sure the house is safe." He didn't give her any room to complain, a trait that most Culpepper cops seemed to have, and took her keys to go inside. He was out in less than five minutes with two thumbs up.

"Thanks," Sophia said, trying to keep her tone pleasant. Though her aggravation was tested at what he said next.

"Let me know if you need anything. I'll be out here in the car."

"You're staying?"

"Yes, ma'am."

"For how long?"

"Until I'm told to leave." He smiled and lifted his hands to stop her from responding. "Sorry, ma'am. Those are the orders."

Sophia didn't have the energy to protest. She thanked him for the ride and walked straight through the front door and didn't stop until she hit the bed. No guilt wound its way up as she sunk in between the loud, multicolored pillows.

For the first time in days no amount of worries could keep her awake.

SUNLIGHT FOUGHT ITS way through the blinds and lit the bedroom in a pleasant glow. When Sophia awoke she felt disoriented but oddly content. It was peaceful here. There were no car horns or sirens competing for airtime, just the buzz of the air conditioner and the soft hum of the ceiling fan. It was relaxing.

She rolled onto her back and stretched. Even though she had slept, there was still a blanket of exhaustion wrapped around her. The stress of everything didn't help. Sophia sat up and looked at her phone. It was barely nine on Friday, meaning she had slept for almost five hours. Guilt rose hot and fast at the realization. Were Lisa and Amanda able to sleep? Did their captor keep them awake, chained up to make sure they didn't escape? Were they even alive? She jumped out of bed, trying to erase the last thought. Feeling guilty wasn't going to help them.

Sophia took a quick shower to wake her up. The rest of the house may not have looked lived in but the bathroom was stocked with all the girly products she needed. Lisa had always been adamant about proper hair care.

When she finished she dressed in another pair of blue jeans, a gray T-shirt and tennis shoes. She didn't bother with makeup or working on her hair. Instead she flung it up into a ponytail, the ends dripping water onto the tile floor. However, she took a moment to spray some perfume on, unintentionally thinking of Thatcher as she did it.

He hadn't called or texted while she had been asleep. It concerned and annoyed her. Had they not found anything to use? Or had they found something that they didn't want to share with her?

The cop car was still sitting in front of the house. He *had* to know what was going on. She'd just have to get it out of him, a much easier task, she bet, if she had a peace offering. Though the pantry was almost empty, she spied a bag of blueberry muffin mix on the bottom shelf. The only ingredient they called for was water, taking twelve minutes to bake. Surely, the cop would be more willing to give her details while he munched on free breakfast.

Fifteen minutes later she was plating the delicious little confections when the doorbell rang. Her heart skipped a beat at the sound. She braced for bad news as she opened the door.

Sophia had never seen the man before. He was tall, fit and had a head full of dark red hair. He looked like the stereotypical Florida beach bum—a floral print button-down opened to show the white undershirt, navy swimming trunks, sandals and a pair of aviators over his eyes. He moved these up to the top of his head when the door opened, revealing eyes as black as coal.

"Hello," the man greeted, smiling wide. He outstretched his hand. "My name is Nathanial." On reflex she shook back. "You must be Lisa's sister, Sophia?"

"Correct..."

"I wanted to come by and give you this." He produced a handful of envelopes.

"What are these?"

"Lisa's mail from work. It was piling up and I knew some were payments for her services so I thought they'd be safer with you." She took them, looking over his shoulder at the stationary cop car as she did. Though she couldn't get a clear view of the officer's face, she could see his outline dutifully seated in the driver's seat. He must have known Nathanial to let him come up to the house.

"Thank you, I'm sure she'd appreciate it. Are you two friends?" Sophia's face heated slightly. She hadn't meant it to sound like that. She just didn't know much about the social circles Lisa had been running in the past year. Nathanial's name didn't sound familiar but, then again, neither had anyone else's minus Richard. "I'm sorry if that sounds rude, I just don't have the best memory when it comes to the names Lisa has told me."

"Oh, don't worry. We're more of acquaintances than friends. I work at Kincaid's Wood World next door to her office. We share a mailbox and I noticed her mail was piling up." His voice softened. "Have the cops made any headway?"

Sophia cocked her head to the side, confused. As far as she knew the general public had been left in the dark about the women's disappearances. Less panic meant more uninterrupted investigating. Nathanial caught on and explained before she could voice the question.

"This is a small town, Sophia. Word travels even when you don't want it to," he said with a sympathetic smile. She couldn't disagree with that.

"They may have found something this morning, so

we're hopeful about that." She decided gossiping to a stranger about Trixie's death wouldn't hurt anyone.

"I suppose all we can do is pray for the best." Sophia nodded. "Well, I'll leave you alone for now. Try not to worry too much, Sophia. It'll all work out in the end."

"Thank you, for these. *When* Lisa comes back I'll tell her you brought them."

Nathanial grinned. "That's the spirit."

She scanned each envelope to make sure there wasn't some kind of ransom letter or runaway note in the pile. Every piece had a return address. She dropped the mail on the counter, fully intending to sort through it later just in case. Privacy, be damned. She grabbed a plate of muffins for Officer Murphy. She would invite the officer inside if he told her what she wanted to know. If not, outside he would stay, she decided.

The Florida heat was back, making her regret the choice to wear jeans. The short walk across the yard to the cruiser was already activating her sweat glands. There was a forecast of potential rain later in the day, but that seemed like a long shot—there wasn't a cloud in the sky. For the past two days the only thing Culpepper seemed to revolve around was the shining sun, leaving sweat-inducing heat and hair-frizzing humidity. A drop in the temperature would be welcome at this point.

Officer Murphy had his head leaned back, eyes closed shut. She didn't blame him one bit. Watching a house would be boring to her, too, especially when operating on a lot less sleep. A part of her wanted to leave him be but a bigger part wanted some insider information.

"Officer Murphy?" Sophia knocked on the glass, the sound loud against the silence of the street. The man didn't budge. She knocked again. Nothing happened. He was really out cold, she thought with a smile. She won-

dered for a moment if she should give him some privacy
and let the man sleep a little longer, but a quick gauge
of her patience squashed that idea. She rapped against
the glass once more before putting her hand on the door
handle. "I'm going to open the door so please don't shoot
me," she said more to herself than him. It wasn't locked,
which she found odd. If you were trying to nap in a car,
wouldn't you lock it? Especially if said car housed guns
and the like? She pulled the door open wide and bent over
a little to look at the man. He seemed peaceful enough—
his face slack, head resting against the seat. "Officer
Murphy?" she said gently, yet loud enough to actually
wake him. The man remained as still as a statue. Sophia
took a breath and prayed the man wouldn't shoot her.
Being killed before Lisa was found just wasn't an option to her at this point. She moved a fraction closer and
prodded his shoulder.

What had seemed like such an easy task—give a
man some muffins in exchange for information—took
a frightening turn. Around the man's neck were ugly red
marks. Frozen, she looked at his chest, waiting for it to
rise and fall. However, the only movement within the car
was from her. Sophia's heart raced. With a shaky hand,
she placed her fingers against the man's neck.

The plate of muffins crashed against the asphalt.

"Oh, my God."

Officer Murphy was dead.

Chapter Eight

This time Sophia had no problem locking herself in the bedroom. In fact, she ran there already dialing Detective Thatcher's number. All the while fighting the bizarre urge to clean up the broken dish left against the curb.

"Officer Murphy is dead!" she practically yelled when the detective answered. "I think someone strangled him! There are red marks around his neck and he isn't breathing!" There was no hesitation in Thatcher's reaction.

"Sophia, I want you to go lock yourself in the—"

"I'm already locked in the bedroom!" she said, cutting him off. "Officer Murphy is still in his car out front. I—I didn't know what to do with him."

"I want you to stay where you are and don't let anyone in or come out until I get there, you got that?" She chalked up his lack of surprise to his profession that called for calm and order in extreme situations. He was all business now. Normally, his orders would have rubbed against her stubborn side but she found herself agreeing adamantly. "I don't want to hang up but I need to make some calls. I'll be there before you know it. Call me if anything else happens."

He disconnected, leaving Sophia with her back against the wall, staring at the door. Someone had to be either incredibly stupid or incredibly reckless to kill a cop.

Whoever had killed Officer Murphy wouldn't bat an eye at killing her. Once they did that, there was no going back.

"Two dead bodies in one day," she mumbled. "I hate this town. I really do."

Sophia couldn't describe the relief she felt when sometime later she heard footsteps against the hardwood, followed by Detective Thatcher's voice. Belatedly she realized that in her rush to feel safe she had managed to skip the very important step of locking the front door. In hindsight it was a mistake that could have ended horribly but now all she could do was be thankful Thatcher was there.

"Sophia?" he called through the house.

"In here!" She undid the lock and opened the door wide.

"Are you okay?" There was no mistaking the worry in his voice. His eyes pierced into her as he closed the space between them. For a moment she thought he was going to embrace her—to fold her into his arms—but something stopped him. He took a slight step back. She tried to ignore the sting of the movement.

"I'm okay, just shaken up," she said, letting out a long breath, trying to calm down. "Did you see Officer Murphy? Is he really, you know, dead?"

He hung his head, a mixture of sadness and anger written plainly across his face. "Yes. Tom is out there with him. I need you to tell me what happened."

"Well, I hadn't heard from you when I woke up. I saw that he was still out there and thought that maybe he might know something. I was going to give him some muffins to try and loosen him up." She paused. It sounded silly when she said it out loud. "I went out there and thought he was asleep, but he just wouldn't wake up. I saw the red marks around his neck, felt for a pulse and freaked out. That's when I called you."

"You didn't see anyone or hear anything strange?"

"No, I woke up around ten then jumped in the shower. The only person I even talked to—" Her eyes widened. She had talked to someone. "There was a man who came by to drop off some of Lisa's work mail." Thatcher's body tensed so visibly she almost stopped talking. "He said he works at Kincaid's. You know, the wood shop next door to Details."

"Did he give a name?"

"Yes. It was Nathanial."

Thatcher grabbed her arm, a little too roughly.

"What did he look like?"

Sophia described the man, showing height and width with her hands. It was the second time the detective had an odd reaction to a piece of news. When she was done, he let go of her and took a few steps back. He ran a hand through his hair, his eyes wild.

"Do you know him?" she asked.

He didn't answer her but instead opened his cell phone to dial a number. "I want you to pack a bag," he ordered, the phone ringing.

"What? Why?"

"You aren't staying here anymore."

"Where are we—" He put the phone to his ear to cut her off.

"Go pack," he said with such resolution that Sophia didn't have the nerve to question him any further. He walked off as the person on the other end of the line answered. "It's Nathanial," she heard him say. "It's Nathanial. He's here in Culpepper."

That didn't sound good.

It wasn't a hard task to pack in a hurry—most of her

things were still in her bag. Thatcher's urgency had also lit a large fire under her bottom. She shoveled in her toiletries, plus a few she borrowed from Lisa's stash, and paused to look around the room. Sadness lurched across her heart. The death of Officer Murphy had, in a way, tainted the warmth of the house. His death felt like an omen—a great foreshadowing—of what was to come, though, Sophia hoped and prayed that the killing would cease.

The front door opened and closed, breaking through the dismal cloud that had spread around her. Without thinking, she grabbed the picture frame from Lisa's nightstand and put it in her bag. It was an old Polaroid of them as kids—a reminder of their bond before childish arguments had frayed it. With one last look at the brightly colored room and its equally loud pillows, Sophia turned off the light and started to go outside.

"How are you holding up?" Detective Langdon asked as soon as she cleared the door.

"I'm okay." The man patted her on the shoulder with a sympathetic smile. All in all Tom seemed to be a pleasant man. "I'm sorry about Officer Murphy."

"Thank you," he said, though his smile faded. "He was a good man. He was a friend." The moment could have turned into another wave of sadness but Tom soldiered on. "Where's the mail that Nathanial gave you?"

"On the counter. I glanced through the pile but didn't open anything. I'm sure my fingerprints are all over them, too."

"That's fine." He started to walk off but Sophia wanted an answer.

"Detective, it was Nathanial who killed Officer Murphy, wasn't it?" she asked, though she had already jumped to that conclusion herself based on Thatcher's reaction.

Tom didn't hesitate.

"We believe so."

Fear pulsed through her again.

"Then why didn't he kill me when he had the chance?" If Officer Murphy was already dead when he gave her the mail, then there was nothing stopping him from doing what he pleased. Why had she been spared when the cop was not?

"That's what we're wondering, too," he replied.

"Oh," she said, unsure how to respond.

"But we're glad you're okay," Tom tacked on. It made her smile but the expression didn't last.

"Tom, who is Nathanial?" Like Thatcher, his whole body visibly tensed. He looked at her with sympathy when he answered.

"Let Braydon tell you."

Tom ended the conversation without another comment and went to collect the mail. Sophia, having nothing more to do, settled into the front seat of Thatcher's truck.

Thatcher.

Sophia realized she had been referring to Braydon by his last name while she had no problem calling his partner by his first. It wasn't that she disliked the detective, in fact, it was the opposite that kept her from saying his name she realized. Somehow calling him Braydon felt more intimate and that was a feeling she needed to distance herself from. Thatcher was the detective on her sister's case. That was a fact she needed to respect, no matter how much the man intrigued her.

Two more cop cars and an ambulance showed up before he joined her. The sidewalks were filling up with Pebblebrook residents. Soon the gossip mill would be turning full circle, at its core Sophia and the deceased officer. One of the cops kept yelling at the bystanders to back up, but it wasn't hard to see that there was a body in the cruiser. Braydon kept quiet as he navigated around the ambulance and out of Pebblebrook. Sophia had so many questions. She didn't know which to ask first.

"What the hell is going on?" That would have to do for now. The direct question didn't unlock his lips. He was stuck on a cycle of checking his rearview mirror, a look of concentration on his face. "You're scared of him, aren't you? Nathanial."

This got a reaction. He laughed. It was unkind.

"I'm not afraid of that man," he said, slowing down for a stop sign. He met her gaze for a moment. "But I am afraid of what he'll do."

"He seemed nice enough when we talked."

"He was lying to you," he snapped.

"How do you know?"

"Because Nathanial has never worked a day in his life at Kincaid's. He also hasn't lived in Culpepper for almost eleven years."

"So you *do* know him."

"Yes," he admitted.

"But how? Who is he?" Sophia was tired of all the unknowns from the past few days. She wanted certainty. She wanted answers.

"It's a long story." He stalled. "Just know he's a—"

"No, sir!" she interrupted, raising her voice. "I don't want this runaround you're giving me. My sister has been missing for almost six days, I've barely slept during three of those and in the span of less than twelve hours I have seen two dead bodies. I'm not stupid, Detective. I know that finding Trixie, the second woman to go missing, doesn't bode well for Lisa. I'm trying to find hope here. So when I ask a legitimate question, I don't need you to patronize me just because 'it's a long story.' *You* need to tell me what's going on, starting with this Nathanial person." She could feel herself blush as she said it, but she meant each word, along with the heated persistence behind her appeal.

A silence filled the cab. It sent a chill down her spine.

"You're right." Thatcher's voice had softened. Another quiet settled—a bloated hesitation that hid an elusive truth. "You deserve to know, but before I tell you who he is, I need to tell you why he hates me."

BRAYDON DIDN'T WANT to tell this story. Hell, he didn't even like *thinking* about it. He could keep her in the dark if he wanted to, but if Nathanial was back, then he needed to tell her. She was now involved and he needed Sophia to understand the lengths that the man had already gone to and would attempt to go to ensure Braydon's misery. He needed to warn her to keep her safe.

"I was a bad teenager," he began, looking straight ahead. "I drank and partied, acted recklessly, stole, did drugs, and had a short fuse and a big temper. I was eighteen and thought I was invincible and no one could tell me differently. My parents tried, though. They tried to reach the sensible side of me, show me the error of my ways, but I was just a selfish kid. I didn't care about them or anyone else, except for one person. Her name was Amelia. She was my sister." He smiled. It was involuntary—a normal gesture that happened when he thought of his sister before the incident. "You talk about smart and beautiful with a good heart, that was Amelia. Though her jokes were lame." He laughed as he said it, lost in the feeling of remembering. "She never seemed to be able to say the punch line right. One time she—" He stopped, remembering the purpose behind the story. It wasn't a time to reminisce. He cleared his throat and continued.

"Amelia could have had any guy she wanted but decided to date Terrance Williams. They were together all of junior year and seemed happy enough but one day Amelia came to my room and said she didn't feel the same way about him anymore. She asked what she should do. I told her to break up with him—to end it. It didn't make sense for her to be with him and be unhappy."

He hit the steering wheel so hard it made her jump. "If I could take back that advice, if I could go back to that moment, I would."

"What happened?" Sophia asked. It was a gentle prod to keep the story going but was also laced with true curiosity.

"She ended it, but a few days later said they were going to meet up at what used to be 'their' spot. Just to talk, she assured me. I let her go with a nod and some teasing. An hour went by and I got a panicked call from Nathanial, Terrance's older brother on break from college. He said his parents found a suicide letter that Terrance had written and their handgun was gone. I told him where they'd gone and jumped in the truck and raced off to the Bartlebees' dock. Or, at least it was then. Now it belongs to the Alcasters. The Bartlebees traveled a lot so the kids used to use their dock to hang out around," he explained as an aside, remembering Sophia didn't know the local history. "I don't remember getting there but I do know I didn't once hit the brakes. I had the worst feeling sliding around my stomach—the feeling that something horrible had happened. I was right. I found Amelia's body there, two bullets in her chest." Braydon stopped, struggling with reliving the emotions. They dredged up anger so potent he could taste it. Sophia put her hand on his knee. The touch was enough to rein in the building rage and finish the story. "I looked around but couldn't find Terrance.

That's when I noticed the tire tracks. He had gone back to Dolphin Lot. I followed, ready to kill the little bastard, but he had already done it for me. Found him parked in the field, dead in the backseat with a gun to his head."

"Oh, my God, just like Trixie," Sophia realized.

"Turns out Nathanial was a few minutes behind me the whole time. He saw his brother just as the cops came in."

"So, what…he killed Trixie and set her up like that to send you a message? To taunt you?"

"Nathanial publicly blamed me and Amelia for everything. He said I had told Amelia that Terrance wasn't good enough for her and that Amelia had poisoned Terrance's mind, playing with it until he snapped. It was a big relief when the Williamses decided to leave town. Up until today, as far as I knew they haven't been back since." He sent her a significant look. "Other than the cops and coroner, Nathanial and I were the only ones who saw Terrance that day."

"So when you saw Trixie like that, you knew," she said, hand still on his knee. Its warmth could be felt through the material of his jeans.

"I wasn't a hundred percent sure that it was Nathanial. Everyone in town knows the story and he could have told someone all of the gritty details. I mean, I even entertained the thought that maybe the kidnapper put it together to throw me off—to bring up the past to try and confuse me, but then Nathanial showed up. It's all intended to be personal, I'm sure of that."

"You think he took Lisa and Amanda, too?"

"Yes. It would be too much of a coincidence if he didn't." He cast a worried look at Sophia. She took her hand off of his knee and placed it on her lap. There she began to wring them together in small circles. Braydon was coming to find out it was her nervous twitch.

"But why Lisa, Trixie and Amanda? What's the connection between them? And why did he talk to me? Why didn't he kill me like the officer?"

"Nathanial is a complicated man. Always has been. As of right now, I have no idea why he chose to take those women, kill a cop, yet not try anything with you. Maybe it was convenient, maybe it was random… Either way, I'll find out. We still don't know his endgame. I can only assume he just wants to show me who he is right now."

That's what worried Braydon the most. Setting up Trixie's body like Terrance's then talking to Sophia and killing the officer outside, these were the actions of a man who wanted his presence known. Why? It almost ensured he didn't have any place to run, to hide. Letting Braydon know who he was had effectively ended the man's normal life.

Why? Why now?

Sophia remained quiet. It was Braydon's turn to try to comfort her. He took her intertwined hands in his. There was a new feeling of guilt as her smooth skin pressed against his. Getting too close to her hadn't been his plan but he couldn't deny it seemed to be happening. Sophia was a part of the investigation. It wasn't professional of him to entertain a closer relationship than cop and civilian. It could endanger the case or, even more, his career. Yet, as he felt her hands in his, he pushed that guilt and worry out of his mind. He wanted to help her, to be there for her.

"Nathanial has a plan he's working through. Lisa and Amanda are still out there. We'll find them."

Sophia gave him a weak smile. He hoped he hadn't just lied to her.

Chapter Nine

Braydon drove to the police station, reasoning it was the safest place for Sophia while he worked. He hadn't said it out loud, but he was sure she was Nathanial's newest target. However, why he had taken Lisa and Amanda he could only guess. The Nathanial he had known before the incident had been a smart guy. This Nathanial was completely foreign to him.

The station felt like a modern-day tomb as they walked inside. All officers, minus the two assigned to stay, had been dispatched to Dolphin Lot and Lisa's house. No one would be getting speeding tickets today. The only other person left was the part-time receptionist named Lynda Meyer. She met them at the door with a flurry of blond curls and Press-On nails.

"Is it true, Braydon?" she asked. "Is James really dead?"

He nodded and a cry erupted from her throat. She threw her arms around Braydon for what she hoped would be a bonding hug. Braydon returned it, albeit awkwardly, before she let go and noticed that he wasn't alone. Her eyes turned into slits as she finally acknowledged Sophia. The blonde had been the most territorial woman he had ever dated, even if they had only gone on a handful of dates two years ago. She had more jealous bones in her body than probably even she knew what to do with. Braydon reached back and took Sophia's hand, showing Lynda that she needed to watch herself.

"Lynda, if you see Nathanial Williams at all I want you to lock the doors, grab a gun and call me immediately," Braydon instructed.

"Nathanial Williams…" Her eyes widened. "Is he the one who killed James?"

Braydon didn't answer but instead led Sophia through the door to the main room. Even with everything going on, he took small pleasure in how perfectly her hand seemed to fit in his.

"The conference room has a couch in it. You'll probably be the most comfortable in there." He ushered her into the room. The couch he referred to was a worn, uncomfortable piece of furniture that gave more neck and back cricks than anything the Culpepper PD had to offer, but Braydon didn't want Sophia sitting in his office. He didn't think Nathanial was stupid enough to walk into the station with a gun or a bomb, but, on the off chance he did, at least Sophia wouldn't be in the one room the crazed man would immediately search. Plus, he had to remember that this was the same man who just strangled a cop to death. "I need to go make some calls and I'll be back. The break room is the next room over and the bathrooms are off the hall that leads to the lobby." He dropped her hand, though he realized he didn't want to let it go, the heat their touch had generated leaving as they parted. "Will you be okay?"

Sophia nodded.

"I need to tell Richard what's going on," she said. Braydon was still unhappy with the rich man giving a stranger the key to Lisa's house, knowing Sophia was staying there, but he had to admit that same stranger had given them a big clue.

"That's a good idea. See if he's found anything." Like they all knew would happen, Richard's attorney had cleared the man with relative ease. He had returned to his house on Loop Road as far as Braydon knew. Unless the stranger and Richard's usefulness took a turn for the worse, Braydon might as well let him do what he was going to do anyway.

"On it." She took out her cell phone and sat at the conference table. He hadn't noticed until now how petite she looked not dressed in her power suit and heels. It was deceiving to think she was fragile. He was learning that Sophia Hardwick was anything but. She had been through a lot more than most and yet her head remained level, her resolve unbreakable. It alarmed him how much he wanted to protect her, to see her happy and to reunite her with her sister.

If Nathanial harmed Sophia in any way, Braydon would kill him.

THE CLOCK ON the wall was broken. It ticked with an uneven rhythm while the second hand was frozen over the six. For the past hour Sophia had begun to despise the clock and the stream of time it was tasked to track.

Sophia felt a stab of guilt in her stomach. She had been so wrapped up in worry for her sister that she hadn't given much thought to Trixie Martin's death. According to Thatcher, this woman had chosen to live a life away from normal social interaction. If it hadn't been for her boss, Cal Green, she may not have been flagged as missing for quite some time. The thought created a pocket of misery within her chest.

Did she have family or friends who would mourn her?

Surely, her boss and coworkers would? Had they already been notified? Sophia closed her eyes, overtaken with sadness. She hadn't thought about any of these things until now. What did that say about her character? The image of Trixie's lifeless body flashed behind her eyelids. Sophia shuddered. Her eyes flew open.

What about Amanda? Did she care about the other missing woman? It was a horrible question to ask herself but she knew it needed confronting. She was so determined to find Lisa that her concern for Amanda had been minimal. It put ice in her blood to realize it. *I do care,* she thought. *I just want my sister back. She's all I have.* The guilt that stabbed at her cut deeper.

"Knock, knock." Officer Whitfield stood in the doorway, a cup in each hand. She offered one to Sophia. "It's not the best brew in town but it'll keep you awake."

"Thanks." She was grateful for the warmth. It soothed the troubling doubts surrounding her quality of character. "I managed to sleep for a few hours but I still feel tired. This definitely helps."

"Can I join you?" Cara asked.

"Of course. It *is* your conference room, but I'd love the company." It was something Sophia didn't often confess but in the moment it rang true. She was dancing dangerously close to self-loathing while she was by herself.

Cara took the seat opposite and sipped at her coffee. Her eyes were red and puffy. She had been crying.

"I know you probably don't want to, but can you tell me what happened to Officer Murphy?" She looked sheepish, yet determined. "I've heard the condensed version but I need to hear what happened from you." There was a desperation there, underlined in shed tears and visible heartbreak. Officer Murphy had clearly meant something to her.

"Sure, I don't mind."

Sophia recounted everything that had happened from the time she began to bake to Nathanial's appearance to feeling for a pulse on Officer Murphy's neck to running inside. What Thatcher had told her about Nathanial on the car ride to the station only reinforced her past reasoning to flee the scene. Though, when she said it aloud, she felt that self-loathing again.

Cara was quiet when Sophia finished. She stared down into her coffee, a deep frown etched in her dark skin. Sophia wanted to comfort the woman but what could she say that would ease her sorrow? Officer Murphy had been found dead less than two hours ago. There was nothing she could say to Cara that could heal the pain. She instead gave her the silence she needed to sort through her thoughts. The clock ticked unevenly in the background.

"James was a good man," Cara finally said, her eyes beginning to water. "He was a damn good man." Sophia grabbed her purse and pulled out a pack of tissues. Cara didn't seem like the kind of woman who would appreciate being consoled with hugs and soft coos. She was like Sophia in that regard. Sometimes a person had to mourn alone for a while before she could mourn with others.

Sophia slid the pack across the table. Cara didn't look up as she took one and blotted at her eyes.

"He had a kid, you know?" A deep waver shook her voice as she spoke. "He's in fourth grade. James always was bragging on him, showing off his soccer trophies and honor roll ribbons. It got annoying after a while." She laughed. It was laced with tears. Grabbing another tissue, she wound it in between her hands.

"You two were close?" Sophia asked. She hoped it wasn't too much of an intrusion but the way Cara spoke seemed to tell two different stories. The cop nodded.

"When I first transferred here five years ago, I was the only female cop. Not saying that it was anyone here's fault, it's just that no woman had ever applied before. Most of the cops here now are good people but there are a few I could do without." She gave a weak smile. "When I first came in there were a few that didn't like that I was here. It didn't help that I was black, either. One night after my shift, I went home to find my house had been trashed. Windows broken, horrible things spray painted on the walls, my flower beds destroyed, and I won't even tell you what I found in the mailbox."

"That's horrible!" Sophia exclaimed. The woman waved off the concern.

"It's okay now, but back then I was devastated. It was clear that the people who did it wanted me gone but I didn't have enough money to leave. I also didn't have enough money to pay someone to help me repair everything. I remember sitting on my porch just crying my eyes out when a truck pulled up."

"James," Sophia guessed.

"Yeah. He got out and without saying anything he just started pulling out buckets, sponges, garbage bags and almost everything I needed to fix the house. When I told him I couldn't accept all that he had bought, he just smiled and told me I'd owe him one day. He came over after every shift and helped me repair everything. He wasn't the only one, Tom, Braydon and a few others helped, too, but it all started with James." She smiled. "We became close friends throughout the years."

There it was again, that feeling that the cop was leaving something unsaid. Sophia didn't question her this time. She didn't have to ask to understand that Cara had loved James. Had he realized? Did he love her, too? If

Sophia wanted to know, she was sure Cara wanted those answers with every fiber of her being.

She looked up to meet Sophia's gaze. There were tears and fire swirling in those brown eyes. "We'll find him, Sophia. We'll find Nathanial and make him pay for everything he's done. Braydon will see to that, especially since—" The cop caught herself. "There's history there," she amended, trying to keep Braydon's past personal.

"Braydon told me on the way here." There was no mistaking the surprise that jumped into the officer's eyes. She tried to hide it by blowing her nose again. Sophia took it that Braydon didn't often talk about his sister's murder. Not that she blamed him. If Lisa was killed, how would she handle it? That would be a bridge she would cross if the time came.

"I'm sorry about James," Sophia said, shaking herself. She had to keep hope that Lisa was still alive. That Nathanial was a man of theatrics with an unknown, devious plan and Lisa's turn in the spotlight hadn't yet come.

Cara wiped at a few tears that had escaped, then blew out a shaky breath. "Thank you." They fell into a silence that stretched between them, lost in their own thoughts, but connected by a common enemy. Nathanial could blame a lot of emotional trauma on the death of his little brother, of finding him in a field with a gun to his head, but he would never be able to justify the lives he had taken since.

Cara excused herself to the restroom, leaving Sophia alone once again with the unforgiving clock. After a few minutes of its broken ticking, she pulled out her phone and, for the first time in days, checked her email. Nothing new but advertisements and newsletters she had signed up for then promptly forgotten about. There were no messages from her boss, which made her nervous, though in comparison to everything that had happened so far it was almost silly to worry about job security. He'd given her "as much time as you need." She would have to take his word that her position as office manager would be waiting for her when all of this was over.

Thatcher won't be. She blushed at the unexpected thought. *He won't be waiting there for you. He'll be here.* The blush only seemed to deepen as the detective chose that moment to enter the room. The worry across his face hadn't ceased to exist—it was a constant mask he wore each time she saw him.

"I need your help." He handed her a large Ziploc bag with a thick, spiral notebook inside.

"This is Lisa's!" she cried, recognizing the blue book that rested inside. She'd given it to Lisa when she had started her business. It was jam-packed with sticky notes, magazine clippings, and had enough dog-eared pages to make a librarian cringe in disgust.

"We found this under the passenger seat of her car. I need you to look through it to see if you can find any information about who contacted her about going to Dolphin Lot and why. Also look to see if you can find a time that she went there. I would look through it myself but I figure you know her best and have a better chance of catching something I could miss. Plus, we're being stretched thin at the moment. We need all the help we can get." He ran a hand through his messy hair, only making it messier. She wondered briefly what it would feel like to run her hands through it. Would it be soft? Would it be coarse? If she pulled her hand away from it, would the smell of his shampoo linger across her fingertips? "We know *who* took them but we still need to figure out where. Maybe we can answer that by figuring out what happened at the beginning."

SOPHIA HAD FORGOTTEN how much of a scatterbrain her sister was until she was wrist-deep in the notebook. It seemed every idea she had ever produced had been transferred into the small pages in the form of sloppy notes, picture cutouts and the occasional doodle. Not only was the notebook filled with the aftermath of an ADD bomb, but it was also hard to navigate. For the first fifty pages or so, the notes were in chronological order. After that, as far as Sophia could tell, her brain had seemed to skip around, writing whatever she needed to in any space she could find. It was like looking into the mind of a hyper child. Sophia downed her coffee while trying to find reason within the chaos.

Thatcher had taken root at a desk closest to the conference room door, trying to figure out what Nathanial had been up to since he left Culpepper all those years ago. Cara had been ordered to go through all complaints filed in the past month from anyone and everyone in the hopes of finding one that involved Nathanial. Braydon believed that the man had been in town a lot longer than the past week. The crime scene on Dolphin Lot had been dissected and was still being processed, while a K-9 unit was searching the immediate area.

Sophia didn't know where Detective Langdon and the rest of the officers were at this point but she did know that Richard was at Lisa's house. When she had called him from the police station to update him on the situation he had already known what was going on.

"I'm well connected, Sophia. There's not much that goes on in this town that I don't know about." He had grown quiet for a moment. He didn't know where Lisa was, but she knew she didn't need to point that out. Braydon had come in then and spoken with the local tycoon. Richard had offered to stay in Lisa's house just in case

Nathanial decided to come back. He reasoned that the cops needed to be out in the streets looking for the madman instead of watching a house.

"Plus, I own several guns," he'd said.

When Braydon asked about the man with the missing tooth and his current whereabouts, Richard had admitted that the man had left town saying kidnappers he could deal with but killers was where he drew the line. Sophia guessed everyone, even those who tangoed with the line between legal and illegal dealings, had a limit and that had been his, though she was disappointed that there was one less person looking for the women. So there she sat, going through Lisa's almost hieroglyphic handwriting, trying to find a missing piece to the puzzle of what had happened Sunday.

"Any luck?" Cara asked after another chunk of time had slipped by. She had brewed a second pot of coffee and refilled Sophia's cup without asking. A gesture Sophia was grateful to receive.

"I can tell you what Lisa had for breakfast two weeks ago, I can tell you about the nightmare about clowns she had in April, I can tell you about the color scheme she's been playing with for a new marketing plan, I can tell you what kind of wedding dress she wants, and I can tell you, with certainty, that she hates counting calories." Sophia blew out a frustrated sigh. "But what I can't tell you is why she wrote down 'Dolphin Lot.' Why a twenty-nine-year-old woman can't seem to write in coherent sentences is beyond me." Cara reached over and patted the top of her hand. "What about you? Anything?"

She shook her head. "All the complaints filed have been small ones." She picked up the piece of paper closest to her. "Mrs. Miller called last week about the neighbor's dogs barking. A week before that it was Mike Anderson fussing about a rusty car that was parked outside of the Realtor's office." She lowered her voice. "He's a real stickler about keeping up good appearances." She put the paper down and took a gulp of coffee. "Other than that, there's not much in here, but I'll keep looking."

Sophia decided to take the break in work to ask something that had been in the back of her mind.

"Why are you being so nice to me?" she asked the officer without any relevant conversational segue.

"What do you mean?"

"Well, I understand being professionally polite but you seem to…I don't know…" She paused looking for wording that didn't make her sound rude. "You just have been genuinely nice to me and you don't even know me."

Cara didn't smile at first, which made Sophia afraid she'd offended her, but after a moment the officer's lips pulled up into a grin.

"You know that saying, 'Be kind, for everyone you meet is fighting a harder battle'? Well, I'd say you're in the middle of one of those." Her smile fell. "Plus, we're all in this together now."

The two women jumped back into their jobs, each digging for some kind of clue. Sophia looked up every so often to see Thatcher answering calls, pacing back and forth, talking to Tom and the captain who was now heading the Dolphin Lot investigation. When the phone calls were through he would sit back down at the computer, his fingers clicking away at the keys. It wasn't until three-thirty rolled around that he rose from his chair and came into the conference room.

"I think I know why Nathanial came back," he announced, leaning against the table. That grabbed Sophia's and Cara's attention. They looked at him expectantly. "I found a local news story from a paper in Arlington,

Texas, where a Lucille Williams overdosed on pills two months ago."

"Lucille Williams?"

"That's his mother. Apparently Dave Williams passed away five years ago, though I couldn't find the cause." He rubbed his eyes. It was the first time she noticed the matching baggage that hung beneath each.

"So, his mother supposedly kills herself and he snaps?" Sophia said.

"He wants someone to blame and picks the person he already holds responsible for his brother's death," Thatcher finished.

"Terrance kills himself and then his possibly still-grieving mother goes the same route. Two suicides in one family… That has to be hard," Sophia said.

"Tragedy isn't a free pass to do whatever you want, though," he added.

"True. Have you been able to track him? Do you know what he's been doing since her death?"

He shook his head. "That's the kicker. The last trace of him I could find was two years after he left Culpepper. He finished up his undergrad then disappeared. The only mention of him since then was the article about Lucille and it was just one line saying she was survived by her oldest son." He turned to Cara, sliding her a Post-it with a number and a name written down. "I need to run to the hospital to talk to the medical examiner about Trixie. That's the number of the newspaper that covered Lucille's death. I want you to talk to that reporter and find out if he knows anything about Nathanial." She nodded and left the room. Thatcher faced Sophia. His eyes softened, those pools of blue putting her at an ease she shouldn't have been able to obtain in this situation. "Stay here and keep working through that. If anything happens or you find anything—"

"I'll call you immediately," she finished with a smile. "I've proven that it's my first reaction anyway."

It was his turn to smile, though it only lasted an instant. "Be safe." With that, he was gone.

Chapter Ten

The Culpepper medical examiner confirmed what Braydon had already known—Trixie hadn't killed herself. In fact, like Officer Murphy, she had been strangled to death. The shot through her head had been postmortem, staged to get Braydon's attention and keep it.

"She was dehydrated but not starved. There's also no sign of sexual assault." She moved the sheet aside and brought Trixie's hand up to show him something.

"What am I looking at?" he asked, stepping closer.

"Nothing," she said.

He tilted his head. "I don't understand."

"That's the point," she said. "There is no dirt or cuts, no skin or blood under her fingernails."

"She didn't fight back," he filled in.

"I don't think she did, no." She put the woman's hand back down. "Did you know her, Detective?"

"I might have seen her once or twice at Green's but beyond that, no I didn't."

"I didn't know her all that well, either, but I did know she was an avid runner. I would see her running past my house occasionally. Her health before her death was impeccable—her muscles were strong."

"Then why didn't she fight back?" he questioned aloud. The ME snapped her fingers.

"That's what I wondered, too." She walked to the head of the table and uncovered Trixie's head. Braydon tried not to look too closely at her face, remembering the way Amelia looked when he had found her. She pointed to a red bump on the woman's neck.

"A mosquito bite?" It was a normal occurrence in the South. The little bloodsuckers fed off of the masses like a plague. "At first, that's what I thought, but I think it's an injection site."

Braydon's brow furrowed. He leaned closer to inspect it.

"You think he drugged her? With what? A tranquilizer?"

"I don't know yet but I sent the blood work out a few hours ago. I should hear something back by tonight," she said. "When I do, you'll be the first I call."

"Thanks." He stood straight, ready to leave when the ME sighed.

"It's sad, really. I saw her just last week running her little heart out."

Braydon nodded in sympathy when a thought occurred to him. "If you don't mind me asking, where do you live?"

"Sophia!" Cara yelled from outside the conference room. The sudden sound made her jump. She wasted no time in rushing out of the room.

"What? Are you okay?" She expected to see Nathanial standing in the room, ready to exact his wrongful revenge, but she was met with a giant smile from the female cop.

"He changed his name!" she exclaimed before turning to the computer.

"What?"

"I finally got a hold of the reporter who wrote that

story," she said, beginning to type. "I asked if he knew Nathanial. At first he said no but then he told me that he was threatened by the son to not include his name in the article. So, I asked what *that* son's name was. You're never going to guess what he said." She hit Enter and a list of search results showed up in the browser. Sophia came closer and gasped.

"Terrance."

"Yep. He took the name of his deceased little brother." Cara whistled. "That's a special kind of creepy right there."

Sophia had to agree. She looked at the list of articles. The fourth from the top was an article congratulating those awarded a Founder's Scholarship almost eight years ago. Sophia took the mouse and clicked the link. The article popped up along with a picture of a group of college students. Among them stood the younger Nathanial but in the picture credit it said "Terrance Williams."

"It's almost brilliant if you think about it," Cara said. "That's the one name we wouldn't have searched."

"Thatcher especially," Sophia agreed. It was an entirely different level of crazy. They took a moment to read the article. Due to his high test scores and grades he was being awarded a scholarship that would help pay for the pharmaceutical engineering program he had just entered in New Jersey. The man may have had a few screws loose, but Thatcher had been right—he was smart. This fact did not help ease her worry.

Cara clicked out of the article and to the next one. "But at least now we have a name to search."

Sophia went back to the little blue book while Cara went to work putting together as much information on Nathanial/Terrance she could find. She flipped through the pages again, having already looked at each one. Her mind began to wander, despite her determination.

They were working under the assumption that Nathanial had snapped after his mother's death, but what if he had been crazy all along? Sure, it wasn't unheard of to name a child after a loved one, but to rename yourself? And only two years after the death? That kind of mind frame wasn't a stable one.

It made her wonder if he had changed his name as a misguided sentimental gesture or if it had been a part of a plan to drop off the grid—to hide from the eyes of cops almost nine years later. Was Nathanial's grudge that powerful or had it just worked out for him in the end?

She sighed. Her coffee was wearing off. The lack of caffeine wasn't helping the questions that buzzed around in her head like hundreds of angry bees. She took the pen she had been chewing on and started to doodle what they might look like. First, a big circle head with long hair and a stick body; second, the round insects with stingers and wings; third—

She stopped, remembering something she had seen in the middle of the notebook. Her heartbeat sped up as she flipped through pages. After a minute she found what she was looking for—Lisa had drawn a picture the size of a dime.

It was a dolphin.

Chapter Eleven

Lisa had always been horrible at Pictionary. Her drawing skills were less than desirable. Sophia had refused to be on her team whenever they were asked to play. It wasn't like she was much better, but Lisa couldn't draw any semblance of a circle and she even managed to mutilate stick figures. However, right then, Sophia could have kissed her sister's cheek.

The dolphin Lisa had drawn wasn't half-bad. Sure the fin was bumpy and the tail was crooked, but she was able to recognize it for what it was—an ugly, yet informative dolphin.

On top of the dolphin's head was a cone with wavy lines coming out the top. Sophia couldn't figure out what it was at first until she took another look at the dolphin's deformed tongue. It was a party hat, the tongue an uncoiled party horn that the dolphin was blowing out. Lisa had drawn one more addition to the festive creature— the number 630 on the edge of its fin, no doubt put there to look like it had a tattoo.

Lisa hadn't written out the message. She had drawn it.

She had gone to the Dolphin Lot at six-thirty in the morning to talk about a party.

It was her turn to yell out that she'd found a clue, just

as it was Cara's turn to jump in her chair. She showed the cop the drawing and watched as its meaning sunk in.

"Don't ask me why she couldn't have just written it out," Sophia said. "Just be thankful her drawing skills won this battle."

Sophia grabbed her cell phone and dialed Thatcher. She didn't know how the information would help but she was glad to announce she had found a clue. It brought her a sense of purpose, a sense of usefulness. She was helping find her sister, not just sitting on the sidelines wrapped up in self-pity.

"You okay?" he answered, worry thick in his voice. It made her blush, something she seemed to do a lot when involved with a certain detective.

"Yeah, I found something. Well, we both did. Can you talk?"

"Shoot."

Sophia told him about the dolphin and then about Nathanial's name change. Cara had already texted him about it but had compiled more information since. She handed over the phone and listened as the woman listed the highlights of "Terrance" Williams's past eleven years.

After Nathanial had left Culpepper, he went to finish the last two years of his bachelor's degree in chemical engineering. The name change came soon after and as Terrance he was accepted into a pharmaceutical engineering master's program in New Jersey. Two more years went by before he graduated with flying colors. Even as Terrance he disappeared for three years before showing up in a collegiate newspaper article as a source from a government research company called Microne, located in Texas. They specialized in running a national research lab, testing drugs created to target behavioral and mental disorders.

Sophia shook her head at that. It was like the pot calling the kettle black in a way. He was in charge of finding the right drug to help people who weren't stable. She had to wonder again if that had been the whole reason he had entered the field—to find something to water down his own crazy or if it was just a coincidence.

He showed up one last time before he was mentioned in his mother's overdose article. It was in a quarterly science publication less than a year ago. He had written a few paragraphs on his thoughts about sleeping disorders, but Cara admitted the words had been too big and she didn't understand any of what he'd said.

The cop quieted as Thatcher commented on the new information. Sophia felt like a child, suddenly annoyed that she wasn't in on the conversation. She had found a clue and now she wanted what? A pat on the head? A kiss from the detective? *I wouldn't mind that,* she thought with a quick smile. Cara passed the phone back, unaware of the odd grin, and began a new search in the browser.

"I'm on the way to Dolphin Lot right now," he started.

"Did the K-9 unit find something?" Hope and fear welled up inside. Hope that it was an even better clue to finding her sister, and fear that what they found *was* her sister.

"It looks like Nathanial had been camping out in the trees near Lisa's car."

"Why?" she asked, though didn't expect a completely sane answer at this point. The more she found out about Nathanial, the more unbalanced he seemed to be.

"My guess?" His voice stiffened. "He was waiting for me to find Trixie's body."

"That's starting to sound just like him," she admitted, feeling uneasy. "Do you think he was there when we found her?" There was a pause in which she imagined he shrugged.

"I don't know, but I'm hoping we can use whatever we find to track his location now. I'll give you a call if we find anything."

"Okay, be safe." It slipped out before she could stop it, but she truly meant it.

"You, too."

THE HEAT MIGHT have been bearable but the humidity was an altogether different story. It surrounded the men like invisible coffins—confining and inescapable. Braydon felt as though he was suffocating as he wove through the trees, following a cop from the county over. He didn't envy any of the officers' dark uniforms.

Captain Westin stood in a small clearing, looking like the only cop in Culpepper who wasn't sweating. A task Braydon attributed to the man's khaki shorts and white T-shirt. His badge hung on his belt and there was a cigarette lining his mouth. He looked like a regular Joe simply stopping in the woods for a smoke break.

"Captain," Braydon greeted. He had barely seen the man since Sophia had arrived. Westin grunted an acknowledgment and motioned to the scene around them.

There was a camping chair set up in the middle of the clearing. It was positioned so it faced out with a view unobstructed by trees, yet far enough away that it would be hard to make out a figure from where Lisa's car had been. A person would have to know exactly where to look and know what they were looking at to be able to see a man sitting there. Next to the chair sat a medium-size red cooler with its lid open. There was one unopened beer submerged in water. Empty beer bottles littered the area around both the chair and the clearing. Some were broken, lying at the base of a few trees.

"I'm guessin' he got bored waiting and did some target practice," the captain said, throwing an invisible bottle at the tree to their left.

"I'm just sorry it took me so long to find the car…and Trixie. He shouldn't have had time to get bored." The captain turned and clamped Braydon on his shoulder. The older man hadn't meant his comment to sound accusatory but Braydon still felt it. "The beer is local," he noted, looking at the Florida orange on the label. Only one place in town even sold it. He looked at the captain, comprehension dawning.

"Yep. I sent Tom out to get the security tapes from Tipsy's. I guess that's how he met Amanda Alcaster. Must have struck up a conversation with her while she was working behind the counter."

Braydon was getting ready to leave, blood pumping faster. He had finally gotten a break. "I'll go help him look through the footage."

"Not so fast, Thatcher." Braydon stopped in his tracks. "Sir?"

The captain took a drag of his cigarette and blew out a long stream of smoke.

"When's the last time you slept?" The question caught him off guard. His first reaction was to lie, knowing what would happen if he told the truth.

"Yesterday," he said. Westin gave him a look that said he knew that wasn't true.

"I want you to head home for a few hours and get some sleep. Tom and the rest of us can handle things in the meantime."

"But, Captain—"

"That's an order," he said sternly. "Just because Nathanial may want to play mind games with you, doesn't mean you're the only one who can take him down. This isn't a movie, son. Go get some sleep before you're useless to us."

Braydon knew better than to fight the issue with the captain. He also knew better than to attempt to sneak behind the man's back and continue working. On the way to his truck he called Tom and threatened that if he didn't keep him updated he would tell the entire force about Tom's want for Lynda. Once that can of worms was opened, there was no going back. His partner groaned but agreed to keep him in the loop.

The next call he made was to Sophia. He'd only known her for two days but it felt so natural to hear her voice.

"Do you want to sleep with me?" he asked after she answered the phone. He immediately slapped his forehead. Maybe he was more exhausted than he thought. "I mean, I'm being sent home to get a few hours of shuteye and I figured you might want a place to crash, too."

There was a small delay before she answered. He knew she was going to do what he wanted to and complain that she didn't need sleep.

"We found a lead in the clearing. It'll take a little bit to sort through but Tom and the captain are on it. They promised to let me know as soon as they have anything." He could still feel her hesitation. "If we don't get some sleep we're useless, Sophia. They are good, smart men. They'll more than make up for our absences for a few hours." He had basically regurgitated what he had just been told but, he had to admit, it was reasonable. Sophia relented.

"I'll be there to get you in fifteen minutes."

They hung up and Braydon was left in the silence of the cab. It had been one hell of a week. He could feel it in his bones. He resisted the urge to check the mirror to see how many gray hairs had sprouted since he learned that Lisa, Amanda and Trixie had gone missing. It seemed like years had passed since Tom had joked about the job of detective being boring. Now Braydon wished he could claim such a thing.

Never would he have thought the young man he had known so little of in his youth would turn out to be a psychotic killer—an apparently *brilliant* psychotic killer. He imagined himself as a comic book character, constantly trying to battle evil while Nathanial was his nemesis whose life's mission was to ensure the destruction of the hero. Not that Braydon thought he was the hero. He was just a man with a new job, people counting on him and a madman to stop. Like the captain said, just because Nathanial had focused his sights on Braydon didn't mean they were alone on the playing field.

The detective's thoughts slid over to the glossy-haired, green-eyed, feisty Sophia Hardwick. She was a bomb in a sexy, stubborn shell. Most of the women he knew would have stayed at home and let the cops deal with the investigation or, if they wanted to help, they would stop at the word *no*. Not Sophia. In a way she reminded him of his sister, Amelia. When she had her mind set on something she went for it full tilt, not once stopping to question herself. Braydon's mother, while in a cloud of grief, had said that it was that specific quality that had been Amelia's undoing, but he had disagreed and he still did now. Her undoing had been a seventeen-year-old, mentally unstable boy and the handgun his parents kept around for safety.

Wondering about Terrance's sanity led him to the subject of Nathanial's. What Officer Whitfield had found was yet another reason to be extremely worried about the man's stability. Every time they learned something new about Nathanial, Braydon's concern for the safety of Lisa, Amanda and Sophia intensified.

He ran a hand down his face as he pulled up to the station. He may not have killed Trixie or James with his bare hands, but he was the reason they were dead. The kidnappings, too, were just Nathanial's scheme to punish his mortal enemy. If anything happened to Sophia… He punched the steering wheel.

He wasn't going to let anything happen.

Chapter Twelve

Braydon lived in a small, traditional two-bedroom, one-bathroom house in the middle of Gothic Street. Though the name inspired dark images, most of the houses sported a variation of tan, beige, yellow and orange siding. His was a rich cream color with a blue front door and a large wooden front porch. That front space had sealed the deal the moment he saw the house.

The house at 2416 Gothic Street was the first and only property Braydon had ever purchased alone. It might not have been the biggest house but it had hardwoods throughout, nice butcher-block counters, and a backyard that was big enough for a Great Dane. He was proud to call it home, and he couldn't deny it felt good to see it. Inside he pictured his king-size bed that barely fit the room, the tall shower that he no doubt needed after such a humid day and the refrigerator that was full of food. He sighed. The last time he had been grocery shopping was the week before; aside from a bag of chips and canned vegetables, the food selection was slim.

"This is nice," Sophia said as the truck came to a stop in the driveway. "I like the porch." Braydon smiled a genuine smile.

When they got inside he gave her the grand tour, which wasn't much. The front door started a hallway that led to the back door and screened-in porch, splitting the living room to the right and the kitchen to the left. Behind the kitchen was the bedroom that stood opposite the bathroom and guest room that doubled as his office. She was politely interested as he pointed out each room and once she even complimented his taste. He knew it was her reaching for a generic compliment—his decor was wood on wood on wood with two leather couches thrown in. He was what some people would refer to as "married to the job." When he had time off, he had higher priorities than decorating.

"Make yourself at home," he said, walking to the kitchen. He opened the refrigerator to confirm its near emptiness. Sophia peeked around his side.

"Looks like you don't cook much," she said. "I guess you go out a lot?" It sounded like an innocent question but Braydon had a feeling it was pointed. Sophia wasn't meeting his gaze. He realized with a smile that, while he knew she was romantically unattached, the subject of his dating life hadn't been discussed in detail. All she knew was that he wasn't married.

"I admit, I'm a big fan of takeout." He shut the door. "Looks like it's time to order some now."

"Hold that thought." Sophia walked to the open pantry and picked up the bread. She checked the expiration date, nodded when it was okay and went back to the refrigerator, taking out the lone pack of cheese. When she made sure it was good to eat, too, she held up both in victory. "How do you feel about grilled cheese sandwiches?"

"Marry me," he said, taking the hand that held the cheese. It was supposed to be a humorous gesture but as soon as their skin touched, he knew neither of them were thinking about sandwiches. The kitchen became heated. It felt exceedingly smaller and much more quiet than it was seconds before the contact. Her hand, soft and warm, was cradled in his own large, slightly calloused hands. They fit together like two puzzle pieces. Braydon looked down at them, convinced the warmth he felt was a moving, tangible entity.

Sophia returned the gaze, her head tilted up a few breaths away from his lips. He could do it. He could kiss her, let her know that what he felt for her had changed and was still changing. Her sage-green eyes were wide yet soft.

"So I take it you like grilled cheese?" There was an undercurrent to her question. He didn't let go of her hand.

"It's grown on me," he answered, wondering if they were even talking about sandwiches anymore.

A small smile started to form across her red lips. Braydon wondered if the color was lipstick or natural. He wondered what they felt like, too.

Why not find out?

Sophia held the bread and cheese as if they were life preservers and she was a drowning swimmer. Which wasn't too far off in her mind. This was uncharted territory she was sailing. The desire she felt for the detective had seemingly come out of nowhere. True, it had been two days since she had met the man, but that still didn't discount the way she felt.

On the outside it must have looked odd—the two of them standing there, her hand and cheese clasped in his, but she didn't care. She was mesmerized. Raising her chin a fraction, she was able to get a better view of those calming aquamarine eyes. Something inside her ached as he searched her face. She wondered distractedly what it was. She decided that it didn't matter. Her feelings were turning out to be just as mysterious. She definitely couldn't ignore them, either. There was the possibility that their chemistry was a result of their heightened emotional states and desperation to find the missing women. However, there was also the chance that Braydon Thatcher could be the answer to a question her heart needed to know, and, if he wasn't, she could at least give the man a trial run.

Sophia had spent the better part of the past four years trying to climb the career ladder through Jones Office Supply, starting as low as an unpaid intern. She had liked the stability the job had offered and her focus had been on building a financial foundation and not much else. She had been friendly and had socialized regularly, but nothing had seemed to stick. Acquaintances became friends but not close ones. Once she fell into the sad loop of leaving work to go home to an empty apartment, it was hard to break. She hadn't purposely secluded herself, she had just worked long, unnecessary hours in an attempt to get that heavenly raise or the ever-elusive promotion. It hadn't bothered her then, but being with Thatcher, smelling his cologne, feeling the heat radiate off his skin, imagining what his body felt like against hers, she realized there was a hole inside her. It had been empty for years.

Overcome with a longing that raced from the top of her head to the tips of her toes, Sophia pushed up on her heels and kissed the detective full on the lips. She believed she was a proactive sort of woman—if she wanted something she went for it—but kissing Braydon Thatcher had been impulsive and an action she hadn't intended to take when they first entered the kitchen.

At first it was just Sophia's lips pressing hungrily against his, marveling at the rough skin. Then, after a moment, he returned the kiss with a slow deliberation.

Sophia felt a thrill of pleasure as their lips moved in tandem, unveiling a common desire. It may have started off slow but that wasn't the case for long. It picked up speed and momentum. All of the desperation, anxiety and fear that the past few days had brought had evolved into a single need for each other. A need that burned red hot between their lips. In that moment Thatcher became Braydon in her mind.

Braydon didn't drop Sophia's hand after the change in action started. Instead he used the grip to bring her closer into his chest while his other hand wound to the back of her neck and knotted in her hair. His tongue parted her lips and invaded her mouth with his intoxicating taste. Sophia wanted him closer still. She moved her free hand up his back and around his neck, becoming her anchor in the sea of uncertainty that was the town of Culpepper.

There they stood, intertwined in the kitchen, moaning against each other's lips, all thoughts of the world around them falling away.

Bliss, as Sophia had learned at any early age, didn't last forever. Their kiss was interrupted by the loud buzz of Braydon's phone pulling them out of the moment like a gunshot in the empty house. He dropped her hand just as she released him, though she didn't want to, and stood back in anticipation. If there was a lead in the case, they needed to know and they needed to know right then.

"Braydon here." His voice was filled with grit, his lips a dark red. Sophia couldn't hear what the female voice on the other end was saying. Judging by his calm facial expression, she assumed it wasn't the call that said they had found Lisa, Amanda or Nathanial. Braydon lowered the phone. "Officer Whitfield found out some more information on Nathanial. Give me a sec."

Braydon took the rest of the call in his office while

Sophia took a minute to try and cool down from the heated exchange. It wasn't as if she had never been kissed before. She'd been kissed enough. However, kissing Braydon had stirred up a new feeling inside. One she hadn't expected lived there, but one she definitely wanted to explore. It wasn't until her stomach growled loudly at her that she decided food was important. She searched the kitchen for a pan and began to make what she believed was one of the detective's favorite foods while her body rode out the remaining highs of passion.

It had been a long while since she'd been with a man and that relationship had just been overshadowed by a minute of kissing Braydon Thatcher. She put her fingertips against her lips. They were tingling with excitement. She could still feel him against her. It was a foreign yet familiar feeling.

Sophia smiled to herself as she cooked alone in the kitchen. Not only had she kissed him, but he had also kissed back.

"I'm going to jump into the shower real quick," Braydon said when he came back into the kitchen. His face was drawn, a frown living where his smile had been. It pushed the remaining thoughts of being wrapped in his embrace away.

"What did Cara have to say?"

"Nothing that leads us to him yet, but enough to make everything more complicated." He sighed. "Let me take a shower, then I'll catch you up. Deal?"

Sophia nodded. The moment between them was gone, replaced by overwhelming concern for Nathanial's victims. They didn't have time for a kiss to become anything more. They needed to stay focused. Though, Sophia wondered what that "more" would be like.

Braydon came back smelling of men's soap and wear-

ing a white undershirt and a slick pair of gym shorts. He
certainly looked more comfortable than he had before.

"Sorry, I needed a shower really badly," he said, looking sheepish. "I haven't been home in almost three days."

"You could have fooled me," she said with a wink, the
aftermath of the kiss making her feel more comfortable
with flirting with him. He laughed and sat down at the
small, round dining room table. It sat four but with their
plates and cups on top, only two could fit comfortably.
Sophia bit into her grilled cheese while Braydon started.

"Nathanial was fired from Microne a month after his
mother killed herself. He had been caught doing unauthorized testing on a new product for people suffering
from severe sleeping disorders brought on by high levels
of anxiety and stress."

"Unauthorized testing?"

"He apparently thought it was a good idea to take it
home and use it on himself, which, I don't have to tell
you, is a big no-no," Braydon said. "Cara talked to a former member of his research team who described Nathanial as meticulous and almost obsessive when it came to
this specific drug."

"What was the drug?"

"They couldn't tell us because it's still in the first
stages of testing. Which is another reason Nathanial got
the boot. Human trials were at least a year away, if not
more."

Sophia took another bite of her sandwich, absorbing
this new information.

"Let me tell you why this information is a little more
interesting to me," Braydon said. "Trixie Martin didn't
put up a fight when she was strangled, or at least as far as
the medical examiner can tell. Trixie is a strong woman
so the ME suspected she was drugged." Sophia's eyes

widened and her mouth gaped. "There was a welt on her neck with a tiny hole in the middle."

"Like from a needle?"

He nodded. "The ME sent off the blood work to confirm if it was or wasn't a drug that kept Trixie from fighting."

Sophia rubbed her neck, subconsciously thinking of Trixie being strangled. Officer Murphy had met with the same fate. Did that mean he would do it to Lisa and Amanda, as well?

"Was there anything else the medical examiner found that could be useful?"

"Only that she was strangled around Monday morning and the gunshot was postmortem. Everything else is just speculation at this point. I also think that she was killed there in the field."

"But her boss said she hadn't been to work in two days, right? She couldn't have been killed Monday," Sophia said, not understanding.

"Cal confirmed that Monday was her day off. She lives alone and keeps to herself so no one knew that she was even missing then."

"But what was she even doing there? Why did Lisa go to the lot on Sunday, then Trixie on Monday?" Sophia blew out a frustrated sigh. Braydon put down his sandwich and held up his index finger.

"I might have the answer to why Trixie was there." He left the room. Sophia finished off her sandwich with interest.

"This is a map of Culpepper," he said, coming back with a pocket-size road map. He put it on the table. "This is where Trixie's house is." He pointed it out with one index finger. "And this is where Dolphin Lot is located." He placed his other index finger on it. "It's roughly 10.5 miles apart." The detective slid his fingers across the space until they touched. Sophia still didn't understand. She shrugged and cast him a look that said "So?"

"Trixie was big on running. When we searched her house there were runner's medals and trophies everywhere. A lot of those were for marathons and triathlons. The medical examiner said she saw Trixie run by her house almost every day for part of training." He pointed to an area that was within the 10.5 distance between Trixie's and Dolphin Lot. "I think the Dolphin Lot road was part of Trixie's running route."

Sophia was alarmed. "But that's a twenty-one-mile run!" she exclaimed.

"Marathons are around twenty-six. Twenty-one miles wouldn't be unheard-of for her."

She sat up straighter in her chair. "Okay, so she goes for a run and then what? She sees something she isn't supposed to? Then he gives her some kind of weird 'pass out in a hurry' drug and then kills her before staging her death just like his brother's?" As she said it out loud, she felt a chill run up her spine. Braydon nodded.

"I think that's exactly what happened to her. I think she was running that route and maybe saw Lisa's car or Nathanial. In his sick mind he saw it as an opportunity he couldn't pass up."

"But why did Lisa go to the lot? I mean, I get it was about a party but who called it in? Nathanial? Was Amanda there, too?" There were too many questions surrounding Dolphin Lot. Why hadn't Lisa told Richard or called Sophia to tell either of them where she was heading?

"We'll find out." He clasped his hand over hers and gave it a squeeze. Unlike the electricity of the kiss, his touch held a blanket of comfort. "We found some good evidence in the woods on Dolphin Lot. I'm hoping it can give us some new information to follow." He proceeded to tell her about the clearing and its creepy contents, including the mass amount of local beer bottles. He put his full confidence in Tom and the captain to sort out the videotapes from Tipsy's and connect a few dots while Braydon took a much needed break. The news brought forth more hope than she'd had in the past twenty-four hours.

"Did Cara figure out where Nathanial went next? After he was fired from Microne?" Sophia wanted to know as she cleaned up the empty dishes. Braydon patted his nonexistent gut, appreciative of the power of a good grilled cheese.

"We still aren't sure. We checked with the apartment he lived in since he got the job there but he got out of the lease just after he was fired. They have no idea where he went. No forwarding addresses or a valid phone number to reach. He fell off the radar."

"That's not disturbing or anything," she said sarcastically. "Does he have any more family?"

"No, ma'am. His mother was the last bit of his family."

Sophia didn't want to empathize with the insane man, but she could do it. If she lost Lisa she would have no more living relatives that she was connected with. She would also lose her closest friend. It was a thought that wasn't fun to entertain but had to be downright horrible to live through. Although, it didn't excuse going on a killing and kidnapping rampage.

The kitchen quieted. Sophia rinsed the dishes off while Braydon pulled something from the freezer. A grin broke out across his face.

"I may not have all of the necessities but you have to give me credit for this." He held up a carton of chocolate ice cream. Suddenly, he was more attractive than ever.

They settled back around the table with bowls filled with frozen deliciousness. Sophia could pretend to have self-control all she wanted, but put some chocolate ice cream in front of her and it was game over. She attacked the sweet goodness with speed and vigor.

"So, if you don't mind my asking, what happened to your parents? I haven't heard you really bring them up."

Braydon waved off her discomfort. He didn't mind her asking.

"Oh, they're alive and well. Living in Utah near my father's relatives. They moved to Culpepper after they married, following my dad's job at the automotive plant that used to be downtown. They used to love it here but after Amelia died they moved. They said they couldn't stand to live in a place where their daughter was killed." He was so candid about it. Sophia wondered if it was easier that way—to state is as a fact.

"What about you?" she asked, sincere. "Why didn't you leave, too?"

"The reason why they left was the same reason I had to stay." He shrugged nonchalantly. "This town was the last place Amelia was alive," he said. "I left once and considered never coming back, but no matter how much pain I felt in Culpepper, the good memories outweighed it. Where my parents saw reminders of Amelia's death, I saw reminders of her life." His lips turned up in a small smile. "We grew up here so when I'm feeling low and want to remember the good times with her, I have an entire town to help me. I can go to the park and see her playing there when she was younger, the high school stadium where I'd take her to games when she managed to bug me enough for a ride, Jefferson Road where she tried to learn to drive and took out Mr. Jensen's mailbox." He let out a breath and licked his spoon. The small smile was

still attached. In that moment he seemed years younger—
no lives on the line, no killer on the loose, no worries.
She quite liked it on him. "It's true, these memories can
sometimes be depressing but they also do the soul good.
I could leave Culpepper if I had to, but it's because of
these memories that I don't want to." He pushed the last
bit of ice cream into his mouth. His eyes shone bright as
he met Sophia's gaze.

"That's a beautiful way to remember her," she said.
He smiled for a second before his face darkened like a
storm surging through blue skies.

"Nathanial hates me because he knows that I would
have killed his brother had Terrance not done it first. Not
only would I have killed him, I would have made him
suffer. I *needed* him to suffer—to pay for what he had
done—and I didn't care what that meant for my future."
Braydon grabbed her hand across the table again, urging
her to pay attention to what he said next. "That's how I
know that Nathanial won't stop. Not until he knows I've
suffered. I don't think he's dangerous, Sophia. I *know*
he is. I'm sorry for all that's happened. If it wasn't for
me, then Lisa and the others wouldn't have been taken."

He tried to let go of her hand but she held firm.

"Braydon, I'm only going to tell you this once. I don't
and will not blame you for the actions of a psychotic man.
You did *nothing* wrong."

"But now I'm afraid he's after you." She may not have
known Braydon as long as his partner or even Lynda,
his ex—according to a conversation she'd had with Cara
earlier—but she did know that the vulnerability he was
showing now was rare. It pulled at her heartstrings.

"We don't know that for certain," she said.

"He wants to make me suffer. What better way than
to use you?"

"You care about this entire town and all of its people. He can use any of us." She said it to lighten the mood. They were skating around saying something significant again. Sophia could feel it. She watched as the conflicted man next to her chose his words carefully.

"He knows you're different."

Sophia's stomach fluttered with pleasure as if she was in high school again. Braydon, however, was still frowning. This wasn't the time for another moment between them. The burden he believed he placed on her seemed to be crushing him.

"What makes you think Nathanial going after me has anything to do with you? Have you seen me smile? I'm just too adorable," she joked. He looked as though he was going to argue with her but stopped short as she grinned wide, showing teeth and gums. Braydon squeezed her hand and the corner of his mouth quirked up. "Now, if you don't try to get some sleep I'm going to tell the captain on you."

He let out a loud breath, exaggerating his feigned annoyance. "Fine. I guess a few hours might do the brain some good." They parted hands and stood. "It wouldn't hurt you to catch some shut-eye, too. You can sleep in my room. I threw on some clean sheets when I got out of the shower."

"Where will you sleep?"

Braydon laughed. "Don't worry, I'll be out here on the couch." Sophia hadn't been worried. She could share the bed with the detective, though if they did that sleep may not be what happened.

"You don't have to do that. I don't mind taking the couch," she said instead.

"I'd feel more comfortable staying out here." He motioned to the front door and then the back. "If anyone tries to get in, I'll be the first to see it."

"Ah, Detective Watchdog." She smiled.

"That's my job. If you need anything you know where I'll be."

They said their good-nights and Sophia headed back to the bedroom. She hadn't noticed how heavy the bags beneath the detective's eyes had been but she suspected that as soon as he put his messy head of hair down he would immediately fall sleep. She switched out her outfit for a matching tank top and shorts combination, wishing for an instant it was sexier, and slid under the cotton covers.

The next day would mark the seventh day that Lisa had been missing. Seven days with the off-balanced, vengeful Nathanial Williams. If she ever saw that man again, Sophia didn't know what she would do but she knew it wouldn't be good. He may have lived through the tragedy of Terrance dying, then the passing of his parents, but punishing Braydon and killing and kidnapping wasn't the answer. He had lost his sanity. The time for intensive therapy or religious salvation had passed. He had condemned himself the moment he decided vengeance was the answer.

She crawled farther under the covers and inhaled deeply. Braydon's scent surrounded her, clinging to the cotton she was nuzzled in. If someone were to tell her she would be in Detective Thatcher's bed when she first came to town, she would have laughed in their face. Her affection for the man had snuck up on her through the course of the investigation. He was strong, determined and wholly committed. The way he had kissed her tonight…it sent a thrill across her body and soul. She imagined how it would feel to press her lips against his again, to run her hands through his dark hair, to feel the warmth of his embrace, to lose herself completely in him.

It was enough to temporarily ease the emotional turbulence over Nathanial Williams.

SOPHIA BOLTED AWAKE, terrified and disoriented. *This isn't my bedroom,* she thought. *This isn't Lisa's bedroom, either.* She looked around the dark space with wide eyes trying to figure out where she was and what had woken her. The dresser opposite the bed had a pair of men's jeans folded on top. *I'm at Braydon's.* She remembered. *But what woke me up?* Sitting still, she listened.

There was a faint noise that was coming from the living room. It came in rhythmic bursts but she couldn't quite place it. Pushing her legs over the bed, she crept across the wood floors and opened the door slowly.

The mystery sound belonged to Braydon. He apparently was a man who snored quite heavily. She tiptoed toward the living room and looked at the prone man.

"Oh, my." She said out loud before slapping a hand over her mouth. Braydon had shed his shirt and shorts after she had gone to bed. Now she had an uninhibited view of a rock-hard six-pack with a smattering of dark hair that led from his pecs down to a region the blanket just barely covered. There were muscles everywhere, it seemed. She stood there looking at them, bathing in all of their sexy glory. *And to think, I was kissing that earlier.*

Feeling as if she was getting close to being creepy, Sophia turned to retreat back into the bedroom when a loud *thump* stopped her. She froze in the hallway. Then the sound of a car door slammed. She turned and walked to the front window, moving the curtain to the side. The road outside was void of people and cars but there was a large lump on the front porch. With dread filling her veins, Sophia turned on the light.

"Braydon!" she yelled before opening the front door. Behind her she could hear the man jump up. She was already on the porch when she called for him again. "Braydon!" She dropped to the ground next to the body. Fear cascaded down every inch of her, pooling along with the blood that surrounded the woman. Immediately Sophia knew it wasn't Lisa. This woman was too short. A small ounce of relief sprouted. "Braydon!" she yelled again.

Braydon ran through the living room to the front door, bare feet slapping against the hardwood. The man always came to her when she called, but this time it wasn't her who needed him. He flung the screen door wide.

"What the—"

"I think it's Amanda." Sophia moved the woman's long hair aside to feel for a pulse. She ignored her shaking hand as she felt a faint beat. "She's still alive!"

Braydon ran back inside to grab his phone. He was back in a flash, phone to his ear.

"Find out where she's bleeding from," Braydon commanded. "We need to see if we can stop it." Sophia looked down at the woman resting on her stomach. Her cheek was pressed against the wood of the porch, eyes shut and lips downturned. In the poor light of the porch's singular bulb, Amanda looked unnaturally pale. Sophia surveyed her back and legs but couldn't find the source of all of the blood.

"Help me turn her over." Braydon put the phone on speaker and told the operator his address while they grabbed Amanda and flipped her over as gently as they could. Blood had soaked into the front of her shirt yet there were no holes or tears in the fabric. Sophia grabbed the hem of the shirt and pushed it up. The source of the crimson made her gasp.

Braydon swore. He finished up with the operator and ran inside to grab a towel. "We need to stop the blood flow!" he yelled back.

Sophia's body had gone numb. She couldn't believe her eyes. Carved into Amanda's stomach was her name.

Chapter Thirteen

The Culpepper hospital was a twenty-minute drive across town. Sophia rode it in the back of an ambulance while Braydon sped behind. If there were any doubts of Nathanial's intentions to use Sophia against the detective, they were gone now. Even Sophia couldn't deny that the crazed man had targeted her. After Braydon had returned with the towel he gave Sophia his gun and all but pushed her inside. There she had waited until the sirens came closer.

Braydon was so visibly shaken and equally on alert that Sophia was surprised she had been able to talk him into letting her ride in the back of the ambulance at all, but there had been no way she was going to let the poor woman ride alone. Plus, if she woke up, Sophia *had* to ask the one question that had burned inside her chest since she had come to town. Where was Lisa?

However, Amanda didn't wake up. The EMTs bustled around her, strapping an IV on and checking her vitals. They didn't talk to Sophia the entire ride, but after they saw her name carved into the young woman's flesh, they couldn't keep their eyes off her. She didn't blame them one bit.

In the back of the ambulance, Amanda looked a lot worse. Her clothes, a band T and cargo shorts, were fully intact but covered in blood and dirt. Her feet were bare and stained with a mixture of red and brown while her hair looked as though it was wet with sweat or grease. The pulse Sophia had felt was weak and, as one of the EMTs said, Amanda had lost a lot of blood. Seeing her lying on the stretcher, body sliced and bleeding, Sophia hoped that Amanda had at least been unconscious when Nathanial decided to brand her stomach.

When the back doors of the ambulance opened, Braydon's face was the first that swam into view. He helped lower Amanda's stretcher down and ran alongside her, telling the nurses inside the situation. Sophia ran behind them, keeping out of the way but just within earshot. A doctor came out, evaluated Amanda and told an orderly to start prepping a room for surgery. Apparently her condition was worse than Sophia had thought.

"He cut her too deep," Braydon said after the chaos had died down a fraction and the woman was being taken into surgery. He gave Sophia a significant look. "There was a bump on her neck."

"From the drug," she stated. Instead of nodding he threw his fist into the wall of the waiting room. A few nurses eyed him warily before turning back to their jobs. Sophia reached out and grabbed the fist. He met her eyes, the fire in them almost burning her.

"I'm going to make him pay," he said. "You just wait."

Sophia couldn't blame him for the reaction. Now Lisa was alone with the man, if she was even still alive.

"So what now?"

Braydon ran a hand through his hair. At least the bags under his eyes had lessened with the few hours of sleep they were able to get.

"Amanda is going into surgery in the next twenty minutes. There was a welt on the back of her neck, so I told them about the drug we suspected she was injected with. They are trying to figure out what it is before they put her under. If they can't, then it could kill her." His frown deepened. "I called the captain and Tom on the way here. They'll look for him while an officer stays with the surveillance tapes. I also called Marina Alcaster. She needs to be here just in case Amanda doesn't make it, so she can, I don't know, see her daughter alive once more." His jaw tensed and Sophia was afraid he was going to strike the wall again. "I'm going to go downstairs to talk to the ME. She took a night shift so she could examine Officer Murphy's body and wait for the blood results."

"Can I stay here?" Sophia asked, eyeing the room they had Amanda temporarily in. "I think Marina might need a little support."

Braydon's phone vibrated in his hand. He looked down at the number and back at her. She could tell that, if he could, the detective would shrink her and place her in his pocket for protection. However, seeing as she was a full grown woman, he couldn't very well do that. Though he looked as though he was about to try.

"Detective," someone called. "Detective?" They turned to see the doctor standing in the doorway of Amanda's room. "She's conscious." He didn't have to say anything else. Braydon and Sophia were already running toward him.

"She's awake?" Braydon asked, stopping as the doctor held up his hand to halt them.

"Just barely. You have less than one minute before we wheel her out." He turned to Sophia. "You need to stay out here."

"But—" Sophia started to complain.

"This woman has been put through hell. The only reason I'm even letting the detective in is because it could potentially save another life." Braydon went into the room without a look back. Sophia nodded and moved against the wall to try and listen. Thankfully there were no other patients in the rooms on either side making the task easier. More than anything she wanted to be in that room, but she stayed strong, remembering that it wasn't just Lisa's life on the line.

"Amanda?" Sophia heard Braydon ask. "Was it Nathanial Williams, a man with dark red hair, who took you?"

Sophia's body was still, her heart thumping in tandem with her anxiety.

"Yeah," Amanda croaked out, voice hoarse.

"Where was he keeping you?"

The woman was struggling to answer—that much Sophia could tell.

"Dunno."

"We believe that Nathanial also took Lisa Hardwick. Did you see her? Is she still alive?"

Sophia felt time slow. *This is it,* she thought. She braced herself against the wall, waiting for a stranger to give her hope or destroy it.

"Lisa's there," she said simply.

"But is she alive?" Braydon prodded.

Every fiber of Sophia's being stood up, waiting for the answer she had sought since Day One in Culpepper. Amanda Alcaster didn't realize it then, but what she was about to say was going to change Sophia's life. In one way or another, she was about to know of her sister's fate. "Amanda, is Lisa alive?"

"Yes," Amanda said so low that she almost missed it. "But, he wants Sophia."

Marina Alcaster must have broken the speed of light to get to the hospital. Seconds after Amanda's ominous message, she flew into the ER in a bout of tears and high-pitched squeals. Sophia wordlessly waved her over and had only a second to move out of the woman's way.

"My baby!" she yelled, hysterical. "I'm so sorry about our fight. I don't care about that land more than you! I love you, baby!"

The second nurse went in then and said Amanda was ready for surgery. Marina, knowing nothing of her daughter's condition, was told to follow them to the doctor but then she would have to go back to the lobby to wait. Not once did the older woman look at Sophia, though Braydon followed her to the end of the hallway quickly explaining the situation.

Lisa was still alive. It was a thought that made Sophia's heart soar. After all the time that had passed since she'd been taken, she was still alive. Not only was she alive, but they knew for a fact who had her.

"I feel like I can breathe a bit easier now," she admitted to Braydon when he made his way back. Lines of worry were etched across his forehead, each a cavern of concern.

"He wants you" was his response. His tone was cold. Sophia wanted to ease the detective's stress but knew there wasn't a thing she could do.

"I need to tell Richard," she said instead. "Go ahead and talk to the ME. I want to stay here to see how the surgery goes."

Braydon managed to tense up even more.

"I'm not leaving you alone," he said.

"And I don't want to see any more dead bodies," she snapped back before letting out a long sigh. "Sorry, I'd just rather stay up here for now." That didn't seem to change his resolve, so she added what she hoped was reassurance. "Listen, there's a full staff on this floor, including security." She motioned to the hospital security officer who had appeared after all the commotion. He stood talking to a nurse at the nurses' station at the end of the hall. "I'll be fine for a few minutes."

Braydon, ever the protective man, waged an internal battle. His eyes never left hers.

"Fine," he relented. "But you stay here and call me if *anything* and I mean *anything* happens. Okay?" She nodded. "Be safe." He waited a moment more before turning and walking over to the elevator, already pulling out his phone to make some calls. She watched him disappear behind its doors.

Sophia went to reach for her own cell but realized, too late, that it was still attached to its charger on the detective's nightstand. She sighed and made her way to the nurses' station.

"May I use the phone?" she asked the nurse behind the partition. The woman obliged and even went so far as to walk away and give her some privacy, the security guard following her lead. Privacy. Something that would have been rare in the city, Sophia thought fleetingly.

Richard answered on the first ring and after she broke the news, he told her that nothing but the devil himself could stop him from coming to the hospital. Even if Amanda was in surgery, he wanted to be there. Sophia knew the feeling. Amanda was the closest they had been to Lisa in days.

The traumatized woman was their first real link to Nathanial, too. If she didn't make it, then finding the madman and her sister would continue to be horribly difficult. Sophia fell into a lobby chair and put her head in her hands. The image of her name etched into Amanda's stomach was stuck in her mind like glue. What was Nathanial playing at? If he did get Sophia, what horrible things would he do to her?

"Oh, I can't take this," Sophia said aloud, standing. The news had been good to hear but now horrible images of what the madman could do raced through her head. Marina Alcaster was still nowhere to be found and so there was nothing to distract her.

"Could you tell Marina Alcaster, the woman who just ran in here, that I'll be right back to talk with her?" Sophia asked the nurse who had let her borrow the phone. She had decided that, dead body or not, she wanted to know as much about this case as she could. It was better than just sitting around and imagining the worst. Plus, she doubted Nathanial would show up at the hospital of all places. He'd have to know Braydon would be with her and that the detective would be more than willing to cause the man harm. "My name's Sophia. I'm friends with Detective Thatcher." The nurse agreed to give Marina the news and then told Sophia how to get to the room where Braydon and the ME would be talking. When the elevators took too long, Sophia headed to the stairs with a newfound purpose to her stride.

The medical examiner had an office in the basement of the building. It also happened to be smack-dab in the middle of the morgue. Sophia realized that made sense but it didn't put her nerves at ease. Each step she took downward was more nerve-racking than the last. She half expected a little girl from a horror movie to pop out just as the lights burned out. Once she was at the ground level, she almost sang with relief.

The hospital's basement was the polar opposite of the ground floor. It was like a wasteland. Sophia crept down the hallway, getting halfway through it and still not spotting a single soul. The lights that buzzed overhead were more loud than bright and more annoying than helpful. Instead of bouncing off all the white surfaces, they cast shadows on everything.

"I wouldn't suggest you run," said a voice from behind just as she passed another light emitting a high-pitched buzz. "That action wouldn't bode well for your sister."

Sophia spun around. She should have listened to Braydon and stayed put on the first floor.

Nathanial Williams was standing in the mouth of the hallway, smiling from ear to ear. He was nothing like the man she had met before—the warm, inviting personality had burned out and in its place was a man on the brink of madness. Shadows crept around him as if he were creating them; they poured out over his facial features, forging a sinister mask with eyes as dark as coal. Maybe it was just her imagination. Maybe Nathanial didn't look different at all. Maybe now she knew too much about the man to ever see him for anything other than a monster.

He stayed still as she looked him up and down. He wore a blue janitor's jumpsuit with a faded name tag. In his right hand was a black rectangular box.

Sophia didn't know which emotion would spring out first, but she was glad it was anger before fear. She straightened her back.

"Where is Lisa?" she asked The distance between them made her feel much more confident than she should when in the presence of a brilliant killer.

"Your sister? Oh, it doesn't matter. She won't be there for too long."

Fear pulled at the pit of Sophia's stomach. "What does that mean?"

"It means, Miss Hardwick, that I have a proposition for you." He waved the box in the air before sliding it across the floor. It stopped a few feet from her.

"Where's Lisa?" she asked again, not moving an inch. Nathanial seemed to think the question was funny. He laughed—the sound was hollow.

"Miss Hardwick, I believe we've moved on from that particular question, but I suppose I'll humor you. She's somewhere and I won't tell you where. Will that answer work for now? I'm trying to strike up a deal with you to save your sister." He was speaking as if they were playing a game, and maybe it was to him.

"What kind of deal?" She practically spat out the words. His smile grew wider.

"Open the box first."

Sophia hesitated. The morgue was down the hall and to the left. If she ran fast enough Braydon might be able to catch up to the madman. At the very least, she bet if she yelled he would hear her. It wasn't as if anyone else was down on the floor with them.

"If you're stalling in the hopes that Detective Thatcher will magically appear, saving you in the nick of time, I would advise against it." He sighed. "Every second you *do not open that box* is one more second that I'll tick off of Lisa's life. Now open it or I'll leave before your knight in shining armor can stop me."

Sophia felt her confidence receding. She took a step forward and picked the box up. To her surprise, it was light. Inside was the most confusing combination of items. The first was a piece of red satin clothing, which, after a moment, she realized made up a dress. The second item was a small needle and syringe. It looked odd sitting in a sea of satin.

"What is this?" she asked.

"That, my dear Sophia, is my offer. I want to make a trade."

"What kind of trade?"

He was almost giddy when he spoke next. "You for your sister, of course." Sophia was almost certain her eyebrow had disappeared into her hairline. The man wasn't making the most sense. He held up his finger to keep her questions at bay.

"Let me elaborate." He cleared his throat. Despite the distance between them, it sounded as though he was right in front of her. "You may or may not have figured out that my ultimate plan is to make your detective suffer."

"Revenge," she stated.

"I wouldn't call it that per se, but I'm not going to stand here and say that you're wrong."

"But why? Braydon didn't kill Terrance. There's no revenge to be had. You need to accept that," she tried.

"I've also been asked to accept that God is real, but that doesn't mean I have." His smile cracked. "I do have my own set of beliefs, although they may not be religious in nature, they still ring true—Braydon Thatcher damned my family, Miss Hardwick. There isn't a force in this world that could convince me otherwise. So, if I were you, I'd stop right there."

A coldness settled in the pit of her stomach. In that moment she realized her own truth—Nathanial Williams would never see reason. He had left all sanity behind. If he'd ever had any at all.

"Okay, so where were we? Oh, right, destroying Detective Thatcher!" His cheerful smile returned. "On Sunday, Richard Vega will be throwing the annual Culpepper Fund-raiser. I want you to tell him to make sure it stays on course and I want you to attend." He pointed to the box. "Wearing that lovely little number."

"What? Why?" she couldn't stop from asking. It was a bizarre request that didn't fit the situation.

"At the fund-raiser I will trade you for your sister." He

paused, waiting for Sophia to respond, but she couldn't find the words. He then continued, unperturbed. "That is *if* you wear that dress. You may have also already realized that I'm a fan of theatrics. See, over the years my world has been submerged in numbers and theories and formulas. It instilled a secret love of all things dramatic within me and I just can't help but employ my own version of poetic justice against the man who ruined my family. Sure—" he took a step closer and stopped "—I could have killed Thatcher without all of this fuss and, sure, I could just kill you right here, right now, but there's honestly no fun in it for me. I want the *drama*. I want the *suffering*." Nathanial seemed to be vibrating with excitement. Sophia's confidence had completely gone and fear housed itself inside her very core. She dared not speak. She dared not breathe. The man kept his monologue going—a broadcast that couldn't be muted.

"You, however, were not in the original plan. I took Lisa with every intention of keeping her just out of Braydon's reach while making him look a fool in front of Mr. Richard Vega, who I've heard, makes no issue about taking down those who displease him. I meant to cripple Braydon's career by torturing and then killing the lover of the town's most powerful man. Then, when he was completely crushed, I would finish what I came here to do, but then I saw the way he looked at you—the way he cared. I saw a way to cut him deeper. I want you, Sophia, not your sister. Everyone else, the women of unfortunate timing, mean nothing to me now. Only you do and that's why I'm presenting you with an option here. I'd like to tell you I'm not as cruel as you think—I want to give you the chance to save your flesh and blood because I know the pain of having them taken." Sophia wanted to point out that her death would leave Lisa in the same boat, but held her tongue. The man seemed to be finishing his long speech. "You show up to the fund-raiser and I'll let Lisa go."

That was the bottom line.

"Why take me at the fund-raiser?" she finally managed.

"Because when I take you, I want it to be a challenge… one that, when I successfully pull it off, will make Braydon feel even more desolate."

"How do I even know Lisa's still alive?" It was one thing to hear it from Amanda. She wanted assurance from the man himself.

"I'll let you see her one more time. Give you a moment to say goodbye. Again, Miss Hardwick, I'm not a monster." Sophia had every doubt in the world about that. "Now, let's talk about that syringe before your friendly neighborhood detective comes back." He took his finger and pressed it to a spot on the side of his neck. "I want you to grab that needle and put it right here on your neck."

Sophia didn't have to ask what was in it. She knew it was his sleep-inducing cocktail.

"It won't kill you, but if you don't inject yourself with it I *will* kill your sister. Of that you can be completely certain." The smile oozed off of his face as he said it. "Braydon will think you're dead when he finds you. He'll get a taste of his future."

Sophia's world slowed. Her vision blurred. She hadn't taken the drug yet but she knew he had already won. With shaking hands she took out the syringe and stared into the eyes of a man filled with hate.

"Right now, you're probably thinking of saying something to the effect of Braydon Thatcher will, undoubtedly, stop me. That he'll save Lisa and then you, but remember, Sophia—he didn't stop me from killing Trixie, he didn't stop me from cutting up Amanda, and he didn't stop Terrance from killing his sister. I suggest, once more, you heed my advice. It's the only way to save your sister."

Sophia didn't hesitate this time. She placed the needle against her neck and pushed the liquid into her body.

"You're heartless," she said as cold pain began to spread through her. Nathanial laughed once more as his joyful smile returned.

"You're wrong, Sophia," he said. "I have a heart and that's the problem."

Chapter Fourteen

Officer Murphy had been helpless to defend himself as Nathanial choked the life out of him. The medical examiner confirmed that the same drug that had disabled Trixie had been found in the cop's bloodstream. Braydon reasoned that he had opened the door to question the man and had been stabbed with the needle before he was able to do anything more.

"I haven't heard back yet about what specific drug it is, but I think it's a safe bet that it's the one Nathanial was working on while at Microne," she had said after being filled in on the man's academic and work background. "He must have taken quite a few samples with him when he left. The best I can do right now is to equate the drug to Ambien which is used to help insomniacs sleep. Though, this particular mix seems to work much, much faster."

Braydon didn't have to agree; the fact that two people hadn't had the time to fight back was proof enough of the drug's power. Instead he thanked the woman for her help and left. He didn't know what he had hoped for when he had come down. At least he could tell James's family that he hadn't been awake when he was killed. It wasn't a lot but the idea of a painless death might be comforting.

It was something he had wished Amelia had.

He brought his phone out and was about to call the captain to tell him the news when something down the hall caught his eye.

"Sophia!"

Instant fear exploded in his chest as he closed the distance between them, his heart already thumping at a nauseating pace. The way she was sprawled on the ground, unnaturally still, tore a wound inside him open, letting an overwhelming feeling of anguish pour out. He couldn't lose her. He wouldn't lose her.

He crouched down next to her, immediately checking to see if she was breathing. For one long second her chest didn't rise and the world seemed to darken because of it, but then she took in a breath and let one out. It was the most beautiful thing he had ever seen.

"Sophia?" he tried again, quickly scanning her body for any blood or obvious marks. His eyes stopped on her neck where a small red bump had formed.

His fear for her life switched gears as he realized that the man who had done this to her wasn't far off. He pulled out his gun and with his free hand dialed Tom.

As soon as his partner answered, Braydon started talking, "Nathanial is in the hospital, or was. He drugged Sophia. We're on the bottom floor."

"I'm pulling into the parking lot now" was Tom's response before Braydon disconnected. The urge to search for Nathanial seared through him but he would not leave Sophia alone.

With one more look around, he put his gun back in its holster and carefully pulled her into his arms, trying to ignore her absolute lack of resistance. It was then that he noticed the box at her feet. Without putting her down he managed to kick off the lid. Inside was an empty syringe atop red material. He didn't have the time to look in any more detail. There was no guarantee that what she had been injected with was the same drug as the others. Sophia needed help as soon as possible. Braydon refused to lose her.

With as much caution as he could afford while still trying to hurry, he got her into the elevator and together they rode to the first floor. During the seconds between he focused on her breathing. It continued to be a beautiful sight.

The first floor of the hospital was in a frenzy. Cops, hospital security guards, and staff were bustling around forming one loud commotion. John the Ticketer ran up to them as soon as the elevator doors slid open. He yelled for help but instead of waiting for hospital staff to come to them, Braydon marched Sophia into one of the small ER rooms before depositing her on a bed. A doctor he recognized but whose name he couldn't place ran up and started to check her vitals while Braydon filled him in.

"Tom took the stairs to the basement and we have two bodies going through the second floor. A nurse called the ME and told her to lock her doors, too," John said as the doctor and a nurse worked. "The captain is outside and Cara just walked in."

Braydon nodded but kept his attention on Sophia. Her face was slack, her lips downturned. He wanted to touch them, to kiss them, until the sleeping woman awoke. The doctor turned and, on seeing his gaze, seemed to soften.

"Her vitals are normal. She's just asleep right now," he said. "I'll move her to a room to keep a better eye on her but, for now, she's fine."

A weight lifted from Braydon's chest and for one moment he felt pure elation. However, it didn't last long. He took a few steps out into the hall and called the woman officer over.

"Is she okay?" Cara asked, looking over his shoulder.

"For now. I need you to watch her," he said. "You do not leave her side for any reason, do you understand?" She nodded. "Once she's in that room only the captain or the doctor go in there."

"What are you going to do?"

"Nathanial is too smart to stick around. I'm going to go look at the security tapes to see if that can't help us somehow." Braydon cast one more look in Sophia's direction. "Don't let her out of your sight."

Finding a security guard wasn't hard since all of the hospital staff had been alerted. Braydon followed him to the room that held all the security feeds for the entire hospital and ordered him to play the ones from the bottom floor. The guard didn't seem to be offended at the lack of kindness in him and started to pull up the right tapes. Under Braydon's direction he rewound the footage to where Sophia exited the stairwell and then pressed Play. The two of them watched as she walked down the hallway while Nathanial walked behind her before stopping.

All Braydon saw was white-hot rage. It was as if he was eighteen again, the difference being instead of wanting to kill Terrance Williams, he was focused on his older, more sadistic brother. He looked at the computer monitor and willed the man he saw on its screen a horrific, slow death.

"Turn it up," Braydon barked out to the security guard. Sophia's lips were moving but he couldn't hear anything.

"I can't. The audio hasn't worked on these recordings in years." It took everything he had not to slug the guard.

"Then why haven't you had it fixed?"

"Look, man, we don't have that kind of money right

now," the guard defended. "Just be thankful this camera is working. Two more on the same floor have been down for weeks."

Braydon didn't say any more. Instead he watched the scene unfold on the security tape with rage boiling in his veins. There she was, caught in the killer's sights. Nathanial slid her a box and must have said something interesting enough to entice her to open it. Braydon knew now what was inside.

Even though they couldn't hear the exchange, Braydon continued to watch with heightened concentration, focusing on Sophia's facial expressions. When Nathanial had first stopped her, he could make out the stubborn anger that made her posture go straight. Then, the more Nathanial had talked, the more she had sagged at the weight of his words. Her apparent fear translated through the computer screen and right into his heart. Then, Nathanial pointed to his neck. There was more talk and, all of a sudden, she was injecting herself.

"She did it to herself," said the guard, just as Sophia crumpled to the ground. Braydon was completely taken aback. When he found Sophia he had assumed she had been given the injection against her own will.

Braydon swore as Nathanial walked over to Sophia's prone body. He knelt next to her and brushed the hair off her face. Then he turned and looked straight into the camera. With a smile that almost mirrored his brother's, he waved.

"Why did he do that?" the guard asked.

Braydon was so angry it felt as if his body was vibrating. "He wanted me to see him." Nathanial left Sophia and went to the elevator where he rode to the main lobby and walked right out through the front doors of the hospital.

John the Ticketer came into the room then and was ordered to stay with the guard and find out when Nathanial had come in.

"I also want to know how he came in, if he talked to anyone, and if he made any detours," he ordered. "You don't leave this room until you figure all of that out, okay?"

John nodded and then Braydon turned to the security guard. "I want you to make sure that man does not come back into this hospital. You notify every staff member on shift. I don't care if you have to go to every damn room to do it, either. If you see him, you call me *immediately*. Got it?"

"Yessir."

"Good." He gave the man his cell number and went back to Sophia's new room. Officer Whitfield was standing guard at the door, currently being yelled at by Richard Vega.

"You know I'm not the killer, for heaven's sakes!" he yelled, throwing his hands into the air in frustration.

"I'm sorry, Mr. Vega. I'm not supposed to let anyone in here unless authorized by Detective Thatcher or Captain Westin."

"I'm only here because Sophia called me—" He stopped midrant when he saw Braydon arrive.

"You can't talk to her now," Braydon said, glazing over any greeting. He didn't have time. Sophia was a few feet away, unconscious in a hospital bed. Just because the doctor said she would be fine didn't mean she wasn't still in danger.

"I'm guessing he's no longer here," Richard said after a moment.

Braydon didn't respond. He didn't have to. The two men glanced at the room next to them.

"What do we do now, then?" Richard wanted to know.

"We find the bastard."

THERE WAS A TICKING AGAIN—a clock saying to the world it knew exactly what time it was and it wanted everyone to know. Sophia hated it. She wished it would shut up. Clocks in Culpepper were the bane of her existence as far as she was concerned. She opened her eyes to find the source of her annoyance and was surprised at how hard it was to do—each lid was heavy and, once up, wanted very badly to go back down.

"Sophia?" a man asked at her side. Even in the haze she was currently seeded in, she knew it wasn't Braydon. This man was shorter and had blond hair. Her eyes slowly slid to Richard's mouth. It held a small smile. "How do you feel?"

She looked around the hospital room and thought about that for a second. Like opening her eyes, this was also a difficult task.

"Awake" was all she could come up with as an answer. Richard laughed.

"Well, I suppose that's good."

She nodded and her head swam at the movement. She shut her eyes tight until the world settled. The clock continued to tick.

"Do you remember what happened?" Sophia opened her eyes at his abrupt change in tone. It softened to almost a whisper. His face was as open as she had ever seen it— kind and patient. He was dressed down in a plain T-shirt and jeans, looking nothing like he had the first time she'd met him. He looked like just a regular guy. "Sophia?"

She realized she was staring.

"Sorry, everything's kind of fuzzy," she admitted. He came to the side of her bed and patted her hand.

"I'd imagine so—you've been out for almost thirteen hours." She didn't have the speed to react with a worthy response. He seemed to realize this and patted her hand once more. "It's okay. Don't rush it. I'll go get the doctor."

Sophia watched him go. She wondered where Braydon was but wasn't quick enough to answer. It was as though she was submerged underwater. Everything felt slow. What *did* happen? The last thing she clearly remembered was kissing Braydon in the kitchen—the thought made her cheeks heat despite whatever weird fog she was in—but she knew that wasn't the last thing that happened. She scrunched up her face in concentration.

That's when she remembered a grin that made her blood run cold.

Nathanial.

SOPHIA COULD HEAR Braydon running down the hall toward her room. Cara paused what she was doing.

"Want me to tell him to hold on until we're done?" she asked.

"Please." Sophia leaned back against the bed and waited while Cara slipped outside to hold off the detective. She could hear his annoyed tone as he agreed to stay put. Cara came back in, careful to shut the door quickly, and went back to Sophia's side to finish the task they'd started.

"Thanks again for helping me with this. I don't think the nurse likes me much." Sophia held on to Cara as the officer steered them to the bathroom.

"No problem. When you gotta go, you gotta go."

It had been almost a half hour since Sophia had woken from her drug-induced sleep. The doctor had come in twice to check her vitals and, with a lot of head scratching, he had declared her as healthy as a horse. The only way the doctor would allow her to leave was for her to give them a urine sample they could test. Sophia didn't have any room to argue and two bottles of water later, she was about to burst.

The only problem was that her limbs didn't seem to want to function together. Her legs quaked like jelly when she attempted to stand on her own. Whatever had made her mind fuzzy had made her body just as sluggish. It had been a blessing that Braydon had assigned Cara to watch the room. She suspected he had noticed the friendship that had formed between them. The bathroom trip just made it more official.

When the mission was complete and the sample collected, Sophia sat in one of the two armchairs next to the bed. She didn't want to look so helpless when Braydon came in.

"Are you good now?" Cara asked. "Ready for Detective Thatcher?" There was a smile in her voice, though her face remained serious. Sophia had told Richard and Cara the same story about her run-in with Nathanial. She wanted them to understand how unbalanced, and therefore dangerous, the man was.

"Yes, thank you. Send in the bull," Sophia teased. She wanted the mood to lighten if only for a second. Cara finally smiled, then slipped out as Braydon came in.

"Hi," Sophia greeted. She meant it to sound strong but couldn't deny its smallness. Braydon stopped next to her and openly looked up and down her body. She adjusted her hospital gown subconsciously. The detective, apparently approving of what he saw, grabbed the other chair and moved it so he was sitting right in front of her. They were so close their knees were touching.

"Tell me what happened," he said. The time for playing was over. Braydon Thatcher was a man on a mission, except his had nothing to do with bathroom functions. His was much more dangerous.

"Cara said you watched the security footage," she started.

"But there was no sound."

"So…you want to know why I injected myself."

He nodded, his jaw set hard. "Yes, I want to know why you injected yourself instead of running, yelling for help or even attacking him."

"You're mad at me."

"You're damn right I am!" he yelled, standing. "You could have died, Sophia! What could that man have said that would make you think what you were doing was a good idea?" There was no mere undercurrent of disapproval in his voice—it was a tidal wave rushing across the surface. He wasn't going to like what she had to say. She sighed before recounting what had happened. She didn't stop once, ignoring the fists he had balled on his knees.

"What if he'd been lying about what was in there? You could have died, Sophia," he said, bringing his voice down and sitting back in his chair. "Then where would we be?" Sophia flinched at his words but her resolve stood firm. She didn't know who the "we" was but she knew it wasn't the time to ask.

"Remember when you told me you *knew* Nathanial was dangerous?" She waited for him to calm down enough to nod. "Well, I *knew* he wasn't going to kill me. I did what he told me because I also *knew* that if I didn't he would have killed Lisa."

"Sophia—"

She put her hand against his cheek. "Please don't be mad at me for what I did," she said, voice low. "It was a gamble that I wasn't ready to lose. You tell me you wouldn't have done the same thing."

"I would have killed him," he responded, though his tone was calm again.

"Well, all I had was a syringe. If I had messed it up, he probably would have killed me right then before going to do the same to Lisa." She dropped her hand back into her lap—holding it up had been a feat all its own while Nathanial's drug worked its way out of her system. "Plus, he's right—only he knows where Lisa is. If he had died and we couldn't find her, I would have blamed myself for the rest of my life."

Braydon sat still as another internal battle waged within him. Sophia waited for the victor to show. She knew he understood why she had listened to Nathanial but the protective part of him was screaming that the risk had been too high. The conflicting viewpoints waged behind his pools of blue. Eventually, the more reasonable side won.

"Just don't do it again, okay? That's all I ask." Sophia nodded but now she had to approach a more delicate topic.

"What Nathanial wants me to do…you know I have to do it." Braydon's eyes almost bugged out of their sockets while his lips stretched thin.

"You aren't seriously wanting to go to the fund-raiser are you?"

"I wouldn't use the word *want* but yes, I *am* going." Her voice was calm—level in sincerity.

"Sophia, he's asked you to hand yourself over."

"I don't have a choice," she pointed out.

"Yes, you do," he stressed. "Sophia, he isn't asking you to go watch a movie or to take a stroll around the god-damn park. He wants you so he can torture you *before* he kills you. He wants to kill you as my punishment. *My* punishment." He grabbed both of her hands. "There's no question about if he'll keep you alive or not. He won't. He'll only let you live long enough to torture you. That's all." There was fire in his eyes. Sophia hoped she had the same fierce gaze placed on him.

"Then don't let him take me," she said. "Let's take Lisa instead."

BRAYDON KNEW THAT the younger Hardwick woman wasn't going to budge on her decision to attend the Culpepper Fund-raiser. If he was honest about it, he already knew what her choice would be before she said it out loud. She loved her sister with a passion that the threat of death couldn't destroy and would stop short of nothing to prove it. He respected her immensely for it, though he tried a few more times to talk her out of Nathanial's trap. She, of course, refused to reconsider. So instead of beating that dead horse, Braydon switched into planning mode.

He excused himself, or rather was shooed out of the room so Cara could help Sophia change, and found Richard down the hallway. He was staring at a vending machine with his hands in his pockets and mind somewhere else entirely. It took him a few seconds to realize Braydon was standing next to him.

"Sophia told you everything?" he asked, eyes still on the rows of candy bars.

"Yes."

"I'm assuming you're not comfortable with her plan?" he asked, looking at the detective.

"It's not *her* plan, it's his." Braydon was trying not to sound accusatory but he couldn't stop what he said next. "Are you comfortable with her plan? Her life for Lisa's?" He knew it wasn't a fair question to ask but he didn't know where the man stood. Richard had Lisa while Sophia was single. To the general public she didn't have someone who had her back. "Because I can't help but hate the plan." He didn't like the idea that he was the only person stepping forward in an attempt to fight the deadly idea of her sacrifice. He wanted her and everyone else to know that he *was* in fact defending her. Richard took a moment before he answered. For once, it didn't sound full of his normal energy.

"Do you know I'd never met Sophia before the other day?" He didn't wait for Braydon to answer. "I hadn't even talked to her on the phone until after Lisa went missing. She didn't like when we started seeing each other and she certainly didn't approve that we kept on dating. That alone could give me reason to not like her, but…" His face became thoughtful as he searched for his next words. "I feel like I've always known her. They may have been at odds lately, but that never stopped Lisa from telling me all about her little sister. After a while I realized she didn't even notice that she was telling me stories about Sophia. She would see or hear something that reminded her of this memory or that memory and then tell me all about it. For instance, every time we get into bed at night she throws all of the pillows on the floor and smiles. Do you know why?" Braydon shook his head. "When they were young, Lisa used to fill up their bedroom floor with all of her pillows and Sophia hated it, for a while at least. Then Lisa would pull her down on top of them and they'd laugh, Sophia would smile and everything would be fine again. However, one night Lisa told me a secret—she hated the piles of pillows. When *she* was little, Lisa had a bad habit of rolling off the bed in the middle of the night. She became so afraid that she would roll off and hurt herself that she stopped sleeping altogether. So, her dad bought her enough pillows to cover the floor while she slept to cushion the ground, just in case. She didn't think it would work so he demonstrated, rolling off onto them. It became a nighttime ritual, she said, but then he died. She said she hated the sight of the pillows after that."

"Why did she keep them, then?" Braydon asked, genuinely curious.

"Because one day a very young Sophia cried about not remembering her father. She was a toddler when he died so she didn't have the memories that Lisa did. Their mother had no business being a mother and didn't know or care about helping the little girl. So, when Sophia wouldn't stop crying, Lisa did what her father had done every night before bed and rolled onto the ground over and over again until Sophia finally stopped." Richard smiled. "It may not seem like that much of a story but after all of these years Lisa could have told Sophia that the whole routine used to make her sad—make her miss her father—but instead she's kept the act up and even stocks her house *and* mine with tons of odd pillows because in her words 'Sophia deserves them.' Lisa believes with all of her heart that Sophia deserves to always be happy. So, you tell me, Detective, do you think Lisa would say that Sophia deserves to be brutally killed by a sadistic man?"

"No," he answered.

"Then why would I?"

Chapter Fifteen

Sophia felt 50 percent better once the hospital gown was
off. There was something about the way they looked that
set her on edge. Maybe it was the fact that if a person was
wearing one it meant they were in the hospital and therefore not in the best of shape. Either way, after Cara helped
her into her normal clothes, she gave a loud sigh of relief.

"You okay?" Cara asked.

"All things considered, yes." She sat down in one of
the chairs and went to work putting on one of her shoes.
The doctor guessed the drug would leave her tired and
wobbly for a few more hours but she would fully recover.
He equated Nathanial's injection to taking one very large
sleeping pill before chasing it down with some whiskey.
Sophia could attest to this assessment—her body wasn't
as off-kilter as it had been, but she wouldn't be passing
any field sobriety tests in the near future. Good thing she
was already in the hands of the Culpepper PD. "I still
can't believe I was out for almost *thirteen* hours. I guess
Nathanial knew what he was doing when he made this
stuff." She quieted as guilt pushed out her next question. "How's Amanda doing? Braydon said she still hasn't
woken up."

"The doctor said she had a lot more of that stuff in
her system but they were able to stop the bleeding and

stitched her up good. So that's a plus," Cara said. She tossed Sophia's wayward right shoe at her. "Since she was injected before y'all brought her in, they think she'll wake up by tonight. Marina sure hasn't left her side, though. I've never known that woman to be quiet this long. It kind of makes me nervous."

"It's good that she's staying with her."

"Yeah, normally you can hear the two of them fussing at each other from a mile away but...I think they're pretty close when you get down to it."

"That's a relationship I can understand." Sophia smiled.

"We're also leaving them an officer just in case." She folded her arms across her chest as her face hardened. The last officer they had left to guard someone had ended up dead, but they both knew it wouldn't play out like that with Amanda. Nathanial had made it clear that he only had eyes for Sophia.

"I'm glad she's going to make it," she said truthfully. "I just hope her stomach doesn't scar." Cara gave her a sympathetic look. They both knew it would. She felt guilty that Amanda had been used as a personal message to her and Braydon. It also didn't help that it was her name that had been cut into the woman's skin.

The doctor came soon after and gave Sophia the okay to leave, though he tried to make her stay for observation at least twice. Braydon took over helping her walk to the truck. His closeness allowed his beautiful scent to envelop her. It stirred up the feelings from their first kiss, which felt like a lifetime ago. The thought sent a pleasant tingle through her. She was almost sad when he helped her into the cab. Cara, though off duty, followed behind the truck as they left the hospital.

"Where are we going?" she asked, settling into her

seat. Once again, she marveled at how familiar this routine had become.

"Back to my place for the moment. I didn't have a chance to grab your things earlier today."

What with a crazed man dropping a half-dead woman on the porch, she thought.

"Then where are you putting me?" She was half teasing. It seemed like every time she had gotten into his truck he had taken her somewhere new.

"You and Cara will be headed to Château Vega."

"Isn't Cara off duty?" she asked. It wasn't fair to keep sticking the officer with her if she didn't have to.

"Everyone on the force is working this case, off duty or not." There was a note of pride for his peers in his tone. "Small towns are stereotypically close, remember? If you mess with one of us, you mess with all of us."

"How much *does* the town know of what's been going on?" She hadn't had the chance to really wonder how everything that happened looked on the outside. She suspected that, under different circumstances, she wouldn't have been kept in the loop of knowledge during the investigation. Plus, aside from the hospital, she hadn't really been anywhere truly public without an officer or Braydon. If there was gossip going around Culpepper it fell on deaf ears where Sophia was concerned.

"After James's death, Captain Westin made an announcement about Nathanial being a dangerous man and to take safety precautions until we have him in custody. Knowing how unstable he really is now, I'm glad we let the town know that he's running around."

"And what about Lisa and Amanda?"

"We've tried to keep their names out of the public, if only because people around here can get really riled up and turn into vigilantes." He sighed. "Normally, it might be a good thing to have an entire town looking for them, but it's too much of a risk with Nathanial. He has no empathy—if someone got in his way, he'd only drag them into his little play of evil." She had to agree there. Culpepper had already lost enough because of the man. "Richard and Marina kept quiet as best they could but, you know how gossip is—I'm sure it isn't as much of a secret as we want it to be."

She nodded and yawned. The Nathanial Cocktail was one heck of a drug.

"So why are Cara and I going to Richard's?"

"I'm not comfortable with the security at Lisa's or my place anymore," he said bitterly. "Richard already has guards and a gate."

"He has guards?" she asked incredulously. Was Richard *that* big of a man that he needed not one but multiple people to watch over him?

"He has two on rotation year-round—cousins Able and Dwight Stevens. He brought them with him when he moved here. They live in a house at the back of the property with Able's wife. From what I know of them, they're pretty dependable guys. Honestly, I should have taken you there instead of my place." He paused, about to say something, but then stopped himself. He turned his neck to the side and popped it before continuing. "I guess I just felt better with you near me."

Sophia felt herself blush, but wasn't embarrassed by it. She was used to the effect he had on her and didn't care to make excuses for it. Instead, she turned to face him and smiled.

"I felt better, too." That seemed to ease his mind. He didn't smile but he stopped frowning. "So, while we're at Richard's where will you be?"

"Hunting."

The house at 2416 Gothic Street hadn't changed in the past seventeen hours or so since they had been gone but to Sophia it felt like a different world. Captain Westin was sitting on the front porch looking down at the spot where Amanda had been when they pulled into the driveway. Sophia felt more confident in her abilities to walk alone. She shooed off the helping hands of Braydon and Cara and walked right up to the captain and shook his hand. He returned the gesture with a firm grip.

"Glad to see you're okay, Hardwick," he boomed. "Pretty gutsy move you pulled."

"Thanks," she said, "at least I think."

"Don't worry, that was a compliment," Braydon whispered just over her shoulder. His breath tickled the exposed skin of her neck. Suddenly she was self-conscious of the fact that she'd been holed up in a hospital bed all day without a shower or a good teeth-brushing.

"Right," she said, making sure to turn her breath away from the man. She excused herself to his room and began to pack up her things. When the EMTs were loading Amanda into the ambulance, she and Braydon had grabbed a change of clothes to throw on in lieu of their pajamas or, in Braydon's case, the lack thereof. He had flung open his chest of drawers, grabbed a pair of jeans and a black shirt then put them on as he ran back outside. Sophia had taken more time with her jeans and tank top. Now, standing in the middle of the room, she looked at the combined mess they had made in their hurry. It was like a small bomb had gone off.

"You okay?" Braydon popped around the corner. She could hear Captain Westin and Cara talking in the living room.

"Yeah. I'm just…sorry for making such a mess." She didn't know why, but at the moment she was pushing down the urge to start cleaning the entire room. Because *that* made sense. Braydon began to laugh.

"You didn't make a mess. I believe it was me who did all of that." He pointed to the pile of clothes on the floor. "Plus, my bedroom floor is usually covered with clothes anyway." Sophia felt her eyes narrow in abrupt jealousy, imagining women's clothes littering the room. Which was a reaction, she reasoned again, that didn't make sense to have in their situation. The detective cleared his throat and quickly continued, "I mean I *am* a single guy living by himself. It's normal for me." He rubbed the back of his neck and tried to act as if he hadn't purposely thrown the word *single* in for her benefit. Sophia's eyes reverted to round and amicable. It was nice to know that Detective Braydon Thatcher wasn't swimming around the dating pool. Especially since they had shared a kiss—one that Sophia couldn't quite get out of her head.

She finished packing and together they went outside to Cara's 4Runner. Braydon put her bag in the backseat and stood with the passenger door open as she scooted into the seat. Cara sent a questioning look to Sophia, then to the detective when she, too, got into the car.

"I want you two to be careful—to be safe, okay?" He looked between the women, then to Cara. "Don't play hero if you see him." Then, very noticeably he inclined his head to Sophia. "Got it?"

"Yessir."

He gave her a quick smile. "You know the drill then, call me—"

"If I need anything or anything happens," she finished.

"Exactly. Let me know when you two get to Richard's. I'll stop by later." He shut the door after one prolonged shared look with Sophia and headed back inside. An odd feeling of loneliness moved against her chest but she shook it off. There were more important things happening than her selfish feelings for the man with aquamarine eyes.

Chapter Sixteen

Braydon ran a hand through his hair. He was standing in front of a closed door and wondering why he was even there. The afternoon had flown by with no new leads and them no closer to finding Nathanial or Lisa. Wherever he had her, it was one hell of a hiding place. The only person who could help them was still asleep in the hospital, though the doctors were positive she would wake up soon.

He sighed.

Amanda shouldn't be the only person who could help them break the case. He was a detective and, although newly appointed, he liked to think he was good at his job. However, the longer Lisa was out there—scared, possibly hurt and in the hands of a madman—he felt he was losing any claim he once had. Not only was he unable to stop Nathanial but he was now afraid he had lost Sophia's confidence.

She'd said she had injected herself because she'd known that Nathanial would kill Lisa if she didn't. In her mind, that only damned the sanity of "Terrance" Williams when in fact, it also quite clearly sent the message that she *knew* that Braydon wouldn't be able to find Lisa. It was a thought that frustrated him to no end.

He stood in the hallway of Richard Vega's second story. Cara and Richard were having a late-night dinner—both unable to sleep—while the Able cousins stood guard at each entrance to the house. The only other entrance was locked and between the two. If anyone managed to break in from that door they wouldn't be able to move throughout the house without one of the two seeing them first. Tom was sent home to rest for a while, the captain heading the search. Officers from the next county had been told to stay and help. Braydon hated the feeling of being useless. Maybe that was why he stood outside the bedroom Sophia was staying in. He wanted to comfort her, but at the same time he wanted to be comforted.

The realization made his mood sink lower. He didn't wait for guilt to rise in him—it had already surfaced and made a home after finding the body of Trixie Martin. Anger was its constant companion while an unhealthy sadness weighed down the edges of his mind. Having Nathanial's vendetta unveiled had made the memory of Amelia's death that much more prominent. Braydon hated to admit it, especially everything considered, but it made him miss her so much it hurt.

He let out a breath. It was almost midnight and Sophia was probably asleep. She didn't want or need him there. He had nothing new to deliver. With his mind made up, he turned to leave when he heard something that made him instantly reconsider—Sophia was awake and she was crying.

"Sophia?" He knocked on the door. "Are you okay?" There was some movement in the room but she answered right away.

"Yeah, hold on." His hand was already on the handle, but he waited until she gave the okay. "You can come in."

The guest bedroom was one of six in the entire house. It held a queen-size bed, a dresser and a love seat comfortably—all were pale pink and dark wood. Sophia was sitting on the love seat when he walked in, but the covers of the bed were pushed to the side and the floor was covered in pillows. She was trying to act normal but her swollen eyes and tear-streaked cheeks gave her away.

"What's wrong?" Braydon asked, immediately on alert. He had never seen the woman cry before—the aftermath was so unsettling he didn't realize at first she was only wearing a long T-shirt. Sophia tried on a smile, pushing her hair over her shoulder, but it slid right back off.

"I—" She paused and to Braydon's horror tears began to roll down her face. "I don't want to die," she finished, burying her face in her hands as she began to openly cry.

Braydon closed the space between them and knelt in front of her. He gently took her hands and pulled them away.

"You aren't going to die," he whispered. "I won't let you." He kissed her hands, keeping them in his own. She watched the movement while tears continued to come.

"But what if something happens tomorrow and—and he *does* get me," she said, close to sobbing. "He'll do awful things to me."

"Don't go, then. We can dress someone as you or—" He stopped as a loud sob escaped her.

"But then what if he kills Lisa?" she asked. "She's all I have!" She seemed to fold into herself at that, bringing her bare knees up to her chest. Braydon released her hands and took the seat next to her. Not caring if it was too brash of a movement, he put an arm around her shoulders and pulled her to him. She didn't protest and was soon leaning against his chest, his arms encircling her.

Up until that moment, Sophia Hardwick had been a rock. She had remained so calm, so collected, so confident. Sure, she had cried after finding Trixie but that had been an in-the-moment response—one that most anyone would have had. Since then she'd taken everything in stride, showing courage in the face of a madman who wanted nothing more than to see her dead. Braydon had liked her determination, her courage but, as she wept into his shirt, he realized that her vulnerability didn't diminish her strength in the least. She was a strong woman who had finally let her worries catch up to her.

"Sophia," he said, stroking her hair, "he won't kill Lisa, and I know I can't keep asking you to trust me—I know I don't deserve it—but please believe me when I say that I will kill Nathanial before he ever gets a chance to hurt you." There was a hardness in his tone—a stone-cold promise he refused to ever break.

Sophia's sobs quieted and soon her tears ceased. She pulled back to look him in the eyes, but Braydon didn't drop his arms from around her.

"But I do trust you," she said, her voice and its meaning wonderful music to his ears. He smiled, relief flooding through him. "You're a good man, Braydon Thatcher. I hope you know that." He was about to respond but stopped when she leaned forward. Her lips pressed against his in a soft kiss.

At first he didn't return it—she was vulnerable—but then so was he. Bringing his hands to cup her face, he deepened the kiss, parting her lips with his tongue. She moaned into his mouth, which seemed to awaken the rest of his body. He wanted her—all of her.

"Wait," Sophia said, pulling away. Braydon froze. "Just, hold on." She stood up from the couch and walked to the door. He looked on, afraid they had gone too far, moved too fast. Then, she did something that made him give a little laugh.

She shut the door with a smile.

THERE WAS A KNOCK on the door. It was an annoying, continuous sound that brought Sophia out of her sleep and back into the real world. She stretched, thankful it wasn't a clock's ticking, and looked at the empty spot next to her. Instead of her spirits dropping at Braydon's absence, a smile bubbled up at the memory of his presence hours before.

She could still feel his lips on hers—their warmth, their passion. The way he had commanded her body's attention. It had been a long while since she'd been with a man, but, somehow, with Braydon it had been more than a physical connection.

Hunger had fused them together in a dance filled with much more than the need to momentarily escape their current situation. The way he had touched her, kissed her, held her...the way he had looked into her eyes. Sophia had felt a connection in those moments that she had never felt before—all encompassing and filled with fire.

The knock came again, pushing the memory of a perfect, naked-bodied Braydon to the back burner. Sophia let a sigh stream from her lips.

"Hold on," she called, stretching one last time. A pleasant soreness radiated throughout her body as she hurried around the room, grabbing clothes from her bag and putting them on. A quick glance at her phone showed that it was almost noon. That surprised her. She didn't think she would be able to sleep after doing nothing, thanks to Nathanial's drug. When she was finished dressing, she looked once more at the empty spot on the bed, then opened the door.

Cara stood in the hallway looking simply devious. She held up her hands. One held a cup of coffee and the other a chocolate muffin.

"I was sent here to try and coax you awake," she said.

"Who sent you?"

"Okay, fine, I sent myself," she confessed. "Braydon had me at the end of the hall to give you some space, but Jordan came around and has been talking to me for almost two hours and I just can't take it anymore." Sophia stepped aside to let the woman into the room.

"Jordan?"

"Richard's nonstop-talking assistant. He keeps whining about every little thing while the vendors and decorators set up for tonight. Also, I think he's scared, too, and likes being around someone with a gun. I told him we had this place locked down but I guess some people are just naturally nervous. Though, I can't say I blame him right now. I hope it's okay that I woke you. I wasn't sure how much sleep you got." Sophia's eyes widened and heat started to spread up her neck as Cara glanced at the bed. She took in the rumpled sheets and pillows and, with more horror on Sophia's part, together they spotted a pair of wayward panties on the floor next to the foot of the bed. Cara was kind enough to pretend she didn't see any of it and instead sat on the love seat and held out the gifts she'd brought. Sophia gladly took them and joined her on the couch, the heat from her embarrassment ebbing away as the smell of coffee invaded her senses.

"Coffee is always appreciated where I'm concerned." She took a sip and almost sang, it was so good. Cara let her enjoy it for a moment before bringing reality into the room with them.

"Amanda Alcaster woke up early this morning," she began, instantly grabbing Sophia's attention. "Braydon already questioned her—he was adamant about being the first person to talk to her." Sophia nodded, glad that Braydon had been the one to do it. She trusted him, a fact that didn't surprise her anymore.

"What did she say? Does she know where Lisa is?"

"No, I'm afraid not, *but* she was able to give Braydon and Tom a new lead to track down…" She let her words trail off. There was something she didn't want to say.

"That's good, right?" If the lead came from Amanda, then surely it had to be good, she thought.

"Well, we now know why it's been so hard to find Nathanial. According to Amanda, someone is helping him."

Sophia almost spit her coffee out.

"What do you mean 'helping him'?"

"Amanda said they were kept in a windowless room, most likely in someone's house, and when Nathanial was down there with them, they could still hear someone moving around in the rest of the house. Sometimes they also heard him talking to someone but they never heard the other voice clearly enough." Sophia didn't know which piece of information to tackle first. Nathanial was partnered up with someone, but who would agree to be part of such a sinister plan? They were kept in a windowless room. What were the conditions there? Were they tied up? Were they abused? Cara seemed to pick up on the more intimate questions and continued. "Amanda said they were tied to chairs and were given bathroom breaks and food. She said Nathanial never hurt them."

"Except when he decided to carve my name into her stomach," Sophia said with anger.

"He had already put her to sleep when he did that." Cara sighed. "Small blessings I suppose." Sophia marveled that cutting someone up *after* they were asleep was a blessing at all, but in this case, it was true.

"So what lead did she give if she didn't know where they were being held?"

"We found out that Amanda had been talking to Nathanial when she was working at the gas station through

Tipsy's security tapes." Cara's whole demeanor changed as she started talking again—she was excited. "When we asked her about it she said that Nathanial had been talking to Amanda about buying the Dolphin Lot. He expressed interest one day and she ate it up. When her mama found out they had a big fight. She left, got a little drunk and went back home. Decided to let off some steam and walked back through the lot. She said Nathanial pulled up around then and grabbed her."

"That's what Marina was talking about in the hospital," Sophia started. "She said she loved Amanda more than that land!"

Cara nodded.

"He went through a lot of unnecessary trouble," she thought aloud. Sophia had to agree.

"Let's hope it's his love of theatrics that does him in."

Chapter Seventeen

There were two plans underway with the same goal—
take down Nathanial while saving both Hardwick sisters. However, the route to the finish line varied between
two methods.

The first plan hadn't changed since day one. Just because Nathanial had said the only way to save Lisa was
to make the trade, that didn't stop half the police force
from continuing to look for her. Unlike the first few days
of the women's disappearances, there was more confidence among the searchers. They knew about the connection between Nathanial and Amanda, knew the women
had been in a house, and knew that Nathanial was not
working alone. The last fact dimmed some enthusiasm
but at least now they could broaden their list of suspects
now that they were looking for more than just Nathanial.

Unfortunately, no one knew where Nathanial's car
was. Amanda had only been able to say that Lisa had said
it was old. Between the two of them, Nathanial hadn't
drugged Lisa immediately when he grabbed her. Captain Westin had some of his men finding regular Tipsy
patrons who had been seen on the security tapes that he
and Tom had gone through in hopes that they'd remember something about Nathanial's visits with Amanda.

The second plan, dubbed everyone's least favorite,

was built around Nathanial's trade. No matter how much they disliked the plan, they couldn't ignore it. Since Nathanial hadn't ordered Sophia to come to the fund-raiser alone, the plan was changed to Braydon's liking—instead of handing Sophia over so she could be taken away, tortured and killed, there would be a big ambush and the sisters would be saved. Until Nathanial contacted her, Sophia would attend the fund-raiser with Braydon and Cara at her side. The rest of the police force that weren't out actively searching would dress up in their formal best and mingle as if it was going out of style. Everyone would be on alert.

Everyone would have eyes on Sophia.

She hoped and prayed that the first plan would work, but as the sun went down and night fell over the once-sleepy town of Culpepper, it was time to prepare for option two.

Sophia stood in front of the mirror and looked at her reflection with a mix of anxiety and appreciation. She hated to admit it, but Nathanial's dress was beautiful.

It was a sheath dress, fitting against her body like a glove, and falling to the tops of her knees. Thin, silk straps held it up while the bust of the dress left little to the imagination—cutting low on her chest while simultaneously pushing her breasts high enough that her cleavage could be seen from a mile away. Under different circumstances, she would have loved to attend a swanky function wearing such a garment but she couldn't seem to get behind loving it while a crazy man waited for her. Though, again, she hated to admit that it looked and felt good against her skin. The ruby-red satin emphasized each curve of her body while the color mixed well with her complexion. On reflex alone, she applied some eyeliner and lipstick. Her hair she twirled up into a high bun. It made her feel more prepared for potential action.

"You ready in there?" Braydon called from the other side of the door. His voice sent a thrill through her.

"You can come in," she called back, taking one last look at her reflection. She wondered if it would be the last time she ever saw herself, a morbid thought that she tried to tamp down quickly.

"Wow." Braydon stood in the doorway, with an apparent look of appreciation. She gave him a polite smile.

"You don't look so bad yourself," she responded, walking over to him. He wore a black blazer that was opened up, showing a dark blue button-down. His slacks were also black and matched dark dress shoes. He was freshly shaved while the wild mane of hair she had grown used to in the past four days was slicked back with gel. His entire image had an effect just south of her waist, only made stronger by the memory of what was beneath each stretch of fabric that he wore.

"I knew I'd need to step up my game if I was going to deserve the company of my date." He grinned down at her. No matter how high her heels seemed to be, she was still under Braydon's gaze.

"Your date? Do I know her?" Sophia teased. It was Braydon's turn to roll his eyes.

"I'm sure you'll meet her. She's about your height, has these beautiful green eyes and is undeniably stubborn." He bent his head so that he whispered in her ear. "She also does this little trick in bed where—" Sophia laughed and slapped his chest.

"Okay, okay. I get it!" She took a step back while her cheeks cooled down. "Are there a lot of people here yet? I haven't really left the room all day." She had spent it worrying about Lisa. The night with Braydon seemed to have relieved the fear for her own life. She had cried, and done other things, until that fear had turned to determination—an even calm that left no room for second-guessing. Whatever happened tonight, she knew two things for certain: she would do anything for her sister and she would never blame anyone other than Nathanial if anything happened to Lisa.

"A few," he answered, "but none more beautiful than you."

The detective closed the space between them and wrapped his arms around her. They stood there for a time. The sound of the South played outside the window—frogs and insects stringing their respective sounds together for a chorus that only outsiders seemed to notice. Sophia took a deep breath in and let it out. Braydon kissed the top of her head, sending a wave of pleasure through her. It was the last calm before the storm.

They left the room and made their way downstairs. Sophia, Braydon and Cara walked out the front door and followed the path that led to the area of yard that had been sectioned off for the event. Valets were already standing at attention, ready to park the cars farther down the street, while caterers and Jordan, the newly appointed party planner since Lisa wasn't there, buzzed around, making sure everything was going according to plan.

Richard Vega knew how to throw a party; there were no two ways about it.

Sophia's nerves were on edge. She may have been resolute to making the trade if it came down to it, but the waiting and anticipation had her stomach in knots. She hoped no one could tell. The three of them were smiling as they rounded the house and walked into a wonderland lit up by beautiful hanging lanterns and the moon. The decorations were stunning, but Sophia was starting to realize not to expect anything less than extraordinary from Richard Vega. An elevated stage overlooked the party area behind the house while a mini-orchestra was seated on its beautifully stained wood. A canopy covered half the stage while gold and silver lanterns drooped from the rafters. The party area stretched far and wide with pockets of white chairs and alternating gold and silver tables. Waiters and waitresses walked around with platters filled with hors d'oeuvres while two long buffet tables draped in sheer cloth stood in the middle. Everything was white, gold or silver. It was all beautiful and yet oddly reminiscent of her senior prom.

Men and women wearing cocktail attire were already milling around, eating finger foods and making small talk. When Braydon had said it was the event of the year, she could see he wasn't the only person who held that as truth. Culpepper natives had more than stepped up in their dressed-for-the-best attire.

"Glad you could make it," Richard greeted, after catching their eye while talking to one of the waiters. A few of the attendants moved closer to him as she made her way over. Richard really was like a modern-day prince in Culpepper—everyone seemed to gravitate toward him. "I trust the walk here was pleasant?" he asked with a winning smile. The man sure worked well under pressure.

"It was a breeze," Sophia answered. She tried to mimic his smile.

Richard had already been briefed about the night's plans. All he had to do was pretend that he knew nothing about what was going on. Captain Westin had even gone as far as to tell the man not to mention any of Nathanial's victims, including Lisa.

"If anyone comes up to you and asks about any of them, change the subject," he'd said to all of them. "We don't need a bunch of civilians running around worried or trying to play cop. We'll play ignorant until we finally get him." It had been a hard pill to swallow for Richard, especially given the fact that most everyone would wonder why Lisa wasn't at his side—especially at an event she had originally planned—but he had promised his lips would remain sealed.

"I'm glad." Richard extended his arms in a sweeping gesture. "Welcome to the seventh annual Culpepper Fund-raiser. Feel free to eat, dance and meet some wonderful people." The second part sounded rehearsed, Sophia thought, but Richard had been the host for seven years running. It was natural to him by now. He left to mingle with a new wave of partygoers while Sophia and Cara followed Braydon to the buffet tables. Sophia's nerves had pushed her appetite to the back burner but she didn't mind taking a glass of champagne that was offered to her by a floating waitress.

"You okay there, Miss Hardwick?" Braydon asked with a big smile. It was only for appearance's sake—the concern was sewn into each word.

"Never better," she lied before tipping her glass back for a long drink. It was smooth and delicious.

"Remember, you need to try and keep a low profile here," Braydon reminded her for the umpteenth time. It was his protective side coming out. A part of him didn't want Nathanial to see her, but that was the whole reason she was there in the first place.

"Don't worry," she said in what she hoped was an even voice. "Just wanted to get my feet a little wet is all."

Cara smiled and said, "I like the way you think." She grabbed a glass and the two clinked them together.

"Women," Braydon mumbled.

By the time eight o'clock rolled around, the party was

in full swing. Being the outsider she was, Sophia didn't recognize anyone minus a few cops, and they made sure to mingle away from the three of them. Braydon, however, was a different story. Every time he seemed to turn around there was someone ready to congratulate him on the promotion or talk football scores or share a few pieces of gossip with him. Sophia's favorite local who stopped to chat was an elderly woman named Ms. Perry. She had her flirt turned on high and occasionally would reach up to pinch Braydon's cheeks after he said something that she deemed adorable.

"I'm about to make my speech," Richard said after Perry hobbled off to find another glass of champagne. "But first, can I have a moment alone with Sophia?" He directed the question to Braydon. It annoyed her immensely yet felt flattering in a way, as if Richard was asking her man if he could have the next dance.

"Stay inside the party and in my sight line," Braydon said after a thoughtful pause, clearly weighing the pros and cons. It didn't offend Richard in the least. He agreed and the two of them walked as far back from the party as Braydon would be comfortable with.

Sophia looked expectantly at the man her sister loved. He was handsome in his suit but she found herself comparing him to the detective like she had the first day she'd met both men. They each were dressed right for the occasion but Sophia thought they looked worlds apart. Richard was the authentic businessman—dressed to make money and attract clients. He looked handsome but not necessarily mouthwatering good-looking. Braydon on the other hand was reminiscent of a Bond character—suave and sexy with an overpowering sense of confidence. His suit let the world know he was ready to party but equally ready for any action that might come his way. She knew his gun was at his side beneath his blazer—also ready for a potential fray.

"How are you holding up?" Richard asked when they were out of hearing distance from the closest group of partiers.

"Honestly? I hate this, but I'm trying to stay hopeful. What about you?"

"It's been hell," he admitted. "I've been asked where Lisa is a dozen times. I keep coming up with more lies and excuses to field each question." He rubbed at his eyes. He suddenly looked years older than his thirty-four. "I just want her home." Sophia couldn't help it—she wrapped Richard into a quick embrace.

"I know what you mean." He returned the hug. It was brief but it was the most goodwill she had ever shown the man. "I never said it, but thank you for all that you've done trying to find her. I know I haven't been the best sister about your relationship, but I didn't know you before." She quirked the corner of her lip up into a little smile. "I know it doesn't mean much right now, but you two have my full blessing." Richard's face broke out into the first genuine smile she had seen from him.

"Thank you, Sophia. That means a lot to me…and Lisa. I just hope everything goes well tonight. That Lisa *and* you stay safe."

They made their way back into the midst of the party relatively unnoticed but it was like all of the men's pocketbooks had a Richard Vega radar that blipped quite loudly when he was in close proximity. The whole "keep a low profile" idea had become just that—an idea. One that Sophia was having a hard time practicing, through no fault of her own. There was only so much she could do about her revealing dress. When the men around Richard weren't transfixed on the rich man, they were ogling her chest and legs. She was about to tell the nearest older man where her eyes were located when a sickening feeling crawled through her.

Without looking, she knew Nathanial was out there now, watching. She could feel it. Whether he was out in the trees that stood on each side of Richard's house or hiding amongst the hundreds of people that made up the crowd, a very daring move if true, he was somewhere out there, waiting for her to come forward. Waiting for her to make the trade.

An older man with a thick mustache and flowing gut led the crowd that halted Sophia and Richard as he made a beeline for the host's attention. He gave Sophia a small nod before effectively cutting her off from the rich man. His back became a barrier of expensive satin. She looked around the crowd and noticed more men dressed in meticulously pressed suits eyeing Richard as if he was a juicy steak and they were the rabid dogs. Maybe he was the one who needed police protection.

Among the ones near the buffet tables were Braydon and Cara. She wondered if they'd even moved while she had gone to talk to Richard. They were staring at her—Braydon with a look that conveyed worry with a touch of something else and Cara with an approving smile. Sure a killer had given Sophia a dress, but that didn't mean it wasn't one heck of a great dress.

"You and Richard seem to be quite close," Lynda the receptionist said by way of greeting before Sophia could walk back to her group. She wore a dress that didn't hide any of her assets. It dipped low, had no back and rose up to the middle of her thighs as she walked. Sophia didn't have room to judge, but at the same time she had been told to wear *her* dress. Lynda had poured herself into her slinky number on her own accord. Sophia wouldn't have been so critical had the woman not accessorized her outfit with an outright sneer.

"We just needed a moment away from everyone," she explained, trying not to stare at the cleavage that somehow was pushed up so high, it almost hit the woman's neck. She glanced down at her own and was relieved to see it wasn't as out there. "We needed some alone time to talk about a few things. Talk about Lisa." Lynda was one of the few who knew Lisa had been kidnapped because she worked at the station. She shouldn't have been surprised that the two of them were talking.

"How nice for you two." Lynda didn't dial down the accusatory tone that she was currently carrying; the implications of something romantic or sexual going on between Sophia and the party's host weren't missed. "So I heard that you stayed here last night. I guess Braydon's place wasn't to your liking, huh?" She plucked the toothpick from her drink and sucked the olive off it. It wasn't the classiest thing Sophia had seen, but she was betting Lynda was touching tipsy. "It's a shame, you know. Braydon is *all* kinds of fun."

Sophia wanted the conversation to end fast. There was no time to sit around playing catty. Lynda wasn't even trying to hide her jealousy that Braydon and Sophia had been getting close. And she didn't even know about last night. They weren't in high school and, quite frankly, she didn't have the patience for this. However, she couldn't deny that at the same time, she wanted to stake her claim on the man Lynda had once dated.

"Oh, on the contrary, I am quite fond of Detective Thatcher." She lowered her voice and wiggled her eyebrows. "As for how fun he is, I'm pretty sure if last night was any indication, I'll definitely have to agree with you there." Lynda's mouth dropped open—the half-eaten olive showing. Sophia stopped the look of disgust from covering her features. "Now, if you'll excuse me." She didn't wait for whatever comment was about to spring from the other woman's bright-red lips. "Richard said he is about to make an important announcement and I want to get a front-row view." This did nothing to perk up the receptionist. Her whole body seemed taut with shock and jealousy. She took her leave of the woman and made her way through the crowd to the detective and officer, looking back once to see Lynda staring after.

"What was *that* about?" Cara asked, confusing Braydon.

"Oh, you know, just fun girl talk." She didn't hide the sarcasm. "Why don't we go get us a front-row spot?" They nodded and Braydon took Sophia's hand, leading her through the crowd, Cara and her black cocktail dress in their wake. The olive-eating, jealous Lynda followed, stopping behind them as they made their way to the front of the stage. Cara looked between the two women before giving Sophia a grin and rolling her eyes. It seemed that she wasn't the only one who disliked the scantily clad woman.

"What did Richard have to say?" Braydon asked, oblivious to the silent conversation going on behind his back, but she didn't get a chance to answer. Richard took his place on the stage, which was elevated two or three feet off the ground, and cleared his throat. The sound was surprisingly loud and clear—it cut through the chatter of the crowd and brought silence to the party of people.

"If you would please gather around." He motioned to the empty space on both sides of their group. Braydon hadn't let go of Sophia's hand—it warmed her skin and helped bring back her original calm. His brow was furrowed and his eyes went right through Richard. The man of the hour smiled and turned his focus to the rapt crowd. "First off, let me begin by saying a warm thank-you for attending this year's fund-raising event. Without good people like you in the world, such things could not exist. So, let's take a drink for all of those in attendance." He raised his glass and brought it to his lips. Most of the crowd followed his actions. Richard smiled after his sip, though it was more like a lengthy swallow, and continued. "Second, thank you for any and all donations and purchases you may make tonight. This fund-raiser has become a tradition that helps out organizations and charities throughout Culpepper. Everything earned here tonight will only help further the town's progress and success. Now, speaking of traditions, I'd like to sidestep another one this year—the welcome speech's length. Most of you can recall last year's record half-hour address and I'm sorry about that. I do believe I had a bit too much champagne at that point." He paused for laughter. It came easily. "Tonight I'd like to keep it short and sweet and say welcome to the seventh annual Culpepper Fund-raiser! As always the auction will start at eight-thirty. Cheers!" The crowd shouted back with excitement and took another celebratory swig of alcohol alongside their host.

Sophia finished off her second glass and smiled at Richard. She was proud of her sister for not listening to her when she'd implied that he was nothing more than a rich jerk. *That* was a label that would remain a secret between the sisters. Richard caught her eye and gave a small nod.

"You have got to be kidding me. I think it's time to take a smoke break," Lynda said, all but huffing as she turned on her heel.

"What's her problem?" Braydon asked, though he didn't seem much invested in whatever the answer would be.

His eyes scanned the faces of each and every partygoer he could see.

"She has some issues with my *friendship* with a certain detective. Apparently she used to be really good *friends* with him." Sophia could have laughed at how Braydon's entire demeanor stiffened. He shot a dirty look at Cara who had just found her nails to be fascinating. It looked as though he hadn't been prepared for her to know about his past relationship.

"That was a long time ago," he defended. "I ended it. That woman has more than one screw loose."

Sophia smiled at the red that filled the detective's cheeks. It was the first time she'd seen him blush. The result was oddly charming. He tried to put together an explanation, though he didn't owe her one. She placed a hand on his chest to stop him.

"Calm down, Detective. I told her being friends with you was *a lot* of fun." Cara laughed out loud and Sophia couldn't help but join her. It was nice to laugh. It helped ease her nerves, if only for a moment.

The music picked back up as the first organization prepared for their auction time. If the whole event hadn't been a cover to draw out Nathanial, Sophia would have liked to watch the bidding. When she had first come to Culpepper, she had disliked the small town and its residents, favoring the city. However, the more she was around them, the more fascinating she found the charming place. Minus the obvious bad seed named Nathanial Williams. They all knew each other—they were all connected somehow. Standing between Braydon and Cara, she felt like even she was a part of that connection. She wondered how it would feel if Lisa was here, safe and sound, while Nathanial was long gone.

She didn't get a chance to think about it too much,

though, because just as they were about to get situated in the crowd to watch the first auction, a scream tore through the night air. Like the carrying voice of Richard, its effect on the crowd was instantaneous. The band stopped playing while everyone looked in the direction of the nearest tree line looming ominously behind the boundaries of the party. Another scream sounded, this time with words attached.

"He's here!"

Chapter Eighteen

Lynda came crashing out of the trees and into the haven of lights created by the lanterns that boxed in the party. Her face was fear stricken. "I saw him! He's in there!" That didn't mean much to most of the fund-raiser's guests, but it sure got every cop in the crowd moving as one in the direction Lynda was pointing. Braydon hesitated for a moment before springing to action.

"Sophia, you stay here or so help me—"

"Go!" She shooed him. "Get Lisa!"

Braydon nodded, brought out the gun from under his jacket and ran full tilt after the officers who poured into the woods. Cara, tasked with sticking to Sophia's side no matter the occasion, grabbed the crook of her arm while Richard's assistant Jordan ran to the microphone and tried to calm everyone down. Richard had disappeared, no doubt going after Nathanial, too. Sophia and Cara hurried to the shaking shell that was Lynda.

"I just wanted to smoke a cigarette," she said as they approached, looking wildly between them. "I didn't want to piss anyone off so I took a walk. He was just standing there with a—a big needle in his hand." Fresh tears rolled down her cheeks.

"Was there a woman with him?" Sophia asked. "Was Lisa with him?"

"I don't know." Her voice shook. "I'm sorry. I saw him and just freaked." Sophia's stomach fell. Was Lisa not with him after all? Did this mean that the trade had been a trick? Was Lisa even alive still?

"Do you think Richard would mind if we went inside to sit down?" Lynda asked. "It's too *exposed* out here."

"That's actually a good idea," Cara agreed, eyeing the tree line.

"But—" Sophia started to argue. Cara wasn't having it.

"We'll stay in the living room," she said, already moving with Lynda toward the giant house. "Plus, I have my gun." She pulled it from the purse she had been toting. Sophia relented but looked back, hoping Braydon was okay.

The three of them wove through the crowd to the door that led from the stage into the back of the living area. Jordan eyed them warily from the mic but when he recognized them he waved his approval to go inside. Not that Cara would have stopped had he said no. It was the first time Sophia had seen her in full cop mode. She made a mental note to never mess with the woman.

This was a part of the house Sophia had never seen, sticking to the kitchen, study and second floor during her stay. It was just as opulent and clean as Richard's office a hallway over and, even though she wasn't a fan of animal prints and white as a decor combination, it seemed to work for the space. Lynda held the door open for them but didn't stop once it was shut.

"I need some water," she said, pointing toward the kitchen.

"We need to stay in here," Cara said. The view to the party was uninhibited thanks to floor-to-ceiling windows that lined the wall. "I'd feel more comfortable if we could see everyone."

Lynda gave Cara a slap on the arm. "Come on, Cara, it's only a room away," she tried.

Cara touched the spot Lynda had hit.

"Watch it," she complained, "that hurt."

"Sorry, it must have been my ring. Can I go get some water now?"

Cara sighed but nodded. Sophia wanted to stay by the window but knew she wouldn't be allowed to do so alone. She followed the cop with her own sigh. They hadn't made it more than a few steps into the kitchen before Cara stopped suddenly.

"You aren't wearing any rings" was all she could say before she lost her balance and pitched backward. Sophia tried to keep the woman upright but she was a good few inches taller and heavier. All she could do was slow the fall. "Cara?" she shrieked, hitting the ground with the woman on top of her. "Cara?" The officer was unconscious. Confusion surfaced before Cara's last words registered. Sophia looked at Lynda. She was smirking.

"That took *forever* to work." Lynda held a small syringe and needle up for her to see. "I honestly didn't think she'd ever pass out."

Sophia's face contorted into a mask of rage. "Why?" she asked.

"Why? Well, because you wore the dress. That means you want to trade." She held out the used syringe. "Wasn't that the plan, Nate?"

Sophia felt sick as Nathanial walked around the corner and took the syringe. He wore a black suit with a red button-down shirt that almost matched his hair. His tie was as white as the grin he was currently wearing.

"That's right." He pulled out a bag from his suit pocket

and switched out the used syringe for a new one. Sophia watched in muted horror as Lynda pushed her hair out of the way and let Nathanial inject her with it. "Remember, you might want to lay down. As everyone in the room can tell you, this works rather fast."

Lynda nodded and sat down on the hardwood.

"Good luck with your vengeance," she told him with what Sophia only could describe as a flirtatious smile. "Let me know if you ever want to do this again."

Nathanial didn't respond but instead turned his attention to Sophia. Lynda slumped against the wall and fell the rest of the way to the floor. Her dress was even more unflattering in its rumpled state.

"You weren't in the woods," Sophia stammered, meeting the cold, dark eyes of "Terrance" Williams. "She lied for you."

He held up his index finger and wiggled it back and forth. "She didn't lie for me, Sophia. She lied for money," he corrected. "There is a difference." He came closer and grabbed the gun that had fallen away from Cara's hand. Instant fear seized hold of her chest, but he held out his other hand for her. "Now, let's go see your sister."

Sophia felt bad for pushing Cara off her, but she did it as gently as she could manage from beneath the woman. This time Nathanial didn't tell her to inject the drug into her veins. Instead, he looped his arm through hers and guided her upstairs before stopping just outside the farthest room from the landing—three doors down from the room she had been staying in. Sophia's heart pounded in her chest. She gave the killer a questioning look.

"The deal was you get to say goodbye, remember?" He detached her arm from his before producing another, smaller syringe from his jacket. How much more of that stuff had he made? He opened the door but held her wrist firmly.

The world melted away in a rush of relief so strong that it brought tears to Sophia's eyes. Sitting up on the bed was Lisa and, even though her arms and legs were tied and a piece of cloth was stuffed in her mouth, Sophia couldn't help but smile. She was alive. It was a fact that overpowered her with a rush of courage. In one swift movement she turned and kicked Nathanial hard in the groin. He doubled over and the gun dropped from his hand. She lunged after it, scooping it up just as he pulled her to him. He pushed a needle into her skin at the same moment she pulled the trigger.

A loud bang sounded. Nathanial roared in anger and threw her against the ground. The gun fell from her hands and skidded across the floor and under the bed. Sophia knew she didn't have long. She looked up at her sister. They locked eyes and for the first time in a long while Sophia felt content.

"I love you," she said.

Then the darkness came.

Chapter Nineteen

"This is too easy," Braydon said, stopping to catch his breath. His gun was raised in front of him.

"What?" Richard had been running next to him, undeterred by the fact that he had no weapon to defend himself. The rest of the woods were swarming with cops, yet no one had yelled back that they had made contact or even seen Nathanial or Lisa.

"This was too easy," he said again, already starting to turn around. "I think he's at the party." Richard didn't question him as the detective backtracked, running harder than before. He followed with surprising speed.

The crowd hadn't moved, thanks to Jordan spouting some nonsense on the microphone, but when they saw Braydon run out with his gun raised and their host right behind everything got loud. He didn't care—his focus had narrowed as it swept across the clumps of people.

Sophia and Cara were nowhere to be seen.

"Jordan!" Richard yelled after they fought their way to the stage. "Have you seen Sophia and Officer Whitfield?"

Jordan's mouth was slightly agape as he looked between his rumpled boss and the gun-wielding detective. He pointed to the back door without a word.

"Stay behind me," Braydon growled out of professional reflex. He didn't care about anyone other than Sophia right now. He threw open the door and for the second time in a handful of minutes, felt the sharp stab of dread. Cara and Lynda were laid out on the floor, unconscious, and Sophia was nowhere in sight.

"Call this in," Braydon snapped, not bothering to look back at Richard as he stepped over the two women. His gun remained raised and he quickly searched the bottom floor. He entered each room with his heart in his throat and white-hot anger in his eyes.

"Braydon," Richard called out after his first-floor search ended. He ran back to meet the man at the stairs. "Something fell upstairs." From somewhere Richard had produced his own handgun and started to lead the way. When they reached the top they paused, listening. A second later there was a loud *thud* at the end of the hall. Braydon rushed forward, waiting only until Richard got on the other side of the door, and flung it open.

On the floor next to the bed was Lisa Hardwick. As Richard cried out and ran over to her, Braydon knew he should be happy that they had finally found her, but he couldn't, knowing what the cost had been. Richard removed the cloth from her mouth. That's when Braydon noticed a dark red stain against the hardwood.

"He'll take her to the dock!" she rasped out as soon as her mouth was free.

"She's alive?" he had to ask once he realized what he was looking at was blood.

"Yes, he drugged her and took off after she shot him."

"She shot him?" Richard asked, working on the ties around Lisa's legs.

Braydon heard her say yes but was already out of the room and running down the stairs. *This is it,* he thought, *this is where it ends.*

SOPHIA COULD HEAR the soft lull of water nearby. It pushed against the hard surface beneath her, causing a swaying rhythm. Unlike the last time she had been injected with Nathanial's homemade drug, she wasn't lost in a haze when she came to. It was easier this time around, she thought.

"I'm glad you could join me," said a voice to her side. Everything that had happened came back in a rush. She sat up straight and flinched away from him. Before she could move an inch, Nathanial pulled her toward him and looped his arm around her shoulder. His grip was firm. His eyes were crazed.

"What's happening?" she asked, disoriented by the change in her surroundings.

"What's happening?" he repeated. An eruption of laughter escaped his throat as he turned to look her in the eyes. In the moonlight his face looked more twisted than it had in the basement of the hospital. Darker shadows played across his features while his skin had a pale sheen of sweat covering it, plastering his hair and clothes to his body. His jacket was missing and there was a dark red stain growing on his side. It seeped through the light red of his shirt.

"I shot you," she said with a start, remembering pulling the trigger. She hadn't realized it actually hit him.

"You sure did." He brought his other hand up and wagged his finger at her. She didn't mind the gesture but she did mind the gun in his grip. "It wasn't very nice, you know? I had to speed up my entire plan."

"Speed up?"

He skimmed over that question and motioned around them.

"This is where it all started, Sophia Hardwick."

They were sitting on the edge of the dock, water slapping against the wood. In front of them was an expansive body of water closed in by a line of trees in the distance. Sophia craned her head around to see a house a hundred or so yards behind them. She turned back to face the water.

Nathanial's words sunk in.

"This is where Amelia was killed."

"Bingo!" Nathanial said. "Though technically they found her body over there off to the side." He pointed back to the beginning of the dock. She spotted a car parked in front of the house. She bet that it was his.

"You want to kill me where she was killed."

He nodded. "Was there really any other place to do it?"

Sophia's stomach turned to ice. "Will my death really help you move on?"

Nathanial laughed again before stopping to wince. "I don't expect it will. Then again, I don't expect to live much longer, either. Your lack of aim managed to do more damage than I would have liked." He looked down at the bullet wound. "It's almost poetic that Braydon won't have the satisfaction of killing me, just like he didn't have the satisfaction of killing my brother." He moved his wrist to check his watch. "He should be here soon."

"How do you know?"

He shrugged, all nonchalant. "I imagine your sister has told him by now. That is, if they even found her." He cursed beneath his breath, wincing again. "I may have been too clever about all of this."

"Why do any of it?" she asked. "Why go through all of this?"

"Because Braydon has to pay for Terrance's death," he growled, his composure slipping. "He has to pay for what he did to my family. After my folks left town, they were never the same. Dad took to drinking and dropped dead and Mom…she held on as long as she could. I tried to help her, but—" He paused before lowering his voice. "But I wasn't enough for her." He hung his head like a disappointed child. Sophia dared not move. The man had clearly lost what little sanity he once had.

"Is that when you decided to come back to Culpepper?" If she was going to die, she at least wanted to know.

"Yes…and no. A part of me always thought about coming back."

"Is that why you changed your name?"

He tensed. "Mother told me the name change would make her happy." His head drooped lower. She thought he was going to pass out but he straightened up after a moment. "It didn't. So, I went back to school." It sounded like Nathanial wasn't the only unstable member of his family. To ask a child to rename himself after his deceased sibling was just not right. The air grew thick with silence. Sophia hoped to every god out there that Nathanial would either fall unconscious from blood loss or just outright die. His story may have been sad but that was no excuse for all he had done. However, she had to ask at least one more question.

"Were you the one who got Lisa to go to the Dolphin Lot?" Sophia could tell the pain he was feeling had worsened. His face was pinched when he answered.

"Guilty." He smiled again, as if he was proud of what he'd done.

"What did you say to get her to meet you?"

"I told a few fibs. I said I was about to purchase the lot and was interested in selling some of it to her for her planning business, but first I wanted her to come check out the area to see if she'd even be interested."

"And she just agreed, without telling anyone?"

He shrugged. "I asked her to keep it a secret because

all the paperwork wasn't done yet. She agreed because she was excited. When we met, I told her I planned on killing her. She tried to run, I grabbed her, then took her. It was easy as pie." Sophia felt nauseous. Nathanial spoke as though Lisa was just a pawn in a horrible and twisted game of chess. He may have been brilliant at his job but he was so far off base when it came to basic humanity.

"And what about Trixie? Amanda? Why did you pick them? What was the point?"

"Trixie was a happy accident. I was setting up my spot to view Braydon discovering Lisa's body in the car, that is before I was ready to stage her, when she came jogging by. She saw the car and I had no choice but to keep her quiet. Plus, it worked out wonderfully. I was able to see Braydon's feelings for you." At this he grinned. "Amanda would have been fine had she not followed my car out here when I came to check on everything. I only started talking to her to get information about the land. I took her to Lynda's so she could serve as your message later." He turned and winked. "It's amazing how easy it was to sway that woman to help me. It started as a joke over some drinks at the bar then all it took to make it a reality was the promise of money."

Sophia was about to ask how much money Lynda had been promised when Nathanial let go of her shoulders. He put his hand to his wound, then held it up to the moonlight. Dark red dripped from his fingers.

"Maybe Braydon isn't as fast as I need him to be right now. I guess it's time for you to die, Miss Hardwick. I truly am sorry that he won't be able to see you take your last breath." He struggled to stand and Sophia went with the only option she had left. She lifted up into a crouch and threw all her weight into the man. Startled, Nathanial pulled the trigger before the two of them toppled over the edge of the dock and into the water.

Sophia's adrenaline surged as they hit the cold water, going under in a tangle of limbs. For a man who was so keen on dying, Nathanial thrashed around, fighting to break away from her grip. Though, Sophia wasn't budging. She wasn't sure but she thought she had heard the *thunk* of the gun hitting the dock. Nathanial had already made it crystal clear that he wanted Sophia dead. If he got to the gun, he *would* kill her.

Sophia's plan quickly backfired. Nathanial grabbed a fistful of her hair as his feet found the bottom of the bay. He pushed her farther underwater, using his other hand to press her back down. He didn't need the gun to kill her now. He was going to drown her. She thrashed around, heart slamming against her rib cage. She used her nails to claw at his hands and, when he didn't let up, she remembered the bullet wound. With the last of her energy, she threw her hand out and jabbed her fingers into the wound. Even underwater she heard him yell. He let go and she scrambled to the surface.

"You little bitch!" he howled, the water coming up to his chin. Sophia didn't wait to hear what he said next. She swam around the dock until her feet hit the muddy ground. The air should have chilled her wet body but she was still in the throes of an adrenaline high. She ran out of the water as fast as she could.

"Stop, or I'll shoot!" Nathanial yelled. She whipped around to see him standing on the dock. He picked up the gun and held it firm in his hand. Sophia's shoulder burned, her throat ached, and more than anything she wanted to kiss Braydon Thatcher goodbye. "Before you die, I want you to know that I may have killed you but it's still his fault." He sneered as he said it.

"It's not Braydon's fault!" she snapped. "It wasn't his fault eleven years ago and it isn't his fault now!" She stumbled to the side, suddenly feeling faint. Her adrenaline must have run out. "When you kill me, Nathanial Williams, I want you to remember that it was your fault."

Sophia fell to her knees just as the gunshot rang through the night. She waited for the lights to turn off— to be the victim of darkness that would never let up. She waited for death but it didn't come. Instead Nathanial fell backward into the water, a bullet piercing his forehead. She turned around, confused, to see Braydon lower his gun. He was the most beautiful man she had ever seen.

"Good shot," she greeted, but he didn't smile back at her. The detective grabbed his phone and dialed a number—his brow creased, his lips downturned in a frown. *What a weird time to make a phone call,* she thought fleetingly.

"What's the status on the ambulance?" he barked into his phone, dropping down beside her. He still wouldn't meet her eyes.

"He doesn't need an ambulance, Braydon," she said, looking toward the dock. "Nathanial's dead." Braydon ignored what she said as if he couldn't hear her. Instead he yelled more into the phone before flinging it into the dirt.

"Sophia, I need you to stay awake, okay?" he said. It sounded farther away than it should have with him being so close. She was confused but nodded all the same. She trusted Braydon. She felt safe with him. He put his hand above her chest. It brought on an unexpected, terrible pain. She looked down to see what he had done, ready to fuss at him.

"Oh," she managed.

Apparently, Sophia hadn't been the only one to get a lucky shot in. It looked like Nathanial might have got his wish after all.

Chapter Twenty

The world was bright, warm and horizontal. Sophia opened her eyes to the buzz of fluorescent lights and the face of a woman with identical green eyes.

Lisa was perched on the side of the bed, smiling down at her little sister. There were dark purple bruises that lined the left side of her face and a scab across her bottom lip. Even though her face was devoid of makeup, Sophia couldn't help but be proud of how beautiful Lisa was.

"Your eye," Sophia said, jumping to the most relevant thing. She smacked her lips together—her mouth was unbearably dry. Lisa read her mind and produced a cup of water with a straw.

"Don't worry about this," Lisa said. "Out of everyone Nathanial hurt, I'm the one with the least damage." Sophia was glad to hear that. She pulled on the straw until her cracked lips felt smooth. Lisa took the cup when she was done.

"I'm glad you're alive," Sophia said. Her throat felt better, but her head felt sluggish. "I can't count how many times I almost lost hope that I'd ever see you again."

"I knew you wouldn't give up. You're too darn stubborn." She laughed but then all humor disappeared.

"I was afraid I'd never see *you* again." Lisa's brow

furrowed and her eyes began to water. "Sugar, you were shot. If Braydon hadn't gotten to you in time…"

Sophia reached up and grabbed her hand, squeezed it and smiled.

"But he did and I'm okay." She paused. Maybe she couldn't claim that, considering she'd woken up in the hospital. "I am okay, right?" Lisa's seriousness lessened. She nodded and smiled. Sophia realized how much she had missed the image.

"Yes, you are. Apparently you're *so* stubborn that you won't let things like bullets in the shoulder stop you." She sobered. "You've only been here for a few hours. They had trouble getting all of the bullet bits out, and they were nervous about how much of Nathanial's drug you had been given in such a short amount of time, but in the end the doctor gave you the okay." She reached forward and lightly touched the large bandage that was over the front of her shoulder. "It'll scar, though." Sophia frowned, thinking of Amanda's stomach. Nathanial had branded her without a care in the world.

"Nathanial is dead," she stated with some venom. Again Lisa nodded, her long hair slipping from her ponytail at the movement.

"Yes, he is."

Sophia also liked the sound of that.

"Braydon had to go back to the police station to talk with the captain and deal with paperwork because of it."

Sophia's heart did a little flutter at the mention of the detective. She didn't want to admit it, but when she found that Braydon hadn't been in the room, her stomach had dropped. Nathanial's reign of terror was over. Lisa had been found. The case of the missing Culpepper women was solved. Their romance had started in the heat of extreme circumstances and now that the danger had passed, Sophia wondered where that left them.

Lisa put her thumb between Sophia's eyebrows and pushed down.

"Stop your worrying," she ordered. "You've had enough troubles this past week to deal with. Try to relax, okay?" She moved her hand away and her brilliant smile returned. "And just to let you know, I basically had to kick Braydon out after the captain called him."

"Why?" Sophia tried to keep her voice from showing how much she cared about the man's presence. Although, she was sure Lisa had already picked up on the fact that her little sister was pining for him.

"He wanted to make sure you were okay. He didn't even leave the hospital until you were out of surgery." She winked. "He was stuck to your side like glue." Sophia couldn't stop the smile that crept across her lips. Lisa's grew, too. "I thought there might be something there."

They stayed in a giddy bubble of happiness for a moment before Sophia had to start asking questions about what had happened. Lisa must have realized it was coming. Her smile faded and she pushed her shoulders back, readying for the inquiries.

"What happened?" Sophia started. It was an umbrella question that would lead to all of the answers she wanted.

The Saturday night before Sophia's birthday party, Lisa had received a call from a man she now knew was Nathanial, claiming he was about to purchase Dolphin Lot. Lisa hadn't known the history behind the Alcaster property but she did know that it was a beautiful space and that it was undeveloped. The man went on to say that after he purchased it, he wanted Details to be able to use one of the acres as an event space, but he wanted Lisa to see the lot with him first.

"I jumped at that," Lisa said. "An entire acre of Dolphin Lot could be used for great outdoor parties and weddings. It would double my client base alone. When he asked me to keep it a secret until everything was finalized, I thought it was a small price to pay for such an amazing opportunity. He wanted to meet that Monday but I told him I had my sister's birthday to attend. So, I offered to meet him Sunday morning before I left instead." Lisa grabbed her hand. "If I hadn't done that..." She became quiet. Sophia waited, not wanting to push the woman. "I met him on the road. He grabbed me, threw me into his car and then drugged me. I woke up in Lynda Meyer's enclosed garage."

Sophia's jaw hardened. "I can't believe she helped him." Having Lynda, a woman who worked for the police department, be the variable no one had expected, had been a smart move. She knew the case's progress and where Sophia had been at all times. Not to mention, no one had suspected her.

"After Nathanial took Amanda out, Lynda finally showed herself. She told me that it was nothing personal—Nathanial had just given her a lot of money. He promised her that no one would ever know she had helped him."

"Then why did she let us see that she was in on it? Didn't she know that you and Cara would tell everyone about her?"

"She probably thought you were as good as dead." Lisa paused, not liking those words. "And apparently Nathanial promised that he had left me dead in the upstairs room at Richard's and also would finish off any other loose ends, which I assume meant Cara. Lynda woke up an hour ago in handcuffs." Sophia couldn't deny that seeing Lynda in handcuffs would make her happy.

"I still can't believe any of this happened," Sophia breathed. Lisa had gone missing a week ago but it felt like years.

"I can't believe you shot Nathanial at Richard's," she admonished. "What if he had gotten a hold of the gun and killed you right then and there?"

"We both know he wouldn't have done that. He wanted Braydon to see me die for his big finale or, at the very least, kill me on the stage of his choice."

Lisa frowned. "I'm just glad Braydon showed up in time."

"Me, too."

Silence filled the room again. This time it was loaded. Lisa's eyes began to water again.

"Sophia…" she began, looking down at their clasped hands. "Richard told me what you did at the hospital, taking the syringe when you could have run. Then volunteering to turn yourself over to him…" She met Sophia's gaze. Her eyes were shining green orbs. "You saved me, Sophia. No one else did. It was you. I—I just don't know how to repay you for what you did." Sophia smiled at her sister's emotional gush.

"It isn't a debt, Lisa," she said. "You don't owe me anything because I'm your sister and I love you. So, don't cry because you know it makes me uncomfortable." Lisa laughed but nodded, wiping under her eyes. "Now, is there anything else I missed?"

"Actually, there is." Lisa composed herself enough to smile wide. She held up her left hand. A beautiful diamond graced her ring finger. Sophia copied the smile. "He said he's been holding on to it for a while, waiting for the perfect moment. After everything that happened, he said he didn't want to wait anymore. Plus, I heard *someone* gave him their blessing."

"It's beautiful," Sophia said honestly.

"I could care less about the actual ring. It's the man who makes me happy. There's only one problem, though."

Sophia raised her eyebrow. "What's that?"

"Since I practically live at Richard's anyway, it only makes sense to sell my house. But that can be such a lengthy, unpleasant process, especially when dealing with strangers. If there was someone who I *knew* was interested it would make everything easier. Someone who, perhaps, wouldn't mind taking care of all of my pillows." Lisa winked. "I'd even consider renting it out if that fit the person's needs better." Sophia understood the meaning her sister was pushing. Although she had an apartment and job back in the city, she couldn't deny that Culpepper and one very handsome detective had changed what she thought of as "home."

"Are you sure she'll like this?" Braydon looked around his living room, skeptical of the brightly colored streamers that hung from each corner. The contrast between the purples, blues and pinks of the party decorations and the oak wood and leather was an odd combination to see. Cara stood with her hands on her hips and did a 360-degree turn. She nodded her approval.

"I think she'll love it, especially considering she spent her actual birthday thinking her sister didn't care enough to show up. What with her being kidnapped and all," Cara said. "That woman deserves a little party."

Braydon nodded, he couldn't have agreed more.

A week had passed since Braydon had killed Nathanial Williams, ending the sick cycle of a terrible, violent past. In a way he felt as if he had finally found justice for Amelia, killing "Terrance" before he had a chance to hurt anyone else. Though, he knew he couldn't take all of the credit.

Nathanial hadn't bet on Sophia fighting back. She had thrown everything at the man, wounding him and giving Braydon enough time to get to the dock and finish the job. In a way, Sophia had saved her own life. Culpepper had since returned to normal while those affected slowly started to heal.

Cara had woken up from Nathanial's drug, groggy but unharmed and had personally handcuffed Lynda to her hospital bed before the receptionist had awoken. Lynda was facing charges that would put her away for a long, long time. The money that had been deposited in her bank account by Nathanial had been extracted and used to pay for Trixie Martin's and James Murphy's funerals. Instead of finally getting rid of the Dolphin Lot and moving far away, Marina Alcaster had turned the rights over to her daughter who had decided she wanted to build and run a small bed-and-breakfast on the land nearest the water. She had then sold two acres of the land to Lisa, who had paid for it with her own money. Lisa had told him that before Sophia had been discharged from the hospital, Amanda had stopped by her room and relieved the guilt that had been clouding her mind.

"You didn't physically do this to me, so I expect you to not feel bad about it," she had said after showing the puckered marks that spelled out Sophia's name across her stomach. Amanda even went as far as to joke, "I'm just glad you don't have a longer name."

Lisa also let it slip that Sophia had finally called their mother and the three of them were slowly trying to repair their relationship. It reminded Braydon that he needed to give his own parents a call. At the end of the long story they promised to visit him soon.

Richard had also made a town-wide announcement that the annual Culpepper Fund-raiser would make another visit within the next three months since it had been shut down before any of the auctions started. There would also be an addition of a new program that promoted mental health awareness and was aimed at working with those with issues to help get them the attention they needed. He also announced his engagement, inviting everyone in town to the wedding at the end of the year. Braydon had no doubt in his mind that it would be one of the most extravagant ceremonies he would ever see.

Braydon and Tom had spent the majority of the week completing paperwork and building an airtight case against Lynda. Braydon had, despite everything, made sure that Nathanial was buried next to his brother. In the end, he'd been the sole attendant at the funeral.

During all of this, Sophia had been discharged from the hospital and had holed up with her sister in Pebblebrook. The detective had seen her twice but they hadn't been alone. Once the paperwork was finished and the case was officially closed, Braydon had decided to throw a surprise party for the beautiful, maddening, stubborn woman because, like Cara had said, she deserved it. Just like the pillows.

"Lisa just called. They're on their way," Richard said, coming in from the back porch. Braydon nodded to the man he'd come to respect and started to usher the party-goers into the living room. It wasn't a big crowd—Cara, Tom, Richard, Jordan, Captain Westin and John the Ticketer—but he hoped she would be pleased. Everyone in attendance may not have known the woman all that well, but there was no denying each person's affection for her.

Minutes later there was a knock on the door and everyone quieted.

"I guess I'll just come right in!" Lisa called, feigning ignorance. She opened the door wide, hurried through and turned to her sister as everyone yelled, "Surprise!"

"Happy birthday!"

Sophia's face instantly turned red, but a smile reached ear to ear. The next half hour was spent talking, drinking and eating. Not once was Nathanial's name mentioned. Braydon watched as the younger Hardwick sister continued to smile. She was the most beautiful woman he'd ever seen.

"Why don't you just ask her to dance already?" Lisa teased, coming out of the kitchen with a slice of cake. "I'm sure she'll say yes."

Braydon laughed, the sound drawing Sophia's attention. She excused herself from the conversation she was having with Cara and walked over.

"I have something for you, by the way," she began, earning an eyebrow raise from the detective. He followed her into the kitchen where she handed him the bag she'd been carrying when she first came in. "It's to say thank-you for everything."

Perplexed, Braydon opened the bag. There was a brand-new pan and spatula inside.

"I noticed that your pan was a little too small for making two grilled cheeses at once," she explained, not stopping for him to question it. "I just figured, since I'll be living in Culpepper now, it might be handy to have."

"Living in Culpepper?" It was the first time they'd talked about her future. Braydon hadn't wanted to have the conversation about Sophia returning to the city. It was one he'd been hoping to avoid.

"I've decided to stay," she said proudly. "Lisa is letting me rent out her house." There was no stopping the smile that attached to Braydon's face.

"What about your job?"

"It wasn't actually as hard to leave it as I thought it would be. Lisa asked me to become a partner in Details and I said yes. I have a better knack for numbers and, I have to admit, it would be fun to be around her again." She paused. "So, I thought if you wanted to—"

Braydon interrupted Sophia by closing the space between them. He kissed her long and hard. It said everything the two of them couldn't form into words. It promised a hopeful future and happiness that Braydon had never felt before. It promised him a life with Sophia.

It promised a life filled with grilled cheese sandwiches.

* * * * *

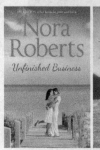 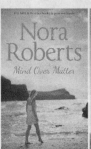 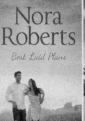 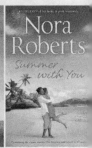

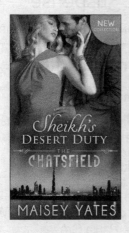 

MILLS & BOON®
INTRIGUE
Romantic Suspense

A SEDUCTIVE COMBINATION OF DANGER AND DESIRE

A sneak peek at next month's titles...

In stores from 17th April 2015:

- **Scene of the Crime: Killer Cove** – Carla Cassidy
  and **Navy SEAL Justice** – Elle James

- **Cowboy Incognito** – Alice Sharpe
  and **Under Suspicion** – Mallory Kane

- **Showdown at Shadow Junction** – Joanna Wayne
  and **Two Souls Hollow** – Paula Graves

Romantic Suspense
- **Capturing the Huntsman** – C.J. Miller
- **Protecting His Brother's Bride** – Jan Schliesman

Available at WHSmith, Tesco, Asda, Eason, Amazon and Apple

Just can't wait?
Buy our books online a month before they hit the shops!
visit www.millsandboon.co.uk

These books are also available in eBook format!

Join our *EXCLUSIVE* eBook club

FROM JUST £1.99 A MONTH!

Never miss a book again with our hassle-free eBook subscription.

★ Pick how many titles you want from each series with our flexible subscription

★ Your titles are delivered to your device on the first of every month

★ Zero risk, zero obligation!

There really is nothing standing in the way of you and your favourite books!

Start your eBook subscription today at www.millsandboon.co.uk/subscribe